BOOKS BY JEFFREY POSTON

ACTION/ADVENTURE THRILLERS

American Terrorist: Where is the Girl?
Contagion: American Terrorist 2
Escalate! American Terrorist 3
American Terrorist Trilogy

The Joshua Experiment (Call Sign: Raven Book 1)
The End of Everything (Call Sign: Raven Book 2)
The Queen (Call Sign: Raven Book 3)

JASON PEARES HISTORICAL WESTERNS

Courage (Book 1)
Legacy of an Outlaw (Book 2)
Warriors (Book 3)
Manhunter (Book 4)

American Terrorist 3
ESCALATE!

JEFFREY POSTON

PROLOGUE

"**P**RESIDENT SHIRLEY MALLORY MUST DIE! That is non-negotiable."

The speaker sat in the darkness of an underground concrete bunker facing another man across a small conference room table. His name was Grainger Koll, though very few members of even the inner circle of Atlas leadership knew his identity.

The only light in the room emanated from the large high-definition monitor on the wall. A three-dimensional wire-frame representation of the Greek Titan, Atlas, rotated on a light blue background on the screen, the figure's muscular body supporting the globe on his broad shoulders. Both men listened to the voices debating over the heavily encrypted comm channel. The encryption was designed to prevent America's NSA keyword searchers from matching voices to known personnel files. Other voices on the comm channel argued the pros and cons of that statement as if it were not a command.

Finally, someone said, "We should at least give President Mallory one last chance to rejoin Atlas. She is valuable, and we need her."

"No, we need control of the US government!" Grainger said. "Mallory knew the price of her betrayal. No one has ever been given a second chance. She dies. Any questions?"

Another voice added, "We've tried that twice."

The second man in the darkened room, Hollis Koll, said, "*Rainman* tried that twice, and he messed it up twice."

"Enough!" Grainger said, and all debate instantly ceased. "The president will die, but first, the American Terrorist must be neutralized. We cannot take the chance that he will interfere again."

"I agree," Hollis replied. "Carl Johnson is on a killing spree in Mexico. For eight months, he's been like a hound with a scent. He will not stop until he finds us. And it appears he is now in an active partnership with the president, and she is providing him with intel, logistics support, and government assets."

A woman's voice, a rarity in the inner circle of Atlas, floated from the speaker grill on the conference table. "He is resilient and resourceful, so another tactical operation against Johnson is unlikely to be effective."

"I agree," Grainger said. "That's why we have a multipronged operation set to begin tomorrow. We believe he is going back to Mexico to terminate the last surviving member of the Triad. We have men on-site waiting for him."

"And if he survives?"

"We have four more ops in motion against him. After he is neutralized, the president will die."

His brother nodded in the deep shadow. "Then Operation Atlas will commence."

Grainger Koll paused for a moment as if the silence itself reinforced the import of his next words. "No one turns their back on Atlas, not even the president of the United States. She rejected our agenda, so she must pay with her life."

CHAPTER 1

"**H**EY, MISTER, ARE YOU AMERICAN?"

Carl Johnson, known to the world as the "American Terrorist," pivoted in the shadows and found the owner of the tiny voice. Clearly, the boy already knew he was American because he addressed Carl in English. The boy looked about eight and was dressed in a tattered T-shirt and canvas pants. What looked like a lamp cord served as his belt. He was barefoot and stood in the doorway of a cheap high-mountain cabin.

Carl nodded. "I am."

"Are you gonna kill somebody?" The boy looked past Carl to the walled homestead across the rural road.

Carl nodded and said, "Mm-hmm."

"Have you ever seen people die?" the boy said.

Carl gazed across the road at his target. He was getting ready to do exactly that in a few minutes—watch people die. "I have." He glanced back at the boy. "Have you?"

The boy shook his head and said, "What does it feel like?"

The question surprised Carl, partly because of the content of the question and partly because the question came from such a young person. There was barely ten feet between the boy's adobe ramshackle house and the next, and the area where they stood was shrouded in dark shadow compared to the bright sunlight of the late afternoon.

The homestead that was his target was in a rural town nestled in the foothills of the Sierra Madre del Sur, in the mountainous southwest part of Mexico. It was an undeveloped town in a location no doubt desired by the owner because outsiders stood out.

Carl pivoted and stepped over to the door, then squatted down in front of the boy. He raised his face shield and gazed into the boy's hazel eyes. "You speak my language very well."

The boy smiled at the compliment. "Someday, *mi papa* is gonna take us to *Los Estados Unidos*."

"Yeah? What part?"

"*Los Anheles*." The boy pronounced the City of Angels by its Spanish translation.

Carl restrained his knee-jerk response that the American dream wasn't all it was cracked up to be, and if you were brown, Mexican, Muslim, Asian, gay, or of original Native American heritage, then the Dream didn't apply. But in his next thought, he admitted that wasn't entirely true. In his life before becoming the American Terrorist, he'd carved out a pretty successful real estate career thanks to the American dream. That had all changed when the TER—Terror Event Response—Agency came for him on that fateful day in November. Fast-forward eight months, and he was discussing his feelings on life and death with a young Mexican boy.

"You want to know what it's like to watch someone die?"

The boy nodded.

"Well, it depends on who's dying. I watched my son die, and it was the worst thing a person can ever have to watch. A month later, I watched some of the men who killed my son die, and it was the greatest feeling ever." He tapped his semiautomatic rifle. "Especially since I was the one who killed them." Then he stood and turned toward his objective.

"Take no unnecessary risks, Zero. And no more reckless engagements." Agent Palmer's clinical voice teased his inner ear through his tiny earpiece.

Whenever she wanted to seem all business with multiple listeners on the comm net, or when she was displeased with him, she called him by his numerical designation instead of his name. He was Zero, she was One, and the rest of his mercs also had assigned numbers.

"What you call risky behavior, I call mixing things up and being unpredictable. It keeps me alive."

"I'm not denying the value—"

"Agent Palmer, you're not going to win this argument with me today. Now feed me intel on my target."

Her response was tinged with frustration, and he knew why.

"Wait for backup, Zero!" she said. "That battle suit doesn't make you invincible. Merc Three has secured the evac site, and choppers are inbound. Six and Sixteen are en route to your location."

Carl's team had infiltrated Mexico as tourists. It was the same method he'd used on his mission to rescue the president's daughter so many months ago. He had minimal support from his mercs and no military backup, but he had a supreme advantage.

He looked down at the black hard-shell combat armor that completely covered his torso and limbs. Purchased on the black market from Peru SWAT, it was constructed of a series of interlocked metal-ceramic plates specially designed to resist penetration by all standard small-arms fire. It could even deflect all but direct, close-range, armor-piercing ordnance. Any impact would hurt like hell, of course, but he would still be fully functional in a firefight.

He stepped from his cover between the two buildings, lowered his Kevlar combat helmet's acrylic face shield, and made a beeline to the entrance of the ranch house across the street. He put the stock of his PDW—Personal Defense Weapon—to his shoulder and sighted along the barrel as he walked. Compact, magazine-fed, and self-loading, the PDW was his favorite lightweight urban street fighter.

Merc Three's voice came over the comm. "Jesus, Boss! What are you doing?"

"I'm going in, with or without intel."

For the third time in a month, he was going into solo combat in a foreign country, Mexico, a US ally. Though *combat* was probably a mischaracterization of his mission. He was going to assassinate the last surviving member of a powerful Mexican political cartel, the Triad. Those were the people Rainman had employed in the kidnapping of President Shirley Mallory's daughter and in the subsequent attempt to murder

Mallory, the first female president of the United States. It was the group ultimately responsible for the murder of Carl's son.

Merc Three said, "Well, Boss, perhaps you and *Miss Government Agent* can put aside your little domestic dispute and get your fucking heads in the game! If you die, the mission ends."

Palmer said, "Copy that." She paused a moment, then added, "Dammit, Carl, wait for Three to arrive."

"Negative," he said. "Intel, please."

She sighed. "The overhead drone shows four hostiles approaching the courtyard fast from the west side of the house—your right. Two more are approaching from the east side. Distance, ten meters. ETA to visual, five seconds."

The homestead reminded Carl of northern New Mexico architecture. The house was earth-colored adobe—*real* adobe, the two-foot-thick kind made of mud, grass, and chicken wire, not the thin kind made of two-by-fours and synthetic stucco. He passed through the open archway in the adobe courtyard wall, his attention laser-focused on the man he would find beyond the front door, and pulled two square grenades from his utility belt. He pulled the black tabs and tossed one after the other, so they both landed just beyond the east and west corners of the house. The battle armor restricted full range of motion, but his aim was true, and debris blasted from the explosions on both sides of the building.

Agent Palmer said, "Two survivors on your right."

Carl stopped, pivoted, and snapped off two headshots from six meters away at the two wounded security guards that stumbled into view. He continued toward the door and grabbed another grenade from his utility belt. He stopped, tossed the grenade, and leaned forward in anticipation of the blast. The explosion annihilated the entire doorway, and debris pinged against his armor, then he charged through the smoke. His thumb found the selector switch, and he flicked it from single-shot to triple-shot.

Agent Palmer said, "Infrared shows one tango approaching your position from the right, forty-five-degree sightline."

Carl shifted to the right, but no one was there. He only saw the stairs, so he shifted his aim upward and fired at the same time the gunman halfway down fired at him. The man sprayed bullets everywhere, but only one hit Carl in the chest, pounding him back two steps.

"Fuck!"

"Status, Zero?"

"Damn, that hurt."

He desperately wanted to massage the sore area but couldn't because of the armor. He looked upward again and found his triple tap had splattered the gunman's blood on the wall, and the man had rolled the rest of the way down the stairs. Carl checked the body. He was most definitely dead, but he looked barely old enough to be called a teen.

"Three tangos approaching your left, ninety degrees, seven meters."

He didn't want to risk shooting down the hallway and missing one or more of the approaching gunmen. Then he'd find himself in an extended gunfight that would be challenging, even with Agent Palmer's surveillance drone assisting. He pulled another grenade and tossed it around the corner. He heard a warning shout barely half a second before the explosion, and more debris blasted across the foyer in front of him. Carl followed his PDW into that hallway and fired three single shots at the wounded men. Three more headshots at point-blank range.

"Your path is clear to the living room at the rear of the house. Infrared shows eight tangos there."

"Copy that."

Carl moved quickly, knowing the grenade explosions would draw the local police. The first wave probably wouldn't have any weaponry that could stop him, but he didn't want to create an international incident for President Mallory. She could disavow any knowledge related to an incident involving the American Terrorist—that was part of his agreement with her—but he didn't want to use that capital just yet.

As if reading his mind, Agent Palmer updated him. "Radio chatter indicates local law enforcement has been called. You have seven minutes to conclude your business."

Conclude your business. Government speak for terminate another human being. Do to them what they tried and failed to do to me but instead did to my son.

Seven minutes was plenty of time for that.

Carl walked into the glass-enclosed entertainment patio. Sliding glass doors were open and stacked to the left side of the twelve-foot opening. Three opulent white wicker sofas decorated the room, adorned by a dozen huge silk pillows. Fruit, sandwiches, and a variety of drinks sat on the glass and steel coffee table in the middle.

His target, Federico Gonzales, sat in the center of one sofa, surrounded by seven people. Two were kids, and five were young adult men and women.

Pointing his assault rifle at the man's chest, he said, "President Shirley Mallory sends her regards."

"I've been expecting you," Gonzales said in clear English with a strong accent. He made a shooing motion with his hands and said something in Spanish before everyone started to get up.

"Stop!" Carl's command instantly froze everyone in mid-motion. "Sit the fuck down!"

He heard Palmer's hesitant voice in his ear. "Zero, what are you doing?"

Gonzales said, "It was not enough for you to kill my daughter and my mother. Now you have to kill my entire family? My grandchildren too?"

"If my son hadn't been a casualty of your scheme, I might give a shit about *your* family."

"Zero, don't do this," Palmer said. "Terminate your target and leave the others alive. They are not your enemy, not the mission."

It had taken a lot of arguing to convince President Mallory to authorize what amounted to an assassination mission into Mexico to terminate the Triad. With the Triad and their military general dead, and with former Vice President Walter Breen—a.k.a. *Rainman*—in hiding as the most wanted man in the covert world, Carl was about to close the book on a political conspiracy that reached to the highest levels of the US government.

What would he do after that book was closed? How would he live without his son? Mark, murdered at age thirty, had been collateral damage in large part because of the man sitting in front of him, and Carl found himself hating the family members of that man because of what he'd taken from Carl.

The Triad leader seemed to sense Carl's anguish. "Please, I give you my life. In all that is holy and decent—"

"Your life is mine to take, not yours to give. And there's nothing holy or decent about me anymore. Your people saw to that."

"Then let me buy the lives of my family with critical intelligence you need. You have an informant on your team, a high-level informant. I can give you the identity of that informant in exchange for the lives of my family."

Carl saw deceit and treachery in the man's eyes, or at least he imagined he saw those qualities because it made it easier to hate the man. Still, he knew the man would do or say anything to grasp the elusive hope of preserving his and his family's lives a little longer. Problem was, Carl didn't believe him. He had faith in his team, but he knew the moment he got complacent or overconfident would be the moment he'd lose the war. And there was no way any of his mercs could be a traitor. No way any of Agent Palmer's limited government team could be a traitor. All had been in combat with Carl, and all had risked their own lives. They were all vetted.

Except the new mercenaries. And the new government agents.

"Zero, you have two minutes to evac. Use the south yard exit."

Carl nodded at the man and lowered his weapon. Even if he did have the name of a traitor, Carl knew he wouldn't get that name right now, so he said, "I'll contact you in one hour for that name. If your intel is not true, we'll have this discussion again…minus the discussion."

Then he walked out the rear all-glass door, walked six paces, and stopped. When he looked over his shoulder, Federico Gonzales was still watching him. Carl glared at his enemy for a few more seconds, then turned and continued his retreat. He only made it a single step farther before his breath rasped in his throat, and he growled. All the hatred, anger, and pain of the past few months boiled to the surface of his consciousness again.

"Motherfucker…"

"Carl?" Agent Palmer said quietly.

He turned and faced Gonzales again, this time pulling out his last grenade. He pulled the tab. The man's eyes widened, and he extended his arms, palms outward, imploring Carl not to throw the grenade.

Agent Palmer, clearly still watching him on drone telemetry, said, "Carl, don't do it! Stick with the plan."

"I don't give a fuck about the plan," Carl said. "And those people around him are not innocent. They understand the business he's in and what he does to people. They choose to benefit from his murderous deeds, so they deserve no mercy."

Merc Three added, "Don't do it, Boss. There are children—"

He released the tab, and with a backhanded flick of his wrist, Carl tossed the grenade back into the glass-enclosed patio. Then he turned away as the device exploded. Glass shards pinged harmlessly off his armor, and the heat of the fiery blast washed over him. He took one final look at the patio and watched the roof cave in, then he turned and walked away.

Agent Palmer gasped. "Carl, what have you done?"

"I have completed my final act as the American Terrorist. I'm done."

Now he had to figure out how to live with everything he'd done—everyone he'd killed.

He had to figure out how to live without his son.

He had to decide if he even *wanted* to live without his son.

I should have saved the last grenade for myself.

CHAPTER 2

"**H**EY!"

Former Special Agent Lenore Cummings tensed when she heard her cell phone ping. It was the distinctive default notification from the Signal secure texting app. Since her discharge from federal service more than six months ago, she'd communicated only through the secure app for both text and voice, and she required the same of her daughter and mother. Carl Johnson, the American Terrorist she'd unwittingly gotten involved with, had set her on the path of paranoia for good reason.

"This isn't over," Carl had said so many months ago. "They'll come for you again if they think we're connected in any way."

The cell sat on the fake granite counter beside her chopping board. She stopped her food prep and looked at the screen. She didn't recognize the number.

The text message read, *Need your help.*

Then the phone pinged again.

"Hey!" the cell said.

The next message read, *Please.*

She rinsed her hands and dried them. The third ping came after a pause, and she sensed the sender of the texts was unsure of himself or herself.

Niece in trouble. People say you know someone who can retrieve.

People? Who were these *people*? The *someone* was Carl Johnson, so she knew it was a trap. She pushed the phone aside without answering the text, but before turning back to her veggie-chopping task, she noticed her mother watching from the kitchen archway.

"Is that trouble?"

"I'm not going to answer it."

"Maybe you should. Ignoring trouble won't make it go away."

"No, Ma. It's not like they can't find us whenever they want. We can't hide. We just have to be prepared."

Lenore had a family, so she couldn't just disappear. They had a new home. She had bills. Her daughter had to go to school. Ma had hobbies and friends. No, they couldn't hide, and she refused to live in fear. She looked at her ma and tapped the sidearm she wore all day whenever she was awake.

"*Hey!*"

She looked at the phone, and the eyes of a pretty teen girl gazed back at her. The girl looked about Lisette's age.

My niece, Tiara, 13, the unknown person texted.

Lenore looked at her mother and waited for the phone to ping again.

I'm LE.

She didn't know anyone with the initials LE.

Can't file missing persons report for 24 hrs.

Of course, Lenore knew that.

Can't go get her myself. No backup.

"Huh…" Lenore looked at her ma. "He's a cop." LE stood for law enforcement.

There were many reasons a police officer couldn't mount a rescue of a family member on his own, and that's why he had no backup. There were reports to be filed, investigations to be initiated, authorizations to secure, and operations to plan—all that took time. If the captive was a family member, well, that was an obstacle in and of itself. She texted her demands back to the unknown officer, if that was, in fact, what he was.

Name, she texted back.

His response was immediate: *Diego Contreras.*

Badge number.

He gave it.

Selfie. She wanted to know what he looked like, so she could match his face with the inquiry she was going to make.

Officer Contreras's face filled her screen.

She called a contact at the local Bureau office she knew would do a quick personnel background check for her. She'd been forced out of the FBI but had associates at the office who still regarded her as the competent agent she'd always been. It was an unspoken protocol between active and retired agents. A professional courtesy between brothers and sisters. As long as she didn't ask for classified information, they'd help her.

The officer checked out, so she texted him a location with a short ten-minute window. If he didn't show up, then he was on his own. He said he'd be there.

Lenore looked up. "Ma, can you finish up here? And make sure Lisette finishes her homework, okay? I should be back in an hour."

Her mother nodded. "You're doing the right thing. You have to be sure. You can't wait for them to come."

In the Signal app, Lenore dialed a number from memory, a number she knew she could only use once.

Carl Johnson's voice was all business. "Talk to me."

"This… This is—"

"I know who you are." Of course, the man would recognize her voice. It had been months since she'd seen or spoken to Carl, once an enemy then a savior, but she immediately felt calmed by the caring tone of his voice. "Sitrep."

"I think the trap you said we should expect is here."

"I was wondering how long it would take them."

"A cop reached out for help. Are you in town?"

"Just got back this morning," Carl answered.

Lenore nodded with the phone to her ear. "Which makes this too coincidental."

"Indeed. We'll be coming heavy. Tell me when and where."

CHAPTER 3

CARL JOHNSON STOOD ACROSS THE street from the trendy Nob Hill diner, listening to the curt operational voices in his right ear. Merc Three was conducting the op.

"Twelve, status," Three demanded.

"The area is secure. All exits covered. No hostiles."

"Seventeen?"

"Two-block perimeter established. Clearing for hostiles. Stand by."

Three said, "Eighteen, you have overwatch?"

Merc Eighteen was the retired Special Forces sniper Agent Palmer had recruited to take the place of Merc Four, who had died in the op to rescue the president's daughter.

"Roger that. Overwatch established. Zero hostiles."

Merc Three said, "Boss, we're standing by for perimeter check. Agent Palmer, request private channel with you and Zero, over."

"Copy that." Palmer's voice was silent for a brief moment, then she said, "Private channel established."

Carl knew what Three wanted to discuss. He knew Palmer wanted to discuss it too, but there hadn't been time.

"I crossed the line in Mexico. I know that." He kicked some rocks on the sidewalk. "But I couldn't help myself. I was so…angry. Rage consumed me, and when I looked into that man's eyes, all I could see was my dead son's face. All I could think about was making him and his whole family pay."

Three said, "Boss, you know me and the guys got your back no matter what. Actually, I wanted to ask you about *what he said*. Do you really think we could have a mole?"

Palmer interrupted, "Maybe if he'd stopped at 'informant' instead of 'high-level informant,' I might have given him credibility."

Carl nodded to himself. "My thoughts exactly. The only high-level people on our team are the three of us and McGrath, and we've all been through the shit together. I trust you and, yes, even McGrath. There's no way any of us four have been compromised. Just to be safe, though, let's monitor all the new TER agents and mercs. I think he was just trying to live a little longer."

Three added, "Or he knew you were going to kill him, and that statement was his last jab, just to fuck with us and make us change our ground game."

Palmer said, "On the other topic, Carl, I'm concerned about… Hold one." She fell silent. "Seventeen is reporting in on the other channel. Perimeter is clear. No hostiles. Reestablishing comm channel."

"Copy that," Three said. "All units, report in."

It was late, so Carl had been standing in the dark shadows of the alcove of a closed clothing store half a block south of Central. Traffic cruised slowly by on the well-lit Central Avenue, but the side street where the restaurant was located was only sparsely lit, and traffic was light. It was a good choice for a clandestine meeting. He scanned the dimly lit street as his team reported in. Three coordinated with Agent Palmer and gave him the all clear.

"Boss, you are cleared to enter the restaurant."

"Entering now."

He crossed the street, crossed the courtyard patio, and stepped through the open front door. It was an old house that had been converted into a mom-and-pop New Mexican food restaurant. He'd eaten there many times over his three decades living in Albuquerque. The familiar aroma of red and green *chile* sauce reminded him of his long time living in that city…before becoming a domestic terrorist. Back when his son Mark was a child visiting for the summers, they'd eaten there so many times he'd gotten to know the owners. But that was a long time ago.

Carl had no backup inside the restaurant, so he paused inside the doorway and scanned the small dining room. The room was dimly lit and comfortable for patrons, and he wore a black T-shirt and dark jeans, so the Glock he held pinned against his right thigh went unnoticed by everyone except Agent Cummings and the cop she sat with. Carl approached their table against the wall, then tensed as his earpiece erupted in chatter.

"Danger close! I have the shot! I'm taking the shot!"

Carl hadn't fully perceived the threat yet, but there was something nonthreatening about the presence he felt quickly approaching him from the smaller dining room behind him, something familiar.

"Oh my God!"

The explosive whisper almost stopped Carl's heart, and he whispered harshly, "Hold! Hold! Hold!"

As he spun to face the approaching figure, he also noticed Agent Cummings and the police officer tensing. Then the young femboy leaped into his embrace. He wrapped slender legs around Carl's waist and his arms around Carl's neck, then giggled and buried his face against Carl's cheek.

"Rainey!"

"Hi, Carl." The boy unwrapped himself, then planted a shy kiss on Carl's cheek.

Carl tucked his Glock in his waistband in the back, gently grabbed the boy by his shoulders, and pulled him into a warm hug. "I thought you were dead," he said, rocking Rainey side to side. "I thought I killed you by infecting you."

"I never got sick. They said I was immune."

Carl held the young man at arm's length and looked him over. Rainey Livingston wore tight black girly shorts, knee-high black boots with brass buckles, and a burgundy button-down blouse. He was just as pretty as when he'd first met him, except back then, Carl had thought he was a girl because he'd been dressed in a miniskirt and stilettos. He had soft facial features and a minimal amount of makeup—clear lip gloss and a bit of eyeliner. He'd helped the boy out of a traumatic situation but had touched him before he knew he himself was infected with the deadly Contagion. He'd assumed the boy and all his family had contracted the disease and died.

"Did you change your hair?" Carl asked.

Rainey nodded. "I just cut it last week." His straight black hair was ear-length on the right and shoulder-length on the left. He pushed a few strands behind his left ear. "You like it?"

"I do," Carl said with a smile. It highlighted his caramel-colored skin and made him look older than his twenty-something years. "Your family…uninfected?"

Rainey nodded. "You want to meet them?" He pivoted and pointed to a group of people that were eyeballing Carl. They seemed unfriendly.

"I have clients." Carl nodded behind him. "Besides, your family looks like they don't approve of you hanging with a terrorist."

"I don't believe what they say about you on the news, and I don't believe you're a terrorist." He nodded at his family. "Besides, they don't know you like I do."

Carl smiled at the boy's naivete, but he also felt a little sad. In his new life in the shadow world of terrorism and government clandestine operations, a normal world of friends and family was forfeit. He shook off the sadness quickly. He'd chosen this life. He couldn't blame anyone but himself.

To Rainey, he said, "What they say about me is true."

"Well, I love you anyway."

That caught Carl by surprise. "You know I'm older than your parents, right?" His words sounded crazy even to himself.

Rainey punched him playfully on the shoulder. "I don't mean like *that*, Silly." He hugged Carl again, then got teary-eyed. "I never thanked you before, you know, for helping me." He kissed Carl on the cheek again.

The gesture of tenderness made Carl smile. "You don't have to thank me," he said. "It's what we do for our kids when we're able." That was his life mantra now because he hadn't been able to save his own adult son. "I'll see you around, okay?"

Rainey nodded, and Carl watched him sashay back over to his family.

A server approached. "Can I get you anything?"

Carl shook his head as he turned to face Cummings and the officer.

The server turned her attention to the others. "Are you two still doing okay?"

They both nodded as Carl sat on the cushioned bench next to Cummings.

"Agent Cummings," he said in greeting.

"Actually, it's *ex*-agent."

Carl grunted. "FBI's loss." He knew how capable Cummings was. He'd seen her extensive dossier.

They looked at each other sideways until it became uncomfortable, then his gaze took in what he could see of her new physique. She'd dropped almost twenty pounds and looked slender and fit. Lethal. Even her brown-eyed gaze was as hard as a rock. She looked ready for action.

"Looks like somebody's been working out. No one is going to catch you off guard again."

"Damn straight."

"Are you armed?"

She nodded. "Every minute of every day."

Carl grunted his approval, then swiveled his head Chris Tucker-style and examined Officer Contreras across the table. The young man was clean-cut and good-looking, late twenties. His police uniform was immaculate. His face looked desperate.

"I hear you have a missing child," Carl said.

The officer nodded. "My niece. She's only sixteen."

"You know, if one of my people had a missing kid, nothing would stop us from getting that kid back, so what's stopping you?"

The young officer looked around and started to speak, but Cummings interrupted him, saying, "She's not missing, is she? She didn't run away."

Contreras looked down at the table and twirled his water glass. Finally, he shook his head. "My sister told me a week ago that Tiara, that's her name, she took up with some people much older than her, in their mid-twenties. Shady people, that's what Sis called them. She said they're trafficking drugs and cars. I thought she was saying that because the guys got high and wore white wife-beaters and because them and the girls are all inked up."

Cummings said, "So all you have is your sister's concern. You have no evidence of kidnapping and so no cause for a legitimate investigation. Yet you are worried. Why?"

"Tiara didn't go home last night. She promised she would because she had a doctor's appointment early this morning." Contreras looked at them both. "I've checked these people out. They are *bad news*. One of the guys and two of the women have records—assault, burglary, theft —and another has kidnapping charges filed against him, but without convictions."

Carl looked to his left at Cummings and said, "Illegal surveillance. My kind of guy." She held his gaze, and in an instant, he was back in time a little more than eight months ago. He'd had the FBI agent strapped naked to a table and threatened her daughter's life because of what she'd done to…

She bounced her knee roughly against his and brought him back to the present.

He blinked several times, refocusing on her serious brown eyes. "Sorry."

She nodded, and he watched her scan the room.

Once a cop, always a cop. He followed her gaze while speaking into his comm. "Three, what's our status outside?"

"All clear, Boss. No threats."

Carl nodded to himself and said, "Officer Contreras, do you have the names of the people your niece is involved with?"

The officer gave him the names of two men and one woman.

Carl was silent as his team researched the names. The cop was nervous. His gaze darted between him and Cummings, and he absently toyed with his fingernails. The officer clasped his hands together and glanced again between Lenore Cummings and Carl. He started to speak, but Carl held up a palm.

Wizard, his ex-CIA analyst, whistled. "These really *are* some bad people, Boss. That police officer's information barely scratched the surface. If the girl is mixed up with them…"

"Officer Contreras," Carl began, wanting to make sure everyone on the channel knew to whom he was asking questions. "Do you have a location on the suspects?"

The officer nodded and rattled off an address with a zip code Carl recognized on the west side, not the best part of Albuquerque by far, but not the worst either.

Wizard said, "Two of the suspects have that address listed on their ID as their residence. I'm also seeing evidence of frequent travel to Mexico. Credit card receipts for El Paso hotels, gas stations, and also in Juarez. These folks don't care about leaving a digital trail."

Agent Palmer said, "Carl, are you thinking they're involved in human trafficking?"

"I am, but it's only a gut feeling." He enjoyed the power of knowing that the people he sat with could only hear his side of the conversation.

Palmer said, "If we wait for evidence, it might be too late for his niece."

"Agreed," Carl added. "Redirect the drone over that address. Let's see who's home."

"Copy that. The house is on the West Mesa. Drone ETA, three minutes."

Officer Contreras raised his eyebrows. "You have a drone?"

"I'm a fucking terrorist. Of course I have a drone. It's why you called her." He head-nodded in Cummings's direction. "Even though it's dark, we have thermal and low-light capability. We'll at least get a body count."

While they waited, Cummings asked, "How did you know to call me?"

Contreras replied, "I called my sergeant. He was involved with Mr. Johnson's operations late last year. He knew of your involvement together and suggested I reach out to you. He thought since the PD has you listed as *hands-off*," the young cop looked at Carl, "you might be able to help."

The officer ended his statement with a nod at Cummings, who bounced her knee lightly against Carl's again.

Carl knew the explanation was a sham, but he also knew that the officer hadn't knowingly compromised them. Carl's involvement with Cummings was highly classified, so only someone connected at the highest level of the local FBI office could have divulged that info...or someone on Rainman's team.

Carl said to his mercenary team, "Everyone, stay frosty."

Three minutes later, they had a body count. The drone showed five adult-sized thermal markers moving in the kitchen and living room of the four-bedroom house. Two were moving, and three were seated together, perhaps on a couch watching TV. There were also six smaller thermal markers in the southwest bedroom, seated in a row along a wall.

Merc Three said, "My guess would be these six are children or young teens, likely hostages, probably zip-tied."

Carl nodded at the report. "Agent Palmer, your recommendation?"

Three interrupted, "Wait. One of the three seated adults is heading toward the group of six in the far bedroom. He's pausing, perhaps at the door, checking to make sure they're still where they should be. Now he's returning to the front room. He's sitting down again. Probably watching TV."

Agent Palmer added, "I believe a retrieval is warranted. We have six personnel at your location. We'll redeploy a team of three for retrieval with the drone and reposition your remaining team members around you for best coverage."

Good plan. He noticed the way Agent Palmer never referred to his men and women as *mercs*. It was as if she couldn't allow herself to utter the true name of his defense force. Eight months ago, four of his *team members* and a drug-addicted ex-CIA hacker, the one now called Wizard, had royally kicked the US government's ass...twice. Or perhaps she didn't care about all that and was simply giving the mercs respect by being politically correct.

He heard his name called from across the room and saw Rainey waving at him as he and his family left the diner. He waved back, wondering if the boy had nightmares and awoke screaming after his assault. Carl knew a bit about trauma and the emotional aftermath and how it could destroy one's life. Maybe he'd check in on the young man from time to time since he knew where he lived.

Carl caught the attention of a server and ordered a serving of chicken enchiladas, light on the red and green *chile* sauce, or *easy-Christmas*, as the server called it. He was conscious of the closeness of the FBI woman, the heat of her thigh touching his, and the scent of her minty fresh breath. His meal came surprisingly fast, and he devoured the food wordlessly. As he wiped with a napkin, he eyeballed the *sopapilla*, a kind of Mexican frybread that, when deep-fried, puffed up like a little air-filled pillow.

He chuckled. "Mark calls these things 'soapy pillows.' He'd—" Carl froze as a pang of grief gripped his heart, and he looked sideways at Cummings. "Well, he used to call them that. I mean, when he was little."

She smiled cautiously.

He said, "He'd bite off a corner and pour so much honey inside that when he ate one, the honey would gush out all over everything. What a mess."

He offered the two sopapillas to Cummings and Contreras, but they both declined, so he ate them himself. He'd just finished when the retrieval team reported in.

"Sixteen here. I have eyes on six children sitting on the floor, all zip-tied."

"Nine here. I have eyes on five adults in the front rooms of the house."

"Twelve here. Rear of the house is secure. Ready to breach on your order, Agent Palmer."

Agent Palmer added, "Sixteen, is the target package present?"

"Affirmative."

"Breach now!"

Carl heard two flash-bang explosions over the channel, followed quickly by two explosions he knew were the front and back doors being blown open. Three seconds of shouting and harsh language finalized the breach.

"Clear!"

"Clear!"

Carl listened for a moment, then looked at the officer and said, "Six children, including Tiara, have been evacuated from the house. All uninjured."

Contreras let out his breath and signed a cross in the air before him. Carl resisted his knee-jerk reaction of discounting the involvement of the man's deity in the rescue operation.

Sixteen said, "Disposition of the suspects?"

Nancy Palmer was first and foremost a government agent. She wouldn't make the call that needed to be made in Carl's world. She couldn't, so Carl did.

"Kill them."

"Copy that."

He heard shots over the comm channel and shrugged at the shocked look on the officer's face. "They kidnapped children," Carl said. "Hundreds of children go missing every year and are never found. Some are sold across the border into child porn or slavery. Same thing probably would have happened to these children, to Tiara. In my book, anyone who preys on children deserves to die. No question."

The officer nodded and looked like he was supposed to say something.

Carl nodded toward the door. "You may leave now."

The officer stood up and adjusted his uniform shirt and utility belt. He was a slender fellow, but his upper body looked bulky due to the vest under his shirt. The officer held his hand out toward Carl. Carl left him hanging, though, and glared at the young man until he made a fist of his extended hand and took a couple steps back. Carl watched him pivot and walk through the open doorway. He crossed the dimly lit patio of diners and blended into the darkness of the dark sidewalk.

Carl looked at the former FBI agent for a moment. He hadn't seen her since the conclusion of the events surrounding the Contagion outbreak. He'd been the carrier, Patient Zero, and had infected a lot of people, including Cummings and her daughter.

"How's Lisette?"

"She's okay. She'll be fine…I think."

Carl looked away. "Lenore, she'll never be fine, not after what I did to her. To you." *Before the Contagion. Before I infected them.*

Lenore Cummings reached out under the table and held his hand. "Carl, we both did terrible things to each other. We have to find a way to forgive each other."

He looked at her again. His voice broke, and he felt his bottom lip quiver. "I'll never be able to forgive *myself*."

She nodded, and this time, she was the one to look away. "I know. Your son *died* because of me, but my child *lives* because of you."

Carl took a deep breath and blew it out slowly. "If it wasn't for me, your child would never have been in danger in the first place."

He pulled a fifty from his pocket and laid it on the table. *A 250 percent tip.* He stood and reached behind him to make sure his Glock was securely tucked in the back of his pants, under his T-shirt, then studied the agent as she studied him. The plain truth was, he never wanted to see Lenore Cummings or her daughter again. It was too painful.

"Watch your back, Lenore. I thought this was a setup. Someone on the police force knows about us who shouldn't, so I didn't expect it to end this neatly." He hesitated for a moment, feeling like he needed to say something else, but no words came. He turned and left the diner.

CHAPTER 4

L ENORE CUMMINGS SAT IN HER mother's rocking chair in the living room all night. It reminded her of her childhood. It smelled like… Well, she didn't know exactly what it smelled like. It smelled like *comfort*. It smelled like *safe*. The brown leather was well-worn, soft, and smooth.

Whenever she needed comforting way back then, Lacey Cummings would hold Lenore in her lap and rock her in that very same chair. When Lenore's father had died a few years ago, Lacey had been so distraught over the loss of her life partner, she had thrown out everything in the house that reminded her of her late husband. Everything except the chair. It remained parked next to the couch in front of the wall-mounted TV.

Now, though, the chair held no comfort for Lenore. She slept fitfully throughout the night, curled up tight in the chair. She kept thinking of Carl and his dead son and wishing she could alter the past—somehow go back and save the innocent young man.

Dawn was just kissing the sky with a wave of light blue color, but the yard beyond the living room's sliding glass door was still in deep darkness. A night light on the wall behind her provided just enough light in the room in case she needed to move around. She turned on the wall-mounted TV with the remote that sat on the stand beside her chair and muted the volume. The next thing she realized, the sun was up, and her mother had just set a piping hot cup of coffee on the stand beside her chair.

"Thanks, Ma." She looked at the pendulum clock in the corner.

It showed seven-thirty. The digital thermometer above the clock read seventy-three. It was going to be another 100-degree day.

"Did you sleep in here all night?"

Lenore nodded. "I can't get him out of my mind." She sipped her coffee. "He sat next to me in the diner. On the same bench seat. His shoulder touched mine. His leg touched mine." She shuddered. "The last time he touched me…"

Her mom knew what Carl Johnson had done to her and her daughter. They had discussed her feelings and her simmering anger many times. They had discussed her feelings on how he had a shootout with assassins to save her and her daughter, how he took a bullet in the back of his body armor for Lisette, and how he had recklessly jumped out of an airplane to save them a second time.

"Do you think he feels as guilty as you do?" Lacey sat on the nearby sofa.

Lenore nodded. "I felt his pain and his guilt." She sipped the warm liquid again. The coffee was strong, and she could smell the hazelnut-flavored cream her ma had used instead of the regular half-and-half. "God, I actually held his hand, Ma!" She gasped with the anguish of conflicted feelings.

"He needs your forgiveness, doesn't he? And you need his." Lacey drank from her cup also. "But you can't forgive yourself, can you? You need to, you know. You can't carry this burden alone forever."

"How can I? I got his son killed." She sipped again, then whispered, "But he can't forgive himself either…for what he did to Lisette. He told me so."

"Forget about the doctors and therapists. You two need to help each other. You're the only ones who can. You have to find a way to reach him."

Lenore was about to agree but gasped at a picture on the TV screen. The morning news showed the police department photo of a smiling Officer Diego Contreras. The scrolling subtitle was disturbing.

"Off-duty police officer gunned down outside his home. Entire family murdered. Motive unknown."

"Oh my God!" The words that escaped her lips were barely a whisper.

"*Hey!*" Her cell phone pinged at her.

The text message read, *Get out now! –CJ.*

"Ma, we gotta go. Right now! Go get in the car," she said as she hopped up from the rocking chair. "I'll get—"

Halfway to her feet, she heard a man's stern voice. "Sit back down, both of you."

The black-clad man standing in the foyer held a wicked-looking P-90 submachine gun. There would be no arguing with him, and he stood between her and her daughter's bedroom.

Lenore and Lacey sat back down. She heard the door between the garage and kitchen open, and five more similarly armed commandos dressed in black entered the living room. The first man who had spoken stepped down the hall, and he returned a few minutes later, towing a sleepy Lisette by the arm.

"Mommy!"

"It's okay, sweetie. Come over here with me."

The man said, "She stays with me."

At five-six, Lisette was tall for a twelve-year-old, but he towered over her by another foot.

"What do you want?" Lenore asked.

"We want the American Terrorist. We want Carl Johnson."

CHAPTER 5

CARL HAD KEPT HIS MERCS at a heightened state of readiness, not because he expected something to happen but because a trap had *not* happened at last night's operation to retrieve the officer's niece. A little over an hour ago, one of Wizard's automated keyword searches had announced the death of Officer Contreras, and Carl knew then that the trap he'd been expecting was sprung, and Lenore Cummings was the bait. An hour ago, he'd sent Lenore a text warning, but she hadn't responded. Now, Carl's team sat near her house in three SUVs, waiting for Agent Palmer to assess the situation.

As usual, Agent Palmer directed the op remotely from the TER covert operations center in Virginia. Because of her tactical experience and because she could literally see everything on-site through the drone cameras, mission oversight and deployment were her responsibility, even though Carl was technically the commander of his team of mercs and agents.

The big black SUV that Carl and his team of two mercs waited in was parked two blocks away from Cummings's house in a suburb of Albuquerque called Taylor Ranch, which, ironically, was where Carl had bought his first home almost twenty-five years ago. On his way, he'd experienced a nostalgic trip through his old neighborhood, even though a lot had changed since he'd lived there. A second SUV waited behind Carl's with two more mercs, and both drivers kept their engines idling and ready for instant movement. They faced directly east, and the sun rising over the north end of the Sandia Mountains blasted blinding light straight through the front windshield.

Cummings's house was a single-story ranch on an eighth of an acre. The floor plan he examined on his tablet indicated the two-thousand-square-foot home had two bedrooms and a bath on either end, separated by the living room, dining room, kitchen, and guest bath. A smaller window on the tablet showed an area map centered on Cummings's house. A third SUV pulled to a stop on the next street, and that assault team had only to go through a yard and hop Cummings's back fence to be in play.

"The drone shows all the blinds are drawn," Palmer said over the comm net. "So, Eighteen, I want you to trade your long rifle for an assault rifle and join the breach team."

Carl knew Merc Eighteen was in the SUV two streets over.

Palmer continued, "High-resolution infrared shows nine thermal units inside the house. The way they are positioned, these six are high-probability hostile targets." A red circle appeared on Carl's tablet, highlighting the six hostiles. "These two in the center are likely Cummings and her mother, based on body size."

Blue circles highlighted those two.

"But this thermal imprint here…" Palmer highlighted the thermal target nearest the front door. "This one's a double target, likely a hostile and the child."

From the SUV behind Carl's, Three said, "Boss, I don't like this. We have hostages all over the place in there, and we can't pick our targets until we get inside. This is clearly a trap, and they're expecting us. They'll have us pinned down before we even get a shot off."

Palmer said, "But it's a tactically inferior distribution of forces inside, Carl. They're all bunched in one room. Amateur nonsense. They're all concentrating on the hostages, and no one's guarding other access points—the garage, the other bedrooms, the backyard."

Three interrupted, "You think there are other tangoes hidden inside the house invisible to infrared?"

"No doubt," Palmer said. "They'd know we're coming fully armed. They know we have drone support, which, by the way, shows no other obvious thermal targets near the house."

"Air support?"

"Negative."

"Boss, what do you want to do?"

Carl said, "Well, it's clearly a trap, so let's pretend we're falling for it. We'll launch a frontal assault right through the front door."

The comm net went completely silent.

Three spoke tentatively. "Um, Boss, I'm not sure I like that plan. If they have support inside we can't see—"

"Right," Carl said. "So, we nuke the two bedroom wings with rocket-propelled grenades. The RPGs will take them by surprise for a second— make them flinch. The backyard team shoots up the living room. Aim high. Lots of noise and shattered glass. That will distract them further, so we can blow the front door and I can get a clean shot at the guy holding Lisette."

Palmer added, "That only leaves five hostiles inside."

"We leave those to Cummings."

"You assume she's armed?"

"I *know* she is. Every minute of every day, she told me. She's in the mix, so let's use her. I guaran-damn-tee you she knows me, so she knows what's coming. She'll be ready."

More silence filled the net.

"I tell you what," Carl said as he adjusted his armor and prepped his PDW. "I'm going in. Anyone that doesn't like the plan can stay safe in the SUVs."

"Whew! Thanks, Boss," Three said. "Since we have that option, I'm staying in the SUV."

Another voice said, "Seriously?"

"Hell no!" Three said. "Six, Eighteen, you're on RPGs. Hit both bedroom wings on my command. Thirteen, use a non-explosive RPG round on the front door to force it open. Zero, you hit the hostile holding the child. Nine, Ten, spray the living room, aiming high. Former Special Agent Cummings takes out the other five hostiles…if she has a weapon. Any questions?"

Carl looked at the merc sitting beside him and in the rearview mirror at the driver. "Well, when he lays it all out like that, the plan doesn't sound too smart."

"Best we have at the moment, Boss," Three said.

Agent Palmer said, "There are quite a few unknowns on-site, Carl."

Carl held out his arm and bumped forearms with his mercs. "Well, let's go eliminate some unknowns. Agent Palmer, send a smiley-face text to Cummings's cell phone. She'll know what it means even if they've taken her phone." He pounded on the driver's backrest. "Drive!"

The SUV rocketed forward and navigated two streets to Cummings's house. Since they were expected, they made no attempt at stealth. When the truck skidded to a stop, Mercs Six and Eighteen fired RPG rounds into the bedroom windows of the brick house, which exploded in billowing flames. At the same time, the backyard team lit up the glass doors and windows of the living room.

Carl raced toward the porch, ducking when he heard a shout. He felt the wind of the passing RPG round, but he didn't stop moving. The rocket-propelled round slammed into the front door without exploding, and the force of the impact literally blew the metal door off its hinges. Carl ran through the destroyed doorway at almost the same instant with his weapon up and ready, and he aimed as soon as he could see the commando holding Lisette in his grip. They both fired at the same time.

The commando holding Lisette sprayed at least a dozen rounds in Carl's direction, and a distant corner of Carl's brain wondered if neighbors' homes would be hit and how many casualties there would be.

But none of the man's rounds hit Carl because Lisette shoved the man's arm.

Carl's single shot bounced off the side of the commando's Kevlar helmet with a ping, which Carl actually heard despite the cacophony of gunfire in the room. The man had to be dazed by the impact, and Carl was on him with one singular thought—kill. He dropped his PDW and pulled his combat blade, then tackled the commando and the girl to the floor. Even as they hit the carpet, he slammed his blade through the man's goggles and into his brain. Twice.

Bullets punched into the wall next to him, literally exploding the pendulum clock. Carl spun and sheltered Lisette as his back erupted in pain. He'd been shot before—several times, in fact—so he was somewhat prepared for the experience. It hurt like hell, and he was pounded against the wall by the impacts, but he remained fully functional.

Behind him, Cummings hollered, "Cease fire!"

"Cease fire," Carl repeated. "All units cease fire!"

In the sudden silence, Cummings said, "Clear!"

Carl repeated the all clear over his comm.

Three said, "Ten, Eighteen, move in and clear the bedrooms. Terminate any survivors. Nine, you have overwatch. Boss, evac ASAP."

"Copy that."

Carl turned with the girl and examined Cummings's handiwork. All five of the remaining commandos were down, and the former FBI agent stood with her handgun pointed at the floor. She wore the same clothes she'd worn to the meeting last night with the now-dead police officer. Carl sensed she had just sent her mother out of the room because the elder woman disappeared into the kitchen. He heard a door open and close. He was just about to issue the evac order when he heard Agent Palmer's panicked voice over the net.

"Missiles inbound! Five seconds!"

Carl repeated for Cummings's benefit, "Missiles! Three seconds!"

But in their millisecond eye contact, they both knew they'd never get out of the house in time.

Cumming tossed her gun aside and pivoted. "On me!"

Carl didn't waste time questioning her intentions. He simply dropped his knife, picked up Lisette by the waist, and ran down the hall two steps behind Cummings. The bedroom closest to the street was totally destroyed and open to the sky. Surprisingly, there was no fire. He followed Cummings to the right, into the master bedroom, and he knew exactly what she had in mind.

"Everyone, disburse!" he said over the net.

"Boss! Get out of there!"

The first missile hit the living room with an ear-shattering blast that blew out the nearby walls and collapsed the ceiling of the master suite right on top of them. With the girl in his grasp, Carl dove into the cast-iron bathtub on top of Cummings. A pile of debris fell on top of them and blocked out all light.

Then the second missile hit, and Carl heard screams of agony over the comm net.

Then the third missile hit point-blank in the master bedroom.

CHAPTER 6

H E BECAME AWARE OF VOICES amid the ringing in his ears. It was Three and Palmer.

"Nine and Eighteen are down, status unknown."

"Thirteen, status?" There was a pause. "Thirteen?"

"Jesus! Thirteen's in a bad way. Real bad."

Agent Palmer said, "Zero is not answering. Is there any indication they might still be alive?"

Three said, "Negative. The entire house collapsed. They're buried under thousands of pounds of debris. The mother drove their SUV right through the garage door right after the first detonation, but she was the only occupant."

"Very well," Palmer said. "Prepare to depart. Can Thirteen be moved?"

"Negative. He's on borrowed time."

Carl listened to the exchange while he tested his voice. "Nancy, can you hear me?" He cleared his throat.

"Affirmative, Zero. What's your position?"

"I'm lying on top of an FBI agent in a bathtub."

"Gawd, sometimes you're so melodramatic, Carl." He heard the relief in her voice. "I meant your position in the house."

"*In the bathtub!*"

Merc Three added, "She means, what part of the house? We're coming in there to get you."

"Oh, my bad. Got my head banged pretty good. Still seeing stars. We're in the master suite. Left rear room of the house as you look at it from the street."

He tried to move but discovered he was solidly pinned in place. A standard size tub was barely large enough for one adult, yet the three of them were entangled in the tub and pinned by a massive portion of the collapsed roof.

"Lenore," he whispered. "You with me?"

"Alive but immobile," came the reply. "Sweetie, are you okay?"

"I'm stuck," Lisette said.

"I know. We're going to get out of here real soon."

"Agent Palmer, mind telling me how we got hit with missiles? We have a goddamn drone on overwatch. I thought you said they had zero air support."

"We're working on that, but those appeared to be ground-launched missiles, probably shoulder-held weapons with low-yield warheads."

"Well, they were pretty damn precise. They had to have air support for that kind of targeting."

Wizard's voice came on the net. "Not necessarily, Boss. They could have been guided by GPS satellite or by a laser target designator on a drone. Or they could even have used a laser designator on a standoff plane, like they used in the old days."

Old days? Carl thought. *That's how we used to fight wars when I got out of the Air Force twenty years ago.*

A sliver of light lit their dark tomb as the mercs shoved debris off the tub. A few minutes later, they got out of the tub and stumbled across the debris field into the street. Lenore and her daughter walked arm-in-arm behind Carl and Three.

"Carl!" Cummings said.

Lisette gasped.

When Carl turned to the girl, Three then stood behind him and also gasped.

"Jesus, Boss!"

"What?" He shrugged.

Cummings reached to his back and pulled away two armor plates, each about the size of her palm. Both were pitted with long grooves.

Cummings said, "Remember what I told you about the P-90 when they came for us the first time eight months ago?"

"I remember. They fire armor-piercing rounds. That's why we procured these battle suits."

Cummings nodded. "Looks like you took several glancing shots."

"Eighty-five thousand dollars well spent, I'd say," Three added. "But we're going to have to get you a new battle suit, Boss. This one's had it. Its integrity is completely compromised."

Cummings added, "Yeah, buy me one too."

They started moving again, and Carl said, "What's our status, Three?"

"You mean other than the fact that we just got our collective asses kicked?"

Carl grunted. "Other than that. Did we lose anyone?"

"Not yet." Three said it like it was not a premonition but rather a certainty.

Carl stopped walking and looked at his field commander.

Nodding toward the big black SUV with its passenger side caved in, Three said, "Thirteen. He's done." The glass and Lexan laminate that made the front window bulletproof was shattered.

Carl rushed around the vehicle, where Merc Thirteen sat in the driver's seat, and climbed up on the runner. The man sat normally in the seat, but his hands were in his lap. He was awake, and his blue eyes were alert. Prominent crow's feet made him look older than his forty years.

"Edgar, isn't it?"

"Yeah, Boss." The man didn't move. He was uninjured except for a sliver of metal that had severed his spine from the back of his neck but hadn't cut his jugular or airway. The metal piece was lodged in the headrest and was all that was keeping the man upright.

"They tell me it's bad." Edgar's gaze flitted toward Carl.

"It's bad." Carl nodded. "You have family?"

"I have a mom somewhere. Haven't seen her in years. Tell her I'm sorry for being such a shitty son."

"I'll tell her the truth. I'll tell her you've been fighting a classified counterterror war for the president."

"Thank you, Boss. It has been an honor serving with you."

"The honor is mine, Soldier."

Carl pulled his Glock and fired a shot into the side of Thirteen's head, then hopped down from the runner. He regarded Lenore Cummings, her mother, her daughter, and the silent mercs that had gathered around. "When it's our turn, that's how we all should go out." He nodded at Thirteen's SUV. "Fast. Without suffering." He holstered his weapon.

Cummings touched his arm and said, "Thank you, Carl." She looked around at the mercs and sideways-hugged her daughter. "Thank you all." She wrapped her free arm around her mother's shoulder too.

Carl could tell the elder woman had heard all about the events of the past eight months, but this was her first encounter with explosions and gunfire. Her eyes were wide, her gaze distant, and her lower lip trembled as she clasped her arms in a self-hug.

Cummings looked at Carl again. "But I'm not real clear on your plan. You came in by yourself, even with battle armor? You had no backup?"

"I had *you*, Lenore. You said you were armed twenty-four-seven, so I knew that's all the backup I needed in there. And you proved me right."

Three said, "Agent Palmer, I hear sirens."

"I'm coordinating that as we speak. Your cover is that you are a covert FBI team sent to retrieve the Cummings family."

"Copy that. Please have the police respectfully dispose of Thirteen's body."

"Copy that."

Carl looked at his team. They looked pissed, like they'd just had their asses handed to them. Lenore Cummings looked angry, like a lioness ready to pounce on someone, anyone. Her mother looked shell-shocked, and Lisette comforted her grandmother with hugs.

What is the world coming to when a preteen girl is so accustomed to violence that she can comfort an adult?

Carl said, "Three, what's our next available designation?"

"Nineteen."

Carl looked at Cummings. "You are now designated as *Nineteen*. I hate to do this to you, add you to the team, but I figure the safest place for your family now is with us, especially if you're wearing an armored battle suit."

She nodded.

"Thirteen was about the same size as you, so grab his weapons and battle armor and get suited up. We have work to do."

CHAPTER 7

GRAINGER AND HOLLIS KOLL GAZED at the monitor on the wall in Grainger's private office next to the bunker's control center. Agent Cummings's house was almost completely destroyed, and the master suite was open to the sky. The high-definition camera of the Atlas mini drone gazed down into the structure from five hundred feet, allowing the Koll brothers to watch the mercenaries haul roof plywood and shingles off the bathtub and Carl Johnson, Agent Cummings, and her daughter leave the blasted-out house.

Hollis growled. "Bastard just won't die."

"He has more lives than a damn cat."

Hollis shook his head. "I've seen dozens of hostage rescue ops, but this—" He pointed at the monitor. "A direct frontal assault? By himself? Through the front door? That's just plain stupid! He just charged in there and went for the girl."

Grainger pointed at the monitor as the drone showed the trio walking into the street, toward the waiting SUVs. "She's working *with* Johnson. He *knew* she would assist. And after what he did to her and her daughter, that scares the hell out of me." Grainger parked his elbows on the conference table and steepled his fingers at his bottom lip. "How could we even have anticipated that? When did they form an alliance?"

"Had to happen months ago, yet they cleverly kept it out of the debriefs." Hollis shook his head. "Doesn't matter. We've got him outclassed in manpower and weapons. It's a numbers game, and it's just a matter of time before we overwhelm him."

Grainger leaned back in his chair. "All of a sudden, I'm not as confident as you are about that outcome unless we increase our pressure. I mean, think about it. Carl Johnson began his operations against Agent Cummings *and* the FBI *and* the Terror Event Response agency *simultaneously* with only four mercenaries and an ex-CIA hacker. And now, he has a dozen mercenaries, all prior Spec Ops men, plus Agent Cummings now. And the president has authorized transportation, logistics, weapons, surveillance assets, and intel support for him."

Grainger looked at his brother. "He's no longer *just* a terrorist. It's like everyone who comes into his orbit suddenly brings their A-game and joins his team."

"Like Agent Cummings."

Grainger nodded. "From his debriefs, we knew he was maintaining surveillance on her family, and we figured she'd reach out to him as some kind of early warning. That's why we didn't ambush his team when they went to rescue the kids. We didn't know if he'd be on that team or if he'd remain at the restaurant. But this—" He pointed at the monitor. "This is a game changer."

They watched Agent Cummings peel hard-shell body armor from a dead mercenary and fit it on herself. "I've seen her dossier, so now Johnson has yet *another* highly trained weapons expert on his team. She's seen combat in a dozen FBI SWAT raids."

Grainger paused for a few moments of strategic contemplation, then said, "It's time to escalate. Put the asset on standby."

"Are you sure? That's going to get messy."

Grainger pointed at the monitor again. "Messier than blowing up houses?"

"Point taken." Hollis leaned forward. "We need to up our surveillance game too. We need live coverage. That drone"—he pointed at the monitor—"stores thirty minutes of compressed video and transmits it in a microburst transmission. That was the only way it could remain undetected by Johnson's government drones."

"I agree. Have one of our government contractors secure us a position on the next space launch. In fact, get that launch moved up to tomorrow.

The president has all the military satellites locked down tight, but we can get some civilian satellites up there. It won't be full coverage, but if we can keep Johnson on the move, keep him guessing, we'll negate his tech advantage."

Hollis nodded. "Okay, and I'll prep the asset to be airlifted to the next location Carl Johnson surfaces at."

"We should also be ready to hit his next safe house as soon as we find it."

"I assume the asset's rules of engagement are—"

"There are no rules, my brother. Carl Johnson and his team must die."

CHAPTER 8

T WO DAYS AGO, HE'D THOUGHT he was finished as the American Terrorist. After killing the last member of the Mexican Triad, he'd been mentally prepared to walk away from that life and begin the painful task of living a lonely future without his son. Then Rainman had pulled him back in with the attack on Cummings. Now he sat in a trendy coffee shop watching a potential CIA informant exit the mailbox store across the street.

It had taken several months for TER Director Aaron McGrath to cultivate this particular contact, though Carl and his team were skeptical of the man's coincidental claims. The man allegedly had intel about a shadow government agency or international cabal called *Atlas,* and he claimed that organization was behind the attempt to assassinate the first woman president of the United States. McGrath, however, had been unable to find any hard evidence of the existence of any such entity beyond three hundred or so odd companies that had the word "Atlas" in their names. The shadow organization, if it even existed, was shrouded in an impenetrable veil of secrecy. They'd had many discussions about whether or not the man was a plant or part of Rainman's master strategy, though eventually, everyone agreed there was only one way to find out for sure.

The mailbox store was part of an old brick strip mall with big glass windows. Posters depicting mail services, color copies, business cards, and myriad other printing services covered almost every square inch of the windows. It was the perfect place for the informant to covertly study the coffee shop because no one could see him behind all those posters until he stepped through the metal-framed glass front door.

The man looked exactly as Carl had been told to expect. Tall and lanky in his mid-forties with shoulder-length, slightly curly blond hair, he was a nondescript man with a receding hairline. No one would ever suspect Frank Pearson of being a high-level CIA analyst. He looked more like an artist or musician. Carl thought he looked like Willie Nelson in his younger days.

Carl gazed into his coffee cup. He'd changed up his regular house coffee for a mocha this time. He didn't know why. He just needed something different. There was a foamy flower-looking design floating in the brown liquid. He took a sip and savored the bitter flavor of the organic coffee, the smoothness of the chocolate, and the cinnamon aftertaste. He thought about his nemesis, Aaron McGrath, growling at the mere image of the man's face in his mind. He'd gotten Mark killed…and yet, he hadn't. President Shirley Mallory was also responsible. And Agent Palmer. And Agent Cummings.

Then he shook his head. No, those people were just doing their jobs, trying to find a missing girl. They thought Carl had kidnapped her because he looked like the man who had. Their actions had gotten Mark killed, but Carl knew he himself was equally responsible because of how he'd responded to the feds' interrogations. That's what hurt the most. Carl could have prevented his son's death.

Even after Carl had gone berserk and launched a war that cost the lives of dozens of federal agents, they'd begged him—*paid* him hundreds of millions of dollars—to go save the president's daughter *because* he looked like the guy who had taken her. So he'd had a choice to make. He'd wanted—*needed*—to kill the agents responsible for Mark's death, but to continue his war, he'd have had to let an innocent sixteen-year-old girl die. He'd chosen to save the girl. And to save her, he'd had to work with the same federal agents who'd gotten Mark killed.

Aaron McGrath still lived. Agent Nancy Palmer still lived. Agent Cummings still lived.

Worst of all, the former vice president, Walter Breen—a.k.a. Rainman—still lived, though in hiding. With the attack on Lenore Cummings's family yesterday, Carl now realized Rainman was still in play. For some reason, Rainman was no longer targeting the president. He was coming after Carl.

Carl chuckled to himself. *Let him come.*

Eight months ago, he'd been just a normal citizen, a fifty-three-year-old commercial real estate broker. During his private war with the government, he'd been mostly lucky—an unpredictable amateur who had managed critical victories with hired mercs against law enforcement and government covert kill teams. On the mission to save President Shirley Mallory, he'd even won a hand-to-hand fight against a highly trained Secret Service agent who was a former Delta Spec Ops soldier, but he'd been lucky in that fight too and prevailed only by a miracle. After that violent encounter, though, he'd realized he needed specialized training. He had no choice in the matter. He was now part of the world of terrorism and covert ops, whether he wanted to be or not. His mercs arranged for a South Korean SWAT veteran named Lieutenant Yeong Dae Jin to train him in self-defense and weaponry. Then over the past few months, Carl had become a veteran of several combat operations…at the ripe old age of fifty-four. With nothing left to lose and a wealth of experience and training under his belt, he wouldn't stop until Rainman was dealt with once and for all.

Carl looked around the nearly empty coffee shop. A couple to his right rose from their chairs and headed for the door. A thirty-something woman to his left concentrated hard on her laptop and her cell phone at the same time. She had pale skin, too much makeup, and blazing red hair that was short on one side and long on the other.

He took another sip and mentally shook off all the conflicting thoughts in his mind about the government agents and refocused on the CIA informant.

The analyst paused in the doorway and locked gazes with Carl, then casually scanned the street right and left. Carl saw him tense briefly, then the man patted his pockets, threw up his hands in despair like he'd forgotten something, and retreated quickly into the mailbox store. In the next instant, two black sedans with stylish white POLICE lettering on the front doors pulled up right-to-left in front of the mailbox store. They stayed in the traffic lane beside the parallel-parked cars across the street and waited.

Their new Dodge Challenger models had darkly tinted windows, so Carl couldn't see inside.

Several seconds later, a man walked in front of the coffee shop on Carl's side of the street. Through the floor-to-ceiling window wall, Carl watched the man stroll casually from left to right, seemingly without a care in the world. He was a tall, slender, dark-skinned man in jeans, a white button-down shirt, and a black string tie. His shirt was tucked in at the waist, and his hands were parked in his pockets. His shirt was stained with wet perspiration under the arms. He wore a high flattop hairstyle, faded very short on the sides, and trendy dark-framed eyeglasses. He looked like an intellectual or an urban artist.

Both front doors on both police cars opened when the pedestrian was almost exactly across the street from them. They spread out like a pincer, and Carl recognized the chilling intent of the maneuver. If the pedestrian chose to run, he wouldn't get far because the cops had him boxed in.

The man seemed to have no awareness of the officers until one of them spoke to him. He pulled his hands out of his pockets as ordered and held them away from his sides. The four officers approached him in an aggressive posture twice familiar to Carl. Each officer had a hand on his holstered gun, ready for instant action. One of them made a whirling gesture with his free hand. The Black man turned away from them and leaned his hands against the window wall of the coffee shop, feet spread wide.

Carl heard someone on his left whisper, "Oh my God!"

He glanced that way and saw the redhead fumble with her cell phone and point it at the altercation.

One of the cops grabbed the man by the back of the collar. Carl remembered this was to restrain any movements the man might make. Then the cop kicked the man's right foot to the side to spread his feet wider and keep him immobilized, but the man's foot slid too far, and he fell to his knees and screamed. A second officer rammed his knee against the back of the man's head. He kneed him so hard, the man's face made a crack in the window glass and left a streak of blood as he slid to the ground. He rolled over and tried to fend away the flurry of fists and boots pounding him. He even brought one of the cops to the sidewalk with a lucky kick to the shin.

He had absolutely no chance for salvation. There were four cops, and they had guns, Tasers, carbon-composite sticks, and pepper spray, but only one of the officers used anything other than fists and boots. Quickly overwhelmed, the pedestrian curled up into a ball.

The cops kept at him, punching and kicking. One extended a telescoping baton and swung it every time one of the other cops withdrew a boot to kick again. The one with the stick had expert aim, repeatedly striking the man on hard bone—skull, elbows, knees, wrists, and ankles.

The fourth cop took a break, stepping back. He kept looking around as if to make sure no one got too close or tried to interfere, though the only other pedestrians Carl could see were across the street. A young couple had stopped to watch, but when the fourth cop eyeballed them, they quickly resumed walking at a hurried pace.

Then that cop looked into the coffee shop.

Carl sat facing the window wall and assumed the least threatening posture he could imagine. He sat with his feet flat on the floor and his palms flat against the metal top of the little table, one hand on either side of his coffee mug.

The officer caught his gaze, and a flicker of recognition flashed in his eyes. Carl's face was, of course, one of the most famous on the planet. The officer glanced to Carl's left and shouted, "Camera!"

The other three officers immediately abandoned their victim and focused on the redheaded woman in the coffee shop. Carl knew then he was in imminent danger. For whatever reason, those cops—those bullies—were lusting to beat the crap out of someone, anyone. They'd just done it to the man on the street, and now, they were coming for the young woman recording the video. No way they'd ignore the two young baristas behind the counter. No way they'd ignore Carl. That's what cops were trained to do.

Constantly evaluate situational awareness. Assess and control all variables that might be a threat. Put everyone on the ground and sort out the innocents later.

When they got close enough to Carl, they'd notice he was armed.

The three police officers moved toward the door while the fourth—the one who had pointed out the camera—did a curious thing. He squatted down and rifled through the bleeding man's clothes. He expertly searched the man's pockets, shirt collar, belt, ankles, and even quickly pulled off his shoes. He was looking for something but didn't find it, so he stood and followed the other three into the coffee shop.

Three police officers charged through the door, heading for the young redhead's table twenty feet from Carl and hollering for her to surrender her cell phone. The fourth paused just inside the door, sizing up Carl. Glancing down at Carl's windbreaker, he saw the bulge of a hidden shoulder holster.

"Gun!" the officer yelled, pulling his service weapon at the same instant the first cop swung his baton at the redhead.

The third officer was just passing Carl, so he kicked the center pillar of his small table and sent it sliding into the officer's path. The table slid right out from under his coffee cup, and the porcelain mug fell to the floor by his feet and shattered.

The officer tripped up momentarily in his attempt to avoid the collision, and in that instant, Carl leaped between him and the second officer. He pulled his Glock and pointed the bulbous black suppressor at the fourth officer just inside the doorway, who could not shoot now that Carl was in their midst.

Carl fired at the trailing officer in the doorway—headshot, three meters—and heard gasps and shouts behind him as the first two officers pivoted toward him. Even as he fired point-blank under the chin of the third officer, he launched a vicious back kick aimed toward the thick vest of the officer right behind him. It was just enough to shove that man off-balance and against the first officer, and both men couldn't get their weapons free in time.

Carl pivoted and dropped to a knee, then fired twice more.

Two more headshots, one meter.

He slid his Glock back into his shoulder holster and zipped his windbreaker all the way up, then scanned the room as he retrieved his four spent shell casings. Amazingly, the young redhead still held up her cell phone as if filming the encounter was more important than her personal safety.

"You okay?" Carl said.

"Oh my God!" she whispered. "Please don't shoot me."

"Sista, if I wanted you dead, I could have just let that cop cave your face in with his stick. Now turn off that video, get your ass up out of that chair, and get that man to the hospital." He pointed at the Black man writhing and bleeding on the sidewalk. He hollered at the young baristas peeking up over the counter against the far wall. "You too! Both of you, get over here and help!"

Carl turned to leave, then stopped by the door. To the redhead, he said, "Email me a copy of that video file." He wanted Agent Palmer to assess his reaction, tactics, and speed, so he gave the woman an anonymous email address and waited while she fiddled with her cell phone. "And don't call any more cops unless you want that to happen to you too." He head-nodded at the bloody man.

He pulled the door open and left the coffee shop. Glancing across the street, he saw his CIA informant peeking around the edge of the glass door. The man had watched the whole encounter, and now, the meeting was clearly off. No doubt the police CSI—Crime Scene Investigators—would scour every available witness and surveillance camera to find out who the shooter had been. The American Terrorist's presence in Chicago would be known, and the manhunt would be on again. Carl couldn't chance compromising his informant's identity. He'd have to try to reschedule.

Carl turned away from the meeting site and mentally cursed the police. But something tugged at his gut. Though the four officers were White, the assault didn't seem like an ordinary case of cops assaulting a random Black man they may have suspected of a crime. This was an ambush. Their victim had not tried to fight back or run. He'd only tried to duck and cover, and no doubt the cops could spin that fact to support their use of excessive force. They'd get away with it, Carl knew from personal experience. They always did, even if caught on camera. The internal police department investigations and the rare Grand Jury almost always found the excessive violence justified. These cops were specifically waiting for *that* man, though. They were searching for something he presumably had. The way the fourth cop had been looking around was troubling too, as was how they'd gone straight after the woman with the cell phone with a vengeance.

He dismissed the thoughts from his mind. Whatever that man or those cops were involved in was none of his business. His only task now was to escape and evade, then check in with Agent Palmer. Still, he was curious about the strategic reason behind the ambush. He executed a near-perfect military about-face in mid-stride and headed back to the assault victim. The red-haired woman and one of the baristas had just knelt beside the man on the sidewalk and were trying to help him to a sitting position. They all regarded Carl with suspicion when he squatted with them.

"Why did they attack you?" Carl said. "What were they looking for?"

It took the man a few seconds to collect himself to the point where he could respond. He was a mess. His left shoulder appeared to be dislocated, and his left elbow was broken at an unnatural angle. His face was bloodied, nose flattened, and lips torn from multiple boot impacts. More than a couple of his teeth littered the sidewalk, and his blood streaked down the coffee shop glass.

"They control the police," the man muttered.

Carl grunted. "Of course they control the police. That's the way the system works."

"No, you don't understand." The man coughed up blood. "It's *real* control. *Behavioral* control. With *technology*. They can make them do *anything*."

"They who?"

The man's head lolled, and his chin fell to his chest as he lost consciousness.

CHAPTER 9

CHIEF OF POLICE JOHN BILDEMEYER entered the office and stood beside and slightly behind his boss on the top floor of the thirty-seven-story Stennhauser Building in downtown Chicago. They both looked out over the city through the expansive window wall. The midday sky was slightly overcast.

The man he stood with wasn't his boss in the same way as was the city mayor, but rather, he had paid a lot of money to have the chief of police do his bidding. Bildemeyer walked the uneasy tightrope of managing the city's police force under the employment and political oversight of the mayor while carrying out certain less-than-legal police initiatives overseen by the man beside him. Mr. Karuhl was a deadly man who served even more powerful and deadly men. Chief Bildemeyer served at the pleasure of the mayor, yet he *lived* at the pleasure of his true boss. He knew that both statuses were interdependent.

"We have a problem, Mr. Karuhl," Bildemeyer said.

"Indeed, we do," answered the man. "Do you have a solution to that problem, or do you need me to solve it for you?"

"There's no way we could have anticipated the American Terrorist would be having coffee here, in our city."

Mr. Karuhl cast a sideways glance in his direction, and his light blue eyes sent a stabbing chill down Bildemeyer's spine. "You don't have to be defensive just yet, Chief. My people know exactly what Carl Johnson is capable of. What I want to know is, how is he involved here? Why was he at the location of the takedown? How did he know of our operation?"

"Unknown. A cell phone video showed he was just sitting there, and he did not take action until one of the officers recognized him. It appears he was waiting for someone."

"Our target?"

"Unclear. If Johnson had been waiting for our target, perhaps to get the data from him, then he would have interfered before the officers converged on the man."

"Agreed." Mr. Karuhl nodded. "He could easily have dispatched the police officers anytime he wanted." The man took a deep breath, seeming to contemplate something. "You released the altered video to the media?"

"As you requested."

"It was not a request," Mr. Karuhl said with a grunt. "But what about the red-haired woman? I find it hard to believe she is just a bystander who just happened to film the encounter. I'd like to know how she is involved. Could there be a connection between her and the American Terrorist? Were they just acting for the sake of the video?"

"Probably some bleeding-heart liberal. Bystanders always film police activity, especially when a Black man is involved."

Mr. Karuhl grunted again. "They still think taking videos will make a difference, but it won't. Not in the coming new world." The man gazed out the window again. "I want those loose ends eliminated."

Eliminated, Chief Bildemeyer thought. *In other words, murdered.* The redhead, Malik Tavares, and the coffee shop baristas.

He said, "Do you think the American Terrorist knows about your experiment?"

"Thanks to the vice president's failed power grab last year, we've had to accelerate our plan past the experimental test phase. We are now in phase two large-scale demonstration trials. My benefactors have been gradually militarizing the nation's police forces for almost twenty years. They've been patiently waiting for technology to catch up with their goals. And for the last few years, the media has been conveniently circulating our disinformation: *Black Lives Matter*." Mr. Karuhl snorted contempt. "The Black population and their White sympathizers have no idea what's coming, and they won't until it's too late. They have no idea other minorities experience the same brutal treatment in almost equal percentages. We've kept the news media and social media focused on White police versus Black people because the implication of modern-day *social slavery* keeps people polarized and distracted from our true operation. Now it appears someone—this Malik Tavares—has connected the dots. We must know who set him on this investigative path. Who are his sources?"

Mr. Karuhl inhaled and blew it out. "And how is this goddamned American Terrorist involved? It can't be a coincidence he was here."

"You said we're in phase two trials?"

The man nodded. "We've had great success manipulating several recent small-scale protests of police brutality by increasing the aggressive behavior of the police. Chicago, however, is the first citywide test scheduled for next week. Just think of it." Karuhl waved a hand at the expansive window wall. "If we can incite on-demand citywide clashes between the police and the civil population here, and later, across the country in multiple cities simultaneously, the population will give up enormous amounts of personal freedom to be saved from a perceived epidemic of *civilian* protests and violence.

"It'll be just like when the Patriot Act was enacted. People will give up their freedom just like they did after Nine-Eleven. And I have to admit, the American Terrorist's activities over the past few months have actually aided our effort. So, while the former vice president was reckless in his attempt to co-opt our plan with his own, he has actually been helpful. His influence and financial backing have now made large-scale implementation of police control practical and imminent."

Chief Bildemeyer got an uneasy feeling in his gut. "Is that what the reporter uncovered? The timetable?"

Either Mr. Karuhl trusted him and was inviting him into the inner circle by divulging these details, or—more likely—he'd outlived his usefulness and become expendable. In that case, revealing confidential information to Bildemeyer was irrelevant. The chief set his mind to formulating an escape plan to isolate himself from the current operation.

Mr. Karuhl said, "Calling Malik Tavares a reporter is like calling a mall cop a police officer. Nevertheless, he did a remarkable investigative job culling our plan from myriad seemingly unconnected data points. Clearly, we don't want this report public, or we wouldn't have ordered the man's death. Unfortunately, Tavares didn't have a thumb drive on his person, and he wasn't foolish enough to store his report in the cloud, where we could easily access it."

Bildemeyer nodded. "I have CSI people I trust going through his apartment. We'll find his data."

"Eliminate every electronic trace of his research." Karuhl fell silent for several seconds. "We've used a large number of scientists and doctors, and all but a trusted few have been eliminated. Tavares must have found a trend in the data our own specialists missed. The public might have fun posting conspiracy theories online about a secret alliance between the former vice president and several corporations to develop biochemical agents that control aggression and paranoia"—Karuhl raised both hands in a quote-unquote gesture—"but if Tavares reports the exact methodology or the fact that we are all ready to begin phase two trials…"

"Mass hysteria."

"Believe me, Chief, mass panic *is* the desired outcome. That would trigger the widespread civil unrest we need to nationalize the militarized police forces and various states' National Guards, all under a single commander…*our* commander. The president and her government won't be safe from their own Secret Service, or from the FBI, CIA, or TER if we can trigger aggressive behavior in any target we choose."

"And the vice president takes over the government?"

Mr. Karuhl grunted. "Trust me, the *former* vice president, Rainman, is a nonfactor, and we have not decided whether or not he has outlived his usefulness. But government control is inevitable with the help of my benefactors." Mr. Karuhl nodded, then continued, "But if Tavares releases his research on the exact biochemical compounds and the activation frequencies…"

Bildemeyer got the feeling that Mr. Karuhl was jockeying for the top position in the *new world order*, whatever that was going to be, but he finally understood the stakes. "Then the plan can be circumvented."

"Police brutality keeps the people focused on the police. However, if the people know that *we* cause police brutality, then their focus will be on us." Mr. Karuhl was silent for a long time. "Okay, here is what I want you to do."

Bildemeyer absorbed his instructions and tried not to betray his shock. What the man was proposing was a bold countermove fraught with risk…for the chief of police.

"I can't use my police officers for that. I'll need to contract—"

Mr. Karuhl tapped his ear. "My people are sending a specialist within the hour. All your people need to do is provide intel."

"Understood," Bildemeyer said. "And if the American Terrorist interferes again?"

"I find it difficult to believe that Carl Johnson would be involved in our little corner of the world. My group has seen intel that suggests he is currently involved in more global affairs, eliminating the people involved in the death of his son. Still, the coincidence of his presence here cannot be ignored. If he interferes again, then our specialist will deal with him too."

"Very well." The chief of police turned to leave.

"You are not to leave these premises until this issue has been satisfactorily resolved. Make your phone calls from here."

Chief Bildemeyer looked around the luxuriously appointed room. All the furnishings were designed in colors of white and gray, including the carpet. He could easily overpower Mr. Karuhl if he chose to do so, and the smaller man no doubt knew this, but then he'd have to escape a dozen or more of his boss's security forces scattered throughout the top floor of the building.

So, in other words, if I don't resolve the issue, I will never leave—at least, not alive.

CHAPTER 10

CARL ENTERED THE OPS CENTER in disguise. His mercs had set up operations in a residential townhouse four blocks away from the meeting site. As soon as Merc Three closed the door behind him, Carl removed his dreadlocks wig and massaged his itching bald head. Even though he and his mercenaries had substantial financial resources as well as government tactical support from the TER, he'd decided to stay with the low-tech operations model that had been successful for almost a year. The fewer digital or electronic footprints they had, the fewer opportunities Rainman had to find or trace them.

Each operation was controlled from a low-key residential house in a nondescript neighborhood. Dozens of single-use disposable cell phones were procured for team members who needed to communicate outside the operations house, and each phone was destroyed after a single use. Disposable laptops were provided for Carl's tech wizard, an ex-CIA hacker named Henry Erickson who the mercenaries had started calling Wizard because there seemed to be no task he couldn't complete with a computer, no computer system he couldn't hack his way into, and no bit of information he couldn't discover.

After Carl's shootout with the police the previous afternoon, he'd gone back to his modest hotel room and packed his few personal items and disguises in his backpack, then took a cab to the nearest department store, went into a bathroom, and came out in his *White-man disguise* consisting of white skin cream covering his face, neck, and hands; nerd eyeglasses; and a straight, shoulder-length brown wig. He took the bus to a nearby mall and changed into his second disguise, Rastafarian with shoulder-length dreads, dark shades, and dark skin cream, and checked into a five-star hotel paid for with a legit fake credit card and ID.

"Status," Carl demanded as he entered the ops center in the living room of the otherwise vacant house.

Wizard replied, "Agent Palmer is on a secure video link, Boss." The tech genius pointed to a large high-definition monitor mounted on the wall in front of the cheap foldout desk on which sat Wizard's laptop. That desk and his chair were the only pieces of furniture in the house, so moving-in activity could be a bare minimum for nosey neighbors, but the mercs slept in sleeping bags in the bedrooms, ready at all times for immediate deployment. Trent Englebaum, known as *Merc Three*, short for his operational designation of Mercenary Number Three, stood guard in the op center with Wizard. From the far corner of the room, he could cover all ingress and egress points. He was dressed in black fatigues and fully armed for combat.

On the monitor, Agent Palmer faced away from her own monitor and camera, discussing something with someone off-screen. From experience in the field, Carl knew Palmer to be an extremely capable field agent. The first female graduate of Navy SEAL training, she finished at the top of her class *of men* and was handpicked by her commander for the elite SEAL Team Six assignment. Two days before graduation, she'd had an altercation with a team member and instructor intent on teaching her that SEAL Ops was no place for a woman. The incident left one man dead, the other hospitalized, and sent Palmer AWOL—Away Without Official Leave. Then she found her way into the covert antiterrorism world, recruited by Director Aaron McGrath of the above-top-secret Terror Event Response agency.

Wizard said, "Heads up, Boss. There's been a development—"

"Carl," Agent Palmer interrupted, facing him on the monitor. "Have you seen the morning headlines on CNN?"

He shook his head.

"Okay, we'll get to that in a moment, but first, I took the liberty of reassigning all but three of your mercenary team, plus Three. Our CIA informant saw your encounter with the police yesterday, and he reached out to us last night."

"I thought we might lose him."

Palmer shook her head. "Apparently, he saw what he needed to feel secure."

"Me in action?"

She nodded. "It pays to have an operations director with field experience. Frank Pearson wants to come in."

"Not just provide information?" Carl said. "Now he wants to *come in?*"

"Apparently, he was holding back in our initial phone contact. As you know, the TER has instant access to all intelligence data of the nation's combined military and civilian police services, but there's still a lot of back-channel unlogged intel to which we don't have timely access. And there's nothing in any database regarding Atlas. Frank Pearson claims to have more information than he initially indicated about that shadow organization and its involvement in the attempt on the president. He wasn't sure he could trust us to act on it, but your performance yesterday evening proved to him he was doing the right thing. Since you tossed your cell phone yesterday, I couldn't reach you, so I assigned five of your people to escort Pearson to Virginia, where he'll be debriefed."

Carl saw Merc Three watching him from out of view of the video camera. In his absence, Three had to agree to that decision, and his posture indicated he wasn't sure he'd done the right thing. Carl knew Three didn't trust government agents, and with good reason. The TER agents under the command of Agent Palmer's boss had nearly screwed up the op to save the president and her daughter late last year, and Carl and his mercs almost couldn't salvage the operation. Merc Three had lost his wife, Merc Four, in that operation.

He nodded at the monitor. "I trust your judgment, Nancy. I always have. And I implicitly trust Merc Three to make the right call here when I'm unavailable."

She nodded in return. "They are en route now, so we can consider your operation in Chicago a success. However, we have this…"

The view on the monitor split into halves, showing Agent Palmer on the left and a live report on the right, depicting a ten-second sound bite video of the coffee shop massacre.

Palmer softened her voice, imparting a level of private concern Carl had come to know and appreciate over the months. "The president called this morning. She's...concerned."

The video only showed the part with Carl shooting the cops. The news ticker at the bottom of the monitor stated the American Terrorist had struck "fear and terror in the hearts of all Chicago residents." The newswoman reported a telephone conversation in which the chief of police related that the American Terrorist assassinated four police officers in cold blood, along with a young male employee of the coffee shop, then left suddenly and savagely beat the pedestrian, Malik Tavares, before more police could respond to the scene. According to the police chief, Johnson had then tracked down the redhead woman who took Tavares to the hospital and killed them both. Then the chief swore that every police resource available would be employed to bring the terrorist to justice.

Carl shook his head and said, "How could anyone believe that stupidity? It makes no sense at all. Why would I let those two live, only to track them down later and kill them? No one is asking *that* question."

Palmer said, "I explained that to President Mallory, and she agrees this looks like a setup. She knows you wouldn't do anything like this, but she's concerned this event might alert the people we're searching for and create a connection with our new informant."

Carl shrugged. "Well, we can't influence Rainman's thinking now, and I'm assuming he's connected with Atlas, so we have to accept that the media has already covered the story. If there's an informant connection, we'll have to adapt or find a way to exploit that knowledge. Meanwhile"—Carl looked down and nudged Wizard on the shoulder—"can you hack into the computer controlling that broadcast feed?"

"Well, it's a national media outlet, but, um, sure. It'll take a minute."

Palmer said, "What's your plan, Carl?"

Carl returned his attention to the monitor and folded his arms across his chest. "I don't mind being blamed for an atrocity because that only strengthens my reputation among the terror community I'm supposed to be a member of. But those cops ambushed that man, and now, the police chief has manufactured this cover story. I don't like being used in this way, as a scapegoat in someone else's crime."

"Agreed." Palmer nodded. "It takes a decision-maker high in the law enforcement hierarchy to fabricate a cover story like this and make it stick."

"Yes, so either the police chief is in on this, or someone close to or above him is."

"Carl." Palmer looked down for a second, then back up at the camera. "Our mission here is complete."

"Mm-hmm."

"What are you going to do when you discover the identity of this person?"

"Nancy, you've known me long enough to know the answer to that question. These dipshits killed innocent people, and now, they've involved me in their nonsense. They'll have to answer for those deaths."

All he knew for sure was that someone related to the chief of police ordered the deaths of three people Carl assumed were innocent civilians. Maybe Carl's coincidental involvement simply gave the commander a convenient fall guy for an illegal police operation. Or maybe the victims weren't innocent at all. Maybe the operation was necessary for public safety.

But wait…the news report made no mention of the second barista in the coffee shop?

That person, if alive, was a witness to the true incident, and they were still in danger.

Wizard said, "Ready, Boss."

"Do it."

Immediately, Carl's face appeared on the right half of the wall monitor, replacing Agent Palmer's image. The news ticker still scrolled at the bottom of the screen, but the newswoman in the small popup window froze in mid-sentence when the American Terrorist appeared on the monitor she was reading script from.

"Um, stand by, please," she said. She glanced off camera and gave a little shrug. *What is this?*

The ticker on the screen said her name was Rebecca Logan. She was a slender woman with short, professional-looking blonde-streaked hair, and her posture gave Carl the impression that she was tall.

A voice off-screen whispered, "You're still on!"

The reporter recovered quickly. "Folks, we seem to be having some technical difficulty with—"

Carl said, "You're not having technical difficulty, Miss Logan. I've hacked your video stream, and I'd like to know why you didn't show the entire video of the shooting."

The young woman glanced off camera again, and Carl imagined her getting a head-nod as permission to continue the impromptu interview.

"The video was provided by the police. Would you like to give your side of this…event?"

Carl dipped his head toward the camera mounted on a tripod in front of the wall monitor because he knew that posture imparted a sinister look, and he definitely wanted to appear threatening. "I know where you got the video. I asked why you didn't play the *entire* video?"

She glanced off camera again, then said, "That's all they gave us. Are you saying it isn't real? That it was somehow altered?"

Carl said, "You're not asking the right questions. You should be asking why I would kill four police officers, then spare the life of a witness who'd just filmed the event and not take her cell phone, then waste time outside beating the crap out of Mr. Tavares, then track him down and kill him and the witness at the hospital later. That holds no tactical logic, and I think I've proven over the months that I don't make tactical mistakes. And why would I only kill one of the coffee servers and let the other live?"

"There was more than one?"

"You better find her before she ends up dead too."

Now that the true story was about to be released, he knew the female barista was in no danger beyond intimidation and threats. Having seen the entire ordeal, she no doubt got the hell out before more police showed up, and now, her death would just prove Carl's point.

"I'm emailing you the full two-minute video, which I require you to play right now in its entirety. If you do not do this, we're going to have this conversation again face-to-face, you and I, except there won't be any words to that conversation."

She gasped and looked off camera, and a voice said, "Nothing."

Carl said, "I didn't say I was sending it to your office. I sent it to *you*, Miss Logan. To your cell phone."

She stared at the camera, and Carl got the feeling she wanted to ask him how he got her private number. She said nothing, and he gave her bonus points for maintaining her professional composure and not giving up her power by asking the question. Instead, she gestured to her right. A young man ran to her with her purse, then darted back out of view. She pulled a smartphone out and fiddled with the device. A few seconds later, the video replaced the newswoman.

The world watched as the four police officers beat and kicked the man on the ground outside the coffee shop. There was blood smeared on the window, and the cell phone's owner said, "Oh my God, they're going to kill him." Then one of the officers pointed at the camera and yelled. Three raced into the shop while the fourth briefly searched Tavares's broken and bloody body. The police officer closest to the camera pulled his telescoping baton from his utility belt and flipped his wrist to extend the assault tool. He and the other two yelled at the camera, and he swung his baton seemingly at it. The video scene fluttered around as the woman raised the cell phone in self-defense. At the same instant, a man's voice hollered, "Gun!" The two lead officers spun around. Carl Johnson could be seen lunging into the midst of the officers and shooting them methodically, even as they tried to pull their own guns.

The shaky camera view centered on Carl as he said, "You okay?"

"Oh my God!" she whispered. "Please don't shoot me."

"Sista, if I wanted you dead, I could have just let that cop cave your face in with his stick. Now turn off that video, get your ass up out of that chair, and get that man to the hospital." He pointed at the Black man writhing and bleeding on the sidewalk. He hollered at the young baristas off camera. "You too! Both of you, get over here and help!"

When Rebecca Logan's and Carl's faces replaced the video, there was a moment of silence as an obviously stunned news crew struggled to cope with what they'd seen. Carl imagined people watching the breaking news story all over the country were equally stunned.

Finally, the reporter reengaged. "So...um, why were you there? In the coffee shop."

Carl notched an eyebrow at the irrelevant question. "Well, I was having coffee, of course."

She hesitated, then said, "Why do *you* think the police lied to us?"

"Sista, I can think of a dozen more relevant questions. For example, since I killed the cops who tried to kill those two, you should be asking who actually *did* kill those people. Was it *more* cops, or was it a hired killer? As to your question about *why* the police lied, there are two answers. Answer number one is the police lied to cover up the murder of three people. And they conveniently blamed it on me because they didn't think I would care or do anything about it."

Carl took a breath and lowered his voice a bit. "Answer number two should be more disturbing. The police lied to you because they can. Because they control you, the news media, and the information you report. Because they know you will report whatever they tell you, and you won't do any investigation. They clearly have someone at a very high level of authority backing them up. They did this, Miss Logan, because they didn't think anyone would or could stop them. They did it simply because they thought they could get away with it since they don't answer to anyone."

"But that makes no sense, Mr. Johnson. The police wouldn't—"

"It makes no sense only because you don't know their motivations, but I agree with you. Police have been beating the crap out of Black men, even shooting and killing them *on video*, without penalty, for years. Why did these particular cops object to their escapade being filmed? What you did not see on the video, what *I* saw, was that those cops were waiting for that fellow. They ambushed him. Why? You saw that fourth officer search that man—so what secret did Mr. Tavares hold that was important enough for the police to murder three people?"

Some of what Carl said was melodramatic, he knew, but he wanted to influence the coming media battle. The opening media salvo had been victorious for the police, and his media response would be equally successful in swaying public opinion. Still, the police would attempt to discredit the video and him simply because of his history of violence against the government. They'd use disinformation tactics well-known to many levels of the government. They'd spin the events and try to make the story about the American Terrorist, not about the police department, and most certainly not about the victims.

Either way, the four cops in the video had been destined to die. Of that, Carl had no doubt. Even if the woman had not filmed the event, the police officers probably still would have entered the coffee shop to threaten the customers and baristas to keep them quiet. At that point, they would have realized Carl was armed, and he would have had to kill them.

The reporter said, "Why does a terrorist care about these people?"

"I don't care about those people, but I do care about media reporting a story about me without fact-checking. And I care about the abuse of government power. That's what got my son killed." That much was true, but he only added it to give the media some fodder to debate over the next couple days. "I killed those cops because they most certainly were going to do the same to that woman—you saw that on the video. The simple fact is bad cops murdered some people and blamed it on me. I don't like that."

She started to speak again, but Carl interrupted her, saying, "Your file says you're an investigative reporter, so do some investigating."

He made a hand signal to Wizard that was not visible on camera, and his face disappeared from the television monitor.

To no one in particular, he said, "Now we wait to see how the powers behind the police respond."

CHAPTER 11

LESS THAN AN HOUR AFTER the airing of the full video, civic leaders and activists were calling for a peaceful march downtown to protest the abuse of power as well as the assault and murders. The mayor and police chief's response was swift and decisive. The police would have zero tolerance for any civic disobedience and would be authorized to do whatever was necessary to protect lives and property. The planned protest was declared illegal, and the mayor made it clear that protesters would be immediately arrested.

Carl was mildly surprised when Merc Three and Agent Palmer ganged up on him against leaving the city.

"So, what do you want me to do about it?" Carl said with a shrug. "These protesters need police to protect them from the police."

"I agree. They need protection," Merc Three said. "If not us, then who?"

Carl shook his head. "We're not police, and it's not our mission."

Three objected. "That's what Agent Palmer said before you gave the reporter the real video. So, you kinda started this, Boss."

Wizard was silent. He simply watched the exchange between Carl, Merc Three, and Agent Palmer.

"Carl," Palmer said. "Officially, even if you were to do something, the TER cannot take a position or get involved in an unsanctioned operation against civilian police." Her tone indicated she wanted him to take a position.

"Understood," Carl said with a nod.

He and Nancy Palmer had been through a lot together. At first, they were enemies when she and her TER agents mistook him for the real terrorist who had kidnapped the president's daughter. Then they teamed up together for the rescue operation and again later to prevent the assassination of the president. She wouldn't abandon him, but she couldn't help him in an official government capacity.

Palmer made some gestures to her assistants off-screen, then held her cell phone to her ear. An instant later, Carl's cell phone rang, and he chuckled. Palmer chuckled too. Her nose crinkled up when she smiled or laughed, and it gave her an innocent-girly quality, if you could consider a Navy SEAL who could kick your ass with pretty much any weapon on the planet a *girl*. And they had shared a passionate kiss once, though that event was never repeated, and both had considered the kiss an accident—a mistake. He pulled his disposable flip phone from his belt and opened it, then placed it to his ear.

"Go for Johnson."

Palmer giggled, then the wall monitor went dark. Clearly, she wanted to talk off the record. He enabled the cell's speakerphone so Wizard, Three, and the other three remaining mercs could hear.

"Carl, you have to help these people, these protesters. The hardline position of the chief of police is going to get some of these people hurt or killed."

Carl glanced sideways at Merc Three but said nothing.

Palmer continued, "Our mission was complete, but you put the video out there, and now, these people are protesting because of it. The police chief has said he's going to come down hard on them. You—*we*—have some responsibility for the coming confrontation."

Carl said, "If these protesters want to avoid getting arrested or getting their asses kicked, they probably ought not protest. That's just common sense. The cops have guns, and the protesters don't. Besides, the police are not our enemy. They're just the tools being used to subdue the people. We don't even know why yet. We *think* the mayor or the chief of police is behind this, but we have no grounds to intercede." He took a deep breath. "These people are not our mission. I say we leave it alone."

Merc Three said, "Boss, you of all people know what the cops can and will do to these people. And the authority to do it comes from the top. There will be no consequences if the cops go postal. These people don't understand the danger they're in. They still think they have rights. They still think being on camera will protect them from the likes of the cops you encountered yesterday."

Carl had firsthand knowledge of police brutality—twice—and at that time, there wasn't a damn thing he or anyone could do about it. Until he went insane, became a terrorist, and declared war on the government.

He shook his head. "That's not how police operate. They don't just *go postal.* They have a threat matrix to assess danger and an escalation matrix to determine their response just like I do."

Merc Three chuckled. "Boss, your escalation matrix has one level above calm, and that's *blow shit up!*"

That got chuckles from the others.

Carl said, "Look, these people have a choice. They can be protesters or activists if they want, but don't think because they're Black and I'm Black that I owe them anything. They're not part of my world, and I'm not part of theirs. If they want to be martyrs—"

Three said, "They're going to be out there *because of you.* Look, I know you're the boss, and we'll follow whatever decisions you make, but personally, I think we owe them at least *some* kind of protection. All we have to do is distract the police. Lead them away from the protesters. Then the people get to blow off some steam while the police can't escalate against them if they're concentrating on us. Then we disappear."

Carl regarded the fabric of the window curtain to his left. It fluttered in the light breeze from the AC vent.

Three said, "Look, Boss, you knew the day would come when you'd have to make a choice either to be the terrorist the world thinks you are or the hero we and the president know you are."

"I'm no hero," Carl said, shaking his head. "We...*I*...have killed good—"

Agent Palmer interrupted, "Yes, you have, Carl. But you've also killed bad people to save other good people. You saved the president and her daughter, as well as Agent Cummings and her family...*three* times now."

Three said, "Hell, Boss, you saved the whole damn country. But you can't *just* be a killer. You can't let the bad guys define you as a terror-ist because it fits their plan. You have to step up and do the right thing because you know what's going to happen to these protesters."

"I agree, Carl," Palmer said. "You can make a difference. You *have* made a difference."

"Damn, Nancy, I go away for one day, and y'all go and start a mutiny." He heard a slight chuckle over the phone's speaker.

Three said, "Are we terrorists, Boss, or are we going to be heroes and save people?"

Carl shook his head. "See, I knew this was going to happen. I buy you guys guns and rockets and shit, and you went and got all soft." He looked around the room at his team for a long moment, then nodded.

Somewhere along the path to terrorism, Carl Johnson and his band of mercenaries had become a force for good. He just hadn't fully realized it until that very moment.

"I *do* know what these protesters are destined to suffer because I certainly remember how it feels to be brutalized by police," Carl said. "I remember how much it hurts and how long it hurts. I remember what it did to my dignity. And to be honest, I've never been completely com-fortable being labeled as a terrorist. At first, it was exciting having that kind of power, but that was when our enemies were clearly labeled. Now everything and everyone seems shrouded in shades of gray." He stuck his hands in his pockets and considered their strategy. "Just because we call ourselves 'not terrorists' doesn't mean the rest of the world is going to do the same. Rainman still has powerful friends within the government and within this Atlas group, whoever they are, and they are still coming after us. If we do this, if we take sides, there will be bloodshed. And these Chicago cops aren't our enemy—at least not all of them—but they will be if we hit them. There are good cops out there too."

Merc Three nodded. "Unfortunately, Boss, we are *their* enemy, and the good cops aren't going to think any different of us. But if there's going to be bloodshed, at least this way, we can control that bloodshed and limit collateral damage."

The other merc and Wizard nodded also.

"Agent Palmer, what's your assessment?"

"To keep control of all variables. You'll have to distract, then disengage."

"So you're on board with this?"

"Affirmative. I dismissed everyone on this end, and we've been off the record since I shut down the video feed to you."

"Is the drone still airborne?"

"I actually forgot to recall that asset."

"Forgot, huh? And the bird has jamming capabilities, right?"

"Correct. You'll have RF and cell phone jamming at your disposal."

Because of his high profile and the sophistication of his enemies, Carl never engaged in an operation without military surveillance drone coverage. He knew his government tech package provided C4 support—command, control, computer, and communications—which was impervious to anything the local police could deploy against his team. Still, he wasn't taking his team into an armed conflict with militarized cops without a plan for absolute victory. No way he was going to fight to a stalemate.

He looked around the room again. "Okay, we're a *go*. Three, it'll be you, me, and Twelve on this op. You two"—Carl pointed at Mercs Sixteen and Ten—"fall back to the civilian op center with Nineteen, Agent Cummings."

They nodded and left.

"But I want to be clear. I don't do *distraction*. I do *escalation*." He smiled at Merc Three. "But we won't blow shit up unless we have to."

———————— ·◆◆· ————————

Four hours later, Carl waited directly across the street from the coffee shop he'd visited the day before. Yellow police tape cordoned off the sidewalk in front of the window wall of the coffee shop. He peered between the posters on the front window of the mail store, where his CIA contact had waited the day before. There were no cars parked on either side of the street today.

A sea of black-clad police officers converged on a huge crowd of chanting protesters outside. The officers wore bulky combat vests, but Carl guessed the vests were only Level II or III protection for the officers' torsos. Considered *soft body armor*, it would protect the officers against most normal bullets, like nine-millimeter or forty-four caliber rounds traveling under fifteen hundred feet per second. Still, they had no protection below the belt or for their neck or any of their limbs, but that was standard procedure for normal police operations. The strategy wasn't to be bulletproof as much as it was to survive a gunshot.

The police had an overwhelming advantage in weaponry and body armor, and the protesters, if they decided to get ornery, would be totally outclassed. On the other hand, Carl and his two mercenaries held an equal advantage over the unsuspecting police. Their strategy *was* to be bulletproof. He and the mercs were outfitted head-to-toe in hard-shell body armor. The protective outfit weighed almost thirty-five pounds compared to the ten pounds of soft armor the police wore, and it would limit mobility. In a free-for-all gunfight, though, if a confrontation came to that, Carl and his team would be virtually impervious to police weapons.

A single row of lightly armored officers stretching from curb to curb marched in-step toward the protesters. They wore black helmets with clear acrylic face shields, and their arms were all clasped together. In time with their steps, they hollered, "Move back! Move back!"

It had to be an intimidating chorus for the protesters to hear, especially for the front row of civilians.

Directly behind the shouting cops marched dozens more riot police, all similarly armored and carrying clear acrylic riot shields with a black stripe across the middle and "POLICE" printed in white letters on that black stripe. They all held their batons at the ready. Behind the riot police marched even more cops, some holding their handguns in a two-handed grip, barrels pointed at the asphalt, and others pointing assault rifles at the ground.

At that moment, Carl felt a shiver of fear grip his spine, not because of the police weaponry, but because of what he did *not* see. None of the police carried gas masks as riot police normally should. He assumed deploying tear gas was a standard procedure as the first nonlethal weapon to be used to disperse protesters, followed perhaps by rubber bullets. Carl felt his own gas mask hooked to his utility belt.

Agent Palmer's voice reported through the transceiver in his right ear, "Twelve has overwatch duty." The tactical term referred to sniper support from high ground. "Three, stand by to engage the front line. Zero, engage SWAT as necessary."

Carl said, "Heads up, people. They're not equipped to deploy nonlethals."

Merc Twelve added, "I don't see any either. Negative on rubber bullets. Negative on soft-shell impact bags."

Merc Three replied, "This is not good, Boss. This could get messy real quick."

"I think that's their intention." Carl recalled Malik Tavares's warning. *They can control the police.*

He still wasn't sure what that really meant, but he was certain he saw it in action.

Carl squatted behind a quarter-inch steel plate Mercs Three and Twelve had anchored to the brick wall under the metal window frame two hours earlier. He listened to Agent Palmer's voice as she provided the sitrep.

"Three, Twelve, maintain your cover. You have a police helicopter orbiting the park half a mile away and a television news chopper directly overhead at five hundred feet."

Palmer's unmanned drone orbited at twenty thousand feet for this op. The mercs were on the roofs of the two-story buildings, one on each side of the street and hidden under tarps the same color as the roof to prevent discovery by the news or police helicopters. Both were positioned two stores east of Carl's position, up high in front of the police force, while Carl brought up the rear on the ground.

Because the police force didn't anticipate any kind of organized resistance, they unwittingly created their own *Fatal Funnel* with the street itself acting as a narrow pathway where they could be ambushed. With the mass of protesters in front and storefronts to both sides, the police and SWAT were now at a chokepoint. Carl's team essentially had the police force in a deadly cross fire.

Palmer continued, "Zero, you have a three-man combat SWAT team on both sides of the street, clearing stores and checking doors. Looks like SWAT Level IV body armor."

Carl had glimpsed the SWAT cops before the riot cops started to march. The SWAT guys were outfitted for their threat expectation. They, too, were dressed in all black similar to the riot cops, but they no doubt had hard Kevlar-ceramic plates inside the front and back pockets of their vests. They also wore knee and elbow pads, shin guards, shoulder and neck guards, and a groin protection pad extended down from the front of their vests. But they wore no butt or thigh guards, and their Level IV armor offered upgraded protection only where the extra plates were. It wouldn't matter, however, because the mercs' armor-piercing bullets would go right through any of that armor.

Still, the police and the SWAT team in particular were an intimidating sight. Most of them wore black facemasks and sunglasses under their helmets so none of their faces could be seen. To a normal citizen, they weren't men. They were unidentifiable *entities*, monsters. Carl was convinced that anonymity and intimidation was the intent of the blackout gear.

Carl ducked his head behind his steel barrier as the SWAT trio walked in front of the shop. He wore a Kevlar helmet with its acrylic face shield lowered to protect his eyes from shrapnel. He knew the cops wouldn't see him in the dark store, if they could even see between all the posters taped to the windows. He was prepared for someone to test his locked door but still flinched when the door rattled. When the squad moved on, Carl reached up and slowly turned the deadbolt to unlock the door. He pulled it open a bit, then shoved a box holding several packages of five-hundred-count copier paper against the open door to keep it from closing.

"Zero, you are clear. Three, Twelve, you are cleared to engage." Carl stood and prepared to step through the doorway. "Engage only if the police engage. Copy?"

"Copy," Twelve said.

"Roger that," Three added.

Part of him still hoped the police only sought to intimidate by a show of force, but the protesters squashed that hope very quickly. At the command of someone with a bullhorn, the front rows of civilians imitated the police and interlocked their arms. The protest was somewhat organized, and clearly, they intended to remain peaceful since they could not fight police if they were all holding each other's arms. That had to be part of their strategy. The police could not later claim the crowd was violent. The cops would have to employ violence first, and the whole event would be captured live on national TV by the news crew advancing alongside the marching protesters.

The riot cops understood this too, because after a few moments of pushing and shoving against the line of interlocked protesters, a single command split the air over the chorus of police shouting. The front row of cops stopped in unison and unclasped their arms. The front row of cops opened up, and the riot police swarmed in between them and to the front.

A sergeant's voice boomed from a loudspeaker, announcing a litany of laws the protesters were breaking and ordering them to disperse. His orders had no effect, and the riot police pushed forward with batons raised.

An instant before the first carbon-fiber baton cracked a civilian skull, Carl said, "Engage!"

CHAPTER 12

CHIEF BILDEMEYER STOOD BESIDE MR. Karuhl as they gazed down at the growing sea of people gathering far below. From the thirty-seventh floor, the people looked like ants, and the police chief viewed them with a certain detachment even when the black tide of the police force closed on the protesters. But when he glanced at the wall monitor to his right, the street-level view on the TV monitor of the protesters was far more disturbing.

Within an hour after the American Terrorist had forced the broadcast of the full video showing the assault of the four White cops on the Black man, civic leaders and activists had called for a show of solidarity against police brutality at the site of the attack. Now, four hours later, the noon crowd outside the coffee shop grew fast, quickly numbering in the hundreds, then thousands.

Bildemeyer was surprised to see several well-known state senators and representatives present, along with city council members. They were in the front row of the protesters at *ground zero* of the protest, right in front of the coffee shop. They were going to be arrested, and they knew it, but the chief sensed they weren't there to win points for the next election. They were angry, and he understood their emotions completely. He'd had the whole affair wrapped up nice and tidy with no loose ends, except there was no way he could have predicted the American Terrorist would show his face on national TV with the raw, unedited video, feigning anger at having been used.

Bildemeyer snorted. Like the terrorist cared about what people thought of him. More likely, he probably only grabbed the video because he figured he'd use it as leverage against the Chicago Police Department someday.

Social media carried the video across the country in a firestorm of public outcry against the violence of the brutal police attack. Millions actually cheered the terrorist for killing the guilty police officers in an ocean of comments, likes, and shares. They cheered because Johnson had not waited for any kind of trial. He'd administered his own vigilante justice right there on the spot. The mayor was asked if the American Terrorist was a folk hero, and the politician stammered and side-stepped through an explanation of what he was going to do to rid the force of any other rogue police officers.

Thousands more citizens were expected to join the protest, some journeying from far outside Chicago. The brand new East Main Street Park was the rally site for what was being tagged as the March for Justice, which had not officially started yet, though hundreds of protesters by-passed the park and gathered directly at the coffee shop. Hundreds more protesters had left the park earlier and brazenly walked in the middle of the main boulevards, effectively shutting down a large portion of the downtown area in the middle of the workday, and the city's police force had not been fully deployed in time to stop them.

It's Tuesday, Bildemeyer thought with a grimace, *and rush hour traffic will soon become a quagmire of stalled traffic.* He said, "If we don't get control of this, things will get real ugly, real fast."

Mr. Karuhl said, "Your response was appropriate. I assume this time, you are prepared for escalation."

"Absolutely. If Johnson shows his face at the protest, he will be dealt with."

"We don't want him dealt with. We want him killed."

By years of habit against such verbal bait, the chief refused to respond.

On the wall TV, Bildemeyer's voice was accompanied by the text of his announcement an hour earlier. The reporter had stated that the chief of police was calling from an undisclosed location, and the chief's voice sounded distorted, like he was calling from a cell phone with poor coverage, which he was. At first, he had urged calm and tolerance, promising

73

a full-scale investigation into the assault. When Rebecca Logan asked him to explain the discrepancy between the snippet of video provided to the media and the full video provided by Johnson, Bildemeyer simply brushed aside the challenge.

"You have to consider the source of the video, which may, in fact, be altered. Anything is possible nowadays with a powerful laptop. Carl Johnson is a wanted international terrorist responsible for releasing a virus aimed at killing the president. He killed several hundred innocent people in Mexico when he destroyed five office buildings without reason, and he murdered several thousand more around the world by infecting them with the Contagion. Before that, he ambushed and murdered dozens of police and federal agents in Albuquerque. Why would you trust the word of such a man, or any so-called evidence provided by that man?"

On the TV, the chief's voice paused. "Look, I understand people want answers, and I promise to get answers, but we need time to investigate and do our jobs. Let me be very clear, though. We will tolerate no civil disobedience. Riot police will be out in force to keep order and ensure the safety of our citizens and property. This is not Ferguson or Baltimore or New York, and violence and looting will be dealt with quickly and decisively."

As Bildemeyer gazed down to the street, he could see that his plea for restraint had fallen on deaf ears. The people were outraged, and the crowd at the park was growing. They needed to wrap their brains around something concrete, and the full video provided by the terrorist gave them that—a video loop the media kept replaying of White police officers beating a helpless Black man. Even though the terrorist had pro-vided instant justice, the people needed accountability from the person in charge. From Bildemeyer. From the mayor. He had to admit, Carl Johnson had masterfully manipulated the event by controlling what the media reported.

Even as the chief watched, the huge crowd spilled out of the park and began the half-mile march to join the crowd already at the downtown coffee shop, where the police brutality had taken place the day before. From his perch, Bildemeyer could see black-clad riot police officers gath-ering on the next street around the corner from the coffee shop. Rather than have police try to contain the massive crowd between the park and downtown, Bildemeyer had recommended to the mayor that the protest be terminated at the bottleneck in the middle of the block, directly in front of the coffee shop that was the protesters' destination. Thirty minutes later, the riot police marched around the corner and confronted the protesters.

From the top floor of the Stennhauser Building, the crowd looked like a mob slowly crawling up the street. On the monitor, though, the crowd was orderly and peaceful. Many held signs ranging from "Let There Be Peace" to "Police the Police." The TV news cameras picked up chants and a few shouts, but Bildemeyer knew that if violence sparked the protest, the clash would forever be remembered for exactly what he saw on the monitor: a crowd of unarmed brown people beaten down by militarized police, mostly White men with automatic weapons and body armor. And that, Bildemeyer knew, was what Mr. Karuhl and his people wanted. It was the test that should have occurred next week.

Bildemeyer had planned his exit strategy to coincide with the up-coming test event. He was not prepared for the test to happen *today*. Mr. Karuhl had seized an immediate window of opportunity, and the chief knew he was going to be the fall guy. His entire police force had been corrupted as part of the experiment, at the risk of a significant portion of the city population, and there was absolutely nothing he could do about it. He'd wanted to be ten thousand miles away when the big test began. Now, he was faced with witnessing that test, not on TV but simply by looking out the window. Hundreds would die in a proof-of-concept test to show that a handful of power players could control any given police force and, therefore, an entire population by using artificially induced aggression. And he had no escape.

Mr. Karuhl seemed to sense his concern. "This is all part of the plan, Chief. It is the way it must be."

"We will have a riot on an unprecedented scale. There will be billions of dollars in damages and lawsuits."

"The violence will distract the media from their original story and the investigation of Malik Tavares. They'll have more pressing events to cover. The nation can never know the truth about Tavares or his knowledge of us."

Bildemeyer stood straighter and faced Mr. Karuhl, hoping to show his loyalty. "And they won't as soon as we locate Tavares's research."

Far down below, the two crowds seemed to merge, and both men faced the TV screen. The camera crew stationed right in front of the coffee shop showed the pushing and shoving as the riot police met the protesters. The helicopter camera showed two three-man squads of SWAT cops armed with automatic weapons flanking the riot cops. Then the front line of police stepped back, and the shield-bearing riot officers stepped in front. A cop in the center of the group swung his baton at a protester.

The front line of the riot police collapsed, and the armed men started falling.

CHAPTER 13

THE KOLL BROTHERS WATCHED THE proof-of-concept experiment from Grainger's office deep in the bunker. At first, Grainger sat back in his leather chair with his hands behind his head, fingers interlocked, wondering just how high the body count would reach. His mind started to wander a few months into the future when Atlas would literally control the world's population by controlling the various police forces and military units.

Hollis's hushed, urgent voice brought him back to reality. "The hell?"

Grainger refocused on the wall monitor and saw blood splattering, acrylic riot shields splintering, and cops falling.

"He's there, in Chicago!" Grainger growled. "That bastard Carl Johnson is on-site. How the hell did he know?"

He willed the TV news crews to pan their cameras around so they could find Johnson, but the cameras remained centered on the massacre in the middle of the street where the cops and protesters met.

Hollis said, "He played us."

"Masterfully."

"He hijacked our media story and turned it to his own advantage. Why?" Hollis stood and pointed at the monitor. "Why didn't he just leave town? Why did he stay?"

Grainger stood as well. "He knows." The senior brother nodded to himself. "Malik Tavares must have talked. He must have given Johnson the data."

Hollis shook his head. "If he had the data, we would have heard of it in the media. Johnson would know that's his smartest play to cripple us." He locked gazes with Grainger. "He either doesn't have it, or he doesn't realize what it is yet."

"Let's keep it that way." Grainger touched a button on the intercom control of the conference tabletop. "It's time to add another layer to the cake."

"And what if that's not enough to stop Johnson?"

Grainger smiled, confident now that he knew the stakes. "We're only halfway into a multilayer plan to handle the American Terrorist."

A voice answered the intercom, "Yes, sir?"

Grainger said, "Put the asset in play. *Right fucking now!* Kill Carl Johnson!"

CHAPTER 14

C ARL SAID, "AGENT PALMER, KILL their comm."

It must have been a surreal and totally unexpected sight for everyone except Carl's people. Still locked arm-in-arm as one, the entire front line of protesters turned their heads away from the surging riot cops and their swinging batons. They were as shocked as anyone when the attacking police fell back and not a single protester was struck.

The well-practiced squads of riot police fell into momentary disarray as blood splattered from the front row of advancing officers, their acrylic riot shields shattered, and wounded officers fell back screaming in pain. After a couple seconds, some of the police officers recovered from their shock. Seeming to sense that shots had been fired, they looked around confused, not having heard gunshots and not being able to tell where the suppressed gunfire was coming from.

Someone in the second row of officers yelled, "Medic!"

Another officer in the rear of the riot squad hollered, "Ambush!"

SWAT cops twenty meters in front of Carl brought up their weapons, scanning the protesters for targets. Carl didn't know for certain whether or not the SWAT cops would shoot into the crowd, and he wouldn't risk waiting to find out.

"Merc Three, engage SWAT on the north sidewalk." With his rifle set to single-shot, Carl stepped through the doorway and engaged the SWAT tactical officers on his sidewalk on the south side of the street…from behind.

He squeezed his trigger three times in rapid succession. His rifle wasn't suppressed, and with the confrontation stalled, the gunshots echoed into the suddenly silent street.

Three headshots, ten meters.

Carl ducked back into the mail store as a hail of bullets destroyed the glass door and windows of the storefront. The fusillade showered his armor with shards of glass, but no bullets penetrated the brick wall or steel plate that shielded him. He pulled a square high-tech grenade from a side pocket of his armored thigh, pulled the tab, and tossed it through the doorway—not at the police, but close enough to knock a few down without killing anyone.

The blast was deafening, and in the absence of sound that followed, Carl heard the moans of the wounded, more calls for medics, and a wave of gasps from protesters as they tried to distance themselves from the gun battle. The civilians retreated slowly, though, because there was a lot of inertia behind the hundreds of frontline marchers.

Palmer's voice said, "Both Three and Twelve's positions took some fire, but both are unharmed."

"Copy that." Carl was still bewildered at the resourcefulness of his mercs. He'd probably never know where they found the sheets of metal for their bulletproof barriers, or where they found appropriately colored camouflage netting, or how they got the heavy metal plates secured on the roofs, or where they acquired the bullhorn Carl had placed beside his own barrier. Yet again, the mercs had proven themselves quite capable at logistic acquisitions.

Carl's voice boomed out to the street over the bullhorn. "Hold your fire! Police officers, surrender or you will be killed!"

A bellowing voice countered, "Stand your ground!"

Carl peeked above his steel barricade and aimed the bullhorn through the partially open door. "The next grenade I throw will land right in the middle of your unit. Lay down your arms! No more blood needs to be spilled!"

A mix of tactical commands coming from different directions among the police units was undecipherable.

Merc Three's voice came over Carl's earpiece, saying, "They're trying to retreat."

"Discourage them," Carl answered.

Several muffled shots split the air, and another officer howled in pain. A few officers tried to return fire to the roofs, but their shots merely pinged off the metal sheets the mercs hid behind.

"Hold your fire! Hold your fire!" came the response from the street. "Okay, I'm willing to discuss this. Come out and talk."

"There will be no discussion," Carl answered. "Make no further attempt to retreat. Disarm or die! Right now!" The unit commander did not respond, so Carl added, "Your team is at a significant tactical disadvantage. We hold the high ground and the choke point, and we're using armor-piercing ordnance. Surrender and live another day. You cannot win this fight."

"What do you want?"

Carl held out the fist in which he held a second grenade. His voice echoed into the street through the bullhorn. "Here is the second grenade. Note that the tab has been removed. Lay down your weapons."

The sound of metal and plastic hitting the asphalt came almost immediately.

"Clear," said Merc Three.

"Clear," said Merc Twelve.

Agent Palmer added, "You are clear, Zero."

Carl rose and stepped from behind his shield, his assault rifle at the ready in his right hand and the grenade ready in his left. He left the mail store and approached the police, stopping in front of the unit commander on the fringe of the riot squad. They looked defeated and shell-shocked. Some simply stood idle in a daze while others helped the wounded. Two or three appeared dead, and a handful had critical injuries. A dozen more had minor wounds. The six SWAT commandos were all dead.

"Do you know what this is?" he asked the unit commander as he gestured with his weapon. The man was a big guy, forty-something, very fit with a thick neck and a shock of black hair visible when he removed his Kevlar riot helmet. The man said nothing, and Carl could tell by the look in his eyes that he was not familiar with the weapon.

Carl raised his voice so the rest of the police officers could hear him. "It's a PDW, a personal defense weapon. It's the only weapon of its kind designed entirely by computer before a prototype was even manufactured. It fires six-by-thirty-two-millimeter rounds, which you now know are armor-piercing. It has a folding stock, which makes it ideal for close-quarters urban combat." Carl's stock was unfolded. "It has minimal recoil, so I can fire it accurately with one hand if necessary, and all the gunpowder burns in the barrel, so it has almost no muzzle flash. That makes it very useful in night operations, unlike your weapons. All in all, it's the perfect lightweight assault weapon to use against armored bullies who like to pick on unarmed civilians."

The commander said, "You're interfering with lawful police operations. When—"

"Just because it's lawful doesn't make it right." Carl head-nodded at the silent crowd of stunned civilians to his right. "These people have a constitutional right to gather and protest peacefully, and they are unarmed. Yet you are attacking them with automatic military weapons. To me, *that* is not legal. That is *oppression*, and I'm putting a stop to it." Carl scanned the officers. "You think you're above the law because no one can stop you. Until today."

Through his face shield, he smiled at the commander. Then he put the barrel of his rifle against the chest plate of the man's thick vest.

In his ear comm, Carl heard Palmer say, "Zero, you have incoming, both airborne and on the ground. ETA, fifteen seconds. SWAT is mobilizing two more units from the park. Our drone can't jam their signals that far away. Their radio chatter indicates they don't know the tactical situation at your position, but they heard the gunfire. ETA, three minutes. You also have the riot squad's backup incoming as we speak. You'd better wrap things up, Carl."

To the commander, he said, "My people are better trained than yours, my tactical position is superior to yours, and my weapons are superior."

A sleek, black, track-wheeled APC—Armored Personnel Carrier— that looked like it was derived from a Humvee body frame with dual narrow, green-tinted bulletproof front windows skidded around the corner at the end of the block. A police helicopter banked from behind the nearest skyscraper and pivoted a hundred feet above the APC, the sniper in its open doorway already shooting at Merc Twelve.

The commander grunted and said, "You were saying?"

Carl glanced from the APC to the commander and calmly said, "Three, kill that APC. Twelve, kill that chopper."

The commander narrowed his eyes.

Before Carl had finished uttering the commands, a swoosh had accompanied a flash overhead, and an armor-piercing RPG had slammed into the APC with a tremendous fireball. The deep *boom-boom-boom* of Merc Twelve's antiaircraft 50-cal echoed down into the street as the merc stitched the chopper with explosive-tipped rounds. One round blasted the main rotor clean from the top of the cabin, and the dead aircraft fell right on top of the burning APC.

"Yes," Carl said, "I *was* saying."

The police commander reminded him of the last Triad leader. He held the same look of defiance in his eyes, like he still had some leverage—like he was still in command. This was the kind of man responsible for all the chaos of the past eight months. This was the kind of man responsible for Mark's death. Carl pulled the trigger.

"Carl!" Agent Palmer said.

The defiant commander howled in pain, and the cop behind him yelped as Carl's bullet blasted through the front of the commander's armored vest, then through his thick chest, then through the back of his vest, and embedded itself in the other cop's arm. Both officers fell to the street, the commander mortally wounded. Two of his fellow officers rushed to attend to him, peeling his vest off to get to his wound.

Carl pointed his assault rifle at the fallen commander and said, "You men should probably step away from him."

Palmer's voice sounded cautious as he said that. "Carl, get control of yourself! This isn't Mexico."

Another officer's voice boomed, "Hold your fire! Everybody, hold your fire. Please." The black-armored man stepped forward, removed his Kevlar helmet and anti-flash goggles, and tossed them aside, then stood with his hands spread wide at his sides. Like the fallen commander, he was a big man, thick in body and neck, and wore buzz-cut gray hair. "You're in control, Mister. What do you want?"

Carl wasn't about to start negotiating with the man. Besides, he knew control *given* was not the same as control *taken*. "Hands up."

The cop complied.

With that simple gesture of surrender, Carl now had complete control over all the cops. "Remove your body armor," he said, looking across the crowd of officers.

The new commanding officer tented his eyebrows. "You can't be serious."

Carl pointed the business end of his PDW at the fallen commander's head. The new leader looked around and nodded, and he and all his men peeled off their body armor.

"Your uniforms too," Carl said. "Everyone, down to your undies and T-shirts."

"Zero, you don't have time for this." Palmer's voice sounded urgent.

The police complied, and inside of a minute, three dozen men stood barefoot, mostly in white undies with a few oddball-colored boxers or briefs mixed in.

"On your knees, hands behind your heads."

With the surrender complete, Merc Twelve said, "You have a young woman approaching your four o'clock position, threat-negative."

Merc Three added, "I have her covered."

Carl turned his head toward the person approaching from his right, slightly behind him. It was a brown-skinned slender man, not a woman. He wore a spaghetti-strap cream-colored blouse, tight white pants, and lots of makeup. The young man didn't look like a girl. He looked like a boy with a lot of makeup. At the sight of the young man, Carl suddenly knew exactly who was behind the mystery that Tavares had uncovered.

"Speak," Carl said.

The camera crew and the reporter had taken refuge in a recessed store entrance, and they eased closer along the sidewalk to Carl's right.

The young man's voice was soft and timid. "Malik Tavares was my boyfriend. I know why he was killed. He was doing an investigation and was going to publish an article on the internet."

Carl nodded, then squatted in front of the cop who had assumed command. He looked into the cop's blue eyes as the man knelt with his hands clasped behind his head. He looked mid-forties with severe crow's feet at the corners of his eyes, and he had a narrow nose.

Seeing the police on their knees in surrender filled Carl with a burning rush of anger he'd been carrying for almost eight years since his first throw-down by cops in Downtown Albuquerque. His arrest by FBI and Homeland late last year for a crime he didn't commit had only served to reignite the flames of anger and humiliation that had never really faded. He felt those emotions course through him again. He felt contempt for the unjust system that protected cops but not citizens.

And the innate fear of armored men in black.

And the pain of getting his ass kicked by a gang of armed bullies with badges.

And the helplessness.

And the loss of dignity he could only pretend to have reclaimed despite his power as the world's most wanted terrorist.

And the fact that if he ever tried to return to being a normal citizen, any cop in any city could steal his dignity again anytime, without cause.

"Zero…status," Agent Palmer said.

Carl barely heard the words.

Palmer softened her voice. "Carl, are you with us?"

Her voice brought him back to the present and calmed him as she always did. He glanced around, aware he'd been breathing hard and shallow, almost hissing. Without realizing it, he'd aimed his weapon at the new commander's face. He moved his finger away from the trigger, gave the man a half-smile, and lowered the barrel of the PDW. A small part of him wanted to kill all the surrendered officers just because he could, just to teach a lesson to the unseen men who had commanded the cops to do their dirty deeds. He wanted to punish these police as substitutes for the ones who had arrested and tortured him and gotten his son killed. He had the power and the weapons to get even, but deep inside, he knew the justice *system*, not these particular cops, was responsible for destroying his previous life. He stuffed his burst of anger back inside, knowing the officer he faced saw it and realized how close he'd come to dying.

"Look at all that," Carl said.

The cop glanced to his side.

Three dozen sets of body armor, helmets, boots, and black fatigues made a huge pile, and the pile of weaponry was just as large. Each cop's utility belt held a radio, two metal handcuffs, plastic zip cuffs, a Taser, a handgun, multiple reload magazines, and pepper spray. The pile also held dozens of automatic and semiautomatic rifles, Glock handguns, acrylic riot shields, shotguns, and carbon-composite batons.

Carl said, "Tell me why you need all that military hardware if you're not going to war? Why do you need all that for peaceful protesters?"

"You are not peaceful, nor are you protesting."

"Nice try," Carl said. "But you didn't know I was coming to the party. You brought all those weapons to kill unarmed civilians. Why?"

The cop stared silently at Carl, but his eyes flinched, betraying his real fear.

Carl leaned over the cop as he said, "Here, hold this *live* grenade." He pushed the device into one of the man's fists behind his head. "Be careful, though, because my guy on the roof has you in his sight. If any of your people do anything foolish, he'll shoot you, and you'll drop the grenade, and all your people will die."

His voice low and rumbling, the cop said, "My people need medical attention. How many more have to die before you're satisfied?"

The man was well-trained, but Carl could tell this particular policeman had never seen death up close. He'd only mixed it up with untrained street thugs or domestic bullies, where the odds were always ten-to-one or twenty-to-one in favor of the police. He'd never been challenged in a combat situation completely out of his control by someone who could actually kill him.

"You're missing the point, Officer. This moment right here." Carl nodded. "The emotions you're feeling right now...*this* is why I became a terrorist. This is how your unarmed victims feel when you terrorize them. And make no mistake, you're just as much of a terrorist as I am. Except you're worse than me. You have the law on your side. You *say* you protect and serve the community, but you really protect and serve the politicians that control you. And you protect and serve the corporations that control the politicians. They give you orders because it fits their agenda, and you don't care who gets hurt along the way because you don't have to answer to anyone for your crimes."

Palmer said, "You have incoming, thirty seconds. Three, Twelve, E-and-E, right now. Get out of there, Carl!"

E-and-E meant "escape and evade," but Carl continued addressing the cop. "Right now, you're feeling a mixture of humiliation, embarrassment, and fear of imminent death, but tonight and tomorrow and for the next ten years, you'll nurse this anger and this feeling of helplessness like a bad, unending hangover because you've been humiliated on national TV. Your dignity has been taken, there's no recourse to help you get it back, and you can't punish the ones who've done this to you. That's how your victims feel every day for years after you beat the crap out of them." Carl looked around at the defeated troops. "The weak ones will quit the police force out of fear. You're strong, though. You'll hold your anger and fear inside for months or years, pretending you've gotten over it. But you never will. You'll wake up at night screaming and sweating. You'll break down crying in anger and frustration. Maybe you'll lose control and beat your wife or kids because you can't hurt me." Carl grunted. "Your shrink will call it PTSD and give you some pills." Carl stood and drank in the man's fear and anger. "Or maybe you're not man enough to suck it up. Maybe you want to rush me and take a bullet—take the easy way out so you don't have to suffer the humiliation."

The man opened his mouth to speak, but no words emerged.

Carl ended his statement with, "Welcome to *my* world. This is my life every day. This is the life of every innocent Black, Brown, and Red man ever assaulted by bullies with a badge."

It occurred to him that the first two times FBI and police assaulted him—eight years ago and eight months ago—they'd seemed like faceless, larger-than-life men in black armor with all their weapons. Now, looking at them in their white undies, they looked normal. They looked vulnerable, just like their victims.

Carl took the gay man by the arm and walked away from the officer. He stopped by the camera crew and pointed at the hostage police, saying, "These are the men that murdered a helpless man, a woman with a camera, and the coffee server who witnessed their illegal deeds. These cops dress in black armor and use military weapons to intimidate citizens. When they strike, they are merely unidentifiable ghosts in black fatigues and black sunglasses, so no one knows who they are. But under that black armor, they're flesh and blood just like we are. They bleed and they die just like we do. Now you know who they are. You can see their faces. You know their names. And"—Carl paused a beat for effect—"*they* know they can be hurt. They know they can't get away with police brutality anymore. And before the mayor decides to escalate against me, he might want to call the White House and see how that worked out for the FBI and Homeland Security last year."

He just added that last part as the verbal equivalent of movie special effects because everyone on the planet knew about his war with the US government before he found the kidnapped girl. And it wasn't strictly those officers who had starred in the now-viral coffee shop video, but Carl was using the media for his own disinformation campaign, same as the government did. Viewers would believe what they saw, whether or not what they saw was the actual truth.

Carl turned his attention to the young fem-man. "You're with me." He walked backward toward the shot-up mailing store but kept his assault rifle up and ready. "Stay behind me."

Pausing at the door, Carl looked to his left and right. The street was a war zone. Raging flames rose from the shell of the APC and the crumpled helicopter on top of it. The disorganized gaggle of cops on their knees looked utterly defeated. The massive pile of body armor and weapons framed the defeat. The wounded moaned, and the dead still bled. Red darkened the street. To his right, hundreds of protesters stood in shock and complete silence. They watched him, a figure clad in black armor even more scary than that of the cops, and he imagined every single one of them knew who he was. He wondered if they realized he'd just saved many of them from injury or death.

The camera crew remained focused on him as though they expected him to start shooting again, and the reporter stammered to say something meaningful for the watching world. He gazed at the camera, at the world, and felt absolutely nothing—no remorse, no fear. It was always that way for him after combat. Other people died. He didn't.

CHAPTER 15

CARL LED THE FEMBOY THROUGH the mail store. "So, what's your name?"

"Chrissy," the young man replied. He had short black hair in a girly perm style that was plastered flat against his head. He had dark brown skin, and his face had hard features, though it was clear to Carl he used a lot of makeup to make himself look soft and gentle. "Well, it's Christopher, really, but…" The young man talked through the entire brief trip to the townhouse op center.

Carl saw through his pretense. The man was a killer, an assassin, fem or not. He worked for Rainman.

Carl led the way up the steps to the brownstone porch and took a final look around. He felt invincible, like a medieval knight in black armor. Curiously, all the protective armor plates he wore didn't make a sound. He moved in almost complete silence. The door was unlocked, so Carl twisted the knob and pushed the door open, then moved them both inside quickly.

He hollered inside. "Wizard, pack it up. We gotta go!"

Agent Palmer's voice said, "I've already—"

Carl said, "And Chrissy, secure that door, please."

Chrissy turned and reached for the deadbolt.

Carl pivoted and kicked him in the side of the head with as much strength as he could muster. Almost.

Had he connected, the boy would have been out like a light, but he must have expected the attack, and all that heavy hard armor slowed Carl. The fem-man got a shoulder up that deflected most of the power behind Carl's kick.

Still, Chrissy squealed like a girl when he bounced against the wall. "Ow! Motherfucker!"

It was then Carl realized his tactical error. One of the best advantages of his lightweight assault rifle was the ability to maneuver with it in enclosed combat zones like narrow hallways when the stock was folded in. But he'd neglected to fold the stock. Now he was standing too close to the wall and had wasted a precious half-second clearing the weapon. By the time he aimed it, Chrissy had recovered.

The boy kicked out so fast, Carl barely saw him move. The ex-Delta Force killer he'd fought eight months earlier was fast and strong, but this kid moved in a blur. His open-toed shoe kicked the weapon out of Carl's grip, and the boy kicked him five more times in the space of a mere two seconds.

Had he not been wearing body armor, Carl would have had a string of broken bones up and down the left side of his body. The last kick really rocked his world, and he heard the impact echo inside his skull as the top of Chrissy's foot rammed his helmet into the wall.

Then the assassin went for the PDW.

Carl kicked the weapon down the hall and tried to stay in tight proximity with the killer. The first three or four minutes were basically a free-for-all wrestling match between the two. The narrow hallway was barely three feet wide, so Carl quickly learned that if he stayed in the middle of the hallway, his assassin couldn't use his powerful roundhouse and front snap kicks. Still, the young man was extremely capable with his elbows, feet, and knees, and had Carl not been wearing his body armor, he would have been dead already several times over from the assassin's strikes.

Even though he had maybe fifty pounds on the slender man, the killer was fast, nimble, and surprisingly strong. He used Carl's helmet as a weapon, grabbing it from behind and trying to use it to strangle Carl. The assassin got behind him and literally rode on his back, legs locked around his torso. Carl rammed them both backward against the wall, but the killer succeeded in twisting the helmet almost off his head, essentially tightening the noose. Unable to breathe, Carl had no choice but to yank the Velcro strap to release the helmet. Then the killer snatched the Kevlar helmet from Carl and literally beat him over the head with it multiple times before Carl could wrestle it away.

Most of the assassin's strikes bounced harmlessly off Carl's armored forearm, but the assassin still landed a couple of very painful blows. His combo fist-elbow punch took its toll on Carl—he'd punch with his fist, and instead of pulling back to punch again, he'd follow through with an elbow strike. Each time, Carl had virtually no warning. The boy was just too fast. He kept landing blow after blow against Carl's darting head until he got lucky.

Carl heard his nose bones crack and immediately felt the warm, sticky flow of blood. He launched a flurry of counterstrikes in return, but wrapped together like they were, he couldn't get sufficient leverage to land punches hard enough to hurt the assassin.

Carl released him and rolled to his feet. He had the man trapped in the narrow hallway near the door, so the killer didn't have any maneuvering room. Blood flowing freely from his busted nose, Carl pulled his combat knife and advanced slowly. The weapon had knuckle grips like brass knuckles so he wouldn't have to worry about dropping it. He held it blade-down in front of him like he'd been taught and held his left arm in front of his head as a guard against the six-inch stiletto the assassin had magically produced from somewhere on his body. The plates of his armor would easily deflect all but a lucky stab into one of the joints, and he could see in his opponent's eyes that the young man knew this also.

Chrissy wasn't afraid. His eyes were wide with excitement, and he was smiling. He enjoyed the battle.

Carl knew then the killer had been in life-and-death conflicts many times, and the fact that the young man was there told Carl he'd been victorious in all of his previous confrontations. One thing was certain to Carl. Only one of them would leave the op center alive. The assassin had the advantage in youth and skill, but he wasn't wearing body armor, and Carl, though older, wasn't without training.

They regarded each other during the pause in the fight, each looking for a weakness in the other.

The young man said, "How did you know?"

"I've gazed into the eyes of many killers in the last few months."

Then they went at each other again. Sparks flashed off the colliding blades, knees and elbows glanced off muscle and armor, fists bounced painfully off skulls—well, painfully for Carl.

He heard Palmer's voice through his comm device over his own heavy breathing. "What's your status, Carl?"

He gasped as he struck at his killer again. "I'm attempting to interrogate the assassin."

"It doesn't sound like an interrogation."

"Yeah. He's resisting."

"Well, wrap it up quickly. He has support moving in on your position. ETA, three minutes."

"Copy that." If his support team were moving in, then they were tracking his position electronically because Carl was certain no one had followed them. They had to be using different frequencies than the police. "Find his frequencies and kill his comms."

"Done."

The young man was a tornado of kicks, punches, and stabs in the confined space, but in the end, physics won over talent. Carl weighed 170 pounds, and the killer might have weighed 120 after a heavy meal. He forced the smaller man into the corner, all the while dodging his expert stiletto jabs. When Carl moved in for the kill, Chrissy raked his stiletto across Carl's forehead. It was a fast swipe that burned like a paper cut and started bleeding immediately and profusely. But finally, Carl rushed him and buried his combat knife in the young man's shoulder.

The assassin screamed a high-pitched wail of pain. When he tried to twist away, Carl picked him up by the waist and body-slammed him to the floor WWE-style. Then he pulled the knife from the man's shoulder and stabbed it deep into his thigh. The assassin screamed again, and Carl twisted it. He pulled it out and rolled off the killer. The beaten man tossed his stiletto away and curled up against the far wall, a growing pool of blood on the floor beneath him. On his knees, Carl pulled all the quick releases of his armor suit, and the hard black plates fell from his body.

Carl crawled to Chrissy, rolled him onto his back, and parked the tip of his knife against his chest. "Talk." He pulled a handkerchief from his pants pocket and held it against his forehead wound to quell the blood dripping into his left eye and down his face.

"Don't kill me."

"Talk!"

The assassin confessed to the murders, then said he'd been hired by someone named Mr. Karuhl.

"Where can I find him?"

Chrissy grimaced and groaned. "I went to his office. I met with him and the police chief. His name was Bildemeyer."

"Where?" Carl roared.

"The Stennhauser Building, on the top floor. I spoke with them by cell just a few minutes ago. I think they're still there."

"Both of them?"

Chrissy nodded.

Palmer's voice said, "ETA, one minute."

Carl raised his blade.

"No, please," Chrissy whimpered. "I can give you intel."

Carl nodded and slid his knife into its scabbard.

The assassin continued, "It was some kind of experiment in a new crowd-control technology." Chrissy groaned again. "They can control the police. I don't know how, but it's like a prototype test. I was hired to eliminate the survivors from the coffee shop and engage you if you showed up at the protest."

As bizarre as all that sounded, Carl was unsurprised since he'd heard something similar from Malik Tavares, the police assault victim. But he needed confirmation of his gut feeling that Rainman, the man responsible for the attempt to kill President Shirley Mallory, was involved.

"Why you? These people could have hired any number of assassins."

"They called me because you got involved yesterday by eliminating their kill squad, the four police officers. They said I fit your profile. They said your weakness is your need to help the helpless. I was supposed to act vulnerable so I could get close to you."

Palmer said, "ETA, thirty seconds. Get out of there, Carl."

"Unfortunately for you, they misjudged me." Carl stood and retrieved his PDW. "Vulnerable is not part of my profile." He pointed it at the assassin's head. "*This* is my profile."

"Please don't kill me."

"You murdered three innocent people." Carl pulled the trigger. *Head-shot. Point-blank range.*

"Breach is imminent," Palmer said.

Carl sprinted up the hallway and ducked through an exit hole his mercs had several days ago cut in the dining room wall shared with the vacant brownstone next door. Inside that room, he found the mercs' normal stash of defensive weaponry that might be useful in covering an escape. Since the equipment was untraceable, the stash was always left behind in a hurried escape or, in the current situation, when none of the other mercs were coming back.

He dropped his PDW and quickly opened a green metal case holding several RPGs, grabbing two. He made his way up to the fourth floor—the roof access door—and found Wizard waiting inside the door, shakily pointing a gun in his direction.

"Jesus, Boss!" Wizard blurted. "What the hell happened to you?"

"Yeah." Carl put down the RPGs and held the now blood-soaked handkerchief against his head. "Forehead cuts bleed like a stuck pig and are the hardest to clot, but it's not as bad as it looks."

"I dunno, Boss. It looks pretty bad."

"Get our reporter friend, Miss Logan, on your cell. Let's do a video call." He leaned over with his palms braced on his knees to catch his breath.

The assassin hadn't seriously hurt him through the body armor until he got his helmet off, but the young man's feet and knees had knocked him around and bruised him pretty thoroughly. Carl was tired, and his whole body ached. His nose throbbed, and his eyes burned from the blood running down from his cut forehead. He had to breathe through his mouth because of the blood clogging his swollen nose. His jaw hurt, and his lips were split. He hadn't had two fights in his entire life, and in his mid-fifties, he'd had to go up against two highly trained professional killers half his age. And he won! Not that you could tell that by looking at him.

As Wizard worked, he said, "Agent Palmer canceled the jamming of cell phones, but the police comm is still being blocked, as is the hit squad's comm. She says the assassin's support team just breached."

Carl nodded. He'd heard the report through his comm as he climbed the stairs.

"We've detected their mini drone. It's still orbiting at one thousand feet. Ours is at twenty thousand feet."

A mini drone was the perfect surveillance tool for a hit squad to deploy because it was small, mobile, and could be deployed wherever the hit squad set up camp. A military drone like the TER asset Carl's team used, however, was larger and far more capable, though less mobile. The sensors on the TER drone could collect data from all directions, while the mini drone only had lookdown capability.

That was the targeting device for the missiles that had hit Cummings's house, though Carl hadn't known it at the time. It made sense, though, and Agent Palmer had set Wizard and her government team to locating it. It was difficult because, as Carl suspected, the tiny drone was almost entirely nonmetallic, invisible to radar.

Wizard spoke quietly into the phone, then said, "The reporter is ready." He pointed the back of the device at Carl.

"Oh my God!" The reporter gasped at what she saw on her video link. "What happened to you?"

"Just make sure you broadcast this to the world." Carl wiped blood from his forehead and looked into the cell phone camera. "A man named Karuhl sent an assassin to kill me. It was the same assassin he sent to kill those innocent civilians yesterday. The assassin succeeded yesterday, but he fell short today. By the way, this Karuhl fellow ordered Police Chief John Bildemeyer to send those rogue cops to ambush Malik Tavares, and he ordered the police to assault the protesters."

Agent Palmer transmitted the killer's confession over the cell phone channel. In Carl's comm earpiece, she said, "The support team is withdrawing."

Wizard followed with the cell phone camera as Carl picked up two RPG tubes and went out onto the roof. He laid one on the roof near the ledge, then leaned over the waist-high parapet. He pointed the second RPG at the car in the street below. Wizard pointed his cell phone down at the car as the hit squad abandoned the brownstone and got in. Carl pressed the trigger, and the warhead shot down, trailing smoke and flame. The last man getting into the car must have heard something because he looked up. He locked his gaze with Carl's for a millisecond, then he, his team, and the car were consumed in a fiery explosion.

Carl straightened up and glared into the camera.

Rebecca Logan's voice floated unsteadily from the speaker. "Oh my God!" She seemed to be having difficulty deciding whether she was reporting a real-life terror event or a covert operation. "What now?"

Carl said, "The people protesting want justice, so now I'm going to kill the man and his puppet police chief responsible for those murders yesterday."

Agent Palmer directed Carl's attention to the correct building. He dropped the used RPG tube and picked up the second RPG, then sighted through the targeting reticule.

"Wait!" Logan said. "You can't—"

"Can't what, Miss Logan?" Carl notched an eyebrow at the cell phone Wizard held. "I can't do what they did? I can't murder people?"

"Vigilante justice is not justice!"

"What would you have me do, Miss Logan? Call the police?" He smirked. "Do you really think they'll go over there and arrest their own police chief and the rich man he works for?" Carl was using Logan's international broadcast to convict Bildemeyer and Karuhl of their crimes. "They murdered people yesterday, and if I hadn't intervened, they would have murdered hundreds of unarmed protesters using cops armed with military weapons. How long do you think it would take for these rich people to make bail and escape the country?"

"So two wrongs make a right? Murder begets murder?"

"Don't go thinking I'm some kind of folk hero, Miss Logan." Carl turned his attention back to the RPG on his shoulder. "They call me the American Terrorist for a reason. The police and people like Chief Bildemeyer and his masters operate *above* the law, so I operate *outside* the law."

Agent Palmer said, "The thermal sensors on the drone indicate only one office on the top floor is occupied. Two heat signatures are standing by the window that faces your position. Numerous other heat signatures are stationary in the hallways outside that office. I'm painting the top-floor office on the west end with the drone's targeting laser. The RPG has a sensor that can home in on the laser."

He pointed the RPG in the general direction of the Stennhauser Build-ing's top floor and depressed the firing button halfway. He was rewarded with the target acquisition tone.

"Target acquired."

"Confirmed," Palmer said. "Fire when ready."

CHAPTER 16

CHIEF BILDEMEYER LISTENED AS RAINMAN'S scathing criticism blasted from the speaker of Mr. Karuhl's encrypted cell phone. The voice was heavily distorted, but finally, the tirade ended.

"Mr. Karuhl, your people monitored the unsuccessful test, didn't they?" He didn't wait for a response. "Transmit the raw test data now."

Mr. Karuhl accessed the live data file on his laptop and transmitted it. "Done. Even though Johnson interfered with the actual outcome of the test, a high body count was not essential to meet our test objectives. Only the violent clash between the police and the protesters was critical."

"I disagree," Rainman said. "You know very well our stakeholders needed to see the body count."

"Nevertheless, the primary test objectives were met. I'd say this was a resounding success, and we can move immediately to phase 2A and then to phase three on schedule."

Rainman was silent for a long while, then said, "I agree. Phase three is nationwide and expected to take four to six months to launch. However, as you are aware, phase 2A is a more targeted short-term local objective."

Karuhl and Bildemeyer looked at each other.

Rainman continued, "Mr. Karuhl, I was going to suggest you leave the city since your identity is now known. But since the American Terrorist also knows your identity, even leaving the country likely won't be far enough away."

Chief Bildemeyer had listened while Mr. Karuhl updated Rainman about the assassin's infiltration and his hand-to-hand fight with Carl Johnson. The chief had remained hopeful even though the team's comm was mysteriously interrupted…until he saw Johnson on TV. The terrorist was a bloody mess, but it was clear the assassin had failed in his mission. The shaky video was obviously being shot from a handheld camera, likely a cell phone. Johnson's termination of the enforcement squad was spectacular, and it was being broadcast *along with his name* around the world.

How the hell could a domestic terrorist acquire military-grade armor-piercing RPGs and fifty-caliber antiaircraft guns? How would he know to bring such weaponry to a civilian protest? How could he acquire sophisticated RF jamming capability to disrupt police frequencies?

Mr. Karuhl said, "Contracting a gay assassin was your idea, Rainman. Clearly, your profile of Johnson was not as complete as you led me to believe."

"Irrelevant. Your team of enforcers should have been more than enough to handle Johnson. They had the element of surprise. There's no way he should have won that encounter."

Mr. Karuhl countered, "Just as there's no way Johnson and two mercenaries should have been able to disarm trained SWAT and riot police?"

"What's done is done, though he always seems to have multiple layers to his defensive strategy." Rainman took an audible breath. "Johnson has proven himself to be a tactical genius, so I'd distance myself from Chief Bildemeyer if I were you. He's the next likely target, thanks to the assassin's confession that we just heard on national television. Fortunately, your moniker is not your real identity, but the chief is another story."

Mr. Karuhl glared sideways at Bildemeyer.

The chief said, "A recorded conversation between a killer under duress and an international terrorist can hardly be used in court. My lawyers will tear apart that argument, and no judge in the state will issue an arrest warrant—"

Rainman said, "I mean *physical* distance. The American Terrorist doesn't *arrest*. He *kills*. And it's already too late. Look at your television."

The two men had been facing the wall monitor though concentrating on Mr. Karuhl's cell phone. When they looked up, both gasped. The shaky video showed Johnson picking up another RPG. He pointed it into the distance, where the very tower they occupied could be seen. A flash of smoke ejected the tiny rocket from the tube, then its engine ignited, and the missile zoomed into the distance on a horizontal plume of fire. Both men looked out the broad expanse of wall glass and watched the trail of fire rise up to meet them.

"Goodbye," Rainman said.

CHAPTER 17

TWO HOURS AFTER HIS FIGHT with the assassin, Carl Johnson sat aboard his private Gulfstream 850. He still felt uncomfortable on the plane after all these months. It was, after all, the same model used by the government special ops team that had kidnapped him and carried him to an interrogation facility, where he underwent eleven days of experimental torture because Palmer and McGrath thought he was *that other guy*. He was headed back to one of his secure compounds in central Mexico. Alfonso Reyes, the mid-level drug lord who exactly resembled Carl, had owned the compound where Carl was now headed, but that man had died in the custody of the TER agency during an extreme interrogation session. By some creative financing, Carl had inherited all of Reyes's personal and business assets for his terrorist persona and his mission to find everyone associated with Rainman, the perpetrator of the plot to kill President Mallory.

A contract medic Agent Palmer had sent to attend Carl's injuries during the flight was the only other person on board the plane besides Carl and two pilots. The medic was an older gray-haired gent, maybe ten years Carl's senior, and Carl could tell from the man's stocky build he'd seen his fair share of military or covert medical service. Still, the man had friendly eyes, and he kept apologizing for perceived pain he caused Carl with his treatment. The medic closed the cut on Carl's forehead with some gel and flesh-colored adhesive tape, then reset his broken nose. He inspected Carl's jaw and cheekbones, determining they were bruised but not broken. Fortunately, Carl had no broken teeth.

Carl gulped down several painkillers and dismissed the medic to sit in the cockpit jump seat so he could converse privately with Agent Palmer over the secure commlink. He reclined his leather chair as far back as it would go. He put the doctor's cold gel pack over his face and closed his eyes. Listening to Palmer's voice in his ear, he thought about his nemesis. Rainman's plan to coordinate a bloodless coup and take over the US government and the entire western hemisphere had almost succeeded except for the accidental involvement of Carl Johnson.

"You remember in my debrief about that event at the restaurant in Old Town, Albuquerque? The night I retrieved the president's daughter?"

"You shot three men who attacked a transgender man who identified as a woman. How is that relevant?"

Carl took a deep breath and winced at the dull throbbing pain in his face. "In his position as vice president, Rainman had access to all our after-action reports up to the point when we discovered his role in the attacks on the president. He thinks he has profiled me. He thinks he knows my weakness. He thought he could send a fem-assassin to play on that perceived weakness."

"But you saw through that ruse and led the assassin back to the op center so you could interrogate him."

Carl chuckled. "Correct." The interrogation had been successful, though painful.

Palmer quipped, "I probably would have handled the interrogation differently."

"Just so you know, I only let him kick my ass to make him overconfident, you know, so I could get intel out of him."

Palmer chuckled, then said, "Rainman plays large, so if he's involved in Chicago, there's something strategic happening there that is much more than just police brutality. We need to know what it is. The police chief seemed to make a great effort to ensure violence *would* occur. He could have de-escalated his response to the protest at any point, but he instead made sure his police force escalated the conflict. Except I can't imagine how a local civilian protest, even in a city the size of Chicago, fits into Rainman's agenda."

"Well, there's no doubt Rainman is involved, even though I can't show proof." Carl was silent for a moment, then added, "Both Tavares and the assassin said something about technology capable of controlling police behavior, and the assassin said it was some kind of prototype test. If we investigate this further, though, we tip our hands that we know Rainman is involved. He'll know we're onto him and go into hiding again."

"Yes." She was silent for a moment, and Carl got the feeling she was considering the same plan he was. "So we pretend we don't suspect his involvement?"

"Indeed, and I'm thinking the CIA analyst is a plant. His request to join us is too convenient, the timing too coincidental."

"We vetted him. For him to withstand the level of scrutiny we employed in his background check, his alias has to be very deeply placed. We literally know everything about the man going back to his parents' elementary schools. If we now suspect him of being an infiltrator, standard procedure is to put him in isolation and interrogate him."

"Yes, but that's exactly what I *don't* want to do," Carl said. "Let's pretend we don't know either Rainman or the CIA asset is involved. Let's pretend we think our new CIA analyst is a worthwhile asset. Debrief him, then let him go about his business. Let him be seen in public, so if he's being monitored, they'll know he's not a prisoner. Let him stay in his job and feed us intel."

"Okay."

Carl notched his eyebrows under the ice mask even though she couldn't see him over the voice channel. "Nancy, there are so many assumptions in this plan, I expected you to be more skeptical."

She said nothing.

"Unless you know something I don't know."

"The drone picked up some interesting data. I just now got the analysis."

He waited, then said, "Well, don't make me beg, Nancy."

"There was an encrypted phone call originating from the top-floor office. We couldn't decrypt it, but we traced it."

Carl folded his hands across his lap and smiled to himself. "You know where he is, don't you?"

"Rainman is in New York. In Manhattan. I have his address."

Finally, after eight months, I have a lead to the whereabouts of my nemesis. Carl said, "I know the correct tactical action would be to deploy human intel surveillance and satellite assets—"

"But if we deploy assets against him, he'll see us coming," Palmer added. "He's probably at high alert right now since whatever he was doing in Chicago failed. He no doubt has an escape plan in place."

"Agreed," Carl said. "Let's let Rainman reduce his readiness, and in a few days, we'll go visit him, just you and me."

"We might lose him."

Carl nodded to himself. "If we go after him now, we'll definitely lose him. But the president has given us a free hand in pursuing Rainman, hasn't she?"

"She has." Palmer was silent for a few moments. "And *pretending* is something that is definitely not in the government playbook. It might just work."

The FBI and TER had never been able to profile Carl Johnson because he'd always taken random, unexpected actions in his ops against the government and Rainman. If his nemesis now thought he had profiled Johnson, then that was all the better for Carl and his team. If Rainman thought he could predict Carl's actions, then they could bait the man, and his counteractions could be predicted. That gave Carl the tactical advantage.

Twenty-four hours later, as Carl sat on the oceanfront veranda of his opulent mansion on the west coast of southern Mexico, Agent Palmer sent a video to his cell phone showing the aftermath of the protest. After Carl had left, a small band of protesters went over to the disarmed police and offered first aid to the wounded while waiting for paramedics. The rest of the protesters disbanded, but the next day at noon, many more protesters again converged on the coffee shop.

Thousands of marchers filled the streets. There were hundreds more police also, along with snipers on many roofs. Carl saw a dozen more APCs. Even the National Guard had been called out. Clearly, the police were ready for any type of escalation. They were ready for Carl Johnson even though he was thousands of miles away. There were a dozen camera crews lining the sidewalks. Then the black-clad police made their approach, same as the day before. Thirty feet shy of the protesters, though, a surprising event occurred.

A cop hollered a command, and all the police stopped. Then that solitary cop walked over to the front line of the protesters, fully armed and in uniform, removed his helmet and dark shades, and dropped them to the street. He turned around and faced the rest of the police, held out his elbows, stepped back into a newly formed gap in the civilian frontline, and linked arms with two of the protesters. For several long minutes, nothing happened, then a reporter and her cameraman raced over to get the interview.

Carl muttered, "Huh… Well, ain't that something?" *One white face among the sea of brown faces. One hero making a difference.*

When the camera zoomed in on the officer, Carl saw it was the police officer who had assumed command of the defeated riot squad yesterday—the officer Carl had lectured, then almost killed in his own personal rage.

The reporter stuck a microphone in the man's face and asked him why he was there. She asked him if the American Terrorist had made him rethink his duty and responsibility to the citizens.

"I'm first and foremost a police officer," the man said. "If I see the terrorist Carl Johnson again, I'm going to shoot him dead, and there won't be a trial." He looked left and right. "But I'm also a citizen of this city, just like all these people. Sometimes we forget whom we serve. People have a legal right to protest peacefully, even if the politicians or the powers-that-be don't like it. If protesters get violent or start looting, I'll be the first one to make some arrests. But our job is to preserve the peace and protect our citizens. We don't have to escalate. In fact, our job is to *not* escalate whenever possible."

The officer looked around, then continued, "I may get fired for this, but I'm protesting something too. I'm protesting the series of orders yesterday that led to the murder of six SWAT officers, two of my team, and the crews of that chopper and APC. Those decisions also resulted in over a dozen officers being seriously wounded. I'm protesting the illegal actions of a handful of bad cops that cost the rest of us good cops the trust of the citizens. The city lost a valued citizen, along with two witnesses to that crime. These people have something to say about it. They want to be heard, so let's hear them."

The police force kept its distance, and after some time, the protesters began to disband. Thanks to the officer, their voices had been heard. Some patted the officer on the back or shook his hand. Others got interviews with any of the news crews who would give them airtime.

Carl felt a wave of emotion as he watched a single man defuse a crisis that could have spiraled out of control into a full-blown race riot. He felt hope for his country and for humanity, but he also felt fear.

"Nancy, we didn't do anything good here. We just made it worse by getting involved. There're ten times as many cops as yesterday."

"You stopped the violence."

"I didn't. That officer did."

"Because of what you did yesterday."

"I can't help but wonder if every protest from now on will be faced with even more police. Maybe they'll use the excuse that I might be there to justify bringing out the big guns. Maybe they'll be even more brutal than ever before."

Agent Palmer added, "You've given the topic of police brutality a new conversation thread. Traditional and social media are on fire with the discussion of creating a federal entity to police the police at the local level. Not under the control of a vigilante or a terrorist, of course."

They both chuckled.

"The current thinking," Palmer said, "is that it would be more of a monitoring or watchdog agency that is not a part of any law enforcement organization."

Carl was silent.

Palmer continued, "The assassin, Chrissy, spoke of an experiment or test. Along with the encrypted phone call, there was an unencrypted data stream transmitted from the Stennhauser Building. It was a brief test report summarizing the proof-of-concept experiment Chrissy men-tioned...in *biotechnical behavior control*."

"I can see controlling police activities from a systemic or policy perspective by creating rules of engagement, but controlling their physi-cal or mental behavior? I can't even begin to understand what kind of biochemical mechanism might be in play here."

"They've done it. You stopped the violence, but this data suggests the experiment was successful, though it doesn't explicitly mention the biological technology used." Palmer took a deep breath and said, "Carl, the report says they'll be ready in a few months to launch in a dozen major cities with actions that will make yesterday's protest look like a Sunday school picnic."

She took a deep breath, and Carl figured she was about to drop the bomb on him.

"That's phase three, but the report conclusion mentioned phase 2A, the manipulation of a compartmented protection unit."

Carl stood up so fast, he almost dropped the phone he held. He disabled the phone's speaker mode and put the device to his ear. "Christ, Nancy, he's going after the president again!" He continued to gaze out at the Pacific Ocean, but he no longer saw the tranquil beauty of the undulating surface. "They're going to target the Secret Service to make them kill her."

"Agreed."

"Do you know when?"

"Yes, Carl. Rainman is going to implement his plan in twenty-seven hours. We have that much time to save the president."

CHAPTER 18

ARL'S GULFSTREAM CRUISED AT FORTY-THREE thousand feet en route to Virginia for his mission with Agent Palmer to retrieve the president. He sat in one of the four captain's chairs in the front part of the cabin, his laptop open on the table that folded down from the bulkhead to his right. He had a split-screen videoconference app open, waiting for TER Agent Nancy Palmer and Director Aaron McGrath.

As Carl waited, he opened his brown lunch bag and pulled out a sandwich. For an instant, he was launched forty-five years into the past when he'd been the only kid in school that carried his school lunch in a brown paper sack instead of a superhero lunch pail. He chuckled at the memory, then remembered he'd packed his lunch on the plane so he wouldn't have to eat one of the government MREs provisioned on the plane. The government interrogators who worked for Palmer and McGrath had used MREs as psychological torture when they'd captured him eight months earlier. Sometimes, they'd let him eat them, and other times, they'd snatched that hope away in the most hideous way possible. If he never ate another MRE for the rest of his life, that would be just fine.

He thought about Lieutenant Yeong Dae Jin, still struggling with his mixed feelings about the man's death. The Korean SWAT and Hostage Rescue Teams veteran had sculpted Carl into an aged but effective killer. Now, Carl was a near-expert shooter with several handguns and assault rifles, and he could hold his own in hand-to-hand fighting with trained soldiers and assassins half his age, thanks to three months of intensive training by the lieutenant. But the man was a sadistic bastard.

At first, Carl had been excited when the lieutenant said his training would be like "SEAL training, except you won't have to play in the water like those kids do." He'd soaked up his trainer's advice and techniques like a sponge, but he soon learned the unfortunate reality of trying to undergo intense training at an advanced age. He felt renewed respect for any *young* person who completed SEAL training. It was one thing to watch it on TV, and quite another to actually experience what SEALs went through.

He learned that fifty-four-year-old muscles could take the extreme training, but the ligaments and tendons could not. In one's fifties, those connective tissues are much more brittle than those of a person in their twenties or thirties. Carl's training exacerbated existing tendon micro strains, stretches, and tears he didn't realize he had. He was in constant pain for the whole three-month training program, but his trainer gave him no respite and no quarter. End-of-day ice packs on knees, elbows, and shoulders were part of his daily regimen.

Until that final sparring match.

"Carl?" Agent Palmer's voice snatched him back to the present. "Are you okay? I know that look."

He grunted and looked out the window at the blue sky. "I was thinking about Lieutenant Yeong." He tried to calm the feelings of hatred that he knew Palmer saw on his face.

"His death was…unfortunate." She gazed at him from the laptop monitor, then said, "We never talked about that, but we have a few minutes while we wait for Aaron. I mean, if you want."

Palmer's serious face took up the left side of the screen, and the right side was a gray box where McGrath's image would soon be.

"Everything was fine until I bested him in a sparring match in the second month. I got lucky, but he took it as a sign that I needed harsher training. He became even more sadistic. He was cruel, evil. I needed tough training, but in the last month, I snapped. To me, he became a bully. So, I killed him."

Fifteen years Carl's junior, the lieutenant was an extremely capable soldier. He was a world-class marksman in multiple firearms, an expert in blade work—knives and swords—and a high-level black belt in several martial arts. Carl had learned a lot in all those disciplines from the man, and he was grateful to him for the extreme training.

"When I fought that Delta Force assassin eight months ago, I was lucky." Carl had been the last man standing between the killer and President Mallory, and he could not retreat. "But when I picked up a knife and went after Yeong in that final encounter, he still thought it was just a sparring match—another training exercise. We went at it for five minutes." Carl took a deep breath and looked out the window again. "And then I cut him. Twice." He looked at the laptop screen again and matched Palmer's piercing gaze with his own. "Right then and there, he knew he was going to die. I saw it in his eyes, and his fear empowered me. Ten seconds later, I cut him again, a life-ending arterial slice in his upper thigh, and then I took him to the mat.

"I could have reveled in my victory, could have stood over him and watched him bleed out, but I didn't. I knelt down and cut his throat." He closed his eyes and said, "It couldn't have ended any other way. I know that now."

Palmer said, "I'm worried about you, Carl. I'm worried that you're going too far to the dark side."

"I know. I can feel it too. I'm losing control of what little humanity I have left." They looked at each other for long seconds, then he said, "I want to see you again, Nancy. I mean, not on a mission or anything. Just, you know, maybe coffee or dinner or something."

She smiled in that girly way that crinkled her nose. "That would be nice, Carl." She returned his gaze with a distant look in her eyes, then said, "I think about…"

That kiss. "I think about it too."

She was about to say more, but Director McGrath's face replaced the gray box on the laptop screen. "Status," he demanded.

Carl raised an eyebrow at the aggressive tone of the TER director's voice. He looked at Palmer's image, but her face showed no reaction. Something new had happened.

He said, "You already know we suspect the president's life is in danger—"

"Yes." McGrath looked down like he was consulting notes. "Another assassination attempt, this time using Secret Service personnel compromised by an unknown biotechnology." He leaned forward with his elbows on his desk and clasped his fingers, and Carl got the feeling the director was ready to drop a bomb.

"Don't keep me guessing, Aaron. Let's have it."

McGrath nodded. "I want to run this op out of our office here in Virginia."

Carl shrugged. "You don't work for me, Aaron, nor do I work for you. You can do whatever the fuck you want to do as long as you don't interfere—"

"Your body count is rising too high and too fast. Eighteen deaths this month alone in Mexico, six in Albuquerque, and now, sixteen *police officers* in Chicago, not counting the initial four officers at the coffee shop."

"If you mean the cops that killed civilians and those that were getting ready to kill protesters… Well, the bad guys are dead."

McGrath leaned toward his screen. "But apparently, not the bad guys that these bad guys were working for! The operators that went for Cummings are gunning for *you*, not us."

"Their mistake."

"Johnson, do I have to remind you that we have—"

Carl leaned closer to the laptop, matching the director's posture. "Don't go thinking you have some kind of leverage on me and my people, Aaron. I'm happy to conduct my ops *my* way without your—"

Palmer held up her palms, and it seemed to Carl that one was for him, and the other was for her director. "Gentlemen, let's stay on task. The president's safety."

Carl leaned back and nodded, as did McGrath. Their relationship had deteriorated in the past couple months, and Carl understood he was primarily to blame for that. Eight months after losing his son in the government ambush, he wasn't getting better. In fact, he felt himself spiraling into depression and his terrorist persona taking over, dragging him further into the abyss. And he liked it. He felt more comfortable and more content as a terrorist. It gave him power. It gave him the advantage over his enemies. He blamed McGrath for the fact that he couldn't get over the loss of his son, and he needed revenge against someone. Aaron McGrath was a ripe target for his anger, so Agent Palmer had assumed the role of mediator between them.

Wizard unwittingly provided the détente. Carl's laptop beeped, and a new conference window opened in place of McGrath's. The director's image slid over to the left half of the display, below Palmer's.

"Good," the computer wizard said. "I have all three of you on the same channel. I'm sending you some telemetry now. Boss, you asked me to monitor keywords associated with Officer Bonhardt, the cop who defused the second protest yesterday, and it looks like a contract for immediate execution has been purchased on him and his family in the amount of two million."

"A contract?" Carl said. "What the hell for?"

"International banking espionage, if you can believe that. The notation states he provided you, Carl, with trade secrets and account information that defrauded three Swiss banks out of hundreds of millions of dollars. By the way, he has also been terminated from the Chicago Police Department for his role in yesterday's second protest. They completely bypassed any kind of suspension or other disciplinary action and went straight to the finish line."

Everyone was silent for a moment as they digested the new information.

Carl said, "Why kill the man because he had a change of heart after I took his unit down? And why kill his family?"

Palmer nodded. "Usually, with these kinds of underworld contracts coming out of Europe, targeting the family is viewed as a deterrent for others considering betrayal or whistle-blowing. But I agree. This seems like overkill. Assuming the people who purchased the contract are the ones behind the police-control test, it's not clear to me what threat he poses to them. He certainly can't expose them since the police chief and the man the chief answered to are both dead."

McGrath added, "I wonder if he might be a threat in another way." Carl watched the director rub his chin. The one thing he respected about the director was his ability to dissect a problem. "He was, after all, a member of the test group of police officers who were subjected to whatever this biotech control methodology is. Maybe there's something different about him."

Wizard said, "You know, now that you mention it, when the quote-unquote American Terrorist intervened, the police didn't blindly continue assaulting the protesters. They turned to face the new threat. And the second day, when Officer Bonhardt provided a buffer between the protesters and the police, they again stopped as if they had to process the unexpected interference."

Palmer said, "You assume Rainman's people were conducting the test again the second day."

Wizard shrugged. "It's a stretch, and there are a lot of unknowns here."

McGrath nodded. "Maybe, but let's go with that for a moment. What if Rainman's people did a test failure analysis for the first day's results? What if they discovered a potential weakness in their methodology?"

"Yes," Carl said. "They would have modified their test. The second day, they sent many more police, yet the test still was not successful."

Wizard added, "We assume it was not successful because the protest did not become violent."

Palmer added, "Bonhardt surrendered his force on the first day because it was his only option to save his people. But the second day, he clearly was not under the same influence as the other police."

McGrath said, "And the fact that the rest of the police paused and did not continue their aggression against the protesters, assuming they were being coerced to assault the people, suggests that this biotechnology control methodology does not yield *total* control."

Wizard said, "Maybe it's more of a *suggestive* control mechanism."

Carl added, "Or maybe they discovered a developmental flaw during the test. If there's something about that cop that makes him immune or resistant, they would have to kill him and destroy his body to prevent someone from doing medical analysis that might help us understand or counter their control mechanism."

McGrath agreed. "Hence, the two-million-dollar contract. Johnson, I think you should divert to Chicago and retrieve him. If he represents a technology flaw, we need to understand it so we can exploit it."

Carl shook his head. "The president's life is more important."

"You'll get no argument from me on that point," the director said. "But think about it. This was admittedly a proof-of-concept test, and it represents a new and very dangerous weapon development program. It may be used for domestic population control, or it may be used, as we fear in the president's case, for political or corporate assassination either here in the US or in any other country. A weapon of this magnitude could be devastating to the political or economic stability of every nation on the planet. At the very least, imagine what a renewed arms race would look like if the mere existence of this weapon is made public."

Palmer said, "I agree, Carl. The president is important, but you know she would order us to move on this threat."

"You'll be without support retrieving the president, Nancy."

She said, "I'll be relying on you and Aaron to come up with a plan to get me close to the president and get her out of DC…by working together."

Carl grunted but nodded grudgingly.

Wizard said, "Well, Boss, Officer Bonhardt certainly isn't going to be happy to see you again."

"Every bounty hunter in Chicago, professional and novice alike, is going to be gunning for him and his family. I've heard Chicago police seize more than six times as many illegal firearms per capita than even New York, so there's going to be a lot of amateurs going after him in addition to the pros. If he knows there's a contract in place, I'm guessing he'll welcome my visit."

"Unless he thinks you're after the bounty too, in which case he might just shoot you on sight."

"Yeah, there's that." Carl shrugged. "All right, ping his phone and tell him about the bounty and that I'm coming to retrieve him and his family, then set me up with whatever comm support you can muster until Three gets a team there."

Wizard nodded, and his image disappeared.

Agent Palmer said, "You realize by sending me after Shirley Mallory, I may unknowingly become a threat to her if I fall under the influence of this technology."

Carl thought about Palmer's disclosure. "I have some thoughts about that." He had Palmer's image on the left side of his laptop screen again, now that Wizard had signed off, with McGrath on the right.

McGrath added, "I don't think we can call any assumptions solid *thoughts* at this point."

Carl snickered. "Oh, we're not even on *terra firma* of assumptions yet. We're still in the quagmire of *wild-ass guesses*. We need to get some serious brainpower on this biotechnology. Figure out what it's capable of, how to defend against it, and what makes Officer Bonhardt apparently immune to it."

"I agree," McGrath said. "TER usually subcontracts this kind of tech analysis to classified university specialty research groups, but the more people outside our circle we involve, the greater the risk of Rainman's people discovering our interest. If they think we know about their experiment, they'll take countermeasures."

"Agreed," Palmer said. "So what are your thoughts, Carl?"

"Well, first, in terms of brainpower, let's use my best friend, Randal. Well, he used to be my best friend." Carl shuddered. "You know him as Randal Cunningham. He does problem analysis for the government. Over the years, we referred to him as the Thinking Machine. During the first Gulf War, when our troops were having friendly fire problems within the tank regiments—because our tanks closely resembled certain models of the enemy tanks—Randal was given the analysis task to put a quick thirty-day, low-tech IFF solution in the field. As you know, that effort was successful."

She nodded. "And you're sure you can convince him to help us?"

Carl pointed a finger at McGrath's image on his screen. "You can, Aaron. He's worked for classified higher-ups before. He knows the gig, but..."

"But what?"

"I'm certain he won't willingly cooperate after your folks grilled him about me, so you're probably going to have to kidnap him." Carl focused a deadpan gaze at the government man. "You know how to do that, right?"

McGrath grunted. "Funny."

"And kidnap his family too, or they'll become a target for Atlas and Rainman." Carl registered his verbal sparring victory with a sly half-smile that never quite reached his eyes. "So here's what I think we know about this biotech weapon so far. I think we know it controls behavior, but we don't know the specific aggression methodology. I mean, how does the tech identify a specific target? There must be some sort of external trigger, some kind of biotech programming. We know there's a targeted delivery system, or the protesters would also have been affected by the same technology and been equally aggressive toward the police. So, I'm thinking Agent Palmer will be safe from the influence of this weapon when she gets to the president because she will have been isolated by physical distance from the effects of whatever trigger this biotech employs. I mean, what are the odds, right? I'm thinking the targeted personnel, the Secret Service agents, will already have been infected or programmed or whatever this thing does."

"I agree with you, Johnson," McGrath said. He paused half a beat, then added, "Wild-ass guesses. Any other thoughts?"

Carl shook his head. "That's all I got."

"Let's proceed then," the director said. "I'll have agents pick up Cunningham and deliver him to the safe house Agent Cummings set up in Kansas. I assume that's where you'll be delivering Officer Bonhardt?"

Carl nodded.

"Very well." McGrath's gaze seemed to dance between Carl's and Palmer's images, and he made a shrug that included his hands. "Any ideas on how we get Shirley out of the White House without arousing suspicion, and how we isolate her for retrieval? Her schedule shows no meetings all day and tomorrow."

"Actually, I have an idea about that." Carl looked pointedly at McGrath. "Don't you think it's time to bring your relationship with her out of the closet?"

CHAPTER 19

CARL LANDED AT THE MUNICIPAL Chicago Executive Airport for the second time in three days. Wizard had arranged a rental minivan that Carl retrieved while wearing his dark-skin Rastafarian disguise. Then he proceeded downtown to check into his hotel on the popular tourist canal.

It was midday and hot. *Insanely* hot. And muggy. So it was with great pleasure that Carl got out of his Rasta disguise and took a long cool shower as soon as he got to his room. Afterward, he stood by the window, looking down eight stories below at the tourists walking along the pathways. He spied the tour boats cruising the inner-city canal in between the one-way streets.

From the shadows on the concrete below, he could tell the sun would still be up for a few more hours, so he decided to drive back to the small airport. From the Gulfstream, he loaded up weapons for him and the cop, water, and two meals for him and each member of the family he was about to rescue, and his battle armor. Then he made his way back to his hotel room, where he ate and studied maps on his tablet. He memorized all the major streets in the area, as well as all the fast exits from the neighborhood.

He had to get the officer and his family safely to the downtown hotel undetected and keep them alive until his backup arrived in the morning with drone coverage. That meant he had to do the retrieval the old-fashioned way, alone and blind. He'd have no high-tech government support, so he wouldn't know where the enemy was or what their numbers were. On the plus side, though, he'd have Wizard and Merc Three in his ear on comms. They'd be monitoring police frequencies, trying to guide him around any law enforcement roadblocks.

The contract on Bonhardt had been active for a few hours, so he figured the novices would park within sight of the house and see if they could prepare a quick nighttime hit. Carl wasn't worried about them. He was infinitely more worried about the professionals. Whether they worked alone or as part of a sponsored team, the professionals would have night vision gear like Carl had. They'd have silencers. They might even have *overwatch*, a military-trained sniper or maybe even a mini drone. He had a scope with a laser to blind such a drone, but he had to see it to laser it, and the damn things were so small and whisper-quiet he probably wouldn't find it if it was more than fifty feet away.

No doubt the contract would spawn competition. Two million dollars was a lot of money, and there would be no sharing. Whoever won the contract had to present clear evidence of the kill to get paid—a video and an identifiable body part, like a head—and the successful killer would then become a target of opportunity by other contract killers seeking to steal that evidence and present it for payment. The professionals would be careful. They'd need to scout an escape route before making the kill, and Carl might be able to use that to his advantage.

As he lay on the bed, thoughts and memories drifted through his mind. Faces panned slowly across the projection screen of his brain. Faces of people he'd killed, people he had yet to kill, and people involved in the death of his son. People like Aaron McGrath.

Agent Nancy Palmer's face popped into his mind, and so did that kiss. Something stirred deep in his soul, something he thought he'd never be able to feel again. He wondered what it was about the young woman that appealed to him. He wanted to see her again, and the thought that she also wanted to see him again felt exciting.

Then he remembered she was also involved in the death of his son, and his mind wandered to thoughts of where she was at that exact moment.

CHAPTER 20

T E R AGENT NANCY PALMER CHUCKLED AS she sat in the bar, watching the news headline ticker scroll across the bottom of the wall-mounted TV.

THE PRESIDENT HAS A BOYFRIEND!

Every major news outlet screamed the same headline, and all the other political issues were immediately relegated to filler material, subordinate to the single-mom-in-chief's sex life. No one would ever know the identity of the low-level staffer who'd leaked the information, but it had happened mere minutes before the daily White House press briefing. The White House Press Secretary had brushed aside the report and related questions successfully for two minutes, but it quickly became clear that nothing else would be on the agenda that morning. Then President Mallory herself crashed the briefing.

"Yes," she said after the initial ruckus settled. "I have a boyfriend, and no, I'm not going to tell you who he is, other than to say we've been dating for many years."

A question rang out from the back of the room, and the president replied, "No, I have no plans to get married any time soon. However," she added, moving away from the podium, "if you'll excuse me, I'm meeting him for lunch right now." She teased the crowd with a shy smile. "And, no, I'm not telling where we're going. I'm having lunch with *him*, not with all of you too!" She waved and was out the door.

Agent Palmer waited in the private bar tucked in the middle of the restaurant that only she, McGrath, and the president knew was going to be Mallory's romantic rendezvous. She heard the entire exchange on TV and through the comm device in her ear. McGrath had texted the president to go on comm half an hour ago and prepped her for the coming leak and press fanfare. Through the president's comm, Palmer heard all the Secret Service chatter. She knew when Mallory left the White House, when her armored limousine arrived in front of the restaurant, and exactly when Secret Service protocol was ignored. No one preceded the president into the restaurant to secure the building, its staff, and its patrons.

Dressed as a server in all black, she had ID ready to pass Secret Service inspection but made a fast dash for her hidden weapon and headed to the front entrance. She aimed her silenced service weapon through the glass pane of the wooden door.

Standard Secret Service chatter came over her comm at first. "POTUS is in transit, entering the restaurant." Then she heard, "Madam President, this is where you die."

The top half of the ornate wood door featured a leaded-glass section with beveled inserts, so her view of the president and her escorts was severely distorted. She could vaguely tell that at least one agent had a weapon pointed at the president, but she could easily see that Mallory stood alone near the door while her agents had stepped back. That's all Palmer needed. Still moving forward, she started shooting through the window at the dark distorted figures. Then she yanked the door open and kept shooting.

"Inside!" she shouted at the president.

As Palmer followed Mallory inside, she saw a disturbing sight. Mallory had three escort vehicles in addition to her limousine, yet only four Secret Service agents had accompanied Mallory to the restaurant door. The rest were just now realizing a shooting had occurred, thanks to Palmer's silencer, and only then started to exit their SUVs. None pursued them into the restaurant. Rather, several were pulling their coiled earpieces from their ears, and one was talking into a satellite radio.

"Aaron, I have the president," she said as she ushered Mallory to the back exit. "But something's very wrong. I expected a more aggressive response. Their pursuit is slow, so we can actually make the backup car I have parked in the alley."

"Negative," McGrath replied. "Even though the agents may be under suggestive influence, they should still follow their training and secure all exits if they want her dead." He paused just long enough for Palmer and Mallory to reach the rear exit. Palmer had just wrapped her hand around the old-style doorknob when McGrath said, "Stick to the primary plan. Use the basement to exfil."

Nancy Palmer hesitated for a split second. The escape car was just twenty yards away from the door. Through the grill covering the outside of the half-moon window in the heavy wood door, she could see the path to the car was clear. But her training was too ingrained, and she implicitly trusted McGrath. They'd had many successful operations since the first days of the TER agency. In fact, the operation against the American Terrorist had been their first and only mission failure. She glanced at the president standing beside her and nodded.

"Copy that. Proceeding with the primary evac plan." She nodded behind them and to the right. "Into the basement we go, Madam President. And Aaron, I want to—"

McGrath's voice said, "Stand by. I'm getting some intel from our new CIA asset."

Nancy Palmer and Shirley Mallory kept moving down the steps to the basement.

Halfway down, she heard McGraths's panicked voice return to her ear. "Get Shirley into the basement. Now, goddamnit. *Now!*"

The only time her boss had ever lost his composure was when he'd thought Carl had murdered his daughter, Anita Chapman, so the terror in his voice spurred her faster. She grabbed Mallory by the arm and yanked her down the last few steps, then pulled her through the basement doorway. She didn't know what manner of assault had panicked McGrath, but it was big. Had to be.

Palmer leaned her shoulder into the thick, heavy door and almost got it closed when a tremendous explosion knocked her into shelving halfway across the basement. Then everything fell into complete darkness.

CHAPTER 21

CARL AWOKE WITH A START, completely unaware he'd fallen asleep, and was pleased to see dusk had settled into the deeper blackness of night. It was time.

He drove the minivan along the route that Wizard had sent to his tablet until he was two blocks from Bonhardt's house on Chicago's westside. The neighborhood was a collection of narrow row houses on narrow lots, and all looked the same with red brick. The homes were all three levels, and the first hosted a single-car garage beside the front door. The homes had tiny front yards and arm's-length clearance on both sides. According to Wizard's overhead map, the backyard was equally tiny. Carl figured they'd all probably be the same floor plan on the inside too. All in all, it was the cheapest home one could afford to own that wasn't a slum house.

He backed into someone's driveway, then got out and opened the driver's side passenger slider. His first action was to get out of his Rasta disguise yet again. It took a few minutes and a dozen wet wipes to wipe the thick layer of skin color off, then he got into his battle suit and geared up.

He noticed there were no streetlights in the neighborhood. Correction: there *were* streetlights, but they just weren't on. "Three, it looks like a team with heavy support is already in the area. All the streetlights are off."

"Stand by," Wizard's voice said over the comm. "Okay, I just hacked into the public utilities. It seems there was an emergency maintenance work order filed an hour ago, and I see a maintenance team was dispatched. I'm guessing they've been eliminated and replaced."

Three said, "Watch your ass, Boss. The bad guys are likely already on-site or close to it."

"Copy that." Carl donned his Kevlar helmet and lowered the face shield into place, then attached auxiliary vision gear. He lowered the low-light reticule in front of his right eye and the infrared reticule in front of his left, then set out toward the officer's home. "I wish I had drone or satellite coverage. It would be nice to know if anyone is waiting in cars, trying to effect an ambush."

"Hold on, Boss," Wizard said. "Let me see if I can hack some cell towers and do some trilateration... Got it. Damn! I see fifteen cell signals *not* inside houses, all within a block of the cop's house. By the way, there are four signals inside his home. I'm guessing one each for him, his wife, and two kids. They're probably home."

Wizard gave Carl the precise locations of the street cell signals on the path Carl was to follow to the officer's house. The first car was parked at the intersection of the dark street, apparently ready to follow Bonhardt's car if they left. Carl transferred his PDW to his left hand and pulled his silenced Glock from his right thigh holster. He walked up to the driver's window, knelt down, and fired a single shot through the window, into the head of the person. The second bounty hunter was parked on the wrong side of the street facing the target house, so he also had no indication someone was going to walk up to his car in the pitch darkness and shoot him.

Carl holstered his Glock and continued his trek toward Bonhardt's house with his PDW ready for action. Stock pressed firmly against his shoulder, he panned the barrel back and forth as he'd been trained. His brain combined the green and red worlds that his separate eyes saw.

"Boss," Three said. "Hold one. Something has changed."

Carl kept walking a few steps until he was even with a curbside tree, then stepped right against the trunk and merged his body into the darkness. "Talk to me," he said.

Wizard said, "The contract has just changed. One million for the family, dead only, and five million for the officer, alive only. That's going out to all hitters as we speak."

"Hmm," Carl said. "There's gotta be something about his physiology they need to study, and for that, they need him alive. The five million is a guarantee no one will slip up and kill him."

As Carl continued to scan the street, his sight was drawn to a bright flare of light coming from each of two cars, both parked nose-in on the driveways of two adjacent homes. As he got closer, he would have eventually seen their thermal signature, but they helped him by checking their cell phones for the contract update.

He thought about crossing the street and firing into both cars with his silenced handgun, but a moving shadow even on the dark street might be detected by an alert observer's peripheral vision. Besides, sooner or later, Carl's presence would be known, so it might as well be now, when he was close to his target.

He scanned his immediate surroundings again, particularly looking for heat targets in cars in driveways, then knelt and sighted his PDW. The weapon had two tactical advantages. It was very quiet and had virtually zero muzzle flash. He fired twice. The six-by-thirty-millimeter armor-piercing rounds punched through the back windows like plastic, and his enhanced vision showed his aim was true.

Two headshots, distance twenty meters.

Continuing up the sidewalk, he found himself directly across from the cop's home. He looked left and right, but he saw no obvious threat, either in low-light or infrared vision. He had just informed his team of his intent to charge across the dark street and kick in the front door when Wizard's voice froze him.

"Hold! Hold! Hold!"

"Copy." Carl knelt and held his position, weapon ready and focused on Bonhardt's front door.

"I see three new cell phone signals emanating from the front of the house. A hit team is in there with the family."

"They're probably threatening his family to get him to leave voluntarily, but they're going to kill them anyway."

Three added, "And one of the cells is active. I'm guessing he's calling for the retrieval vehicle."

Wizard said, "Whatever you're going to do, Boss, do it now! You have maybe fifteen seconds max."

Carl didn't have time to think about options, so he decided on a direct frontal assault. Upon approach, though, he discovered the metal front door was well-insulated against heat loss. It *was* Chicago, after all, the Windy City. His infrared reticule couldn't detect any thermal targets through the door, and he couldn't take the chance that the metal door had a deep deadbolt that might not yield to a single kick, so he moved to the window.

He saw two thermal figures. One stood a few feet away from a kneeling figure with his hands held behind his head. Carl sighted on the standing figure and pulled the trigger. Then he rushed to the front door and decided to try the knob. It was unlocked, no doubt picked open by the hit team. He shoved the door open gently and motioned the now-standing Officer Bonhardt to silence with his index finger stuck in front of his face shield. Then he pulled his silenced Glock from his holster, tossed it to the policeman, and pointed to the front door. Even as he gave his nonverbal commands, he heard a vehicle screech around the corner and accelerate toward the house.

He scanned the next room with his thermal vision and easily identified three figures seated on a couch and two standing figures in front of them. One of them called out, appearing to turn toward the doorway to the front room. Maybe he'd heard Carl drop the hitman, or maybe he just heard him fall or heard the man's weapon hit the floor. Whatever.

Carl fired two quick shots and kicked through the door, ready to shoot again. The family screamed at his entrance, but they were in no further danger from those men.

Two more headshots through the drywall, distance two meters.

The wife and two children stayed huddled in fear on the couch.

Carl turned and went back into the front room, which looked in the darkness like a formal living room. "The bounty is now five million alive for you only and one million for them dead only. Get them ready to move by the time I get back."

Carl stepped through the front door with his PDW blazing as the pickup vehicle, a cargo van that looked greenish with a blazing red splotch where the engine was, screeched to a halt. He stitched the vehicle with three triple-taps, then walked over and calmly dropped a live grenade in the driver's open window. As he walked back toward the cop's front door, the grenade blast blew out the van's windshield and doors and shoved him a couple steps forward, but the shrapnel pinged harmlessly off his battle suit. The distraction, however, was just enough so Carl didn't see the killer step around the side of the house until fire exploded from the tip of his shotgun.

The blast hit Carl full in the chest and felt like a mule kick that knocked him flat on his ass. By the time he recovered from the dizzying flop, the killer stood over him. He racked the loader forward, then stumbled forward, tripping over Carl's prone body. In the doorway, Bonhardt rose from a two-handed firing position and lowered the Glock. He ushered his wife and kids out the door as Carl rolled to his knees, coughing and trying to catch his breath.

The cop rapid-fired the questions at him. "You have a car? Which way? They'll be watching for mine."

Carl simply said, "Fuck! That hurt." He got to his feet. "Wizard, what's the status of all the cell phones in the area?"

"You have four signals you passed up the street. They are unmoving, so I assume those are the hit teams you terminated?"

"Correct."

"Okay, you have the three stationary signals in the house, plus the four I assume belong to the family."

Carl looked at the officer and nodded. The man had prepped his family well and left the cell phones behind because they could be traced.

"There is also a signal in the street, in front of the house."

Carl said, "The cell phone survived the grenade blast, but the occupants did not."

"Okay, your exit route seems clear, but other signals are converging on you. I recommend haste."

He pointed at Officer Bonhardt and said, "Make a right at the corner, go up two blocks, make another right. I have a maroon minivan parked halfway up the street, right side, nose-out. You take the lead, and I'll bring up the rear because that's where the attack will likely come from." He did a quick mental count of the shots he'd heard fired from each weapon. "Here." He pulled a mag for the Glock from his utility belt and tossed it. "You're down five." The PDW was down thirteen with plenty remaining in the thirty-count mag.

The cop pocketed the magazine and turned to his wife and children. Carl guessed the kids' ages at maybe seven and nine. They seemed remarkably calm in the face of certain death.

Bonhardt said, "This is going to be just like we practiced many times because of my work, okay?"

The kids nodded.

To the younger one, the boy, he said, "Now you keep hold of your sister's hand."

The boy nodded.

Bonhardt took his daughter's chin gently in his hand. "And you keep hold of mommy's hand."

She nodded, and the officer stood and gave his wife a reassuring smile.

"All right, team, let's move. On the double!" Bonhardt said.

Carl admired the man. He made it seem like a family camping trip, and they'd clearly practiced before. Just like the military.

Practice so you don't panic.

They took off at a slow trot, fast enough to make haste, but slow enough to react to possible danger. Through his low-light lens, Carl saw the officer glance at the cars with destroyed windows. They made it to the minivan without event, and the officer took the driver's seat and started the engine with the keys Carl had left in the ignition. Carl put the family in the rear-most seats and took the center bench for himself. He powered down both side windows and folded the PDW stock so he could maneuver the rifle in the smaller space of the vehicle if he had to.

Bonhardt said, "I need a destination."

"River Hotel downtown." He glanced at Mrs. Bonhardt. "Your kids sure are brave. But everybody down in back, okay? This could get crazy."

The kids hit the floor behind Carl's seat, and their mom covered them with her body.

Two blocks later, the cop said, "I think we picked up a tail. No, two."

Carl raised his enhanced lenses so he wouldn't be blinded by headlights and looked out the rear. "They probably have air surveillance, so watch left and right. They'll probably try to ram us from the side while you're watching the rear."

"Is that what a terrorist would do?"

"That's what they do in the movies when—"

Bonhardt slammed on the brakes to avoid a car speeding out of a side street, avoiding the collision by mere inches. The offending car bounced up onto the curb and slid sideways, clearly trying to stay in the chase. Carl pointed his PDW out the open window and fired two triple-taps, one at the driver and one into the front grill of the car. No way that hitman, if he was even still alive, was going to follow them after three armor-piercing bullets ripped up his engine block.

Bonhardt floored the gas, and they slipped under the L, as the elevated train platform was called, and followed the Orange Line for several blocks.

"Make a hard right up ahead. Pretend to lose control a bit so the chase cars get closer."

He did so, and Carl pulled the tab on a high-tech grenade. He tossed it out the window just before Bonhardt straightened the car and entered the side street. The device bounced and exploded right under the lead chase car just as that car started to make the turn, and the car flipped over and tumbled right past the intersection.

The second chase car blasted past the rubble and followed them closely down the street, so Carl tossed two more grenades in sequence. To the Bonhardt family, he said, "You folks okay down there?"

He heard an affirmative chorus.

"Okay, cover your ears because here comes some noise." Carl fired seven shots through the minivan's rear window.

Bonhardt hollered, "Hard left coming up!"

Carl braced himself as the minivan turned, but the chase car kept going straight, slowing and trailing smoke. "Get back under the L. I have an idea."

The officer followed the instructions without question, and Carl pulled his laser designator from the duffel he'd left in the minivan and attached it to the PDW housing. It was a special high-intensity laser specifically designed to blind camera and sensors on surveillance planes or drones.

Any doubts that a mini drone was spotting them vanished when yet another chase car careened out of a side street just after they passed. The sedan accelerated much faster than the minivan and pulled alongside their passenger side.

Carl ejected his spent mag, pulled another from his utility belt, and slammed it home. "Panic stop on my mark!"

He braced himself on the floor, legs spread wide with his boots rammed against the wall, then he popped the lock, slid the door open, and pointed the business end of his assault rifle right at the driver's head.

"Now!"

The driver was a woman, and a man next to her was leaning forward, trying to see around her. When Carl shoved the minivan door open, she was looking right at him with the same serious, calculating, killer's eyes he'd seen on many adversaries. She grasped the steering wheel with her left hand and held a silenced handgun in her right, though it wasn't aimed at him yet. Her surprise registered in her eyes briefly, and she did exactly what Carl knew she would. She slammed on her brakes.

But the minivan was also slowing at the same rate, so she stayed precisely in Carl's sights. He fired two carefully aimed shots into the heads of both killers from near-point-blank range.

"Pull over fast." He jumped out even before the minivan came to a complete stop. With his index finger, he turned on the laser designator, aimed behind the car, and waited.

They were still under the L platform, and a drone would have to drop down under the platform to reacquire them. He squatted behind the car and waited but saw nothing. He lowered his low-light and infrared lenses into place, but he still saw nothing.

He was just about to abandon his ambush when he heard the cop's harsh whisper through the shattered back window. "Johnson, front! Eleven o'clock high."

Carl stood and pivoted, and there it was, hovering fifteen feet off the street, about two car lengths away. Black with four nearly silent propellers spaced around the main body, it was small enough for one person to carry. He aimed the active laser at the device, but it pivoted almost at the same instant. It rose quickly and bounced off the bottom of the L platform, then banked hard to the right and hit a support beam. The fragile drone lost some plastic pieces in the impact and spiraled down to the street. Bonhardt hit the gas and crunched his front left tire over the drone.

"Mission accomplished," Carl said as he got back in the minivan.

Merc Three said, "I thought we'd stay off the channel so you could concentrate. Are you secure?"

"Secure for the moment. Heading to the safe house now."

Three said, "Copy that. We'll continue to monitor."

Bonhardt said, "You have a safe house in Chicago? I thought you said we were going to the River Hotel."

"Safe hotel," Carl said. "Yeah, that's what I meant."

"Okay, we'll be there in five." Bonhardt raised his voice. "Is everyone okay back there?"

Carl heard another chorus of affirmative responses as the family members got up off the floor, then said, "Stay low until we know we're safe for sure, okay?"

A few minutes later, they pulled into an automated parking structure two blocks away from the hotel, and Officer Bonhardt parked the minivan front-in against a concrete wall in between two full-size SUVs. He and Carl scanned the garage and listened for cars following them.

"Well, I think we made it," Carl said.

Carl got out and peeled off his battle armor down to his Under Armour tights, and he quickly got into casual clothes while the officer checked on his family. They all got out on the opposite side of the minivan and hugged while Carl bagged his gear. Then they all walked casually toward the hotel, Carl carrying his bag of armor and Officer Bonhardt carrying the weapons duffel.

Carl had chosen the River Hotel because it was touristy. There were lots of people walking around even late at night and lots of lights. It was not the kind of high-visibility area fugitives would seek haven in. At the same time, their hunters would stand out if they found them. Besides, the assassins would be staking out the officer's friends and family first. Either way, Carl had a plan to misdirect the hunters, a head fake that might buy them enough time for his backup to arrive.

Carl listened as the parents put their kids to bed after a half hour of hugs and reassurances. He couldn't begin to understand what the kids were thinking and feeling any more than he could understand what Lisette Cummings thought and felt. How do children cope with terrorists and assassins? How do they normalize gunfire and brutal car chases and grenades? How do they relate to the specter of impending death, of actually *seeing* death take place, or of people trying to kill them? How do they *not* fear an armored gunman, even though that man just saved them? Did it even register to the kids that he'd saved them?

He stood by the window and gazed at the hotel directly across the river, trying to wrap his heart across the thousand-mile gap between himself and the gangly twelve-year-old Lisette. Was she safe? Was she asleep? Was she having nightmares?

Behind him, Mrs. Bonhardt said, "Are we disturbing you?"

He shook his head without looking at her.

"I saw you on the news. Can you tell us what all this is about?"

He nodded. "It's time."

"Time for what?" the officer said.

Carl stepped aside and motioned them to the window. He pointed at the hotel directly across the canal that he'd been looking at. "I had my computer whiz hack your credit card and reserve a room a couple hours ago in that hotel as a distraction. All the lights were off until a few seconds ago. I didn't figure it would take this long for one of the hit teams to locate your room."

Mrs. Bonhardt said, "But why would you lead them so close to us?"

Carl just smiled at her even as the flash of fire blossomed in his side vision. It spread out briefly from the balcony but didn't spread to the adjacent floors.

"Oh my God!"

"Don't worry. It was a small explosion, just big enough to consume the killers who went into the room." They'd gone in and turned on the lights, no doubt confident in their numbers or weaponry or both. "I left some dud grenades in there to make it look like a team found you and blew up the room and just got caught in the explosion."

"CSI will see right through that."

"Sure, in a few hours. Hopefully, the hunters will believe my head fake—that you're dead, along with a couple careless hitmen until after we're safely in the air."

"Why are you helping us?" Officer Bonhardt said. "After the protest, I thought you wanted me dead."

Carl lowered his gaze toward the river walk below. Pedestrians had stopped and were gawking at the scene of the explosion high above them.

"In another life, I wanted people like you dead. But there are other people in the here and now that really wanted you dead up until an hour ago. Now they've upped the bounty to capture you alive."

"But why?" the woman said.

Carl shook his head. "I don't know, Mrs. Bonhardt."

"I'm Claire." She nodded toward her husband. "Richard or Ricky."

Carl nodded, then said, "We're still working on the *why* part."

"We?" Richard said.

"I'm working with the TER agency." They looked at each other, and it was clear to Carl that neither knew what the initials represented. "The Terror Event Response agency is the president's highly classified anti-terrorist rapid-response team. Apparently, Malik Tavares discovered some research data suggesting that *someone* has some kind of biotechnology method to control the behavior of the police, or anyone, for that matter. It seems to enhance aggressive behavior. We're guessing the two protests were proof-of-concept tests.

"On the first day, I intervened, and that broke the cycle of violence. On the second day, you"—he pointed at Richard—"did an unexpected thing, and that also broke the cycle of violence. You appear to be immune or at least significantly resistant to the effects of this biotech. At first, we thought they put the contract on you to eliminate evidence of a possible vulnerability in the test control protocol, but now we think they've learned something critical about you, something that makes you physiologically unique, and that requires an assessment of why you seem to be outside of their control."

Clair turned to her husband and said, "We should go to the police. There are a lot more of them than there are contract killers."

Carl looked at Richard and saw in the man's eyes that he understood the truth of their situation.

"Claire," Carl said, "you don't have any friends on the police force. Not anymore. The people who controlled the police chief, the ones who put out the contract on you, are beyond dangerous because they answer to no one. Any good cops that might help you will be totally outclassed in weapons and authority by whomever they'd be going up against. More likely, any cops that offer to help you will be going after that five million."

She looked exasperated by the bleakness of their situation. "So we have to put our lives in the hands of a terrorist?"

"Me and my people, yes."

"He's not really a terrorist, Claire." He looked at Carl. "Are you? You're a government operator."

In his ear, Carl heard Merc Three chuckle.

"I'm not a government operator, folks. I most definitely *am* a terrorist. Call it a temporary partnership with President Mallory, motivated by mutual goals."

They traded skeptical glances.

"You might want to sit down for this," Carl said. "It's gonna take a minute, and it's a bit hard to believe." He sat on the edge of the bed and waited while they took chairs at the dinette table. "Three, are we secure here?"

"Copy that, Boss. We're tapped into the hotel camera system as well as the city grid in your area. The police have the entire area cordoned off. Homeland is evacuating the other hotel."

"Good," Carl said. "I'm going off comm for a while, but keep the channel open."

"Copy."

Carl removed the comm device from his ear and laid his PDW within easy reach on the bed. "Here's the short story. Eight months ago, I was a commercial real estate broker. Then a Mexican national, a drug lord who looked exactly like me, kidnapped the president's daughter. The TER captured and interrogated me because they thought I did it. My son got killed in the mix. I blamed the TER and the FBI for the death of my son, and with good reason, so I sort of declared war on the government. I became a terrorist and started killing government agents. Turns out, the president asked me…begged me…to go rescue her daughter"—he shrugged—"because I looked like the bad guy. Well, the *other* bad guy.

"Vice President Walter Breen and his partners in the US and Mexico had a plan to use Melissa Mallory to infect the president with the Contagion, and she in turn infected almost everybody at her State of the Union speech. Breen's secret cabal almost succeeded in killing the president and taking over the country, except my team and I worked with government agents to stop them."

Clair leaned forward and parked her chin in her palms, elbows resting on her knees. "Are you telling us that a terrorist saved the president and her daughter *and* the country?"

Carl nodded. "Yeah, pretty much." To Richard, he added, "I have a friend I want you to talk with. We used to call him the Thinking Machine. He has ten different degrees, including three or four PhDs in theoretical physics, laser physics, quantum physics—that kind of stuff. He's a government contractor, and his real job title is strategic analyst. He can analyze problems and technologies to determine countermeasures and may be able to shed some light on what this biotech weapon is and why it doesn't seem to work on you."

Leaning against the dining table, Bonhardt shrugged with his whole upper body, including his arms. His voice hiked up a notch with frustration. "I asked you this before, but why do you even care about me, about us?"

Carl stood and glanced out the window again, then focused his gaze on the officer. "Well, if this test protocol is representative of some kind of mind-control or behavior control weapon, it will have far-reaching, even global, implications. In particular, we've received intel suggesting this technology will be aimed at coercing the Secret Service to murder the president."

CHAPTER 22

RICHARD AND CLAIRE STARTED TOWARD their room, presumably to digest and discuss what Carl had told them. Then the room's phone rang. Everyone froze and stared at the device on the desk.

"We're blown!" Carl grabbed his PDW and armor duffel. "Get the kids ready to move!"

They raced to wake the kids while Carl grabbed the phone.

Wizard said, "Boss, get on comm. We have a problem!"

Then the line went dead.

Carl crossed to the nightstand and stuck his comm unit in his right ear. "Talk to me."

"The Bonhardts have been ID'd on a traffic cam, and the minivan has been found and traced to your alias. Radio chatter suggests some heavy contract hitters are en route to your hotel right now. ETA, ten minutes. Trust me, the police and Homeland won't be expecting this level of engagement. They won't be able to stop them."

"I should have anticipated this." Carl began running scenarios in his mind at light speed, trying to find a way out. "The good news is the minivan was registered to Kyle Fortuna. They don't know it's me yet."

"Won't matter, Boss. They know the cop was driving the minivan, and they probably know by now that your alias is registered in that hotel. They're going to tear that place apart to get to the Bonhardts no matter how many people they have to kill. Wait, here's Three."

"Boss, I've been on comm with Eighteen. He's from Chi-Town, so he has assets there. We've got someone on the way right now, but it's a race to see who gets there first."

"Copy that. Advise me when he's on-site."

"From what I hear, you'll know it when he gets there."

Carl got into his battle suit and stuck as many extra mags in slots in his utility belt as it would hold. Bonhardt filled his pockets, removed the silencer from his Glock, and handed an extra handgun to his wife. She checked the chamber and stuck the weapon in the back of her pants. Carl notched an eye at her.

She shrugged. "I'm the wife of a cop. What do you expect?"

Carl nodded and looked at them. "You folks ready for this?"

Officer Bonhardt nodded. "As ready as we can be. Let's take the stairs. We don't want to get trapped in an elevator."

"Agreed. I'll lead this time. Let's move."

Carl charged out the door, PDW up and ready with the barrel swiveling left and right. He moved swiftly down the stairs, followed closely by Claire towing her kids, and Richard Bonhardt brought up the rear. They arrived in the lobby just as Wizard told him his ride had arrived.

Carl approached the lobby's rotating door. "Damn, Three! You found someone with a real APC?"

The army-green armored personnel carrier was old, but it hopped the curb and went airborne for a moment before crashing back down on the pedestrian sidewalk. It had eight all-terrain wheels that looked like they could withstand anything short of a grenade blast. It turned and skidded sideways until the back end was pointed right at the exit. More tires squealed as several SUVs and cars approached the hotel from both directions of the street.

Carl lowered his face shield into place. "We're going to have to make a run for it. I'll cover—"

The old APC burned rubber in reverse as the vehicle's back end crashed right through the revolving door. Carl and the Bonhardt family dodged debris as the APC stopped five feet *inside* the lobby. The awning collapsed on top of the vehicle.

The rear hatch on the APC dropped open with a clang, and a gruff voice bellowed, "Get in!"

Carl covered the family, and as soon as he ran into the APC, Officer Bonhardt hollered, "Clear!"

The rear hatch rose fast with the noise of grating metal. With little headroom, Carl walked hunched over until he was right behind the driver. The man looked about fifty with leathered skin and a shock of unruly white hair. His extra-large bright green Hawaiian shirt printed with white flowers couldn't hide his massive belly.

"I'm Dutch," the driver said. "Gehrhart sends his regards."

Carl recalled that was Merc Eighteen's real name. He patted Dutch on the shoulder. "Head for the Executive Airport!"

"Shit, that's way on the north end of town!"

"Well, let's not waste time chatting about it."

Dutch turned his head sideways. "Hang onto something back there!"

The APC's engine screamed, and the beast took off east toward Lake Shore Drive. Carl grabbed one of the overhead leather loops hanging from the green metal ceiling. It looked like original equipment and reminded him of the old New York subway cars. He spread his feet wide for stability.

There were two bench seats on each side of the compartment, each big enough to seat two adults, and thick slats of crisscrossed leather took the place of backrests. Between each bench seat was a bulkhead door on heavy hinges midway along each wall of the APC. Claire had one arm wrapped through the webbing, and the other clutched both her kids. They clung to her, rocking with the wild movements of the vehicle. Richard Bonhardt sat sideways on the next bench with one hand holding the bulkhead webbing and a leg braced firmly on the opposite bench.

The approaching SUVs tried to block the path, but the heavy Vietnam-era army vehicle blasted right through them with an explosion of glass and metal. Carl heard the sound of gunfire pinging harmlessly against the vehicle. They were safe for now, but there was no way they'd outrun street vehicles all the way to the airport. Besides, if they had his alias, then they knew he rented the minivan from the Executive Airport. They'd already have a team en route there, and Carl knew the assassins would get there first. Despite virtually no traffic on the road at that late hour, the APC topped out at a mere fifty miles an hour.

When Carl looked out the green-tinted viewport above the rear hatch, he saw seven vehicles chasing them, three abreast. They were hanging back, looking for an opportunity, and it didn't take them long to figure it out. He saw the flash in the darkness and knew what was coming.

"RPG!"

The driver hauled the APC over so fast, Carl was flung against the bulkhead. He probably would have broken something if he hadn't been wearing armor. He looked out the front and saw the missile flash into the distance. Then, when the highway curved a bit to the right, the missile's path intersected that of a car coming the opposite way. The explosion was spectacular, though the driver probably never knew what hit him or her.

The first RPG missed, but the second did not. The left side lifted at a crazy angle, and screams of terror filled the cabin until the vehicle bounced back down. They all heard metallic screeching like something was being dragged under the carriage.

"I think we just lost an axle," the driver said. "Good thing we have three more."

Richard Bonhardt said calmly, "At this rate, we're not going to make it."

Carl had a similar thought. "Three, are you still with me?"

"What's your status, Boss?"

"Grim. Get Aaron McGrath on the line."

That task took fifteen seconds while the driver kept swerving across the highway to spoil the RPG launcher's aim.

"Status," the director said.

"Aaron, we're in the shit here. I don't suppose you have an armed fighter jet nearby, do you?"

"Let me see what I can do." His channel went dead.

Three said, "Gotta love that government guy. Doesn't waste words."

Carl stepped forward and forced the latch open on the left-side personnel door. He yelled at the driver. "On your next swerve to the right, execute a full U-turn to the left. I'll try to slow them down."

The APC swerved to the right, then arched through the U-turn, and for a brief moment, Carl faced the pursuing fleet through the open hatch. He put his PDW on full auto and expended an entire clip at the vehicles. Windshields shattered and sparks showered from the fronts of the cars.

Then the U-turn was complete with the APC now traveling against traffic near the concrete median wall.

Carl reloaded and waited. Five seconds later, they flashed past the disarrayed gaggle of pursuit vehicles, and he raked them again with another full clip. He didn't get them all, but he did a good amount of damage. Two of the SUVs were out of commission with blasted-out windows, smoking engines, and multiple holes in their front grills and side panels. A couple others had minor damage, but he'd given the drivers something to think about, something to fear.

Carl closed the personnel door and hollered, "Can you get through that median wall?" He stepped forward and pointed at the center concrete barriers.

"Let's try!" Dutch swerved as far left as he could without leaving the pavement, then swerved back to the right and gunned the engine.

The tires chirped under the sudden thrust of the big diesel engine, and the APC plowed through the median, knocking two of the heavy concrete barriers off their footings. They were driving south again, this time on the correct side of the highway. Then the APC was hit by another RPG, and the back end was knocked 180 degrees. In an instant, they were racing north on the southbound side of the highway.

"Damn, I think they took out a couple of the starboard tires! These things were built tough back in the day, capable of handling almost any terrain or damage, but I'll be surprised if I can keep it above thirty-five now. They're gonna have us boxed in PDQ."

Army talk for "pretty damn quick." "Next exit," Carl ordered.

The exit they took was actually a southbound on-ramp.

Three said, "Boss, the director found you some help."

An unknown voice began issuing commands, and Carl wasn't about to argue. They were out of options.

"APC, this is Hammerhead Two-Five-Zero. Get back on the highway ASAP."

"Copy that." Carl hollered, "Hard left! Get up the slope and back on the highway."

The APC hopped the curb and headed south on the frontage road, then angled up the dirt embankment and crashed through the guardrail, so they were back on the highway and heading south.

"They're right behind us," the driver said.

The APC was losing speed fast, and the sound of grating metal echoed through the cabin. An SUV followed, closing the distance rapidly. The other two cars sped ahead on the frontage street and sped up the on-ramp half a mile ahead, then stopped in the middle of the highway.

"APC, Hammerhead Two-Five-Zero. Stop and hold your position under the next overpass."

"Copy," Carl said, then relayed the instruction to the driver.

They slammed to a stop, as did the SUV a quarter mile back. Carl saw the driver up ahead prepping another RPG. He fired, and it flashed toward them at incredible speed.

"Well, fuck me sideways," Dutch said. "That's gonna hurt!"

Carl shouted behind him, "Brace for impact!"

Even as Carl uttered the warning, tracer fire from somewhere above lit the darkness and intersected the RPG five meters before impact. The explosion and shrapnel washed harmlessly over the APC. Then more tracer fire literally exploded the RPG shooter into pink mist and turned the two cars into wrangled piles of metal in two seconds flat. The rear SUV suffered the same fate.

A completely blacked-out helicopter settled into a landing on the highway directly in front of the APC. It looked like the FBI assault chopper that he'd seen ambushed in Albuquerque. Clearly, McGrath had learned a lesson and put this crew on high alert in anticipation of the Chicago operation.

Carl patted the driver on the back. "Dutch, you saved our asses. I owe you."

"Can you guys afford to refurbish my baby?"

"Hell, I can afford to buy you a new one."

"Not necessary, my friend. As you can see, this one serves just fine."

"Consider it done."

They shook hands, and Carl followed the Bonhardt family over to the helicopter. It had a futuristic-looking optical surveillance and targeting pod mounted under the nose, and he knew from his days in the Air Force that the belly-mounted minigun that just destroyed their pursuers was slaved to the targeting pod. Both side doors of the chopper's cabin were open, and a gunner in black fatigues stood ready in each doorway with a machine gun that was fastened to a swivel at the top of the doorway.

After everyone strapped in, the pilot launched the chopper.

Carl said, "Aaron, are you still on this channel?"

"I am."

Carl nodded, though he knew the man didn't see the gesture. "Good save with less than two seconds to spare."

"We keep Homeland assault teams on standby in nearly every major city for rapid-response."

"I take back everything I ever said about you."

"Not the good things, I hope."

"I don't recall saying any good things about you, so we're good." Carl hoped the humorous retort might soften the ground between them a bit. "Three, you there?"

"Yes, Boss."

Carl looked at Officer Bonhardt and his family. "The package is airborne and safe for the moment. Is the jet fueled and ready for emergency takeoff?"

"Engines are running as we speak. Jet is positioned for emergency takeoff."

"Pilot? Are you still on this channel?"

"Affirmative."

"I have no doubt our Gulfstream has been identified, and a team has been dispatched. You can expect resistance on approach."

"Resistance is futile."

Carl chuckled. "An Air Force combat *Star Trek* geek."

"Marine Corps, sir."

"Almost as good."

He noticed one of the gunners eyeballing him. He was a big Black kid with a serious face. In the darkness of the cabin, his skin seemed almost as dark as his black combat flight suit.

The young man said, "So, you're the American Terrorist."

"I am."

Gunner nodded. "We heard what you did for the president. Damn fine work, sir. And I'm sorry for the loss of your son."

Carl felt pain rip through his gut at the mention of his dead son. Mark was probably ten years older than this young soldier. He nodded. "Thank you. That means a lot coming from a true warrior."

He also felt a renewed respect for Aaron McGrath. He knew these young soldiers would quickly realize who their cargo was, so McGrath had no doubt focused them on the mission by telling them the truth of his contribution to President Mallory's cause.

The pilot said, "ETA, three minutes."

When Carl looked out the window, he saw three strings of lights converging on the airport from different directions. The closest was still half a mile out when the chopper crossed over the boundary fence.

The combat chopper put them down twenty meters from the Gulfstream, which sat at the end of the east-west runway with its engines screaming. After a quick dust-off, the chopper turned to face the approaching vehicles while Carl and the Bonhardts raced aboard the plane.

Carl hollered upfront, "Go!" He palmed the button to raise the stairs and close the door, and everyone got belted in.

He was forced back into the seat as the plane shot forward under emergency thrust. Then Carl looked out the window and saw six RPGs blast into the sky. The missiles chased the Gulfstream down the runway. He knew the inevitable truth that only military afterburners could outrun RPGs, and the Gulfstream wasn't a military plane.

The nose of the Gulfstream lifted, forcing Carl down into his seat. He kept his gaze on the battle behind him, watching as thermal flares burst from the bottom of the combat chopper. Blinding flashes erupted, distracting three of the RPGs and sending them tumbling to the tarmac, where they exploded harmlessly. Two quick bursts from the chopper's cannon obliterated two more RPGs, but the last missile was locked on target.

The chopper pivoted quickly to keep its optically slaved minigun engaged on the RPG. Tracer fire slipped through the air and chased the speeding missile. At the same time, Carl saw both of the gunners engaging separate lines of headlights on the road. Showers of sparks and explosions lit the ground as the gunners raked the lines of headlights.

Right when the battle looked like a one-sided Homeland slaughter, when it looked like the hit teams had absolutely no chance of survival, a final RPG reached up from one of the vehicles and slammed into the tail rotor of the combat chopper. The aircraft spun crazily and fell from the sky as a missile flashed from its fuselage and sped to the north. Then the chopper hit the ground amidst a blast of sparks from the rotors grinding against the tarmac. To Carl's amazement, the chopper's missile corrected its course as its onboard guidance system reacquired its target, and the antimissile missile zoomed back toward the much-slower RPG that was homing in on the Gulfstream.

The explosion was spectacular and close. The blast rocked the plane, and shrapnel pinged against the metal skin as they continued to climb.

Carl kept his gaze on the fallen chopper. "Aaron, Hammerhead Two-Five-Zero is down."

"Copy that. What is your status?"

Carl was about to answer when he saw a fantastic sight. "Holy shit! They're still in the fight!"

Tracer fire erupted from both doorways of the downed chopper and annihilated the closing vehicles. Sparks and explosions again rippled down the line of SUVs, then all that remained of the hit teams was the burning rubble of their vehicles.

"Gulfstream, Hammerhead Two-Five-Zero. What is your status?"

The Gulfstream pilot responded, "Only minor damage. The board is green. You?"

"Mission complete. All hostiles destroyed."

Carl said, "Casualties?"

"Negative casualties. One minor injury."

The pilot eased off on the steepness of his assent, and Carl stood and began removing his armor. He caught the gaze of Richard and Claire.

Over the comm channel, Carl said, "Officer Bonhardt and his family send their gratitude to the crew of Hammerhead Two-Five-Zero. As do I."

Richard nodded.

"Copy that. Safe journey, sir."

Carl was suddenly famished, as he hadn't been able to eat or drink before they had to leave the hotel. He figured Richard and Claire hadn't either, so he went to the rear of the TER plane and gathered some MRE packets and bottled water from the storage cabinets. The kids were fast asleep.

As Carl returned to his seat, he reached out to the TER director. "Aaron, is there any update on Agent Palmer?"

"We've had a situation in DC, and she's been off comm for a few hours. I'm concerned."

CHAPTER 23

PALMER GASPED AS SHE ROLLED to her elbows and knees. "Christ! What the hell was that?"

"Agent Palmer, are you okay?" The president's shaky voice split the darkness.

"I'm okay, Madam President. Are you injured?"

"I busted my right ankle when somebody threw me down the stairs." Mallory chuckled. "But I think I can walk. You?"

"If that had been a lightweight steel or wood door, I'd be dead. But Aaron's people use this place as an evac safe house. He made the basement assault proof, including installing a twenty-four-inch-thick steel and concrete door. The door hit me pretty hard, but its bulk and the hydraulic-assist hinges absorbed most of the blast." Palmer gingerly got to her feet and took a deep breath, cataloging her body for serious injuries. "How long has it been?"

"You were out for several hours."

Palmer pulled a penlight from her pocket and scanned the big room. "It looks like a storage room and, in fact, normally serves that purpose until we need it for a safe room. It has an exit into the next basement over there." She swung the bright-white LED beam to the east wall.

Palmer helped President Mallory cross the room and then hauled open another thick concrete and steel door. Instead of an escape corridor, though, she found tons of debris blocking the exit. She swung the flash-light beam back over to the main door, but that was also blocked. She swung the light around the room, heavy dust dancing in the beam. As she expected, there were no windows in the basement. They were trapped.

"Madam President, wait over there." She indicated a central area relatively free of debris, but shelving and boxes everywhere had been dislodged and tossed about from the blast. "I'll see if I can make a hole to get a comm signal through. Right now, all this thick concrete rubble is blocking radio signals." She started pulling at boards and rebar shafts embedded in pieces of the building's brick walls. "Aaron probably already has a team on-site or en route. I just need to get word to him."

It took a few minutes, but as soon as she pulled a piece of debris that revealed a narrow shaft of light, she heard McGrath's voice in her ear again.

"Palmer, I have your signal again, but I don't have Shirley's. What's your status?"

"Injured, but functional. What the hell happened?"

"Since your signal just now registered, I assume that you're exiting the safe room, but Shirley must stay within. Copy?"

"We're not going anywhere anytime soon. In fact, we're sealed in good, but I'm at the entrance threshold. I cleared a gap in the stairwell debris to get a signal through, but the escape door was completely blocked by debris."

When McGrath next spoke, Palmer heard the sigh in his voice. "That was an advanced tactical air-to-surface missile."

"What?"

"And it was launched from a stealth aircraft. One of our own."

"How could Rainman possibly have put an aircraft in play that quickly? At that point, the announcement that Mallory was leaving the White House for lunch wasn't even half an hour old."

"I know," McGrath said. "Rainman is acting a lot like Carl Johnson this week. He's on the offensive with backup plans and plenty of contingencies. On the plus side, though, we now know Johnson's new CIA contact is the real deal, and he's loyal."

"How is that relevant?" Palmer said.

"He relayed intel that Shirley has been given a radioactive isotope, which is what Rainman's fighter used to home the missile in on the restaurant."

"So Rainman set the Secret Service detail on us and also had a stealth fighter orbiting the city, waiting for her to leave the White House? He's probably just sitting up there and waiting for her to pop up on his radar again."

McGrath sighed uncharacteristically. "It's been several hours, and right now, it's well after midnight. But yes, Rainman had a plan and a backup plan. It wouldn't surprise me if his fighter is fueled and ready to launch again as soon as a satellite picks up Shirley's radioactive signal."

"Well, we can't stay down here forever. Sooner or later, Rainman's people are going to try to put eyes on their target. They'll want to know for sure if they got her."

"You're safe for the moment. I have a Homeland rapid deployment team on-site."

Palmer leaned against the thick door. "They can't protect us from a stealth fighter. Twenty or thirty seconds is all they need to reach us with another missile."

McGrath gave his characteristic pause as he often did during an operation, indicating his brain was turning over scenarios. Carl did the same thing.

Finally, he said, "I keep asking myself, 'What would Carl Johnson do?' "

"When he learns what these bastards have done, he's going to escalate. That's what he'll do."

"I know." McGrath was silent for a moment, and Palmer got the feeling he was already planning damage control for Carl's reaction.

"You're not going to tell him, are you?"

"On the contrary, I think we should—"

Palmer finished his thought. "Unleash the American Terrorist?"

"He'll do whatever is necessary. He'll do *anything* that's necessary. And we need a response that our enemy won't see coming. Johnson is good at that. He's our best weapon right now."

Palmer lowered her voice a bit. "There'll be pushback."

McGrath sighed. "I'll handle the president." When Palmer remained silent, he said, "You don't agree?"

"I agree 100 percent. Let's stop trying to control him. I say we let Carl Johnson be Carl Johnson."

"Agreed," McGrath said. "Let us put together an exit plan for you, but the damage on-site is extensive, so it's going to take a few more hours to get to you. Get comfortable until morning, then here's what I want you to do."

She listened for a moment. "You want me to do *what?*"

———————◆◆·———————

It took McGrath's people ten more hours to clear away enough debris from the basement. Early Friday morning, Nancy Palmer limped out of the wreckage. Her left arm was in a sling, and she had a bloody bandage wrapped around her forehead. Her black jacket was ripped nearly to shreds, and her right pant leg was sliced up to her butt, revealing another bloody bandage wrapped around her upper thigh. One of McGrath's fast-response operators tried to assist her, but she brushed him aside and struggled to walk on the uneven debris of the collapsed restaurant by herself. She nearly fell several times.

The missile had completely leveled the restaurant, along with the two adjacent stores. The president's limo, her three escort SUVs, and all the Secret Service agents near those vehicles had been swept from existence by the blast.

Palmer made her way to the medic van, which was a standard ambulance box truck painted matte black and adapted for military use. Like the TER's fast-response APCs, the medic truck had no distinguishing lettering or emblems on its surface. She saw half a dozen thin radio antennae extending eighteen inches off the roof and a black acrylic dome that she knew housed surveillance sensors.

Nearly a dozen of the armed TER operators in full black battle gear had secured the area on all sides of the destruction. They kept the DC police back, and the police kept the press and onlookers back. Two black, unmarked TER combat choppers hovered over the area and kept the news choppers away. But the operators' posture was solemn, and weapons were at rest. This was clearly a cleanup operation, not a defensive military operation.

There were plenty of cameras, and the secret had been out for twenty minutes. The carnage that was the presidential vehicles was being featured on every channel. Speculation turned to fact when two more TER operators hauled a black body bag out of the wreckage and laid it gently on a waiting gurney.

"The President Is Dead!" blasted the headlines.

The operators wheeled the gurney over to the ambulance and started to lift it into the truck, but Palmer stopped them. She unzipped the bag and laid her forehead against the president's forehead. Mallory's torso was a bloody mess. A moment later, Palmer zipped the bag, and the operators lifted the gurney into the truck. She tried to climb up also but nearly collapsed, so an operator lifted her and helped her into the ambulance. The door closed, but the truck sat still as the operators slowly retreated to their armored vehicles. They clearly were in no hurry. The president was dead.

Inside the ambulance, Palmer ripped off her bandages and stripped down to her black sports bra and panties. One of the medic operators tossed her a plastic bag from which she retrieved a change of clothes. The other medic cracked an ampoule of smelling salt formula and waved it under Mallory's nose. The president was awake in an instant.

She tried to sit up, but the medic held her down. "Lie still for a moment, Madam President. Let me check your vitals."

McGrath's voice came over the comm net. "You okay, Shirley?"

Rubbing her neck, she looked over at Palmer and said, "She hit me!"

"It was Aaron's idea." Palmer tapped her own collarbone. "Brachial plexus nerve bundle. Had to get you unconscious, and I couldn't tell you it was coming."

Palmer smiled as she used wet wipes to get the blood off her skin. The TER operators had been well prepared. They'd dug a hole in the debris over the basement entrance and carried down bandages and blood to create the illusion that Palmer was seriously wounded and the president had died.

"By the way," McGrath said, "that was a nice bit of acting, opening the bag and mourning over the president. A lot of cameras picked that up."

Palmer nodded at Mallory. "Had to make Rainman's people believe they succeeded in killing you, or we'd have been hit by another missile by now."

"Yes," McGrath added. "But that helpless *I'm-hurt-carry-me-into-*

the-ambulance move was kinda over the top. Trying for an acting career next?"

Palmer grunted. "Can't get a man to carry me across the threshold unless he's in full battle gear."

Mallory chuckled and sat up, then rubbed her neck again. The medic handed her a plastic bag that held a black two-piece outfit like Palmer's with a high-neck T-shirt. The two medics turned away as the president wiped off blood and changed her clothes.

"So, what's our next step? They're going to come after us again as soon as they realize I'm not dead."

"Agreed," McGrath said. "Right now, your caravan is en route to Walter Reed. Your physician has already been informed, and the coroner is being cleared. However, you're going to stop at a subway entrance in a few minutes, and Agent Palmer is going to get you underground. At that point, the hunt will be on again, so Johnson and I are working on a plan to get you safely out of DC."

Palmer explained Rainman's use of a stealth fighter with a rogue pilot.

Mallory said, "You can't just order all aircraft grounded?"

"I already have, but Rainman clearly still has loyal high-ranking officers on his team. That stealth fighter is in combat mode with no radar emissions, and its transponder is off, so we have no way to track it. But it won't be able to track your radioactive signature if you're underground, so you'll be safe for a while. That'll give us time to get you out of reach of missiles."

"Us?" the president said, focusing her gaze on Palmer. "Aaron and Carl haven't exactly been working well together."

Palmer nodded. "I'm…managing the situation. We will all do whatever is necessary to get you to safety."

"I don't want to be *safe*! How many people died back there? I want *everyone* to be safe. I want these bastards found!" Mallory sucked in a deep breath and shuddered. "*Before* they kill more people." President Mallory clasped her hands together and gasped in frustration.

Palmer knew the president was reacting to the stress of the attack. From her jump seat, she reached out and laid a hand on top of Mallory's fists.

The truck slowed to a stop, and the driver said through the open slider, "Red light. Caravan is stopping."

"Copy that," Palmer said.

McGrath added, "Stay frosty, Agent Palmer. You must be ready to get underground with a moment's notice if we detect a threat."

President Mallory looked like she was going to stand up, but Palmer held out her hand in restraint. "Stay on the cot. We don't know what the resolution of the jet's detector is or how sensitive it is. The pilot might see you moving inside this stopped truck."

Mallory nodded.

"Green light," the driver said just before the truck accelerated. "We're on the move. Your stop is in two miles. Get ready to exit the vehicle."

"Copy," Palmer said. "Did you bring the weapons package for me?"

"As requested," a medic operator replied, handing her a black satchel.

When Palmer examined its contents, she found a PDW with its stock folded—a weapon choice she'd borrowed from Carl—a Glock, spare mags for both, a sheathed eight-inch combat knife, a dozen grenades of the flash-bang and lethal variety, and an M-203 grenade launcher with a dozen shells.

Mallory said, "Let's hope you won't need all that."

"We will." Palmer looked at her as she holstered the Glock on her thigh and zipped the satchel. "I wish I had one of Carl's armored battle suits, but I figured the Secret Service would search and clear the restaurant before you entered. I figured I could blend in with the staff, but not if I had armor." She sighed. "Didn't figure they'd blow up the whole block." She took a deep breath as much to steel her own resolve as to impart confidence to the president. "Anyway, as soon as we move, they'll realize you're alive. Depending on how far away that stealth fighter is, we might have twenty or thirty seconds max to get underground. Since the fighter can't hit us underground, Rainman will send in a ground team to do it the old-fashioned way."

McGrath added, "If Rainman is thinking like us, then his ground team is already in play, probably on standby like the jet until they verify you're dead, Shirley."

Palmer nodded to the president. "Aaron's people can jam the subway

surveillance system, but it's only a matter of time before they hem us in."
She raised the duffel. "Then we'll need this."

Mallory nodded at the operators. "Are they escorting us?"

Palmer shook her head. "A big crowd of armed agents will be easier
to find. We'll be on our own until Aaron and Carl figure out a way to get
us out of DC."

"We're working on that," McGrath said. "Have the medic withdraw
half a pint of blood from the president for a missile decoy."

Palmer relayed the instructions, and the medic quickly attached
a clear plastic tube to an IV bag, then gingerly stabbed Mallory in the
forearm with the needle. For nearly half a minute, her blood filled the
bag. Then he taped the tiny puncture site with gauze and covered it with
a Band-Aid.

"Ten seconds!" The ambulance swerved to the right. "Subway entrance will be ten meters to your left as you exit the rear door. Good luck,
Agent, Madam President."

The medic grabbed the plastic blood bag and glanced at Palmer.

She nodded. "Let's do this."

The ambulance jerked to a stop, an operator flung open the door, and
Palmer and the medic leaped out. The president stepped out of the ambulance and screamed in pain, collapsing as soon as her foot touched the
pavement.

Agent Palmer caught the president just before she fell over sideways, but Mallory's scream of pain made it clear she wasn't going to be
running. Palmer grabbed the bag of blood from the medic and shifted the
president's weight to him.

"Carry her," she ordered. "And let's move with a purpose. We're on
the clock here."

She knew they had only a few seconds before the pilot of the fighter
jet would realize Mallory was not dead, that her movement was not con-
sistent with the ambulance. He'd need a few more seconds to clear his
next action with Rainman, and then he'd send another missile to their
location. They had thirty seconds *at best*.

The plan had been for Palmer, the president, and the medic to get
underground fast. Then the medic would rush back to the ambulance with
the decoy bag of blood, not to fool the pilot but to draw away the fire-and-

forget missile that would be homing in on the last known location of the radioactive signal from her blood. That would avoid a direct hit on the train station. Now that part of the plan was no longer possible. Palmer and the medic knew it.

He huffed and puffed, carrying Mallory down the entrance stairs. At the bottom, he unceremoniously dumped the president to the concrete floor, then sprinted back up the steps three at a time.

"Blood!" he hollered.

Palmer tossed it in his forward path, and he snatched it from the air.

Palmer hefted Mallory to her feet, and they fled as fast as she could limp away from the entrance.

The president said, "He's not going to make it, is he?"

The blast came before Palmer could answer. The sound was tremendous, even though the TER agent likely got the decoy blood a hundred feet from the subway entrance. But the tactic was successful, and they avoided a direct hit on the station. Dust blasted into the ticket kiosk area behind them, the concrete structure rumbled, and some art-deco tiles popped off the walls, but that was the extent of the damage. It wasn't even enough to set off any alarms that automatically interrupted the movement of the trains.

With the emergency over for the moment, Palmer slowed their pace. Their ride arrived a few seconds after they got to the platform. The electronic sign on the front of the train and on the side of every car of the train flashed red: Not In Service. That was Aaron's idea.

The doors opened, and everyone got off the train. Many of the passengers seemed displeased, even though an announcement informed them that another train would pick them up in two minutes.

Palmer and Mallory stepped onto the train, and the doors closed. Palmer quickly got Mallory into a forward-facing seat, and then the train accelerated. She knew Aaron was watching because the train hadn't moved until Mallory was seated.

Palmer unzipped her duffel and pulled out a military first aid kit. She gave Mallory three painkillers and wrapped two chemical ice packs against her swollen ankle as tightly as she could. Then they sat in silence and waited.

"All those men," Mallory said. "All those people, dead because of me."

"Not because of you." Palmer reached over and held her hand. "Every TER field agent has read Carl Johnson's after-action file. They all know what he sacrificed for you. Even though Carl was classified as a terrorist, he inspired people—mercenaries, an FBI director, USAF Colonel Vesario Reichert, even Agent Cummings. Carl set the bar extremely high when it comes to protecting you, and those TER agents back there gave their lives to do exactly that. It's what we do for our president." Palmer looked at Mallory and squeezed her hand. "It's what we do for *you* because you aren't just the president. You're special."

Carl's voice came on the net. "That's right, Shirley. You are a role model for more people than any other world leader in history. More than Obama, more than Gandhi, and more than Mother Teresa. Little girls all over the world now believe they can grow up and become the president of the United States or leaders of their countries. We cannot allow the bad guys to win. I cannot begin to imagine how dangerous the world will become without you as president."

McGrath added, "And if we all have to die to keep you alive, that's what we'll do."

Palmer patted Mallory's hand and released it. She knew what Mallory was feeling. The president was the leader of the free world, a master politician and statesperson, but she wasn't a combatant. She'd been the target of multiple assassination attempts during the release of the Contagion, but she'd been unconscious during that event. Now she was in the mix, and the most powerful person on the planet was running for her life while her enemy, Rainman, now controlled the Secret Service, the very agency sworn to protect her.

Palmer shook her head as she considered the irony of the president's protectors. The train strategy was Carl's idea, and it was McGrath's idea to use the decoy blood bag to give them time to get underground. Two men were sworn enemies who, at one point, wanted to kill each other for what each had done to the other's adult child. Carl's son had died in an ill-fated sting that turned into an ambush. McGrath's daughter survived Carl's wrath, but she and her family would be traumatized for life by his actions. They were two of the smartest and most dynamic tacticians

Palmer had ever known, one trained by a long covert government career and the other accidentally thrust into the world of terror eight months ago. Now, they were working together to save the president.

"Carl," Palmer said, "I assume you've connected our comm circuit to the rail system? The security and surveillance systems are under Wizard's control?"

"Correct. It won't take Rainman's people long to locate your train, even though they don't have access to the subway system cameras. DC isn't that big. They'll eventually just start sabotaging tracks manually, and you'll be stranded. So you can't hide from that stealth fighter for more than a couple hours.

"Right now, you're on the Red Line, but soon, we're going to divert your train onto the Yellow Line. The enemy is smart enough to figure our best bet is to get Shirley out of DC, so they'll be watching Reagan National Airport because the subway stays underground all the way to the airport. The Metrorails to the other airports all become surface tracks outside DC, so those airports are not options for us. That leaves the municipal airport at College Park, so…" Carl's voice trailed off.

McGrath added, "So you *are* on the decoy train…to Reagan. In about ten minutes, we're going to land a fully armed F-22 Raptor at College Park. The two tactical helicopters that are now flying parallel with your decoy train will bug out at the last moment and provide cover for the F-22 when it lands. The two APCs that were escorting your ambulance survived the second missile attack, though the ambulance did not, so those APCs will converge on a subway station near that little airport, ready to rush you onto the tarmac, get you on that jet, then provide tactical support."

Carl added, "When we leave Reagan Airport completely without tactical support, they'll realize they've been had. They'll think you're going to College Park airport."

Palmer nodded and looked at the president. "That's an elegant head fake, Carl. So, by directing all our assets to College Park, you're hoping to pull Rainman's assets over there too."

"They'll see College Park as the only obvious choice to get the president in the air," Carl said. "When they redeploy, we'll launch the F-22 for intercept duty and hope they would also have redeployed their stealth fighter to that area. When it detects Shirley's isotope back at Reagan, it will launch missiles. When it does, we'll have its position, and the Air Force can kill it. The choppers will be on antimissile defense duty. We'll throw up a curtain defense between you and the stealth fighter."

"No, I forbid it," Mallory said. "What if all these missiles hit the ground? Too many good men and women have died already."

McGrath countered, "Shirley, Rainman *is* going to attack, so our only chance to prevent more deaths is to destroy those missiles before they hit you or the ground."

The president leaned her elbows on her knees and buried her face in her hands. She didn't seem to realize Carl and Aaron could see her through the surveillance system, so Palmer put her hand on her shoulder.

"No." Mallory shook her head. "Aaron, I order you to stop this madness."

Carl said in a flat tone, "McGrath is not running this op, Madam President, and you should know by now that I take orders from no one."

"But you don't understand! These are real people dying because of decisions you're making two thousand miles away!"

Palmer heard a noise in the background like Carl slammed a cup down or hit his desk. He shouted, "Who the hell do you think you're talking to? I know *exactly* what our people are sacrificing." Carl took a deep breath that was audible over the channel, then sounded calm again. "Shirley, the young men and women who are dying…they're soldiers and agents. This is what they signed up for. My son was innocent, and now he's dead because our enemy doesn't care about collateral damage. Your daughter almost died because of these people."

Palmer understood that being in combat, or being a victim or target of combat, is traumatizing. The president had made many life-or-death decisions from her office. Now, however, when thrust in the middle of it, she was in shock. Carl Johnson was probably the only person who could reach her. He was the only one who could disobey her if that became necessary.

Carl spoke softly. "All the lives lost won't matter if Rainman wins. All the things Aaron and I have done to each other won't matter. All the people I've killed…"

Palmer sensed Carl was finding, at that very moment, his reason for living.

Carl continued, and his voice carried more compassion than Palmer had ever heard from him before. "These people—Atlas and Rainman— they must be stopped, but there has to be something beyond the killing. There has to be a reason for all this, Shirley, and you are that reason. You. Must. Live."

The comm net was silent for a long time.

Palmer looked sideways at Mallory, who looked sideways back at her.

She said, "Madam President, you have an extraordinary weapon in Carl Johnson because he doesn't follow any standard rules of engagement, but you have to make the call, and you have to make it right now."

McGrath started to say something, but Carl interrupted, "Actually, the call has been made, Shirley. You just have to get on board with it, or you're going to die. And that's not acceptable to me."

"Or to me," McGrath said.

"Or to me," Palmer added.

Mallory's steel-gray eyes studied Palmer, and finally, she nodded. "I know," she said. "I just…"

Palmer said, "Let us do our job."

McGrath said, "Are you with me, Shirley?"

She took a deep breath and blew it out, then nodded. "So, what's the plan at Reagan Airport?"

McGrath said, "Rainman isn't the only one with high-level military contacts. I have an F-35 inbound, stripped down to the bare essentials. No weapons or ammo. Nothing but extra fuel. Its sole purpose is to get you off the ground as fast as possible and out of missile range."

Merc Three's voice came on the comm channel. "Agent Palmer, we're going to start slowing your train, so get ready to exit in thirty seconds."

"Copy that." Palmer turned sideways in her seat and faced Mallory. "Ready, Madam President?"

"Can I say *no?*"

Palmer smiled, reached into her duffel, and pulled out weapons.

Merc Three dictated the play-by-play. He redirected the TER choppers to the College Park subway stop ten miles away. The APCs increased their leisurely pace to an all-out race to the distant subway stop's street-level access, and the F-22 fighter made an emergency landing and short-runway deceleration. It taxied into takeoff position and waited, engines still blasting.

In response, Atlas's heavily armed paramilitary force in civilian clothes suddenly burst from various ambush sites near Reagan National Airport. Plainclothes assassins deployed from the subway station inside the airport terminals and raced outside to a convoy of SUVs that squealed rubber trying to get across town, where they assumed their target would board the waiting aircraft.

Three said, "It's working, Agent Palmer. Enemy units are pulling out of the airport. Your destination is the Crystal City station, the last stop before the train goes to the airport. Prepare to detrain there and meet your transportation topside. Ten seconds."

Palmer helped the president to her feet. "Aaron, any word on the fighter?"

"Negative," McGrath said. "I have a full squadron inbound in five minutes. We're as prepared as we can be."

Merc Three's voice came on the comm. "Foxtrot Two-Two, you are cleared for emergency takeoff, full military thrust. Buster to Angels Ten and maintain overwatch for inbound missile threats. The TER director authorizes weapons free. Repeat, you are authorized weapons free."

"Copy, full military thrust, proceeding to ten thousand feet, weapons free."

Palmer quickly attached the M-203 grenade launcher to the PDW and loaded the chamber. Then she slung the duffel across her chest and watched Mallory stand and test her ankle.

The president winced and looked at Palmer. "I'll be okay," she said. She nodded at Palmer's weapon. "You don't think all of Atlas's assets were redeployed?"

"Just in case." Palmer shrugged. "Stay on my six"—she patted her lower back—"and keep hold of the duffel strap so I know exactly where you are by direct contact at all times. We'll take it nice and slow."

The train slowed quickly, and she heard Carl's voice in her ear. "Good luck, Nancy."

"Carl, you don't tell someone going into combat 'good luck.' You say, 'Good hunting.' "

"Okay, well, good hunting. And…survive." He paused. "Remember, we have a date."

"Geez, Carl. You had to broadcast that over the comm to everyone?"

CHAPTER 24

MALLORY SAID, "SO, ARE YOU going to go out with him?"

Palmer giggled. "Yeah, but I sure wish he hadn't told everyone. Let's move."

Through the subway car's open door, Palmer scanned the platform with quick glances.

"How does it look?" The president's voice was shaky, but her grip on Palmer's duffel strap was strong.

"Looks clear." Palmer stood from her squat and took half a step outside the subway doors as the glass windows of the car exploded into shards. A bullet tugged at her collar as she ducked back inside.

The offending weapons must have had suppressors because there was no gunfire accompanying the exploding glass. So she couldn't tell where the enemy was hidden. She simply reached her assault rifle out the door and launched a grenade round somewhere up the platform to her left, then did the same to her right. The sounds and blast waves of both explosions merged into a single amplified assault on her ears and mind. She fired off a half magazine into the fire and smoke to the left, then she emptied the clip into the fire and smoke to her right.

Palmer replaced the spent magazine, then glanced left and right. No return fire assaulted them. "Okay, here we go." She stood and started forward but felt resistance on her satchel strap.

"Wait!" Mallory said. "Is it really clear this time?"

Palmer glanced out again and shrugged. "Looks clear."

This time, they encountered no enemy fire and made their first cover point, a thick concrete pillar, in only a few steps. Mallory hobbled quietly without complaining, but Palmer could tell she was in pain. Her breath hissed through clenched teeth.

"Okay, our next goal is to get through that hallway and up the stairs," Palmer said. "Cover your ears."

She yanked a grenade from the dozen she had hooked to her custom utility belt and tossed it into the smoke-filled tunnel, then ducked behind the thick pillar. The blast reverberated throughout the concrete subway platform, but she wasn't taking any chances. She pulled another grenade and tossed it fifty feet behind her, into the cloud of dissipating smoke, then took another and tossed it even farther into the tunnel ahead of them.

"That should give them a little headache for a bit. Let's go." Palmer glanced forward and back.

Soft white light from unseen overhead ceiling panels diffused in the smoke from the multiple explosions.

They were halfway through the tunnel when a large dark shadow loomed up right next to Palmer. The shadow could have been anyone—a disoriented passenger, a police officer, or an assassin. It didn't matter. He appeared too close to the president, and Palmer couldn't take the chance of guessing wrong.

The man wasted precious split seconds turning toward Palmer and Mallory, but Palmer made no such mistake. She simply released her grip on the assault rifle tethered around her neck and reached for her combat knife at her belt. In the quarter-second it took Mallory to suck in a breath of surprise, Palmer rammed her blade twice into the side of the man's face and neck without even looking at him. She had time to wipe both sides of the blade on the man's sleeve before he fell dead to the concrete deck. She slid the weapon back into its sheath, grabbed her assault rifle, and continued forward with the president still grasping her satchel strap.

Total time from blade out to blade sheathed: one-point-five seconds.

The tunnel ahead of them was shorter than it seemed simply because it was filled with smoke. In reality, it was only twenty feet long and was formed by the platform wall on the left and a dual bank of elevators on the right. As the smoke began to dissipate, Palmer saw that the wall to their left opened up to a hallway with two stopped escalators, one up and one down. They crept up the metal steps as fast as Mallory could move. They stepped around two bodies on the way up, which made Palmer think that a similar duo or trio might have fired at them from the other end of the platform.

Almost as an afterthought, she grabbed another grenade from her belt and tossed it back down the stairs so that it would be beyond the wall when it exploded.

She heard someone shout, "Grenade!"

Mallory gasped at the explosion, and Palmer's ears rang, but they forged ahead and passed through the one-way exit gates. Palmer saw light through the haze of the explosions and realized they were exiting onto the street. Through the ringing in her ears, she realized she heard a voice. After a few seconds, she recognized McGrath's voice.

"Inbound!"

At nearly the same instant, she realized a vehicle was bearing down on them from the right. Palmer pivoted and stitched the driver's side windshield of the white minivan with a triple tap, then prepared to tackle the president out of the path of the assassin.

"I say again, your evac is a white minivan, inbound."

"Aw, crap, Aaron! I just killed him."

The minivan swerved to the right and slid to a stop only a few feet from them. The driver rose up in his seat and elbowed the pickled window glass from the door.

He said, "Get the president on board, Agent, and let's get you to the plane."

Palmer womanhandled the president none-too-gently into the van through the passenger sliding door, and the driver sped off with the door wide open.

"I apologize for that," Palmer said.

The man just grunted. "You missed." He floored the gas pedal.

"Aaron, what's our status?" she said.

"We have a fast mover inbound now. It will meet you at the north end of runway one-five-three-three. ETA, forty seconds."

"Forty seconds? There are no access gates, and this van can't tear through the fence. It's laced with high-tension security cables to prevent ramming. You know that."

The minivan sped straight west, then jumped a curb and ended up on a paved road that looked more like a jogging trail. They came out of the trees, hopped another curb, and sped northbound on the George Washington Memorial Parkway. They swerved in tight behind a huge blue garbage truck going at least sixty-five. Black smoke spewed from its front vertical exhaust pipe.

"Agent Palmer," the driver called. He pointed out the front windshield. "Our gate opener."

The big blue truck swerved off the highway, over a curb, and rammed straight through the tough perimeter fence, pulling out fence posts for a hundred feet on either side. Palmer's driver swerved right, and the minivan thumped over the ripped fence. Then the rear and front windows exploded.

With the passenger slider still open, the roar of the garbage truck masked all other sounds, so Palmer wasn't sure exactly what was happening. As the minivan swerved around the lumbering trash truck, she heard the ping of bullets off metal inside the vehicle and saw tiny explosions of seat stuffing around her. She wrapped herself around the president and tackled her to the floor as the driver got the minivan on the north end of the tarmac. Something punched her hard in the back, and she heard her own voice scream in pain. The bullet impacts faded as the trash truck turned into the path of the fusillade.

She heard McGrath's voice, Mallory's voice, and the driver's voice, but she couldn't make sense of the words. The president struggled out from beneath her and helped keep her upright.

Mallory said, "I think she's been shot."

"Agent Palmer, what's your status?"

"Hit...can't...move." She'd been shot before, sometimes with body armor and sometimes without, but this time was different. This *felt* different. There was no pain. There was only numbness.

The minivan skidded to a stop, the driver's side sliding door opened, and the driver looked down at her sprawled against the bench seat. She could see in his eyes that she was dead. Her body just hadn't stopped functioning yet.

Over the net, McGrath said, "Get the president...*on...that...jet!*"

Palmer sat leaning against Mallory's lap, and she had a clear view straight down the five-thousand-foot runway.

It was empty.

There was no jet.

CHAPTER 25

PALMER'S OPEN MINIVAN DOOR FACED almost directly down the runway. She watched as the driver—she didn't even know the man's name—dragged President Mallory over the top of her. There was no time for finesse. Saving the president was the mission. The mission was the only thing that mattered. The mission was everything.

Then she watched a tiny dot coming out of the south, hovering barely a dozen feet over the water of the Potomac River and closing fast. She had just begun to formulate the thought that it would never get to them before the assault force. Then she realized the speck was moving far too fast to be the jet they expected. It was moving too fast to land. What if Rainman had outmaneuvered them, outflanked them? But the dot grew larger very fast as it approached, and she recognized the fuselage and wings of a fighter jet…

Flying ten feet off the deck!

The jet approached so fast—it was flying faster than its own engine noise—that it seemed completely silent as it flashed along the one-mile runway at full military thrust in six seconds flat.

Merc Three's voice highlighted the inevitable. "Missiles in the air! We have inbound from the northeast at Mach 3.2. ETA, one minute ten. The Air Force squadron is engaging the stealth fighter. The Raptor is engaging six bandits."

The president's evac jet seemed to float on a pillowy cloud as the vacuum behind it sucked moisture from the air, turned it into mist, and pulled it along its path. In the last few hundred meters, right before Palmer thought the jet was going to blast right overhead, the pilot flared the jet's nose up to vertical, and the aircraft seemed to slide toward them still ten feet off the runway. Palmer could literally see the broad wing base of the jet shudder violently as the jet belly-flopped against the thick air that piled against it. A cloud of condensed air flared from the wings as the jet decelerated through the sound barrier, then an explosion of sounds—the jet's screaming full-power engines and the thunderclap of its supersonic approach—swept over the minivan. Like trying to swing a flat board through water, the pilot used the maneuver to slow the jet from over a thousand miles an hour to zero in three seconds.

"Five-five seconds. Two bandits splashed. Four remain inbound."

Palmer had seen Russian MiG air-show fighters do vertical in-place full-thrust maneuvers thirty feet in the air, but she'd never seen it done in a combat scenario. For two seconds, the jet sat still in the air, ten feet above ground, its vectored computer-controlled thrusters keeping it airborne. Then the pilot did a pirouette in midair, brought the aircraft level to the ground with the landing gear extending, and cut the thrust. The jet dropped ten feet and bounced once. The canopy was already halfway open.

Suddenly, the minivan was pummeled by the hurricane-force wind of the jet's stalling maneuver. Palmer's head lolled sideways, but not from the blast of air. She was having trouble focusing, staying alert. Still, the spectacle was so sudden, she just then realized that the driver had Mallory halfway to the jet even before it touched down. They were nearly blown over by the blast of air.

The garbage truck swerved into her view and parked right under the fuselage of the jet, and both drivers used it as a platform to get President Mallory into the rear seat of the cockpit.

Wait…if the truck was at the jet, then what was stopping the chase vehicle from attacking? Oh yes, the garbage truck driver must have been armed. Yes, that had to be it. Maybe he had an RPG or something. Or maybe he just ran them over.

"I'll bet that ruined their day." Palmer tried to chuckle but couldn't find the strength.

"Agent Palmer, say again."

Who is that? Who's talking to me?

"Agent Palmer, repeat your last."

She refocused on the jet again. Before President Mallory was even belted in, the garbage truck agent jumped down and drove the big truck away from the jet and toward the rest of the paramilitary force she knew was pursuing them. It roared by her car, but she didn't have the strength to move her head and follow its progress.

She recognized Merc Three's voice in her ear saying, "Five bandits splashed. One remains inbound. One-one seconds."

She heard an explosion of sound as the pilot pushed his engines to full power for takeoff. The minivan driver still leaned over inside the cockpit and belted the president in, even as the cockpit lowered on him. He dropped to the ground in a hard tuck and roll and had just started to race away from the jet as the behemoth roared right over him. The jet thrust extended like an arm of fire out the back end and engulfed the driver in an instant. He was flash-burned and launched by the force out of her view.

With every ounce of her remaining strength, Palmer watched the jet gain speed. Half a dozen heat-seeking RPG rockets flashed into her view from over the minivan, but the jet, under emergency takeoff thrust, shrank into the distance and quickly outpaced the RPGs. In five seconds, the jet was airborne, once again skimming ten feet off the ground.

She saw the stealth fighter's missile streak downward from high in the sky. Two seconds, and it would be all over. There was no way the president's plane could out-accelerate a Mach 3 missile. No way the missile wouldn't miss.

CHAPTER 26

CARL AND HIS TEAM WATCHED the satellite view of the airport. The F-35 quickly accelerated down the runway, airborne after only five seconds.

"Call-sign *Air Force One* is off the ground," Merc Three said from across the room.

Carl nodded at the designation of an aircraft carrying the president of the United States. There was a brief flash of mist as the jet blasted through the sound barrier, then Carl could literally see the jet increase speed. It flashed over the end of the runway and the river. Had to be going a thousand miles an hour, easy.

The intercept missile vectored in at well over twice that speed. There was no way...

A millisecond before impact, a single flare popped high and away, and a high-intensity heat bloom far hotter than the jet's engine erupted right behind the jet. The pilot pulled his plane straight vertical in a max-climb. The missile exploded in the center of the decoy flare, and the president's jet escaped unharmed.

"*Air Force One* is undamaged," said the pilot.

Three answered, "Copy that. Good flying, sir. Proceed to Angels Four-Zero and maintain max cruising speed, heading two-six-zero. Begin radio silence, zero emissions."

On the monitor, McGrath said, "What's the status of the stealth fighter?"

Three said, "The stealth fighter has been shot down over the ocean. No survivor."

On the monitor, McGrath added, "Civilian damage and casualties?"

"Light," Three said. "Pieces of exploded missiles rained over the city, but property damage is minimal. There are some reports of injuries, but no deaths."

McGrath grunted. "We were lucky."

As Palmer's voice came whisper quietly over the comm channel, the room went silent immediately. "Carl," she said. "Can you hear me?"

"I'm here, Nancy. I can see you. We just got our drone over your position."

"Is it armed?"

"It is."

"Good." Palmer took a labored breath. "You did the impossible, Carl. You saved the president because you worked *with* Aaron. You each are brilliant at what you do, but together, you are unstoppable."

"I know." He glanced at McGrath's image on the right half of the monitor as the director nodded. "He knows too." Carl was silent for a moment. "We have help coming for you."

"No." Palmer's voice was getting weaker. "I did a *Carl Johnson*. I took a bullet for the president. I'm done."

"No, Nancy, I'm—"

She coughed. "Trust me, I know injuries, and mine is terminal." Her breathing grated over the comm like she was gasping for air. "I'm going to miss our date, Carl, but I want you to take care of something for me."

"Name it."

"Make them pay." She took a deep, gargling breath that sounded like she was drowning. "All of them, starting with these fuckers right here with me."

"I will."

Carl watched the video feed from the drone. He saw the paramilitary force in civilian clothes surrounding Palmer's minivan. All around him, his mercs were silent. They had all gathered in the living room to watch the explosive escape of the president. Ex-Special Agent Cummings, her mother, and her daughter were also crammed into the room, as were

Officer Bonhardt, his family, and Randal Cunningham. Carl glanced around the room and found everyone looking at him.

On the monitor, one of the men approaching Palmer's position held a cell phone to the side of his head.

Carl pointed at the monitor. "Wizard, I want to know who he's talking to."

"On it, Boss."

"Three." Carl looked sideways at his lead mercenary. "Prep drone missiles."

On the drone's tactical display on the wall monitor, two triangular brackets appeared over the cluster of three chase SUVs and Palmer's minivan.

A man knelt in the van doorway. "Agent Nancy Palmer," the man said, his voice clearly audible through Palmer's comm channel. "I've heard a lot about you. But you don't look so good."

Palmer's tired voice returned, "Have you heard a lot about my friend, Carl Johnson?"

The man chuckled. "In fact, I'm guessing you're on comms with him right now. My boss would like to chat with him, so I expect my phone to ring." The man dictated a number.

Carl looked at Wizard. "Dial it."

"They'll be able to trace me."

"Not if you trace them first." Carl looked behind him at Agent Cummings. She was fully outfitted in her hard-shell combat armor. "Nineteen, I hope you enjoyed your two days of R&R."

"I'm ready to get busy."

Carl nodded at her. "Let's get everyone prepped for immediate evac. You're in command of civilian protection. Get 'em safe and keep 'em safe."

"Copy."

He turned his attention back to the screen.

The man kneeling in the doorway of Palmer's van answered his phone. "My name is—"

"Let's jump to the part where I don't give a fuck who *you* are. I want to know who your boss is," Carl said.

"Let's jump to the part where I have your agent. I can either take

Agent Palmer to the hospital or stand here and maybe shoot her a couple more times." He pulled out a belt knife. "Or maybe I'll just carve her up a bit."

Carl looked at Wizard, who gave him the universal "give-me" hand sign. He needed more time to trace the man's call.

"All right, what does your boss propose?" Carl watched Wizard's fingers fly over his laptop keyboard.

"He wants to meet you and discuss a ceasefire. Rendezvous with me at these coordinates." The man dictated some lat-long digits. "I'll introduce you to him."

Carl said, "Well, it probably won't be *you* doing the introduction, but I agree to the meeting."

Wizard's fingers moved faster, and Carl knew he was close to a discovery.

"Empty threats don't suit you, Johnson. You're lacking leverage here."

Wizard flashed Carl a thumbs-up signal, and Carl pointed across the room to Three.

"Launching," Three said.

"And send the video to this guy's cell phone," Carl added.

The man on the ground said, "What video?"

"The video showing you how empty my threats are."

At first, the man didn't seem to understand what he was looking at. Then he did.

"Fuck!" He turned and looked into the sky. He seemed to look right at the drone for a brief second before three missiles blew him and his group to hell in blinding white explosions...

Along with Agent Nancy Palmer.

CHAPTER 27

CARL FELT A PUNCH TO his gut. He leaned on the table before him, bracing his weight on his fists, and looked down at the floor. He trembled. "Oh God, what have I done."

"Johnson." McGrath's voice was stern but carried an understanding softness.

Carl banged his fists against the table. "Fuck!" He took a deep breath and looked at the monitor…at McGrath.

"We've suffered a deep loss," McGrath said. "But we still have work to do."

"Yes, we do." Carl stood straight and looked around the room at everyone looking at him. He unashamedly wiped tears from his eyes. Finally, he focused on his field commander, Merc Three. "What's the president's status?"

"The pilot reports she's G-LOC. That's pilot speak for *G-induced loss of consciousness*. They pulled a lot of Gs in that max-climb takeoff."

Carl looked at McGrath's image. "Nice move stripping that jet down to nothing but fuel tanks."

"It wouldn't have worked if you hadn't lured the stealth fighter to the other side of the city."

Carl nodded and felt Cummings step up beside him. "Like Agent Palmer said, you two work well together." She raised her voice a little higher as if wanting to address everyone in the room. "I vote we continue this alliance."

McGrath said, "Agreed."

"Look at us," Carl said. He pointed at McGrath's image on the monitor, then at Special Agent Cummings, then at himself. "Eight months ago, we were all trying to kill each other, and now here we are, working together to save the president." Carl shook his head and smiled mischievously at the monitor. "You know, whenever I'd get in a tight spot, I'd ask myself, what would McGrath do." He shrugged. "Well, I'd use the F-word in front of your name, but still…"

McGrath twitched the side of his mouth in what Carl thought was almost a smile. "Agent Palmer and I had that same discussion a few hours ago. She said I should let Carl Johnson be Carl Johnson."

Cummings said, "Well, the president escaped, but we got our asses kicked…again."

Three said, "That's because we're playing defense. I don't mean to be insubordinate, Boss, but I'm tired of this bullshit. The president is safe for a minute, so it's time for *us* to start our own brand of ass-kicking."

Cummings's gaze bored into the side of Carl's head. "So, what would Carl Johnson do?"

Carl looked at McGrath. "I'm going to need some supplies." He dictated a list.

"The president would never agree."

"Good thing she's unconscious."

"I'll get back to you when I have it all." McGrath's image vanished from the monitor.

From across the room, Merc Three said, "Do you think he can get all that?"

Carl nodded. "That man will do *anything* to accomplish the mission, as will I. And right now, the mission remains to save the president." He swiveled his head Chris Tucker-style toward Wizard. "You have a name to go with that phone number you traced?"

Wizard nodded. "It was hard to trace, but I used the new NSA algorithm that—" He shook his head. "Never mind. But these guys' tech rivals ours. They cover their tracks well."

Carl nodded. "Understood. Gimme."

Wizard tapped a key on his keyboard, and Carl's target appeared on the monitor. He absorbed all the details about the man, his family, and known associates.

"So, Rainman's henchman is named Hollis Koll," he said to no one in particular. Then he pointed at the monitor. "Well, Mr. Koll, I look forward to meeting you in person."

Wizard added, "Look at the name of his corporation."

Carl scanned the sidebar, which read "Atlas Consortium." He said, "You think that's the same covert Atlas our CIA asset mentioned? The shadow government entity? They wouldn't be so blatant as to use the name of a covert organization as their company name, would they?"

"Maybe it's a coincidence," Merc Three said.

Wizard added, "Maybe this consortium *is* the shadow government entity."

Cummings sounded skeptical. "But that's a *European* think tank, a multinational conglomeration of tech and banking companies. Not the kind of company that would have extensive infrastructure in the US."

Wizard pointed at the Bonhardt family. "Well, the contract on these folks was for banking fraud. If a tech and banking consortium was going to put a hit out on someone, banking fraud is what they know best." Wizard shrugged, and everyone looked at the Bonhardt family. "Hell of a coincidence."

Lenore Cummings banged a fist against Carl's shoulder. "If this is our guy, if he's part of Atlas"—she nodded at the monitor—"how are we going to find them?"

When Carl met her gaze, he saw a fierce, controlled anger. "Well," he said with a smile that didn't quite reach his eyes, "I'm going to ask Hollis Koll politely to reveal information."

She nodded. "Mm-hmm. I'd like to be there to see that."

"I'll give him your regards."

"Please."

"Wizard, send all this data over to McGrath and let his people chew on it for a while. After all, data analysis is what the government does best. Let's see what they come up with." Carl took a deep breath and scanned the room. "All right, people, the president's jet is going to run out of fuel in a couple hours, and her blood isotope remains detectable for another thirty or so hours." He glanced over at his longtime friend, Randal Cunningham. "Did you just get here?"

The man nodded.

"McGrath briefed you on the way over?"

Cunningham nodded again and stepped closer to Carl and Nineteen.

"Good. I need two things from you. Before the president's plane hits the ground, we have to find a way to get her out of it and transport her undetected." Carl pointed at Officer Bonhardt, who walked over to join them. "And this fellow seems to carry the secret to countering this behavior control biotechnology. I'd like you to investigate why. After the president, he is the most important person on the planet."

Cunningham said, "I've been thinking about that. There's a lot of conspiracy theory chatter online about psychotronic weapons to influence people, you know, through bioelectromagnetic signals from cell phone, RF, or microwave transmissions, but that's all hogwash. Everyone's brain is different, so you can't just blast everyone with EM hash and expect them to do your bidding. Instead, if you want to target and influence a specific audience and, in fact, *every member* of that audience, then you have to have a trigger to cause them to act the way you want—probably an electromagnetic signal—and you have to have a catalyst of some kind—likely chemical or hormonal—that makes them receptive to your trigger signal." Cunningham turned to the police officer. "Since our target audience for behavior control is the police, we need to identify the trigger and the catalyst. Then we need to discover how you, Officer Bonhardt, happened to interrupt the connection between the two."

"All right," Carl said. "You have everyone in this room at your disposal, so get to it."

Cunningham nodded, and he and Bonhardt turned to talk with the mercs who had gathered around.

Carl felt a tap on his shoulder and turned to face Lisette. "What's up, sweetie?" He saw Lenore Cummings, who had stepped over to talk to her mother, glance over. "I apologize, Miss Lisette." He said it loud enough for her mother to hear. "In front of all these professional soldiers, I should be more formal."

The girl grinned and blushed a bit. "That's okay."

Carl nodded and said, "What's on your mind?"

"We've been here too long." She did that soft-stomping bounce from one foot to the other, which he recognized from eight months ago was her way of showing discomfort and frustration. "We should leave."

Lenore agreed from several paces away. "That's a good idea. Let's redeploy in case Atlas has their own Wizard and was able to get our location from that phone call."

Merc Three looked up from his conversation with Wizard. "I agree with the young commander, Boss." He winked at Lisette. "We've got all our eggs right here in one basket. All our weapons and mercs are here, along with the cop and your Thinking Machine, and the civilians."

Cummings added, "That's a mighty inviting target."

Carl nodded. "And if Atlas has more of those little plastic drones—"

"Very hard to detect, those things are," said Wizard. "And they can probably be outfitted with microburst transmitters. They gather a half hour of sensor data and transmit it in an encrypted burst so short our drone would never detect it."

Carl nodded and held out a fist bump to the girl. "Good call, Miss Lisette."

She blushed again and put her whole body into the fist bump, twisting and making a good windup with her own fist. Carl got the feeling the girl hadn't done a lot of fist bumping. She needed some training.

He nodded at Mrs. Bonhardt and her kids. "Lisette, why don't you show the kids how to bag up all the cell phones so we can get ready to go?"

As he watched the girl walk over to Claire Bonhardt, a part of him just wanted to reach out and hug the girl and apologize...again. Cummings cleared her throat and brought him back to reality.

He nodded at Cummings. "Nineteen, I want you to lead three mercs—Six, Sixteen, and Seventeen—to keep the civilians safe. I know someone who has a mountain cabin outside Taos, New Mexico. She's got an underground concrete bunker fully stocked. She built the whole thing herself, completely off-grid. Doesn't even have cell phone service."

Cummings nodded. "Government and civilian surveillance are everywhere. How do we get there undetected?"

Three said, "Our nearest cargo plane hangar is in Oklahoma. We'll charter a helicopter to get you there, and you can take one of our old Twin

Otters to Taos. If there's a hundred feet of dirt road up there, that plane can land."

"You have your own air force?" Cummings notched an eyebrow. "Not bad. Not bad at all."

"I put the money I stole from Alfonso Reyes to good use. I actually had operations against the government in mind when I bought a fleet of cargo planes and Twin Otters around the country. Those old twin-engine props can land on some pretty rough terrain, and those pilots are the continental version of Alaska bush pilots. Their itineraries are rarely scrutinized."

She said, "Since you have so much money, maybe you can buy me another house since you nuked my last two."

Carl smiled with a shrug. "The first one wasn't really my fault."

"Stingy."

Merc Sixteen spoke up. He was a big guy with multiple combat scars on his face, a crew cut, and a black T-shirt showing huge biceps. His neck was thick. Every visible inch of his body and the right half of his face was covered in dark tattoos. "Not to question your authority, Boss, but can we have someone with combat experience in command, I mean, like a soldier?"

Three chuckled, and Carl said, "It's a fair question, and one I've been expecting." He looked at Wizard. "Put Agent Cummings's FBI record up on the monitor. Show her weapons certification and tactical training list."

Five pages of courses and weapons scrolled up the screen, including a variety of handguns, semiautomatic assault weapons, fully automatic military rifles and machine guns, APC-mounted 50-cal guns, handheld grenade launchers, shoulder-launched rockets, and half a dozen sharpshooter rifles. There were only two categories—expert or proficient—and for all but two of the weapons listed, Cummings was *expert*.

"Anyone here an expert on a weapon not on Cummings's list?"

Three raised his hand like a school kid. "Slingshot, Boss." He pointed at the monitor. "I don't see slingshot up there." He shrugged. "From back when I was a kid."

Another voice said, "Credit card! I can spend that money, and I can kill with it too."

"Butter knife."

"Mom's cast-iron skillet."

Carl waved them all off. "You guys…"

Sixteen said, "I know, Boss. She can hit targets, sure, but I mean *real combat*. That's all I'm saying."

Cummings said, "Anyone here ever had a one-on-five gunfight and killed them all with headshots?"

Three raised his hand again. "Well, Boss did. As I recall, he took out six with headshots, and it was at *your house* too!" He ended the comment with a chuckle. "I think you were there, right?"

Cummings seemed nonplussed. "Anybody other than me and Carl?"

No one spoke.

Carl held out a fist, and she fist-bumped him and said, "Okay, is that issue settled?"

Merc Three looked over at Sixteen. "We good?"

"Good, sir." He looked at Cummings and said, "I meant no offense, ma'am."

She nodded.

"All right, Nineteen, move out." He turned to his second-in-command. "Three, I have a special assignment for you. Take seven men and head west. The director and I will give you your instructions en route. After that, you will be completely radio silent until your objective is achieved. I want tight OPSEC, and no one besides you, me, and McGrath will know your mission."

Three nodded.

Carl said, "All right, off you go." He turned and faced his best friend. "Randal, I know this is all crazy and weird for you, but I need you."

"CJ, I never believed for a minute all that terrorist nonsense. I've known you too long. Besides, I've been telling you for a decade how the government uses the media to spin the truth. But this…" He waved his hand around the room. "Goddamn, CJ! I always thought you were too ornery to be a commander type."

Randal had been one of his closest friends for nearly thirty years. They'd practically raised each other's kids together. Randal stayed married while Carl stayed a bachelor, but their friendship had endured the usually incompatible lifestyle. He walked over and hugged Carl.

"It's good to see you again, my friend," Carl said as they separated.

"Problem is, everything they said about me *is* true. All these guys…" He swept an arm over the mercs. "They're all mercenaries. They're all disgracefully discharged Special Forces soldiers, except the cop"—Carl nodded at Officer Bonhardt—"and FBI Agent Cummings."

"And Director McGrath?" Randal said. "He seems legit."

"Yeah, he is. So, I need you to find a way to make the president invisible. We'll never know which satellites can detect that radioactive isotope in her blood. Design some kind of mobile Faraday cage or something so the isotope won't betray her location. If we stash her underground somewhere, they'll eventually find her. And they'll bring a big enough can opener to get to her. Gotta keep her on the move. Then figure out why Bonhardt is immune to this behavior control weapon. At least, I assume it's a weapon." He shrugged. "It's being used as a weapon, I'll put it that way."

"CJ, I've always had your back, you know that." Randal Cunningham laid a hand on Carl's shoulder. "Whatever you need."

Carl nodded and turned his attention to his sharpshooter, Merc Eighteen. "Pick three men, and let's go meet a man."

"Our mission, sir?"

"I plan to cut his throat open, then we'll see who gets angry and comes *out* of hiding or who gets scared and goes *into* hiding."

CHAPTER 28

W HILE RANDAL CUNNINGHAM CONFERRED WITH Wizard and the five remaining mercs, Carl pulled back the edge of the living room blackout curtain and scanned the street. The op center was located on a nondescript residential street. The driveway was now empty since Three had taken his seven mercs in the two minivans on their classified mission. OPSEC—Operations Security—was paramount. Three had no destination yet. Carl had just told him to head west. Carl organized his upcoming conversation with McGrath.

They needed a place to hide the president against detection for thirty-some hours. It had to be mobile in case Atlas found her. It had to be defendable against Atlas's cruise missiles or assault troops. It had to be remote to minimize collateral damage. But first, they had to get her out of that jet fighter undetected.

Carl turned away from the window. With Merc Three, Wizard, and seven mercs gone on their mission, and with Cummings and her three mercs in the garage prepping civilians for departure, there were only four mercs remaining in the living room with Carl and Randal Cunningham.

"Time to wrap up," Carl said.

Cunningham summarized, "We need a mobile Faraday cage. A SCIF on wheels." He pronounced it *skiff*. "Once we get her in the cage, she'll be safe from detection."

The remaining mercs nodded. They all had military pedigrees involving prior work with Special Forces. All had no doubt received classified military briefings in a specially shielded Sensitive Classified Information Facility. A SCIF was designed to be impenetrable to any kind of mechanical, electrical, or laser eavesdropping.

Cunningham continued, "Except instead of shielding our SCIF against radio waves, we'll have to make sure it's resistant to radiation from the isotope in the president's blood, which resonates at a much higher frequency."

Merc Fourteen said, "Sir, just tell us how to build it. Her plane has a little over one hour of fuel remaining. It's heading in our general direction, but we still have to get it to her in an hour. Even with a helicopter—"

"We don't have to build anything," Cunningham said. "We'll just need some shielding material." He shrugged. "And an eighteen-wheeler." He launched into instructions on how to modify an eighteen-wheel cargo transport box, then said to Carl, "If Rainman has access to a satellite to track the president's plane, all this is useless."

"McGrath assures me he has control over all military satellite assets. Atlas may have access to some civilian satellites, but chances are good that none are directly overhead or even in an orbit where they can easily track her in the short-term."

Just speaking his former nemesis's name brought back thoughts of Agent Palmer. Carl tuned out the rest of Cunningham's discussion. He and Palmer hadn't been in the same location at any time during the last eight months of mission work except for a day and a half when they'd flown to Mexico together to find the cure for the Contagion and save the president and her daughter. They'd fought side by side briefly during that mission, but there was an accidental encounter that had changed the boundaries of their relationship.

During a brief downtime while awaiting mission intel, Carl had been looking for an empty room in Alfonso Reyes's mansion to relax and do some yoga and had walked in on Nancy Palmer right out of the shower. She was dripping wet, and her cream-colored skin was flushed from the hot water. They both stood there looking at each other, and she hadn't bothered to cover up with her towel. Then there was a wild and feverish kiss that lasted all of five seconds, interrupted by the untimely availability of mission intel. Later, they both agreed the incident never happened.

She'd always been in his ear over the months, guiding him and his team on their many missions to hunt down and execute the men responsible for the multiple attempts to assassinate President Shirley Mallory. Now she was gone forever. She'd moved from alive to dead in the space of a minute, just like his son.

Carl looked out the window again, only because he needed to do something, to move. He was unprepared for the sudden loss of Agent Palmer. He felt a longing for her, not unlike the longing he felt for his son. Palmer was actually younger than his son, and he'd always promised he'd never get involved with any woman younger than Mark just to avoid the weirdness of his son potentially needing to call a younger woman *stepmom*. It was such a crazy thought that he chuckled aloud.

All conversation stopped, and Carl sensed everyone looking at him. "Sorry," he said. "Please continue."

Agent Nancy Palmer had always seemed invincible somehow. He thought she'd always be there, always in his ear, and he missed her. He missed her tactical guidance. He missed the thought of any potential relationship they had both intentionally avoided. He'd waited a week too long to ask to see her again outside of the realm of their professional relationship. He felt a dark cloud envelop his soul. Her death was another reason to keep killing. He clenched his fists.

He heard his best friend's voice beside him. "CJ, you okay?"

Carl turned, finding everyone was busy with tasks Randal had assigned. Carl looked at his friend and just grunted, but that wordless communication spanned three decades of emotions they had shared.

"She was special, wasn't she?"

"Yes, but not like that."

His friend chuckled. "We'll just pretend the whole room didn't hear you ask her out on a date."

Carl sensed Randal was trying to lighten the mood, but the joke failed to penetrate his shroud of rage. Then the man stepped into Carl's personal space and hugged him. For a few seconds, Carl wasn't sure how to respond because the gesture seemed so foreign to the kind of man he'd become. Soon, the familiarity of his longtime friend melted away the months of violence and isolation, and Carl returned the hug. They stood together for a long time before separating.

Carl said, "I've changed, Randal."

"I can see that. But I've missed you, my friend. The family misses you."

Carl said, "To be honest, I didn't think I'd ever see you again."

They gazed into each other's eyes for a while. Randal had him by eleven years, and—in his mid-sixties—he was always the wiser. Randal's life was the footprint that Carl's life followed. They were both only children and loners in the social world, even though Randy had always been married.

His friend nodded. "I've missed our political conversations over coffee."

They both chuckled. Randal was the only friend, male or female, he'd been able to share his deepest thoughts and fears with, even his vulnerabilities, without the fear that he'd be taken advantage of. They shared *that* kind of bond.

Randal said, "I remember when you first told me how close you and your son were. You said if he ever died, you would probably go insane and kill anyone who took him from you."

"That was fifteen years ago!" Carl said. "That was just nonsense talk. I certainly didn't have the knowledge or the skills back then."

Randal nodded. "But now you do. I can see it in your eyes. And if I'm to believe all the news reports, you've already done a lot of killing. Now, with the loss of this Agent Palmer, I'm worried you're gonna go to the dark side."

"That's what she said—that she thought I was going *too far* to the dark side." He considered the impact of the female agent on his life for a moment. "She grounded me, Randal. Throughout all the months of violence, she stabilized me and kept me sane. She was the tether that kept me from going all the way dark, and now she's gone. I don't know how I'm going to keep it together without her."

"CJ, we've gone through a lot over the last thirty years. We'll get through this too. I don't know how, but we will."

"You don't know the irony, my friend. You know why Agent Palmer kept me sane?" Carl tried to chuckle, but what boiled was more like a gasp of agony. "She did it because she owed me. She was one of the people that—" He turned away from his friend and leaned against the wall, balanced by his fists. His voice was a coarse whisper. "They killed him, Randal. She was one of those government fucks that got Mark killed. Her and McGrath and that one there." He head-nodded at Agent Cummings, who now stood in the entrance to the living room looking at him. She looked ready to take her team and depart. She looked like she needed to talk to him but was now hesitating at the evil look that he *felt* was on his face.

"And now, you have to work with them."

"If I don't, President Mallory dies."

Randal squeezed his shoulder.

Carl grabbed his friend's hand and held on desperately. "Shirley Mallory was in on it too, Randal. The president of the *fucking* United States. How am I supposed to navigate this for the rest of my life?"

His friend gave him a shoulder hug. "I don't know, man. I really don't. But you already tried killing a bunch of people, and that didn't really work, did it?"

His friend was blunt, and it hurt. Eyes closed, Carl shook his head. "I'll never be able to kill them all."

"Your mercenaries tell me you saved the president's daughter. And you saved the president. And that FBI agent's family. And that cop's family." He squeezed Carl's shoulder again and stepped back. "How'd that feel?"

Carl stepped away from the wall and reached into his pocket for a hanky to dry his eyes. He knew what his friend was trying to do. He smiled and nodded at him. "It felt good, but don't be trying to distract me from the mission with that psycho-babble bullshit." They both chuckled, but Carl wanted to change the subject and bury his raw feelings. "How's it coming with the plan?"

Cunningham turned immediately to business, his mission to get Carl out of his funk apparently successful. He seemed in his element, managing a technical team effort. "I think we have a good plan." He pointed at the wall monitor. "The pilot should run out of fuel right about there." He indicated a red triangle on the map. "We're putting him on an altitude-conserving glide path, so he'll drop off radar just before *that*."

There was a low set of hills on the map of central Oklahoma before the ditch point.

"These hills will mask his radar return, so we'll have him execute a hard right turn and do a full-power burn as long as possible. Basically, we'll divert him a few miles up this valley here, where they can eject right where we'll be waiting. We'll lose the aircraft, but anyone searching will assume for a while that they continued straight west for another twenty miles and crashed. They'll search west, but they'll be looking in the wrong direction. We'll get the president on the highway in an insulated cargo truck that looks like any other eighteen-wheeler. It's a two- or three-person job, though, and I need to go to supervise the president's transition into the container. I need him." Randal pointed a finger at Merc Fourteen. "And if Officer Bonhardt goes with us, I'll have plenty of time to debrief him on the road, maybe figure out this behavior technology."

Carl nodded and said to Merc Fourteen, "Once you're on the road, go dark. No comms at all. Dress civilian, blend in, and stay off-grid for thirty-six hours. This will all be over by then, one way or another. Off you go."

They left, and Carl stepped over to where Agent Cummings waited. They looked at each other for a few seconds, and he thought he saw a tenderness in her gaze.

He said, "Lisette doesn't remember, does she? What I did to her. To you."

Lenore shook her head. "The doctors say she will…someday. Maybe next week or next year or ten years from now. They think it's good that she sees you as a savior for now, though. They think it'll soften the impact when she does remember, but it's anyone's guess when that will be, unless…"

She looked at Carl, and he looked at her.

He nodded. "You want me to talk to her."

Lenore touched his arm. "The doctors think if we control how and when she remembers…"

"I will." He looked at the floor. He could barely stand to look at the girl when she wasn't looking at him, and to look into her mother's eyes now was torture. "Let's try to survive the next couple days, okay? Then I'll talk to her." He took a deep breath and blew it out. "That's going to be hard."

"Hard for you and for me," Lenore said. "Harder for her."

Carl nodded and glanced around the op center. The kids, under the guidance of Mrs. Bonhardt, had bagged up all the one-time-use cell phones and supplies, then wiped all surfaces for fingerprints with disinfectant, so now the whole house smelled like a hospital.

He head-nodded to Mercs Eighteen, Eight, and Nine. "Let's move with a purpose."

Cummings whispered to him. "Can I ask where you're taking the president?"

"Out into the middle of the ocean."

CHAPTER 29

MERC EIGHT PULLED CARL'S ARMORED BMW limo slowly to the curb in front of a trendy boutique café at the coordinates relayed by the civilian contractor Carl had blown to hell. He hadn't been to Philly in decades, and the place looked drastically different. On his last visit, he'd toured the Bell, and he could see it from the limo.

"All right, I'm going in."

Satellite imagery showed Hollis Koll had entered the café ten minutes ago, but so far, no support or protection had been detected.

Eight said, "I don't like this, Boss. If there's no outside support team, then they're inside. No way this guy is in there by himself."

Carl pulled a square, high-tech grenade from his pocket. "If they're in there, they can't help him."

Merc Eighteen reported in from his sniper position eight blocks away. "I have clear sightlines on every major nesting point where he could have a sniper, but I see no hostiles."

"They're here somewhere," Carl said. "Stay frosty."

Nine reported in. "I'm across the street, three units west. Everything looks clear, Boss, but you have a shit-ton of civilians on the sidewalk."

Carl noted the lunchtime rush of people on both sides of the four-lane street. He pulled his Glock and screwed on a suppressor, then shoved the weapon as far into a cargo pocket on his thigh as it would go. He left the limo and approached the café entrance. Dressed in black combat pants and boots with a black T-shirt, he held the pistol grip of the Glock pinned to his pant leg so people wouldn't notice. He held the grenade in his left hand, ready to pull the tab.

He shouldered his way through the throng of people toward the door and found it unlocked, though the neon CLOSED sign was lit in red. A quick glance left and right showed him no one seemed to be giving him any undue attention. He entered the empty shop and took a seat in the center of the room.

Carl studied the rail-thin man across the table for a moment, then said, "No bodyguards?"

The man shrugged with his hands. "This is a negotiation, not a confrontation."

Koll didn't look European, though Carl had never been to Europe. In fact, he looked American. He dressed American. His voice held no detectable accent. Maybe he *was* American and just owned a European company.

Carl put his Glock on the table, pocketed the grenade, and matched Koll's stance with his hands on the cherrywood tabletop, fingers clasped together.

"My condolences for the loss of your agent. That was not part of the plan."

"I'm not here for you, Koll. I want Rainman. You can give me that information or"—he nodded at his gun—"I can force the information from you, which would actually be my preferred method of…negotiation."

Koll seemed arrogantly nonplussed. The smug look on his face made Carl wonder why the man wasn't more concerned for his safety. He had the feeling Koll had read a dossier on him but hadn't really studied him in-depth.

"You can't kill me. You need what I have to offer," the man said.

"And what is it you're offering?"

"The world is about the few, not the many. It's about the *haves*, not the *have-nots*. It's—"

Carl held up a hand. "Please don't tell me you're some kind of maniacal despot trying to take over the world. I've seen that movie before, many times."

"We're trying to *save* the world. This planet is going to die unless we do something about it, something drastic, something *now*. We can't afford to wait even another year."

Carl wondered who *they* were, what *they* were going to do, and why the president had to die.

"We're offering you a place in the new world." Koll's eyes defocused for a split second, and Carl saw a despot who actually believed with his heart and soul the nonsense he was dispensing.

"You mean the New World Order?"

Koll nodded.

"The internet is blowing up with all that conspiracy bullshit."

"That's fiction," Koll said. "The reality, however, is that the human race is on a path of self-destruction and is going to destroy the planet in the process. Forget about all the newly mutated diseases that are resistant to antibiotics. Forget about the explosion of new cancers. Forget about the constant threat of war and the proliferation of nuclear and biological weapons. Those are important international issues, granted, but the real danger for the human race is unchecked exponential population growth. The world's population will exceed food production capability within fifty years. In eighty years, global warming will have melted the polar ice caps so much that 90 percent of all habitable land will be flooded."

Carl found so much hyperbole in the man's statement, he wanted to lecture him on the difference between fact and exaggeration, between geometric population growth and exponential growth, just as he would lecture a novice engineer or college student. He said, "Well, I've heard the Antarctic Ice Shelf is melting *from the bottom* because of the influx of ocean currents that are now a few degrees warmer than the ice itself. It's because all that warm water is actually flowing beneath the ice. And I agree this is because of global warming due to atmospheric carbon dioxide adding heat to the oceans. But I've heard it'll take more than a hundred years for the global water level to rise by only ten to thirty feet. That's hardly enough to flood the entire planet."

Koll held up a fist for some kind of emphasis. "Eighty-five percent of the world's population lives in or near coastal cities. A thirty-foot rise in the water level will render most of Florida uninhabitable. It will decimate every coastal city on the planet. Populations everywhere along the Pacific Rim and the Atlantic coast will have to relocate. Almost the entire global shipping and cargo transportation infrastructure is built within two miles of our coastlines.

"When that happens, and we think it will happen far sooner than one hundred years, there won't be enough food or space but for a few. Do you want to be part of the *few* or part of the 99 percent that has to fight over scraps?"

Carl laughed. "I'm a Black man in America chasing the goddamn American dream. I'm already part of the 99 percent." *Well, I was until I became a goddamn terrorist and inherited half a billion dollars.*

Koll didn't even seem to hear him. "The result will be every country desperately fighting for survival. We cannot wait for a nuclear war to cull the population because that will leave only a few survivors on a nuclear poisoned planet. We cannot wait for a biological calamity to create a zombie apocalypse. We want to be the *few*, but on a planet that is *not* poisoned."

Hollis Koll looked down at the table and shook his head. When he looked up again, Carl saw sadness and genuine concern in his eyes.

"Mr. Johnson, even if we stop the population growth *today*, artificial food production needed to feed the masses we already have will cause more disease proliferation because of the poor quality of heavily pro-cessed, mass-produced food. If you don't believe that, all you have to do is look at the last fifty-year trend in the epidemic of cancer.

"And even if we stopped global warming *today*, it's too late to reverse the damage to the polar caps. It has already started, and we can slow it down, but we can't stop it. You can believe this or not, but our experts say we will still lose half of all habitable land in fifty years even if we stop global warming *today*. But that's moot since our global industry and the world economies couldn't absorb such a radical technological change anyway, not even if the world governments *could* agree on how to fix all these problems...*today*."

Hollis Koll sat up straighter, and Carl could tell he was coming to his conclusion.

Carl nodded, then focused his most hate-filled glare on the man. "Let me guess. You and your people have a way to fix all this, except you have to kill the president and her daughter...and my son."

Koll seemed to be only partly in the same room. "We have to force a change, Mr. Johnson. Atlas does not answer to the world governments. We *control* them."

"I get it," Carl said. "Atlas runs the shadow government that runs the real US government."

"Atlas *is* the shadow government," Koll said. "We are the conglomerate that controls the largest and most powerful corporations on the planet. Therefore, we control the politicians. Isn't it better if we control the destination of the world on terms that will eliminate the toxic population but preserve nature, so the few who survive can do so in a safe and healthy environment?"

"Sure, unless you're part of the 99 percent. Or unless you're my son. My *dead* son." Carl took a deep breath. "So, I suppose *the few* get to play God and decide who lives and dies?"

"We're not trying to play God, but yes, someone has to do it, or we all will die."

"And it's okay with you that people get murdered on the path of your plan." Carl nodded. "You need to kill the president for this plan to work."

Koll sighed. "Shirley Mallory is no threat to us. Her death is retribution for betraying us."

The words hit Carl like a punch to the gut.

"Yes, Mr. Johnson. Now you understand the futility of your actions. President Mallory is one of us."

CHAPTER 30

K OLL NODDED. "SHE WAS ONE of the few."

"Mm-hmm." Carl snapped a finger. "Hey, where can I find Rainman? Walter Breen?"

"The Contagion was an accidental opportunity Walter Breen fell upon. Despite orders to the contrary, Breen abandoned the long game and launched his own plan to eliminate Mallory. He forgot his place in the master plan, but he remains useful, unlike President Mallory."

Another gut punch.

"Rainman works for you?"

Koll smiled and spread his hands. "What you're feeling right now is complete and utter futility. You can't protect her, Mr. Johnson. Controlling her Secret Service contingent was yet another successful proof-of-concept test, despite Agent Palmer's interference. And as soon as we locate your mercenaries, it will be a simple matter to have them kill her. Or you can join *the few* now. In a few short months, the planet will be a drastically different place. Chicago was just a prelude. You think that experiment was about controlling the police, but it wasn't. If we also control the behavior of the general population, inciting the masses in many large cities around the globe to violence, then the police will have to respond, and we will also control their aggression.

"You see, we've spent two decades equipping police with military weaponry to combat terrorism, and now, we simply have to incite the police to respond to citizen protests and uprisings even more violently.

After a few million people have died, the world's citizens will beg for government protection."

Koll paused as if for special effect, or perhaps he thought Carl should have reached the inevitable conclusion.

Carl had, and it scared him. "And government protection means government control."

Koll nodded. "It means population control. Our projections show that in four months, the entire world's population can be reduced by 87 percent, and in six more months, our goal of 95 percent reduction will be achieved." Koll spread his hands again. "Without nuclear war."

Carl shook his head. "Have any of your one-percenters actually considered the logistics of disposing of 95 percent of the population?" He gave Hollis Koll a hand shrug. "Six and a half billion bodies is a trillion and a half pounds of flesh. You can't burn that much flesh without polluting the whole planet's atmosphere. You can't dump 'em in the ocean, and it would take a landmass the size of half the United States to bury them." He smirked. "And I wonder which of your one-percenters will undertake that massive grunt work anyways. You?"

Hollis Koll chuckled and waved aside Carl's questions. "That's a simple detail of logistics."

"Well, good luck with that, but you cannot have the president."

"We will succeed. This week or next, or maybe next month, you will fall, and then the president will fall. Don't fight us, Mr. Johnson. Pick the winning side of the *few*."

"Well, Mr. Koll, maybe someone else in Atlas will succeed, but it won't be you."

A flicker of doubt crossed Koll's face as Carl grabbed the man's left hand and pulled him across the table. At the same time, he grabbed his belt knife and rammed it lengthwise into Koll's upper arm, under his triceps and flat against the bone. The man screamed and clawed, but Carl had half of the eight-inch combat knife buried *inside* the man's muscle, the metal blade grating against bone.

Koll flailed with his right hand, found the gun, grabbed it, and pointed it at Carl's face. Then he pulled the trigger, but nothing happened.

Carl had no magazine in the weapon because he wanted his enemy to feel fleeting hope dangled in front of him, then yanked away, the same as Carl's government interrogators had done to him. He pulled his knife from Koll's right arm and slammed it down as hard as he could through his arm near the wrist.

The man screamed again and tried to pull free, but the tip of the carbon steel blade was stuck deep in the wood of the tabletop. Carl leaned back in his chair as the man quieted to a whimper. He gazed down at the top of Koll's head as he lay sprawled across the table and sobbed. Then the man's cell phone began to ring.

"Maybe that's your boss." Carl stood and reached over the table to the smartphone hooked to Koll's belt. He yanked it from its holster, then examined the display. It read, "Unknown." Carl swiped the display to connect the call, then touched the speaker symbol.

"Ex-Vice President Walter Breen." Carl growled the name. "Or should I say Rainman?"

To his surprise, the young voice that emanated from the speaker was not Rainman's. "Please don't kill my brother."

Brother? Wizard's research indicated nothing about family.

"My name is Grainger Koll." The man had a gentle voice, almost feminine. It wasn't the voice of evil or international intrigue and murder. "Hollis can be a bit cocky at times, but he doesn't know you the way I do. What can I do? What can I give you to keep you from killing him?"

"I want Rainman."

"Rainman is no longer relevant."

"So you say."

"Hollis told you the truth in that Rainman works for Atlas. However, he has become a liability."

Interesting, Carl thought. *They're listening and probably watching.*

"Hollis said Rainman remains useful."

"I did not inform Hollis of my decision to terminate Walter Breen. The way he completely botched the Chicago operation and his choice of assassin to engage you was unacceptable."

"I don't believe you," Carl said, though he *did*, in fact, believe the voice. Grainger didn't sound like *part of* Atlas. He sounded like a man who *controlled* Atlas.

"I know, but that doesn't change the fact. The former vice president has been confined to his office in Manhattan. I have a specialist en route to administer his…heart attack."

"That's not acceptable!" Carl pretended to be the deranged narrow-minded terrorist the public believed him to be, growling into the phone. "Nobody kills him but me."

"I can arrange that, but you'll have to spare my brother's life."

Carl pretended to contemplate for a moment, then said, "Agreed. What is Rainman's location?"

Grainger gave it.

"Very well. I'm on my way. ETA, three hours. If Rainman is not there, we'll have this discussion again. I'll find you, wherever you are."

"I doubt that, but Rainman will be secured, pending your arrival. And, of course, you realize we will blame this dastardly deed on the American Terrorist."

Carl didn't end the call. He wanted Grainger to hear his brother scream again as he yanked the combat knife from his wrist. He wiped the blade on Hollis's raw silk shirt, leaving a deep red smudge on the beige material at the shoulder to match the growing red stain on his sleeve. Then he sheathed the knife. He stuck the smartphone in the man's shirt pocket, grabbed the whimpering heap by the back of his expensive shirt, and manhandled him toward the front door.

"Coming out," Carl said.

Eight replied, "All clear."

Nine added, "Clear."

Eighteen added, "All clear. No threats."

"They're watching from somewhere," Carl said. "Stay tight."

At the door, Carl paused long enough to slam a full clip into the hand-grip of his Glock. Then he opened the door and shoved the wounded man ahead of him. He kept his Glock pinned against his leg, ready for action. Six steps later, they stood at the armored limousine.

Koll hissed through clenched teeth, "We're the same, Mr. Johnson."

"No, we're not. You're a wannabe power broker who pays thugs to kidnap and kill people. You and your brother think having a lot of money and aligning yourself with powerful politicians gives you the right to use and discard people like trash. You think that makes you untouchable."

"We're both survivors, Mr. Johnson. You should be asking yourself which team you want to be on—the few or the many."

"I'm on my own team, and the only reason you're still breathing is because I want Rainman dead more than I want you dead. I don't believe for a second that Rainman works for you and your insignificant brother. And good luck with conquering the world. Many have tried. But if Rainman's not where Grainger says he is, you'll see me again. I promise you that."

He shoved the man away, with Koll clutching his bloody arm, and stepped into the limo, certain that Grainger had heard all of his rant.

Head fake.

Two hours later, the Gulfstream landed at LaGuardia just long enough for Carl to get off before continuing west so the three mercs could meet up with Merc Three's team. He got into another armored vehicle, this one a black Cadillac limo with darkly tinted windows and government plates, and was escorted by one of McGrath's heavily armed fast-response teams in two separate SUVs, one front and one rear. Half an hour later, he and his escorts arrived at the address given as the location of the sequestered Rainman. It was the same address Carl and Palmer were initially headed to only a day earlier before they were redirected to separate missions—Palmer to rescue the president, and Carl to rescue the Chicago police officer and his family.

This time, there was no stealth in Carl's approach to the office building. McGrath's black-clad troopers moved to secure the side and rear entrances with their imposing black machine guns. There were dozens of pedestrians on the sidewalk, but like Moses parting the sea, the flow of humanity broke around the armed government troops.

A government agent remained in the driver's seat of the SUV while Carl and two of McGrath's commandos approached the main entrance. With the business end of his Glock pointed at the ground in front of him, Carl approached the solitary man standing in front of the building entrance. He was a big guy, a bodyguard, and stood with his feet shoulder-width apart and his hands clasped in front. He wore a gray two-piece suit over a white button-down shirt with the neck open. He was a light-skinned Black man, bald, with blue eyes and neatly trimmed sideburns that merged into a narrow beard. He looked more like a GQ model than a corporate mercenary despite the small wireless mike attached to his left ear.

The guard said, "The one you seek is secured on the thirty-seventh floor. No one will resist."

He spoke with an accent, maybe French, maybe African. He'd seen combat, Carl could tell. He was a cool customer and didn't bat an eye at all the hardware pointed in his general direction.

Carl nodded. "You have support inside?"

"Only inside the lobby and on the thirty-seventh floor."

"Have your men in the lobby disarm and exit now. Those upstairs stay in place until I get up there."

The guard relayed his instructions, and two similarly dressed men pushed slowly through the brass-framed ornate glass door and stopped next to their partner.

Carl stepped aside and said, "You should probably leave."

The three men got into a silver sedan parked in front of the black SUVs and drove off.

The tech agent on the government team held his wrist up, showing Carl a building schematic on a flexible screen attached to his forearm. "There are two stairwells and two elevators. Recommend we lock down the elevators and—"

"Ordinarily, I would yield to your tactical judgment," Carl said. "But our enemy doesn't fear us. I can't explain it, but to them, we are gnats on the back of an elephant. They sit somewhere else across town or across the globe, sipping cognac and watching us on a monitor. Rainman is their pawn, but I've misled them into thinking I believe they work for him. They think I've tricked them into sacrificing their leader, so let's continue that illusion. Let them think killing Rainman is my endgame."

The tech guy nodded. "I agree if they want to kill us, it's a simple matter to set explosive charges in the stairwells and elevators."

Carl shook his head. "They won't do that. They need to try to follow us in the hope that we'll lead them to the president. I will take the elevator up alone. You and your men secure the ground floor. I should be back shortly."

Carl boarded the first available elevator and emerged on the thirty-seventh floor. He locked the elevator open, and the alarm echoed in the hallway. There were two penthouse offices on that floor, one to the left and one to the right. Two armed guards dressed like the ones on the first floor stood by the frosted glass door of the office on the left. Their posture was relaxed, and their short-barrel machine guns were hanging at rest by their shoulder straps. Carl approached the pair and head-nodded behind him.

"Take the elevator down, but you should probably leave your weapons up here. There are half a dozen trigger-happy government agents down there."

They'd clearly been coached on their exit strategy because both men disarmed without protest and left on a different elevator. Carl tried the doorknob and found it unlocked, so he stepped into the office. The door hissed closed behind him.

The former vice president sat at the far end of an expensive mahogany conference table large enough to seat two dozen executives. As Carl walked around the table toward him, he gazed out the floor-to-ceiling windows at the cloudless blue sky. Far below, thousands of cars clogged the streets, and thousands more people packed the sidewalks, completely unaware of the matrix they toiled all their lives in while mindlessly serving the whims of the corporate power brokers like those Rainman worked for.

Rainman stood as Carl stepped up beside him. He was about the same height as Carl, maybe a dozen years older. Carl knew him to be a former military officer forty years ago, but he'd long ago lost any form of physique remotely recognizable as military. He was round in the paunch and carried fifty pounds of extra flab inside his expensive blue pinstripe suit. The man was silent, seeming to understand there was nothing he could say to get out of his current predicament.

Carl stood right in front of the man. He could see the fear and finality in his eyes. He wasn't trying to intimidate him, but he knew the emptiness in his own eyes that were completely devoid of emotion was eating at the insides of the former power broker.

Finally, the man said, "Can there be a peaceful understanding between us?"

Carl shook his head. "No understanding. No peace."

"I have information. The people I work for… They are still vulnerable because—"

Carl held up his hand. "Deflection serves no purpose here. The Koll brothers already tried that. You're important to them, so they tried to make me think you work for them and their corporate interests. This makes your pending death all the more satisfying to me. You see, I believe *they* work for *you*. People always tend to think corporations are evil, but they're not. They are run by evil people like you. Unfortunately, I can't kill every evil person on the planet whose corporation supports a piece of shit politician. But face it, Rainman, a corporation didn't kidnap the president's daughter and infect her with the Contagion. A corporation didn't try to kill the president twice. *You* did that.

"Walter Breen, you set in motion a sequence of events that got my son killed. You used a sixteen-year-old child as a weapon of mass destruction to kill a quarter of the sitting government." Carl grabbed Breen by his tie. "I may not be able to kill this Atlas Corporation, but I *can* kill you."

He pushed the man hard against the window wall behind him, then stepped back to the conference table. He set his Glock on the tabletop and grabbed the chair the man had sat in. It was a heavy black leather appliance that sat on a five-wheel base. He spun around with the chair, and on the second full turn, he let the heavy chair fly at Rainman.

The man moved surprisingly fast for his size and ducked under it. Otherwise, he would have preceded the chair through the now-shattered window and down thirty-seven floors to the concrete sidewalk.

Carl's ears popped as pressure from the wind racing around the upper floors of Manhattan skyscrapers invaded the office. Instantly, he could hear the drone of street-level city noise, a cacophony of engine sounds and the nonstop blaring of horns. Rainman straightened, then Carl grabbed his gun and approached. He placed the barrel of his weapon against his chest. The elder politician stuck out his chin defiantly, apparently accepting his fate.

Carl wanted to shoot the man, but he realized how desperately he wanted the man alive and fully aware for the next few seconds. He shoved his arm with the gun forward and forced Rainman out the window.

And then the man was gone.

He stepped forward, braced against the wind, and watched his nemesis flail all the way down. Then the man hit the sidewalk in the empty space near the government SUVs with a splash of red.

Carl backed away from the window, feeling an intense dissatisfaction with Rainman's demise. He was unworthy of such a fast and painless dispatch. Sure, he'd spent the last ten seconds of his life scared shitless, likely screaming his guts out during his terrifying fall, but Carl had wanted to punish him more. He wanted him to hurt more. He wanted him to truly feel some of the agony he'd caused other people. But he'd been forced to put his own needs, desires, and hatred aside.

For the president.

And now, the last piece of his head fake had to be played. He spoke into the air, knowing his enemies were somehow listening. "Wizard, is the president secure?"

"Affirmative, Boss."

"Good. What's Aaron McGrath's position?"

"Huh?"

"Off-grid? What do you mean, he went off-grid? Find him!"

"Um…I'm not following you, Boss. He's on this channel."

McGrath's voice said, "Go with it, Wizard."

Carl added, "McGrath probably figured once I dispatched Rainman, I'd be coming for him. He knows he has to answer for my son's death."

McGrath said, "My men tell me Rainman is dead."

Carl stepped over to the window and looked down. "That mission is accomplished. He's a splotch on the sidewalk far below me right now." He continued the pretend conversation. He wanted to paint a picture for Grainger Koll that he was a revenge-seeking man wanting to tie off loose ends. First Rainman, then McGrath.

Grainger Koll no doubt knew from Rainman that Carl blamed the TER director for the death of his son. McGrath had intentionally laid low for the last few months, and their OPSEC protocols had masked the government man's involvement in Carl's operations. TER agents were involved, but Carl had inadvertently created the illusion that McGrath was on the run.

"Relocate all our assets and mercs to my fortified ranch in southern Mexico ASAP, and deploy all defensive packages. I want antiaircraft guns and antimissile batteries armed and ready. Put everyone on-site on a twenty-four-hour war footing. DEFCON 1 everywhere. I want around-the-clock drone coverage too."

"Um, okay, Boss."

"That's right. We need to *find* him first. Now that Rainman is dead and the president is safe, that man is our top priority. He may try a counterattack, but he'll have to bring an entire army if he wants to take us down."

Wizard said, "I assume you're misdirecting listeners, and by *that man,* you are referring to Grainger Koll."

"Correct. When he comes, I'm prepared to escalate again."

McGrath added, "Coating your knife blade with the same isotope they injected into President Mallory was a shrewd move, Mr. Johnson. It's in his bloodstream for the next three days, and we are tracking him now. He's on a private jet that just left Newark. His destination is Europe."

"Let me know when you have his location. I want to hit him first, before he hits us. Meanwhile, everyone, go off comms. Tell the TER agents I'm coming down in the elevator, then I want complete radio silence until we have that man's location. I have a nasty surprise in store for him, and it's something he won't see coming in a million years."

CHAPTER 31

SENIOR ADMINISTRATOR THADDEUS LEAK KNOCKED on the metal doorjamb of Grainger Koll's office and stepped in with a tablet cradled in his left arm. "It took the better part of a whole day, but I found the civilians," he said when both Koll brothers looked over at him. "Well, I found most of them, anyway."

Leak crossed the threshold between the subterranean bunker's control room and Grainger's office. He swiped an icon on his tablet as he walked that put his view up on the wall monitor. Grainger and Hollis sat at the small conference table, so Leak stood at the end of the conference table to their left and faced the monitor, then talked them through what he'd found. "This is a private ranch about thirty miles west of Taos in New Mexico. We tracked their helicopter from—"

Grainger held up a palm. "Never mind all that. What makes you think they're there?" He stood and stepped over next to Leak and also faced the monitor. Leak sensed Hollis didn't want to be left out as the man stood and walked over to Leak's left. The wounded man seemed to breathe with loud gasps, and his eyes were glassy from the massive amount of painkillers he was taking, but Leak decided not to ask him if he was okay when he saw a look of pure evil in his eyes.

"What are you looking at?" Hollis hissed.

"Nothing." Leak turned back to the monitor.

Grainger bent forward at the waist and peered across the front of Leak. "You okay, Hollis? You don't look so good."

Hollis's left arm was in a sling, and he massaged his bandaged upper arm with his left hand.

"I'm making a mental list of all the ways I can fuck up Carl Johnson's life once we eliminate the president."

"Or before," Grainger added. He gestured at Leak. "You were saying?"

Leak made another swipe, and the monitor showed metallic reflections of light from a poorly camouflaged plane. "They attempted to hide the Twin Otter with netting and tree branches."

"Show me more."

He hit more keys, starting a slightly grainy video from a high-altitude spy plane showing the civilians moving about a log cabin. One armored mercenary was always visible near the cabin, and three others had guard duty on the perimeter of the ranch.

Grainger stood. "How soon can we get a mop-up team out there?"

Leak tented his eyebrows. "Sir, it's clear they chose this ranch because they know the territory. They're likely well-armed and have every advantage imaginable. A mop-up team is unlikely to be sufficient."

Grainger smiled and said, "I meant a team for mop-up after the cruise missiles take out the ranch house."

"Oh."

"Is everybody there?"

Leak looked down for a moment. "We're not sure. We haven't seen any indication that Officer Bonhardt is there. His family is, for sure, and so is Agent Cummings's family."

"My guess is Carl has the cop sequestered somewhere, but we'll find him later. It troubles me that only four mercenaries are on-site."

"Four that we can see."

"You're implying the rest are intentionally in hiding."

"It fits Johnson's tactical playbook. He likes to create disinformation."

"Johnson is a former engineer. He's undoubtedly found a way to shield her from our satellite sensors, so she could be anywhere." Grainger paced his small office, examining the featureless concrete ceiling for a few moments. Then he waved a hand at Leak's tablet. "That means this is all a sham. Maybe they left the plane partly visible so we'd find it. Maybe they'll have a counteroffensive in place. Maybe they have an escape plan. Johnson is known for elaborate head fakes."

"Or," Leak added, "maybe it's exactly what it appears to be. Maybe they have limited personnel because Johnson and the rest of his team are somewhere else, hiding and protecting the president. What if…"

Grainger Koll stopped pacing. "Go on. Speak your mind. This is important."

Leak shrugged. "He's a masterful tactician, and Rainman always thought he was a deep-cover operator. And he's always been several steps ahead of us. Have you considered that he'd use these civilians as a distraction…as bait? His primary mission has always been to save the president."

"Bait? No, he wouldn't…" He shook his head. "No, absolutely not! You think he's been pretending to care about the civilians to distract us?"

Leak shrugged again. "Clearly, there was a strategic gain to saving Cummings because she's on his team now."

"There's no way he could have predicted that outcome. No way he could have predicted I'd send a team after her."

"Maybe he simply took advantage of the opportunity. And maybe he figured out the cop is immune to the Chicago experiment," Leak said. "Maybe he's just protecting the family so the cop will cooperate and help figure out what we're doing. Same with Agent Cummings's family. After all, he did order a drone strike on his own agent to kill our soldiers. It fits." The technician shrugged again. "In addition, Randal Cunningham, Johnson's close friend, has gone off the radar, and he doesn't appear to be at this ranch." Leak pointed at the monitor. "That man's a brilliant problem solver, known in the government contractor world as the Thinking Machine. With the president hidden, this guy can help Johnson concentrate on our weapon."

Grainger Koll paced the room again, but his gaze was a thousand miles away. "Okay," he said, turning to face Leak. "Let's rethink everything we thought we knew about Johnson."

"Okay." Leak nodded. "Johnson said over his comm that his next target was McGrath, and he told his people to get defenses in Mexico ready for an assault."

Grainger nodded. "Which is why we sent Admiral Montmarkle's carrier group south. So, what if he's not at any of his estates?"

Leak said, "So we waste a few cruise missiles." He ended the comment with another shrug that included his entire upper body.

"That's a small price to pay to deny Johnson future sanctuary down there if he survives our next assault." Grainger took a deep breath, feeling energized by the direction of their conversation. "Okay, so what if Johnson isn't really hunting McGrath?"

"What if they're working together? Hell, what if Johnson didn't *recruit* Agent Palmer after the Contagion like we thought? What if she was assigned to him...*by Aaron McGrath!* All this time, we thought President Mallory was giving Johnson government assets."

"That's a dangerous thought, Thad. If Johnson and McGrath are working together, then we need to seriously *and quickly* adjust our strategy." He rubbed his chin. "The only place on the planet we're *not* searching for McGrath is actually on Johnson's estates."

Leak said, "What if he's directing ops from one of Johnson's estates?"

"Very well, have the admiral accelerate her timeline. Target *all* of Johnson's estates immediately with cruise missiles. Decimate them all. We'll never know if we actually kill McGrath, but still..." Grainger nodded as if to himself. "And ignore the civilians at the ranch."

"Well," Leak countered. "If I may?"

Grainger nodded.

"We don't know what Johnson is thinking, but if we ignore the ranch, then we tip our hand that we see through Johnson's deception."

Grainger smiled a sinister grimace that never quite reached his eyes. "Brilliant. We employ a head fake of our own."

Leak nodded. "We go in heavy. Don't let Johnson think we know the civvies are just pawns to him."

"Good. Have the admiral dispatch a cruise missile to the ranch, then send in a ground team. How long?"

"The team can be assembled and air-dropped nearby in under six hours."

"Good. Time the missile strike just before the insertion on the ground by the mop-up team. Two dozen men ought to be sufficient to handle four mercs and half a dozen civilians. Make it look good, Mr. Leak—assault rifles, RPGs, hand grenades, flamethrowers, miniguns, tear gas, food, and water for a two-day siege. The whole package."

"Yessir."

"Wait!" Grainger looked at Thaddeus Leak, then at his brother. "Johnson will expect a cruise missile because we've used that tactic before. So he'll make sure his people are ready for that. I want the admiral to send two missiles—no, *three*. Then the ground team will hit them again and again. Shock and awe, Thaddeus." Grainger pointed at the monitor. "We'll overwhelm them with massive and constant force." Then, almost as an afterthought, he said, "And make sure the team is equipped with anti-drone missiles. And antimissile missiles, too, in case they launch at our forces or cruise missiles. That's the kind of thing Johnson would do. Even if he's not there, he won't let his people just sit and wait for us to strike."

Thaddeus Leak cradled his tablet again and headed back to the command center, but he paused in the doorway when the device beeped. "Well, how about that," he said as he consulted the screen. "I just found Carl Johnson and the president."

"Where?" When Grainger looked at his technician, he saw a mixture of fear and amazement in the man's eyes…and a hint of respect.

"You're not going to like this, sir."

CHAPTER 32

OUTFITTED IN HER BLACK HARD-SHELL combat armor, former FBI Special Agent Lenore Cummings led her mother and daughter, as well as the Bonhardt family, from the old propeller cargo plane known as the Twin Otter toward the log cabin. The rear of the civilian detachment consisted of the airplane pilot and Mercs Six, Sixteen, and Seventeen.

The pilot had made a quick deceleration landing, literally using barely a hundred feet of the dirt road connecting the ranch to the paved road known as US 285. They were roughly thirty miles west of Taos, New Mexico, and twelve miles south of Tres Piedras, a town so small it barely registered on a map. The pilot wrangled the plane off the road, and the entire gaggle worked to camouflage the plane with shrubs and netting.

Lenore approached a confident-looking woman standing next to the cabin with a Mossberg autoloader shotgun cradled in the crook of her left arm. A battered old red pickup sat beside the cabin. Lenore noted a sizable greenhouse beside the cabin and a half-buried structure that she recognized as a smokehouse for curing and smoking meat for long-term storage.

"We mean you no harm," Lenore said. Her PDW was prepped and ready, though it was still pointed at the ground.

"Sista, if I thought you meant me harm, most of you would be dead already."

"Sounds like something Carl would say."

The woman looked every bit of the sixty-seven years Carl gave as her age, hardened by many years of frontier life. Her gray hair was well kept but frizzled, and her face was leathered from sun exposure. She wore beige corduroy pants over trail boots and a gray long-sleeve thermal shirt under an unbuttoned blue sleeveless shirt. Lenore could tell she was the real deal—a *prepper*, just as Carl had said. The woman lived out in the wilderness, completely off-grid and apparently ready for the zombie apocalypse or EMP or whatever global disaster might envelop the country. But she wasn't prepared for what was coming. She wasn't prepared for Carl Johnson's war.

Lenore said, "Nice truck." The red four-by-four pickup had a couple of rust holes and some impact dents, and it featured four oversized mud tires, an essential feature for poor-weather off-road mobility.

"Ol' Big Red is gettin' a bit long in the tooth, but she still gets me to and fro."

"Ma'am, this would be a good time to jump in Big Red and leave. We're expecting visitors…of the unfriendly kind. You don't want to be here when they arrive."

"Leave? Pffft! That ain't happenin'." She turned and waved the group to follow. "Come on inside, and I'll put some coffee on." Lenore and her team followed, and the woman said, "I'm Rebecca. You know, I haven't seen Carl since long before his kid died. Ever since he got wrapped up in all this terrorist bullshit, I figured he'd come knocking at my door one day to lay low. Didn't figure he'd send a bunch of civvies."

"You assume we're with Carl."

"I watch the news. You're wearing the same kind of armor he used to take care of that business in Chicago." She waved Lenore silent, even though she faced away. "Nobody else in the northern hemisphere has this kind of armor. Did he tell you where he got that armor?"

"He said the Peru black market."

"And did he say who procured the armor for him?"

"No, he did not."

"Well, I'm glad he respected my privacy."

Lenore paused on the wood planks forming the front porch of the cabin. "So, you're an arms dealer?"

"Hardly, but I have connections throughout South America from my previous career with the State Department." Rebecca entered the cabin. "And if you're expecting company, maybe I can help."

Lenore was about to explain again that Rebecca wasn't ready for what was coming, but then she stepped through the doorway. She stopped so suddenly that the line of followers literally bumped into her.

"Well, damn!"

The outside of the cabin was a pitched-roof rustic log construction, but the inside walls, floor, and ceiling were reinforced with concrete. The edge of the wall near the doorway looked six inches thick and reinforced with rebar. The structure could withstand any assault short of a tank, explosives, or missiles. But that's not what caught her attention.

Mounted on the left wall was a pegboard with metal hooks and brackets like one would find in a garage. One bracket held an RPG with its ordnance loaded and ready. On another bracket hung an old-school 50-cal single-shot rifle with a tripod attached. A couple shotguns, three assault rifles, and half a dozen handguns in a rope bag finished out the wall of weapons.

"Trouble, Boss?" Merc Sixteen peeked his head in the doorway when Lenore stepped sideways. "Well, okay then," he said over Lenore's shoulder. "That can do some damage. Pretty impressive for a civvie. Of course, Atlas will plow through this cabin in five seconds flat after they discover it's bulletproof, but it's a good start."

Rebecca said, "It's going to be a tight fit for everyone since it's only four hundred square feet, but at least I have an indoor bathroom. The shower runs on rainwater runoff from the roof, and it's lukewarm at best. Most days, it's not even that. I sure hope you brought your own food, water, and supplies. I keep a six-month supply of provisions for one person, but a dozen folks will rip through it in a few days."

Sixteen nodded. "Yes, ma'am. We brought everything we need." He looked at Lenore. "Boss, if it's okay with you, me and the boys will set up our defensive placements."

Rebecca said, "Before you do that, let me show you the bunker. Might make a difference in your plans."

"That's okay," Lenore said with a smile that she hoped wasn't condescending. "We saw it outside." It was a small compartment attached to the backside of the cabin with large angled double doors like she'd seen on tornado shelters.

"Oh, no, Honey. That's just the decoy closet with some canned goods in it. That's a head fake."

"Now I *know* you've spent time with Carl."

"He spent some time up here with me a ways back, so I got to know him quite well." Rebecca stepped over to the old woodstove, removed a teakettle from one of the two burners, and poured the steaming coffee into a mug on the table in front of a couch-bed. "You know he's a pretty decent chess player, right?"

She retrieved an ash-covered miniature shovel against the wall and inserted the handle into a fitting on the back of the stove, then leaned her weight into the lever. The stove, its logs still burning inside, and the mismatched ceramic tiles covering the floor in front, all pivoted to the left. The iron bar supporting the stove at the pivot point was encased inside the exhaust pipe that extended up through the ceiling. The pivoted stove revealed narrow steps into the darkness under the cabin floor.

"Follow me and be mindful of splinters."

Cummings said, "Sixteen, you're with us. Six, Seventeen, get everyone comfortable."

Rebecca descended first. A single low-watt bulb lit the narrow stairwell from the bottom, casting shadows on everyone following Rebecca. The rotted wood walls looked like they could cave in at any moment, and dirt that had crept between the boards now covered the concrete steps.

"And don't worry. Everything down here is reinforced concrete too. The wood is just for show."

Lenore said, "Another head fake?"

"Uh-huh."

Sixteen said, "I like this woman."

Lenore said, "How do you know Carl?"

"I met him about fifteen years ago at an art gallery over in Taos. I'd just relocated from New York, and I told him I came out here to build an off-grid sanctuary. It was right after Nine-Eleven. He just rolled his eyes when I told him the government was eventually going to take all our rights and freedoms. Back then, I thought they were going to come and take our guns, but now I realize they were all along just planning to take our internet. With that, they control everything. Everybody using tech is traceable."

Lenore chuckled.

Rebecca led the way down the steps, talking over her shoulder. "That's why I built that little storage unit you saw on the back of the cabin. It's kind of a fake storm shelter. I always told Carl to let them see what they want to see, and make them find what you want them to find."

"I get it. You want intruders to find the small bunker in back of the cabin so they think they've found all your supplies and then leave."

"And I want them to think this wood door is flimsy enough to break through—"

"Because the walls look like the dirt is held in place by rotten boards," Sixteen said.

"And when they force the door open, they find this."

Cummings saw a second concrete door behind the flimsy wooden door. A hand grenade was hooked to a pin in the top-center of the concrete door, and the grenade's pin was wired to an unconnected hook and chain that could be connected to the wooden door. Opening the flimsy wood door would pull the pin and kill whoever was standing at the base of the stairs and anyone else in the stairwell.

"Won't be enough time to retreat back upstairs."

Rebecca hauled the concrete door open with some effort and continued down yet another concrete stairwell to the left. These stairs went twice as deep as the first until Lenore and her crowd passed through another concrete door into a bunker room as big as the topside cabin. The walls were lined with metal shelves of cans, bottles of water, food supplies, and blankets.

Rebecca waved her arm around the room. "We're about fifty feet below ground, and it stays a nice sixty degrees year-round. When the party starts, we'll just wait them out down here."

Lenore nodded. "It's a good start."

Sixteen added, "And unless they have ground-penetrating radar, they won't know this room is here."

"Well," Rebecca added. "Carl made sure I filed electronic floor plans of the cabin with the County to get a building permit. But we accidentally left the bunker off the design."

"The next wave will figure it out pretty quick when the grenade goes off behind the fake door," Lenore said. "But chances are low they'll bring a bunker buster with them."

Sixteen said, "They'll figure out how to get in here, and I'm sure they'll have enough explosives with them. They're not going to quit."

"In that case, we use the escape door." Rebecca pointed at the far wall of shelves. She hauled on a hidden handle, and the whole wall opened on well-greased hinges. The shelves perfectly dovetailed precisely with those on the wall.

Sixteen said, "Your attention to detail is amazing. I'm guessing you built this all by yourself?"

Rebecca beamed. "Not bad, eh? But this was as far as I could get before I ran into boulders."

The path beyond the door was unfinished, just a dark meandering path between huge boulders. The floor of the path was paved with wood boards.

"You know that gully east of the cabin where the seasonal river runs?" Rebecca asked.

"We saw it from the air."

"This tunnel emerges in the gully, in a small cave carved out by the water flow. After that, we're afoot."

Sixteen nodded. "We're going to need a layered defense in the gully, or they'll bury us out there. And let's park that red truck a mile downstream so we'll have a bug-out vehicle if things get real bad."

"Agreed," Lenore said. She looked at Sixteen. "Get back upstairs, get the lay of the land, and get our defenses set up. I figure it'll take Atlas only a few hours to find us. They have pretty much the same computer and satellite capability we have."

"Copy that. We'll get everything set up, then get everyone trained and practicing escape prep."

Everyone filed up the steps, back to the cabin, but Lenore held Rebecca back. "What's your history with Carl, Rebecca?" she said. "I need to know all the variables."

Rebecca regarded her for a moment. "I told you I met him when I first came out here from New York?"

Lenore nodded.

"Well, that wasn't exactly the way it happened."

A distant look in the woman's eyes told Lenore instantly the kind of trauma she was about to speak about. Because of Carl, Lenore herself was intimately familiar with that kind of trauma.

Rebecca continued, "I came out here with a man, and our relationship deteriorated quickly because he couldn't get work, and I can be kind of…" She pretended to straighten some pressure jars of rations. "Well, he became abusive and…" She stood straight and looked Lenore in the eyes. "No, he just got drunk one night and beat the shit out of me, plain and simple. Then he kicked me out of the house. I vaguely remember wandering along the main gallery road of the Taos Square."

Then she smiled at a fifteen-year-old memory. "I was cold and hungry, bloody and dazed, and I had no coat and no money, no place to go, and no one I could call. I was going to die that night. It was going to be way below freezing. So, I stopped in the doorway of this art gallery and was just looking around for a place on the ground where I could just lay down and die. And then he walked out of the gallery and just stood there looking at me. I was humiliated and filthy. I had bruises and dried blood everywhere. His eyes teared up, and he just unzipped his coat and wrapped me up in a warm embrace, and I cried and cried. He pulled me inside that gallery, and the people… Well, it's Taos. They hugged me and fed me and cleaned me up. They took me to the doctor the next day and got the sheriff to arrest my boyfriend. Carl paid for my attorney and drove up from Albuquerque almost every weekend for a whole year to visit.

"I was useless and depressed because I couldn't get a job and support myself. And Carl… He took care of me. Spent all his savings paying my rent and utilities and food. And paying for this." She waved a hand around the bunker and shrugged. "I asked him why, but he just said he sensed I was a caregiver, and he was taking care of me so I could take care of others. He loaned me the money to build and never asked for it back. Probably knew I could never afford to pay him back. But he never asked for anything. Never required anything of me. He would just say, 'It's what we do for our people when we're able.' "

"So this is you paying him back?"

Rebecca nodded. "I know he's been in trouble recently, so when he called, I didn't hesitate. He said he was sending some people up who needed my help. This is the only kind of help I can give, and he knew I would."

Lenore studied the woman as she spoke. She was slender and strong looking, about five-foot-three and had a full head of silver-gray hair. She looked like a woman who had run away from the trappings of civilized society, like someone who had spent her last fifteen years working the land. Her gaze, though, was rock steady. She wasn't someone who could be intimidated.

An image of the Carl Johnson she knew now flooded Lenore's mind. She tried to equate the savage man she'd helped create with a version of him from fifteen years ago. She tried to picture today's Carl Johnson gently holding a domestic violence victim, caring for her for a year. And suddenly, she *could* picture that. At his core, the same Carl Johnson who kept saving her, her daughter, and the president *was* that younger man. He was the same man who held Lisette and gazed at her with those caring brown eyes. He just had training and weapons now, and he had that dark side—a fully developed killer instinct.

The thought hit Lenore like a sucker punch to the gut. Rebecca's Carl was the same man who had strapped her and Lisette naked to a table and threatened to kill her daughter. The shrink said Lisette had blocked out the trauma of what Carl had done to them. All she remembered was that he saved them from the terrorists. He kept saving them, and now, he was Lisette's hero. She loved him like a protective father she'd never known. The shrink said one day Lisette would remember her ordeal, and when that day came, next year or in ten years, her whole world would come crashing down.

How in the world can I let that man hug my daughter after what he did to us?

Rebecca touched Lenore's arm, making her flinch. "Looks like I'm not the only one with history with him."

Lenore growled under her breath. "It's complicated. Let's get topside." *If he touches my daughter again, he's a dead man.*

Lenore stood on the porch long after nightfall, contemplating their chances of surviving to see the next sunset.

Sixteen strode up. "Hey, Boss. Let me update you."

Lenore smiled in the darkness. Sixteen was the merc who had challenged her ability to lead. The truth was, during her long FBI career, she never desired command or leadership. She *could* lead but always preferred to be investigating crimes. The intellectual work thrilled her, but head-butting with the egos of men did not.

"We're all set up out yonder. Even got the plane camouflaged properly."

"Properly?" Rebecca ended the word with a snort. She stood in the doorway, and Lenore hadn't even realized she'd crept up on her. "Hell, I can practically see half the plane from here…*in the dark!*"

"Half?" Sixteen chuckled. "Well, I don't want 'em to see *that* much."

"Oh my gawd. You actually *want* them to see it, don't you?"

Sixteen shrugged. "We know they're going to find us. If they're coming, it's better they come on our timetable. They probably already have a high-altitude spy plane or a civilian satellite over this part of New Mexico, though I'd opt for the spy plane, one with side-aperture radar. It'll find the plane, despite the darkness, much more easily than a satellite. They'll probably send the plane back over in the morning. I figure we'll have guests tomorrow afternoon."

Lenore nodded. "You practiced the evac?"

"Roger that. When the alarm is sounded, we can get all the civvies down into the safe bunker in four minutes, thirteen seconds."

Lenore grimaced. "How much warning will we get if they send a cruise missile?"

"We put a radar unit up on the mesa two miles west of here. If the cruise missile hugs the ground, we'll get a two-minute, fourteen-second warning, maybe a little more if Carl's missile-defense system works."

"Missiles? You have missiles?" Rebecca said.

Lenore nodded. "Carl layers his responses to threats with multiple reactions and head fakes. Atlas used a military cruise missile on his team before and hurt them badly, so he figures they'll try that again. But if we use radar for inbound detection, they'll just take out our radar, and we'll be blind, so we have passive sonic detectors a couple miles away since a cruise missile tends to be a low flier. When the sonic detectors hear it, we light it up with radar and shoot it down before Atlas can take out our radar."

Rebecca didn't seem impressed. "Yeah, well, what if they have two missiles."

"Ha!" Sixteen slapped his knee. "That's what I said! And you know what he said? 'That's why we'll have a second antimissile battery next to the cabin.'"

Lenore added, "Two minutes isn't much warning. We better pack everyone down in the bunker and keep them there." She looked at Rebecca. "Is that doable?"

Their hostess nodded. "We'll need more blankets. We can't use a heater because the bunker isn't ventilated."

Sixteen waved that comment off. "We have plenty of chemical heat pads to put inside blankets to keep everyone warm for a couple days. We can leave the concrete entry door open until the attack is imminent. We'll keep the woodstove blazing to confuse their heat sensors. They won't know we're not in the cabin."

"Okay," Rebecca said. "A blazing fire is believable this time of year. It gets down into the upper thirties at night."

Lenore agreed. "If a missile hits first, the cabin will be destroyed, and they'll eventually find the stairs down to the bunker. If they send in foot soldiers first, the grenade will take out a couple of them on the stairs."

"Um, yeah, about that," Sixteen said. "A grenade is unreliable really, so I took the liberty of replacing it with C-4."

Sixteen explained the rest of their defenses, and Lenore notched an eyebrow at the boldness of his plan.

"Devious," she said. "That's Carl Johnson kind of thinking. I like it."

CHAPTER 33

G RAINGER KOLL HAD JUST GRABBED his coffee mug and was about to take a sip when Thaddeus Leak gave the latest intel on Carl Johnson's whereabouts. He seethed with anger as he followed Thaddeus Leak back to the control room. Trembling with a sudden irrepressible rage, he flung his mug of coffee against the nearest wall. Brown liquid and shards of glass splattered.

"Fuck!" He paced like a caged lion back and forth across the control room, aware of the nervous glances of his three administrators. Then he turned his face toward the bare concrete ceiling and yelled at the top of his lungs. "*Fuuuuuuck!*" He focused his attention back on Leak. "Where is Admiral Montmarkle's carrier strike group right now?"

A tactical map popped up on the monitor showing a white triangle 250 miles off the coast of Baja California. The ledger next to the CSG9 triangle listed the components of the formidable force—one aircraft carrier, two Aegis cruisers, four Arleigh Burke-class guided-missile destroyers, a tender, and six subs.

The group's speed vector showed the strike force was sailing south at twenty knots. They'd be in an optimal position for the coordinated attack in two hours.

"Get the admiral on the line."

"Right away."

He started to pace the room again. He completed only one circuit when the tech made the announcement. "The admiral is on, Mr. Koll."

Grainger looked at the wall monitor. Piercing blue eyes framed by severe crow's feet in a narrow hawklike face gazed at him.

She spoke first, as was her leadership style. "We'll launch in one-one-two minutes. Intel doesn't reveal which of his estates he's at, so we will hit them all."

"Agreed, but he's not there."

"Excuse me?"

Hollis stepped up beside his brother. "He's not at any of them, Admiral. He fucking played us."

Grainger glanced at his brother. "He played *me*." He looked at the concrete floor and nodded his head, then looked at the monitor again. "He let us believe Aaron McGrath was his next target. Instead, we now believe McGrath may be sequestered at one of Johnson's estates and is actually running their ops. They rightly figured we'd never consider the possibility that they'd be working together, not after what they did to each other eight months ago. But it looks like they've been working together all along."

The admiral narrowed her eyes. "I find that nearly impossible to believe, Grainger."

"That doesn't change the reality. I still want you to continue with the multiple strikes, but launch now. Don't wait for the optimum launch window. And I want you to reverse course immediately. Proceed north at maximum speed."

"Destination?"

Grainger hesitated a moment. "We don't know yet."

That drew a raised eyebrow from the admiral.

Grainger added, "You've seen the comm traffic from the naval yard at San Diego?"

She nodded. "There was a massive fire, but fortunately, it's under control. A fuel pumping station on the north end of the pier exploded. No casualties. Limited damage."

"It was a distraction, compliments of the American Terrorist."

"What makes you think that?"

Grainger Koll looked away briefly, then shrugged. "Because he stole a fucking warship!"

The admiral tented her eyebrows like she didn't believe him.

When she started to speak, he interrupted, "We're still not sure how he did it, but he stole the *USS Grace Hopper*, the first US warship named after a woman."

She gasped, and Grainger Koll saw the first crack in the admiral's stone countenance.

"That's not just a warship." Admiral Janis Montmarkle stood from her chair, and for a moment, Grainger could see nothing above her slender waist. Then she leaned down on her desk, and her face filled the monitor.

In her eyes, Grainger saw real fear.

"Sweet Jesus, Grainger, you want me to engage a *US warship*? A Zumwalt-class guided-missile *stealth destroyer*?"

"I know, Admiral." Koll sighed. "It's nuclear-capable."

"Capable, yes. Armed, no. And that's the *only* thing working in our favor. It just concluded three months of sea trials, so it has no nuclear armaments on board yet." The admiral paused for a moment. "The general public and most of the military believe only three stealth destroyers of this class were built, but there was a fourth, the DDG-1004. It's an advanced prototype, far superior to the other three stealth destroyers in its capabilities and systems. It's basically a combat-capable test bed for new weapons systems. It's the most advanced stealth naval vessel ever commissioned, and it's armed with the most effective offensive and defensive weaponry on the planet.

"It has the radar signature of a sailboat, making it completely invisible to radar outside a thousand yards. With its new bow design, it can cut through the water at thirty-five knots in complete silence, and it can sprint up to the equivalent of fifty-eight miles an hour. We won't be able to find her, much less target her, without a dedicated satellite visual, and that's only if we know exactly where to look. And I'm told all Pac-Fleet space assets are locked down tight."

"I know all this, Admiral." Grainger licked his lips.

Admiral Montmarkle nodded. "There's more, isn't there?"

Koll nodded. "McGrath controls all military space assets," he said.

The admiral shook her head. "So he really is working with the American Terrorist."

Grainger nodded. "There's no way Johnson could have hijacked that ship without highly classified intel and computer codes from someone like Aaron McGrath."

"Goddamnit, Grainger!"

"We're launching a civilian bird from New Mexico within the hour. In two hours, it'll be over the sector of the Pacific where we think that ship might be."

The admiral shook her head. "It will take half the armament *of my entire fleet* to take that ship out, and that's if she *only* plays a defensive game. If the American Terrorist has control of that ship, there's no way he *won't* go offensive. A lot of people are going to die. Do you fully understand that?"

"You have your assignment, Admiral. I don't need to tell you what's at stake. The president is on that ship. Find it and kill it. Kill *her*."

"Easier said than done."

CHAPTER 34

THE PRESIDENT'S HELICOPTER SKIMMED JUST above the waves two hundred miles out to sea, but she was not on board.

President Mallory and her pilot had ejected from the fighter jet that whisked her away from the DC assassination attempt. The jet dipped below radar coverage in the hills of western Oklahoma just as the engines sputtered on empty fuel tanks, and they'd bailed out. They'd been safely retrieved, and Mallory was sealed in a cargo container headed straight west on I-40 to Los Angeles, on a cargo truck that looked like any other on the highway. Randal's overlapping and very fine copper mesh screens were mounted to the inner walls of the container and grounded to the eighteen-wheeler's metal chassis.

The heavy-lift helicopter met them a hundred miles outside of Los Angeles at an abandoned pullout two miles north of I-40, near Barstow. It lifted the cargo container for the four-hundred-mile trip over land and water, staying low partly to avoid radar detection and partly because the cargo was too heavy to maintain any significant altitude.

And the president was still in that box!

The pilot hollered into the open bay. "We have five minutes of fuel remaining, sir! There's no sign of the ship!"

Carl had been stewing on the flaw in his plan for over an hour, and there was absolutely nothing he could do about it. Three hours and fifty-five minutes into the four-hour maximum flight time of the heavily laden chopper, they were well past the point of no return. But that was not the problem Carl had discovered. It was a problem no one had anticipated—not Carl; not Aaron McGrath; not Randal Cunningham, the brilliant Thinking Machine; nor any of the mercs or the helicopter pilots.

The president had to stay inside the container to remain undetected. McGrath had a stranglehold on all military satellites, but there was no guarantee that a civilian satellite hadn't been modified with sensors to detect the isotope in Mallory's blood and launched from California.

According to McGrath, seventeen hours ago, a carrier strike group from the Third Fleet had been moving south, no doubt to engage Carl's several estates, so Grainger Koll had at least fallen for that part of the head fake. But that was yesterday. Atlas had to know by now that the hijacking of the US Navy's newest guided-missile destroyer was connected to Carl and the president. It wouldn't take a rocket scientist to figure out the obvious.

Find the ship, and you find the president.

But the Koll brothers couldn't be sure the president was on board. They wouldn't be certain it wasn't another head fake, and Carl was counting on that. They couldn't order CSG9 or any other military unit to fire on another warship without that certainty of knowledge. That would buy them valuable time for the isotope in Mallory's blood to become undetectable if they could get the president onto and deep inside the *USS Grace Hopper* without exposing her to probing satellites. Randal had come up with an ingenious plan to do that, but now that plan was moot.

Carl assumed all along his deception would be temporary. The Kolls had had over twelve hours to figure out his plan, so he had zero doubt that an enemy satellite was now in a geostationary orbit overhead. It might not be directly overhead, but it was certainly high enough to see the entire parcel of water that the destroyer could have traversed. They probably had the destroyer's position already. They might even have the helicopter's position too.

But that wasn't the critical problem. The cargo container wasn't watertight, and nobody had thought about the possibility of dropping the box in the drink. Now, as the helicopter flew on its last drops of fuel, Carl realized if they had to land in the water, the cargo container holding the president would sink like a rock. They wouldn't be able to get her out in time. Even if they did, she'd be visible to sensors searching for her isotope.

Carl sat uncomfortably in the spacious cabin of the helicopter, still fully outfitted in his armor and ready for instant combat, even after almost four hours of flight time. Except for the two pilots, he was the only person aboard, so he tried to clear his mind. He found himself thinking about Agent Palmer. She'd had sky blue eyes that could either provide comfort or pierce one's soul. He'd been on the receiving end of both emotions. Still, when she smiled or laughed, her nose crinkled up like a little girl. Now she was gone forever, snatched away like his son. He tried to compartmentalize the event like she'd coached him months ago, but in truth, he was emotionally unprepared for the loss. Now, without the stealth destroyer, he was going to lose the president too.

So this is how it ends, Carl thought. *Out in the middle of the goddamn ocean.*

The copilot hollered again. "Visibility is only a couple miles because we're on the deck. If we climb, we can see farther, but that'll cut our remaining flight time in half."

Carl stepped forward to the cockpit. "Tighten your sphincters, guys, and continue with the plan. The ship will either be there or it won't, and there's nothing we can do about that. Besides, McGrath says the damn thing's painted the color of the ocean specifically so it can't be seen until it's right on top of you, kicking your ass."

He put his mind to work on stripping out of his armor with one minute of fuel remaining, jumping out of the helicopter, and swimming to the cargo container to get the president out while the chopper hovered high enough to keep the box from sinking. And as soon as he opened the box, the bad guys would arrive within an hour with a bomber, a missile, or a SEAL team. And that would be that.

"Flare, nine o'clock!" hollered the pilot.

Carl looked out the open port door and saw a red flare arching high in the air. Then it drifted downward. The helicopter banked sharply and headed toward *something.*

He hardly saw the vessel until it was only a mile away. It looked nothing like any destroyer he'd ever seen. Its wake and bow wave were almost nonexistent, though the vessel grew so rapidly in size it had to be moving at great speed. Instead of its bow rising forward out of the water, the front of the vessel looked more like a submarine. Its bow raked severely *back* from the waterline and up to the main deck. There were no masts, deck guns, radio antennae, or rotating radar dishes on the deck. The superstructure had angled sides and was built low to the deck. All the normal radar-reflecting elements on deck had to be housed inside that angled superstructure.

The panels of the ship seemed to reflect the color of the sky and the water, which, Carl knew, was why they hadn't seen the ship until it was close. He wondered how tiny the vessel's radar cross section would be with all those angled panels reflecting radar signals in every direction except back toward searchers.

The copilot rushed into the cabin. From the bulkhead over the door, he unhitched a rolled-up cable ladder and tossed it out.

"If they do an emergency stop right under us, we can drop the container on the aft deck."

Perfect, Carl thought. *Then she can step into the mesh suit Randal designed and walk right into the destroyer, grounded and undetected.* Carl reached to strip out of his restrictive armor, but the copilot shoved him toward the open door.

"No time for that, sir. Out you go!"

Halfway down the cable ladder, Carl saw the water behind the destroyer roil as the vessel slowed quickly, almost to a complete stop under the helicopter. The cargo container thumped down on the deck, completely missing the landing circle and, in fact, landing almost halfway over the edge of the ship.

The helicopter's engine stalled two seconds later.

Dangling beneath the chopper, Carl let go and tumbled across the top of the cargo box.

The chopper fell right behind Carl, smashing the president's container.

CHAPTER 35

LENORE CUMMINGS WAVERED UNSTEADILY ON her feet and tried to make sense of what had happened. She reached out for something, anything, to stabilize the dizziness. She grabbed a slender branch of a sage bush on the bank of the gully's slow-moving stream, but it broke off in her grasp, and she fell to her knees in the water.

She looked around but couldn't see more than a few feet around her. Smoke and dust filled the air, its swirling giving life to the normally invisible air currents that wafted through the forty-foot gully. Her fingers clenched the muddy bottom of the ice-cold stream flowing around her hands and knees. She recognized she was in shock, so she tried to steady her breathing while mentally inventorying her body for injury.

Lenore recalled multiple cruise missiles. Atlas wasn't messing around. They wanted Carl's people dead, no two ways about it. She recalled the tablet view of the attack.

The sonic detector had heard the first missile, and the intercept radar immediately went active. Their defenses destroyed the first inbound cruise missile, and the radar and the launcher had immediately been destroyed by Atlas's drone missiles. Through the tablet, Merc Sixteen had manually commanded their second antimissile battery located by the Twin Otter plane to destroy the drone, and the second cruise missile was neutralized less than a quarter mile away. But Atlas also had a backup—a second antimissile drone that made quick work of the second battery. Then, the high-explosive warhead on the third cruise missile had detonated directly over the cabin. The blast had scraped everything from the earth for two hundred feet in all directions.

It was a glorious air battle, Lenore recalled, and both sides had brought their A-game. Still, Lenore's team fought remotely, safely protected in the underground concrete bunker. They barely felt the ground tremble.

Merc Sixteen had wired dozens of tiny sensors and cameras so they could monitor Atlas's ground progress through the tablet. Most of the devices were destroyed in the blast, but three remained active. He had also set up buried proximity explosives and camouflaged claymores outside the estimated blast range of a cruise missile for the impending ground game.

Lenore recalled watching those hidden explosives claim six Atlas troops in the first wave. More troops, over twenty, had converged around the now-cleared foundation of the cabin and easily found the stairway to the bunker. Four more Atlas troops had been consumed in the stairwell trap. A fifth, who squatted at ground level waiting to lead three more men down into the bunker, had his head neatly cleaved from his body by a piece of shrapnel that blasted out of the stairwell.

Lenore got to her feet and gazed around in the swirling smoke. She saw shadows moving slowly, randomly through the smoke—maybe human, maybe friendly, maybe hostile, maybe hallucinations. Everything she heard was garbled and distant, like at the end of a long tunnel filled with cotton, like her eardrums had been...

The blast. That was it. Because of the booby-trapped entrance to the bunker, the assault team was seen on the mercs' tablet preparing to simply blow up the underground bunker. The remaining men gathered a massive satchel of explosives at the entrance, so Rebecca led everyone out of the bunker through the earthen tunnel and into the gully. Lenore had been framed in the exit when the explosives went off and blasted clean across the narrow gully. She woke up in the creek, and everyone else had scattered.

Now she was starting to hear scattered gunfire and more explosions. It had to be assault team remnants stumbling through the claymores the mercs had hidden in the gully to protect the emergency exit tunnel.

Suddenly, Lenore's hearing cleared, and the scattered distant gunfire erupted into full-fledged gunfights at both ends of the gully. For a moment, she was frozen with indecision. Which way should she go? Where was Lisette?

She crept toward the fiercest gunfire, north of the secret escape tunnel, and soon saw human-shaped shadows moving through the smoke. She aimed her assault rifle but held her fire. Friend or foe?

"Nineteen!" she hollered.

"Seventeen!" said one of the shadows.

"Sixteen!" said another.

"Fifteen!" said a fourth shadow, but that designation was assigned to a merc presently with Carl's team in the Pacific.

That man died in a hail of bullets from Lenore, Sixteen, and Seventeen.

"Status!" Lenore demanded as she moved closer to the others.

Sixteen started to answer, then Lenore spun when she heard a scream behind her that ripped her heart open.

CHAPTER 36

CARL TUCKED AND ROLLED OFF the top of the container split seconds before the belly of the helicopter caved in the top part of the president's container with the metallic crunch of ripping frame girders. As he rolled across the deck, he heard the chopper engine cough, then scream. The pilot must have found a final ounce of fuel in the auxiliary tanks and drove the chopper over the side of the ship.

It plunged into the ocean, the main rotor briefly throwing up mountains of water before the blades were ripped from the shaft by thousands of horsepower trying to drive the blades through unforgiving water. The chain was still connected to the shipping container. The whole box flipped on its side and was dragged, ripping through the safety stanchions and rope at the deck edge, then it plunged thirty feet into the water.

In heroic fashion, President Mallory literally dove out of the container just before it went over the edge. She grabbed onto a ripped safety post just long enough for Carl to run five steps to get to her. He grabbed her wrists as she let go, but she was too heavy to hold, and he went over the side too.

Someone grabbed Carl's ankles. Whoever it was held over three hundred pounds of dead weight in his grip.

To her credit, Shirley Mallory didn't scream. She looked up into Carl's eyes as he clung desperately to her wrists. If she had any doubts that he would sacrifice his own life to keep her alive, those doubts vanished forever in a few seconds of intense eye contact.

Then they were hauled upward, and a few seconds later, they sat facing each other on the deck and gasping for air.

"Well," Carl said as he helped the president to her feet. "That wasn't exactly how I planned our arrival."

"I'll say."

He looked up at the vast blue sky. "They know where we are now, so let's get on with Plan B."

President Mallory was suddenly all business. "I want to talk to the captain of this vessel."

Mercs Three and Twelve stood as well, recovered from hauling them both over the side.

Three said, "The senior staff have been taken to the bridge and are under guard, ma'am. If you'll follow me." They all headed to the nearest bulkhead door. "But first, let's get you into an armored combat suit just in case we come under attack."

"There is no *just in case*," Carl said. "They're going to cripple the ship, then they'll send in a SEAL team with orders to kill everyone."

They detoured to the galley, where all their supply duffels were stored. While the mercs got Mallory suited up, Merc Three said, "A lot has happened since you left DC, ma'am, and not all of it was good."

Carl fitted Mallory's chest and back shell plates into position and tightened Velcro straps. "As you know, the plan was to land the container and have you get into a metallic space suit kinda thing while you were still inside the box. Then we'd have gotten you deep inside the ship undetected. Unfortunately, there's no doubt in my mind they know you're here, so they'll throw everything plus the kitchen sink at us. It's probably already on the way."

They were just about to leave the galley when Carl stopped. "What the hell?"

The others stopped and followed his gaze to a universally recognized emblem on the galley wall.

Carl said, "The Navy serves Starbucks coffee?"

"Damn!" Three pounded an armored fist on the bulkhead emblem. "I need to reenlist."

"To the bridge," Carl said. "Three, tell the team the plan has changed."

"Copy that." Three touched his earpiece and made the announcement to the other mercs on the ship as he led the charge through the empty corridors of the destroyer. The president followed Three, then Carl and Twelve brought up the rear.

Carl said, "Three, what's your team complement?"

"Besides me and Twelve here, Eight is on computer control duty in the ops center below deck. Five, Seven, Ten, Eleven, and Fourteen are positioned throughout the ship, ready to repel boarders. Nine and Fifteen are manning the engine room. And, man, you should see the engine room on this boat. It's like a spaceship down there. Everything's computer controlled. Eighteen is on the bridge guarding the officers."

The *USS Grace Hopper* was the first naval warship Carl had ever been on, and it looked nothing like he expected. In the movies, all the navy ships had battle-gray interiors. The inside of this one was white, but not stark white. Everything was clean. There were no smudges on the walls, no dings in the metal doorways or bulkheads from accidental impacts.

Mallory said, "Are you telling me Navy SEALs will kill other Navy men and women?"

Carl replied, "Military personnel will blindly follow orders, not knowing their leaders are traitors, and they'll do it without question because that's the way the military works. They'll be told this crew has been compromised or that terrorists have taken over the ship, which actually is a fact. Or they'll be told you're an impostor. Once they kill you, they'll sink the ship. So whoever attacks this ship or tries to board us, they will simply become my enemy. No question, I will kill them." Carl glanced in an open doorway and saw a row of curtained bunks stacked two-high, maybe eight or ten to a room. "Three, any problems grabbing the ship?"

"Negative." He climbed steep deck stairs slow enough so Mallory could match his pace. "Your plan was flawless, Boss. Merc Fourteen is a demolitions expert, and his team set charges on the northern-most fuel substation of the San Diego port for maximum visual effect and minimal damage. The explosion just before midnight was spectacular. Everyone not on duty was awoken from a deep slumber, no doubt. Every ship at dock put personnel on emergency damage control duty. Setting a tug on fire and nudging it toward a carrier was a nice touch too. Kind of enhanced the sense of urgency, if you know what I mean, though the carrier was never in any real danger.

"I'm not sure where McGrath found a minisub on such short notice, but it got Twelve's team to the pump station and then delivered us onto the *USS Grace Hopper* undetected. It was Friday night, and according to McGrath, the ship had returned for resupply from extended sea trials, so most of the crew was on shore leave for the weekend. Of its 146 crewmembers, only forty-five were on the ship, and most of those joined damage control and rescue parties immediately after the explosion. My force of seven faced only sixteen crewmembers, none remotely prepared to handle us.

"We got Wizard on and off in fifteen minutes flat, and he reprogrammed the crew's cipher keys to the computer system. We're locked in, and they're locked out. We got the ship underway undetected, thanks to the explosions and confusion. Without running lights, the ship's nearly invisible at night." Merc Three led the way up another set of steep stairs to the bridge deck, then stopped and faced Carl. "As you know, Director McGrath informed us that every naval vessel has a contingent of marines for security. We were prepared to engage them, but we still used non-lethals as ordered—rubber bullets and Tasers. The four marines caused no problems, but we did have one casualty." He looked at Carl and the president. "When we hit the bridge, a young ensign on duty took a rubber bullet in the eye. Killed her instantly."

"That's unfortunate, but you did well," Carl said. "I thought there would be more casualties." He'd yielded to McGrath's demand for no killing but privately told Three to do whatever it took to secure the ship. "Randal and Officer Bonhardt?"

Three nodded. "After you picked up the president's container, Fourteen delivered Randal Cunningham and Officer Bonhardt to a location in Marina Del Rey given by McGrath. I wasn't briefed on their destination after that. Then Fourteen met us in San Diego, along with your crew from the Philadelphia op."

"So you don't know where Aaron is?" President Mallory said to Carl.

"Yes, I do," was all Carl said.

He gestured for Three to lead them through the last bulkhead door and into the bridge. Carl slipped around the president to precede her into the control room. They entered through the aft, or rear, bulkhead door. There were narrow windows across the front and sides of the structure, and high-tech personnel stations lined the bulkheads. The four Navy officers stood against the starboard wall under guard of Merc Eighteen. The officers collectively gasped at the sight of President Mallory suited up in battle armor to match Carl and the mercs.

Carl stepped forward between the two command chairs in the center of the bridge, and he scanned all the computerized tactical stations of the bridge. The windows to the outside were smaller than Carl had expected, but he didn't recall seeing windows on the sleek superstructure as the helicopter approached.

Three continued his briefing on the ship's capabilities. "The USS Grace Hopper has more automated systems than the other three stealth vessels of its class. It also features double-hull exterior armor and Kevlar coatings on all interior critical compartments to prevent spalling. Even if a missile or shell doesn't penetrate the hull, it can blast tiny spalls of shrapnel from the inner surfaces of bulkheads, like when you shoot a bullet at a glass pane. That's extremely deadly in a confined space like interior compartments, so the Kevlar coating prevents that. That means the ship can take hard hits, and the crew will survive and keep fighting.

"As you can see," Three paused while Carl stepped over to the forward window. "The hull and decks above the water level are fitted with tiles that absorb most incoming radar signals. The ship's surfaces are also angled to prevent residual radar signal reflection back to the source. Below water, the hull is coated with acoustical paint to resist sonar detection. Her engines can drive her up to the equivalent of fifty-eight miles per hour, and the new bow design, called a tumblehome bow, which is actually how naval ships were designed a hundred years ago, pierces the waves instead of riding them, making for a more stable ride, even on rough seas. Those slanted structures you see on deck"—Three pointed down at the forward deck—"are armored containers that hold two high-energy lasers, one 'fore and one aft, for missile intercept and an electro-magnetic rail gun amidships that can fire Mach 8 projectiles at targets as far away as the horizon. Other armored containers house multiple missile launchers and close-in guns."

Carl surveyed the room again, and his gaze stopped on the officers.

"This ship belongs to me now, and I'm going to need your full cooperation. Any questions?"

The captain of the ship recovered from his surprise. He was a big, barrel-chested guy with serious crow's feet at the corners of his blue eyes and short gray hair. He wore shoulder epaulets with five gold stripes, but his white uniform was disheveled since he'd been imprisoned for almost twenty hours.

"What is the meaning of this?" he demanded. "You have committed an act of—"

Carl pulled his Glock and shot the man, and the three other officers gasped in various degrees of shock.

Distance: point-blank, shoulder *shot.*

A young ensign and a lieutenant tended their fallen captain, but the commander seemed to sense she had a critical decision to make. She looked late-thirties. Her white uniform and her hair looked equally disheveled. She'd been pushed around, but she still tried to keep her command presence. She had four stripes on her shoulder bars.

Carl said to her, "Now, I'm going to need *your* full cooperation."

She notched her chin up a bit in defiance. "You have the gun, sir. That puts you in charge."

Carl cocked his head and raised his Glock. "Sista, that only sounds like *partial* cooperation." He aimed his weapon at her chest. She had a backbone, he had to give her that.

President Mallory stepped up beside Carl and put her hand on his to lower his arm. To the female officer, she said, "Captain, if you'll give me a moment to explain."

"Commander Tracey Eckels, ma'am." The officer's gaze danced between Mallory and Carl. "You're not a captive?"

Carl holstered his weapon. "Madam President, we don't have time for this. They're coming, and we need to get ready. Commander Eckels, order your crew to follow my instructions without question. The president's life is in danger, and I don't have time to explain."

Eckels looked at Mallory, who nodded. The commander motioned Carl to the captain's chair.

"I don't need a place to sit, Commander. I need to talk to the crew!"

Eckels pivoted to a wall console and took down a coiled handset, then punched a button and handed it to Carl. He debated for a second how to motivate the crew quickly.

"This is Carl Johnson, Captain, US Air Force…retired. I don't have time to explain everything, but I will say this: My enemy has been trying to kill the president for eight months, but this time, they're coming heavy." He glanced over at the commander. "The president of the United States is on board this vessel, so now this destroyer is the only thing standing between her and certain death."

Thinking there was an *Air Force One* airplane and a *Marine One* helicopter, Carl wondered if the *USS Grace Hopper* now became *Navy One*?

The commander motioned for Mallory to stand closer to Carl, in front of the panel.

Eckels said, "Tell them to look at their wall monitors."

As he did so, Eckels punched two more buttons on the panel.

"The enemy has doped President Mallory with a radioactive isotope that makes her visible by special satellite sensors. They launched missiles at her in DC, bombing two restaurants and killing dozens of civilians and Secret Service agents in the attempt to murder her. More government agents gave their lives to get her on this ship. Now our enemy knows where she is, and they're going to throw everything they've got at us. The director of the Terror Event Response agency told me this is the most advanced destroyer in the fleet, and that's why we took it. I intend to commit all of its offensive and defensive weapons to the protection of the president. The president must live. So either you're on my team, or you're on the other—"

The president reached for the phone and shoved Carl out of view of the camera, a move that would have been unsuccessful if he hadn't taken a step in the direction she wanted him to go.

She gazed into the tiny camera, then glanced at the commander. "How do I know they can see me?"

Eckels pointed at a monitor at a nearby tactical station. Since Mallory had turned away from the camera, the monitor showed the back of her head.

"Gawd, my hair's a mess." She swiped at it as she turned back to the camera.

Eckels said softly, "Welcome to the club, ma'am."

"This is Shirley Mallory. The world believes Carl Johnson is a terrorist, but he is without a doubt the only reason I still breathe. He saved my daughter twice, and that was after I made a decision that got his son killed." Mallory's voice cracked. "Even after what I did, he still saved my child."

Carl started forward. "Shirley, this isn't the time—"

She waved him back and continued, "This isn't about me. This isn't about the office of the president. This is about the corporate power brokers of an organization called Atlas who aim to eliminate our government and control not only this country, but others as well. Our very freedom is under attack. Mr. Johnson has a plan to survive this day and end the people who are responsible for a great many deaths, and"—Mallory looked at Carl—"I trust him…with my life."

She handed the phone back to Carl, who handed it to the commander. Eckels locked gazes with Carl as if trying to find deceit in his soul.

"This is Commander Eckels. I don't know anything about this man Carl Johnson, but I believe the president. If he can—"

Three turned from where he stood at a tactical station. "The time for motivational speeches is over, folks. Check your radar screen. Kitchen sink inbound, Boss."

CHAPTER 37

Lisette's scream galvanized Lenore Cummings into action. She raced back along the stream, her combat boots making sucking sounds as she struggled through the mud. Then she started seeing bodies. Rebecca lay in the fetal position, knees to her chest, half in the shallow cold water, and rocking back and forth. In pain or shock, Lenore couldn't tell. Beyond her, Merc Six's body laid faceup in the brush beside the stream, eyes wide open and vacant. The front of his armored battle suit was ripped to shreds and scorched. He looked like he'd taken an RPG to the chest.

Lenore was about to take another step when a deep voice to her left said, "Drop the weapon."

She turned her head slightly but couldn't see anyone or anything where the voice originated, so she slowly shifted the aim of her assault rifle in that direction. Her right thumb clicked the selector to single-shot. Clearly, though, the killer could see her.

"I said, *drop it!* Or I kill the girl."

Lenore knew the man was going to kill her daughter anyway. That's what these men did. Carl clearly reminded everyone in his briefing that Atlas and its hired killers cared nothing about collateral damage. They held absolutely zero regard for human life. Her only way to keep Lisette alive was to keep the man talking. As soon as he disarmed her, he'd kill her and then Lisette. Her only chance to save her daughter was to grab her sidearm and go for a kill shot.

At a shadow figure in the swirling smoke thirty feet away.

"Okay, you win." She let the assault rifle fall from her grasp.

She'd just entertained the thought of executing her fastest fast-draw, the kind that every federal cop practices just in case, when she had a clear sight of the man holding her daughter. He had Lisette tight against his chest with his left arm around her neck. His right hand held a black handgun.

Lenore drew her gun and saw the killer's gun flash at the same instant. He shot her in the face.

CHAPTER 38

THREE SAID, "WHATEVER WE'RE GOING to do, we better do it now."

There was a large Lexan, see-through, tactical display mounted ten feet in front of the two command chairs. It showed a 360-degree radar view and thirteen missiles closing from the south.

"Huh," Carl mused. "No sweeping radar line rotating around the screen."

Commander Eckels replied, "We use phased-array radar. We can see and track targets simultaneously, in all directions. Those missiles are a couple hundred miles away." She narrowed her eyes at Carl and then looked at the president. "There's only one place those missiles could have originated from, and that's Carrier Strike Group Nine. They've knowingly fired on a US military vessel."

Carl nodded. "Well, I thought there'd be more missiles."

"There will be, Mr. Johnson, so I'm going to need my officers at their stations."

Carl nodded at Eighteen, who stood aside while keeping a close eye on the Navy personnel.

Eckels turned to her officers. "Leave the captain! Lieutenant, tactical! Ensign, comm! Broadcast friendly identification and tell them to halt their attack. Tell them we have the president on board."

The commander took her seat in the captain's chair and swiveled an armrest computer terminal in front of her lap. The lieutenant, a tall redhead with double bars on his shoulder epaulets, moved to a workstation along the left wall of the bridge. He glared at Carl as he passed within arm's length, and for a split second, Carl thought the young man was going to try to be a hero.

The ensign, a short, barrel-chested kid who barely topped the five-foot mark, took three careful paces around Merc Eighteen and tried to operate a communications console. "I'm locked out, Commander."

"So am I," added the lieutenant.

Carl nodded at Three, who tapped his earpiece. "Eight, grant limited computer access to the bridge. Comm and tactical."

After four seconds, Eight's voice said, "Done."

Commander Eckels pivoted her command chair to face Carl, where he had moved next to the president and Twelve at the aft bridge door. For a brief moment, Carl saw a vision of a woman every bit as no-nonsense as Captain Janeway from the fictional starship Voyager from the old *Star Trek* series.

She said, "I'm going to need my enlisted people at their stations too, and even then, we are severely understaffed. We had a skeleton crew for the weekend, and most of those were assigned to fight the dock fire."

To Merc Three, Carl said, "Can we take on thirteen missiles without the crew?"

Three stood close to Eckels, and Carl suspected it was to keep an eye on her activities. The merc waved an arm around the computer-automated bridge. "McGrath's specs say the ship's normal crew complement is half that of an Arleigh Burke-class destroyer's crew of 276. This ship is so automated, it can operate effectively with a crew of nineteen, but that doesn't include fighting a war. Thirteen missiles is child's play, but if Atlas controls the Carrier Strike Group Nine commander, they're going to kick our ass, Boss. No doubt about that."

Eckels added, "A carrier strike group can put sixty planes in the air along with a few hundred long-distance anti-ship missiles. We'll hold our own for a while, but that there…" She pointed a thumb behind her at the indicator of thirteen missiles on the Lexan display. "That's just their opening salvo. This ship just finished sea trials, but it isn't battle-tested yet."

"Are *you* battle-tested, Commander?"

She nodded.

"Good, so am I."

Merc Three interrupted, "And, Boss…"

Carl wagged his fingers at the man. "Let's have it."

"When the rest of the kitchen sink gets here, we'll start taking hits. You don't want the crew locked up below decks, drowning if we take a hard hit. The hull armor can only protect us so much. Besides, we're gonna need a lot of damage control assistance."

Eckels glanced from Merc Three to Carl. "When they launch the next salvo, we'll definitely take some hits. I recommend we relocate to the CIC."

"CIC?" Carl was unfamiliar with the term.

"Combat Information Center. It's deep in the ship, the most protected compartment except for the fuel and ammo bunkers."

"Intercom, please," Carl said.

Eckels pushed some buttons, and Carl grabbed the wall handset.

"Attention, please. This is Air Force Captain Carl Johnson." Carl searched for the right words to say. "While it's true I control this ship and its computer, you all have a decision to make. Will you believe me and protect your president, or will you believe the distant commander who has sent missiles to kill us? To kill your president? Politics can be messy, and corporate subterfuge is even messier. The people who want President Mallory dead won't come and do it themselves. They will send your military brothers and sisters from a distant carrier group to do the deed. We're all pawns in this game. You, me, this ship—we're all expendable. My son was caught in the cross fire, and now he's dead. I've sent federal agents to their deaths, too, so Shirley Mallory has a fighting chance to survive."

Carl took a deep breath. "And now, I'm going to ask the ultimate sacrifice of you. We're going to war, folks, and this is for real. If we live, you'll be able to tell your kids and grandkids about this battle—that you served on the first warship named after a woman and fought to defend the first woman president. Help me keep the commander-in-chief alive. When we unlock your doors, I want all hands to report to your battle stations. This is not a drill, and I'm giving operational combat command back to the commander. Marines, make your way to the mess hall. I have a special assignment for you."

A serious voice challenged his order. "Negative, Mister. If we're going to war, our place is on damage control teams."

Carl glanced at Three, who said, "That's Lieutenant Nathaniel Hawkins, commander of the marine contingent on this ship. He has three marines under his command. The rest off-loaded to fight the dock fire."

"Normally, Lieutenant Hawkins, I would agree with you, but the president has no Secret Service contingent to protect her. Our enemy will attempt to disable the ship, and then they'll board and try to kill her, so your only job now is to provide security for President Mallory. Nothing else is more important. In the mess hall, you'll find high-tech armored combat suits and advanced weapons. Get suited up and ready for combat. The president *must* live."

Hawkins hesitated, then said, "Copy that. Protect the president at all costs."

Carl hung up the handset, and Eckels narrowed her eyes. "You hijack this ship, and you brought weapons and armor for the marines? You actually expected them to help you?"

"Commander, I expect marines to do what marines are trained to do. I expect them to protect their president." To Merc Three, he said, "Make the computer unlock the brig, then get the captain down to the infirmary and make sure a medic meets you there to tend to his injury. Then have your team report to the aft deck. You know what to do."

Three assigned Eighteen and Twelve to carry the unconscious captain to the infirmary. "The chopper is already fueled, armed, and ready to deploy." Three hesitated. "Boss, you know this ship can't fight an aircraft carrier, right?"

Carl smiled. "Well, we can *fight*." He shrugged. "We don't have to win. We just have to survive."

Three smiled. "If anybody else on the planet told me they had a plan to survive a war against an aircraft carrier fleet with a single boat, I'd call 'em crazy and jump ship ASAP."

Carl chuckled. "Well, the *crazy* part is still up for a vote. How soon can you get that bird in the air?"

"The pilot of the president's transport helicopter didn't make it out, but the copilot is available for service."

"Copy that. Get down there and get airborne. Code word to fire your missiles is 'escalate.' When you hear it, do it. If we lose comm for any reason at all, launch."

Merc Three started to turn away.

"Mr. Englebaum," Carl called.

The mercenary turned.

"Three, you've gone *way* beyond the call of duty."

"C'mon, Boss. Don't go gettin' all soft and start cryin' and shit."

"I'm trying to say *thank you.*"

Three smiled. "You're one of a kind, Boss."

They bumped forearms, and Three left the bridge.

Carl stepped over to the command chair. "Commander Eckels, the ship is yours. Defend the president."

She nodded. "Lieutenant, sound General Quarters."

"General Quarters! General Quarters! To your battle stations! This is *not* a drill!"

Eckels stood and said, "Madam President, if you'll come with me *now!*"

The ensign grabbed an intercom handset and made the announcement. "CIC, Bridge. POTUS is on the move, galley first, then your location."

"CIC, aye," replied the voice of Merc Eight.

A console beeped, and the three officers froze. They conferred with each other from different stations on the bridge.

"Vampire, Vampire, Vampire! Multiple airborne contacts, bearing one-seven-five, speed four-five-two. Target is the *Grace Hopper.*" The lieutenant glanced over at Carl. "They have us, Captain."

Eckels grunted and looked at Carl. "The *rest* of your kitchen sink."

"How many missiles inbound, Lieutenant?" Carl said.

The young man shrugged. "Well, all of them, I think." Fear hiked the lieutenant's voice up a notch. "The computer is showing 326 inbound."

Eckels said, "Stay calm, Lieutenant. We've trained for this. Are you reading EM?"

"Negative radar emissions."

"Good," Eckels said calmly. "That means they're not homing in on us just yet."

The ensign said, "They'll have an E-2D Hawkeye searching for us, ma'am."

Eckels shook her head. "They probably have a high-altitude visual on us, but even the Hawkeye's advanced radar can't see our minuscule radar return from that distance."

Carl said, "We think Atlas may have access to civilian satellites."

Eckels nodded. "That won't be good enough for end-of-flight targeting. And just so you know, those inbound missiles are not by any means the full complement of an aircraft carrier."

Carl pointed at the mass of blips following fifty miles behind the first wave of thirteen. "How many of this second wave can we engage?"

"We can take out maybe 20 percent in the blue zone with the rail gun. That's at the horizon. We have long-range intercept missiles also. Then we have the two lasers that can blind maybe half of the remaining missiles' targeting optics in the yellow zone. That's two to three miles away. We have short-range antimissile missiles for the red zone, within a mile. When they break through that perimeter, we'll engage them the old-fashioned way—with deck guns."

Carl pointed at the Lexan display screen. "So this is over-the-horizon radar?" The horizon was twenty-some miles away, he recalled, but the first wave was still a couple hundred miles out.

"That's classified."

Carl grunted. It probably had more to do with radar imagery combined with imagery from military satellites McGrath had kept accessible to the *Grace Hopper* while denying access to their enemy. Carl had fought against police, FBI and TER agents, and even foreign military elements, but never in his wildest imagination had he ever considered the possibility that he'd go to war against the US Navy.

Eckels continued, "Tactical computer simulations say we can pick off most of them, but we are still greatly outnumbered. We'll run out of ammunition and missiles. That's when they'll send their boarding party."

Carl pointed at the display. "Is this enough to sink us?"

She shook her head. "A few will get through. They'll cripple us, but barring a lucky hit at the waterline or a deep penetration into the fuel bunker, we won't sink."

Carl nodded as he repeated his mantra in his mind. *We don't have to win the fight. We just have to survive.*

"How long do we have?"

"Twelve minutes until we engage the first wave. The second wave is eight minutes behind that."

Carl looked around the bridge. He eyed a white box with a big red plus sign mounted on the bulkhead beside him at shoulder height. "Things are happening a lot faster than I thought. I figured they'd hit us with some land-based planes or surface-to-ship missiles. I certainly didn't think Atlas could send the whole goddamn Navy after us."

The president stepped up beside Carl. "Did you have to shoot that officer?"

"Yes, I quickly had to win their obedience." He stepped around the president, expecting her to follow. "Let's go meet the marines. When we get down to the CIC, I want to call that carrier's admiral and discuss the terms of her surrender."

CHAPTER 39

A FTER LEAVING THE BRIDGE, THE naval officers went deeper into the ship toward the CIC. As Carl led President Mallory back to the galley to meet the marines, he sensed that she had stopped in the middle of a passageway. She seemed to study the ceiling overhead for a moment. It was then Carl noticed that every square inch of the ceiling and walls was filled with something—a control panel, meter, tube, hose, conduit, insulated pipe, first aid kit, fire extinguisher. There was absolutely no wasted real estate on the warship.

What do you even call the ceiling or walls or windows in a warship?

Mallory faced Carl, and he studied her for a moment. Her eyes looked gray, not blue as he remembered from his first meeting with her eight months ago. Back then, her eyes were filled with pain for her then-missing daughter. Now in her gaze, he saw resignation.

He broke the ice. "You look pretty badass all armored up like that."

"They're going to kill everyone, aren't they?"

"They're going to try."

Her gaze danced with his for a moment. "There's something I haven't told you, something you should know about me."

"That you're part of Atlas?" He nodded as her eyes widened. "I've known for a couple days."

"I *was* a part of Atlas. I left. Tried to, anyway. How did you find out?"

"Our mutual friend Hollis Koll was very talkative."

"Is he dead?"

Carl shook his head. "I had a different plan for him."

Now it was the president's turn to study him. "You have a plan for everything, don't you? For every*one*."

He nodded. "Back from my project management days. Having contingencies is great for risk management."

"Your unpredictability was what drove Aaron insane last year." Mallory looked at the floor, then said, "So what's your plan for me, now that you know?"

"The mission has not changed, Shirley. You're the president. You must live."

"But—"

"You're a politician, and sometimes politicians do stupid shit. They follow the wrong leader, get seduced by the wrong promises. I get it. That's the way of the corporate power game. Men like Grainger Koll know how to figure out what people want or need. Then he promises it." Carl pointed at the floor. "You know why the US Navy paints the floors of the main corridors of the ships the way they do?"

Under the durable epoxy nonskid coating, the floor was painted dark blue with speckles that Carl figured were representations of stars in the night sky. The destroyer's motto was stenciled up the hallway floor: The Spear of the Navy.

Mallory nodded. "Pride."

Carl shook his head. "The US military leadership is just like Koll, and the psychology of warfare is the same as the psychology of corporate business. Military leaders tell these young kids what they want and need to hear so they feel they belong to something bigger than themselves, so they can feel special, so they can be heroes. It's all just brainwashing, though. Good guys, bad guys. Doesn't matter.

"The Navy higher-ups know most of these kids will spend their whole careers practicing for war. But in reality, it's just a few years of scrubbing decks. Very few ever see real combat. Fewer still ever have a chance to be a hero. So, leadership reminds these kids every day that they're part of something bigger, that their destroyer is the spear of the US Navy."

"And are you different, Carl?"

He shook his head. "I'm no different. All these kids on this ship, they're just like I was thirty years ago. They all took an oath to protect and defend the Constitution against all enemies, foreign and domestic. But I'm going to twist it and make it seem like their oath is to protect and defend *you*, the president. Because that's *my* mission, and I need them to believe in my mission just for today. I'm going to give them what they want and need. Thirty years from now, they'll tell their grandkids about this battle. They'll be heroes. *Real* heroes."

"If we win this battle."

Carl smiled. "We don't have to win, Shirley. We just have to survive."

"And then what?"

"Then you give me and Aaron all the intel you have on Atlas, and I'll be the American Terrorist. I'll avenge Nancy Palmer, my son, and all the others who have died."

Mallory gasped. "Agent Palmer…Nancy? She's gone?"

He nodded.

"Carl, these people are too powerful. They've always been a step ahead of us."

"They've been operating in the shadows, but now we know they exist. Aaron will find them, and I will kill them."

"They'll see you coming."

"Oh, I'm sure they'll see *something* coming, but they've never seen me and Aaron both coming at the same time."

She scrunched her eyes like she didn't believe him. "You two… You're really working together now?"

He nodded. "It took the loss of someone we both cared deeply about."

She shuddered and looked away. "My God, what have I done, Carl?"

"This isn't your doing, Shirley." He put a gentle hand on Mallory's armor-plated shoulder.

"I want Atlas destroyed."

"That's a goal we share. First, we have to survive the day, okay?"

President Mallory nodded, and they continued to the galley. Carl stepped aside and let her enter ahead of him. As always, he made sure his holstered Glock was accessible and his PDW was prepped for action. The safety selector was turned to the triple-shot position.

The four marines turned toward them as they entered. They were an impressive and fearsome sight. All were decked out head-to-toe in black hard-shell battle armor, and each had an assortment of weapons clipped to their utility belts or slung over their shoulders. They also wore helmets, but their facemasks were raised. They snapped to attention at the sight of the president.

Lieutenant Nathaniel Hawkins stood in front of the others. He was a short, slender mid-twenties man with light brown skin, but Carl couldn't discern his ethnicity.

Hawkins eyeballed Carl with mistrust, then looked at Mallory. "Madam President," he said. He stood ramrod straight, as did his marines.

"Gentlemen," Mallory said.

One of the two larger soldiers spoke, and that was the only indication that particular marine was female. "It is an honor to meet you, ma'am."

Carl got the feeling the marine spoke to tactfully inform Mallory that she was, in fact, not a gentleman. Mallory nodded at the female warrior but did not offer an apology.

The new world, Carl thought. *First, there were only mixed marriages to try to keep straight forty years ago. Then mixed ethnicities—kids like me—then mixed genders, and now even androgyny. In the military, no less. Never noticed that in my day. Probably drives the pure-blood folks crazy. Hard to label folks nowadays. Hard to put 'em in categories anymore.*

President Mallory said, "Lieutenant Hawkins, you and your people are to follow Captain Johnson's orders to the letter. Are you clear on that?"

"Very clear, ma'am."

Carl said, "You people have only one job now, and that's to keep the president alive. If the ship is disabled, you'll have to repel boarders. It'll be hard because they'll be people you've trained and served with. They've been lied to." He looked at Hawkins. "But nothing and no one is more important than this woman." He head-nodded sideways at Mallory. "She cannot die."

Lieutenant Hawkins nodded. "Copy that, Captain. The president must live. We should get her to the CIC."

Carl nodded. "I'll be there shortly if you'll tell me the way."

Hawkins gave him what seemed like a convoluted path to the CIC, then he and his armored marines marched the president out of the room. Carl looked around the empty room. It was the community eating room for everyone who was not an officer. There were four long tables that would normally have dozens of chairs aligned with military precision. The tables and chairs had been haphazardly shoved to one side to make room for the weapons duffel bags the mercs had used to bring the combat suits and weapons aboard from the minisub.

It was McGrath's suggestion to bring armor and weapons for the marines. He was willing to gamble the life of his lover and president on the loyalty of the marines to place their duty to protect the president above all else. He had been right, but Carl had also been prepared for McGrath's assessment to be wrong. He'd been prepared to kill the marines. He flicked the selector on his PDW back to the safe position.

He sighed, grabbed a chair, and sat against the bulkhead near the door. Then he leaned forward and rested his elbows on his knees—not an easy task with his armor—and closed his eyes. It was always so easy now to kill or plan to kill.

Agent Palmer's face appeared on the inner view screen of his mind.

Gone forever.

Like Mark…gone forever.

Like the battle-hardened Merc Four, wife of Merc Three. Like the young Mr. Garcia, who took his own life after his wife and newborn child succumbed to the Contagion. Like dozens of other cops, agents, and civilians whose orbits intersected mine.

Now he'd sent Merc Three and the helicopter pilot off to die. They had to know their assignment was a one-way trip from which neither would return, but they also knew their sacrifice was crucial to the survival of the president.

So many people had died. So many more would die. He was asking these marines to kill other Americans, their military comrades, and they were going to do it to save the president.

Is one woman worth such a sacrifice in lives?

Nations went to war to protect their heads of state. The US government had an entire organization—the Secret Service—with an annual budget of hundreds of millions of dollars to protect the president, and every one of those thousands of agents would willingly lay down his or her life for the person that occupied the Oval Office.

Until some asshat comes along with a biotech weapon that made

Secret Service agents try to assassinate the person they were sworn to protect.

Carl stood and sucked in a deep breath. *Yes, I am doing the right thing.*

His mission eight months ago was to save Melissa Mallory, the kidnapped daughter of the president, and also to save the president, but that mission was also self-serving at the time. It was his attempt to clear the red ink off his ledger, red ink that represented the lives he'd taken in his private war against the government. Back then, he'd believed power-hungry people were trying to kill the president simply because she was the first woman president. Now, he realized there was a larger strategy in play, and she had been involved hip-deep in it until something made her diverge from the interests of Atlas. She had to have known they'd retaliate. Or perhaps she thought she was immune to their wrath simply by being the president with the Secret Service to protect her.

Atlas, this international cabal, had the power, funding, and influence to direct a full carrier strike group to kill the president. Shirley Mallory couldn't stop them. Aaron McGrath couldn't stop them. Only the American Terrorist could stop them, but he couldn't do it alone.

He found himself moving through the silent ship with a purpose. He slid down the arm rails of two ladders without using the steps, just like they did in the movies, made two right turns and a left, and found himself staring point-blank into the business end of an assault rifle. He refocused past that black orifice and looked into the female marine's eyes.

She lowered her weapon and banged her armored fist twice on the bulkhead door of the CIC, then shoved it open with one hand.

"Thank you, Soldier."

"I'm not a soldier, sir. I'm a Marine," she said without malice in her voice.

He nodded. "Apologies, Marine."

"Corporal Inajosa, sir. My mates call me *Ina* for short." She pronounced it *Ee-nah*.

Just inside the door, Carl was confronted by the smallest of the three enlisted marines, but that guy was still bigger than he was. The lieutenant and the other armored marine, a huge Black guy, flanked the president as she and the commander stood in front of the floor-to-ceiling view screen, similar to the transparent heads-up display on the bridge. Two other enlisted naval operators occupied seats at tactical computer stations in the room. The ensign confirmed that the entire crew was at action stations.

The CIC was about thirty feet by sixty, and two walkways traversed the room lengthwise. Flanking each walkway, metal desks and chairs were bolted to the floor and walls, each desk holding a military version of a computer workstation. There was room for maybe forty crewmembers in the room, but currently, there were only six operators, including the commander, her two officers, the enlisted folks, and Merc Eight. The CIC was certainly not built for comfort. Carl got the feeling modern warfare was fast-paced and heavily based on technology, unlike the drawn-out cat-and-mouse pace of old war movies and books.

Merc Eight kept his seat at the far aft end of the CIC, and Carl made his way toward the president and the commander at the opposite end near a horizontal see-through tactical display.

The three officers had changed into what Carl imagined was the CIC combat uniform—solid dark blue shirt and pants with no headgear. They stood at a center command station near the "front" of the room, so Carl made that station his destination. Subdued white lighting lit the room.

Carl examined the tactical display. The USS *Grace Hopper* was a solid blue boat indicator in the center of the screen. Carl thought the symbol looked like the old style of destroyer, not the new stealth version. White circles denoting distance radiated outward from the ship on the see-through panel. The visual representation on the tactical screen was the same as that on the larger vertical screen.

The top of the desktop display was aligned with the bow of the ship and had an S compass indicator. A cluster of red triangles had descended from the top of the display, indicating the thirteen missiles of the carrier group's first wave. Text moved with the red indicators, showing an ETA of one minute, forty-five seconds.

Eckels grabbed the intercom handset and broadcasted throughout the ship, "Attention all hands. Attack is imminent. Gear up, people." She pulled out a gray balaclava from under a nearby desk and fitted it over her head and neck, as did her crewmembers. Then she fitted on an orange life jacket that could be inflated with the pull of a cord. Carl was certain every other naval person aboard was doing the same, preparing for possible contact with cold water should the ship go down.

Into the intercom handset, Eckels said, "Status, all departments." She hit a switch so the audio came out of a speaker everyone in the room could hear.

"CIC, Damage Control. All three teams are ready to deploy."

Carl knew a mere three damage control teams were woefully inadequate for a ship this size under *normal* operations, not to mention during actual combat.

"CIC, Engine Room. I've got all generators available, full capacity, condition Zebra set, time seventeen twenty-one."

One of the enlisted operators in the CIC called, "Fire control radar detected. They have us bracketed."

"Very well," Eckels said. "Lieutenant, light 'em up. Break EMCON. Set SPY to high power, calculate intercept solutions, and stand by."

"Combat, ready rail gun and lasers. Missiles to stand by."

"Combat, aye!"

"Damage Control, make ready for multiple strikes."

Orders were given and repeated as the ship came alive. Carl was amazed at the efficiency of the crew even under the threat of imminent death. Their routine was well-practiced, and panic was kept in check.

An operator hollered out, "First targets, two thousand yards!"

Eckels said, "Ready all weapons. Defensive posture *Alpha*. Prepare to engage yellow targets with birds and red targets with lasers. Stand by, close-in deck guns."

"Brace for impact."

"Brace! Brace! Brace!"

"Fire missile batteries one and two!"

"Fire missile batteries one and two, aye!"

"Reload one and two and stand by."

Carl watched a wall monitor that showed the topside deck of the destroyer from the perspective of an aft-mounted camera. Armored panels slid open in two places, and two boxy canisters, each holding four missile tubes, swiveled toward the bow. Flame and smoke blasted from the back of each battery as intercept missiles quickly disappeared into the distance. The front laser housing swiveled continuously, accompanied by a slight dimming of the CIC lights as the device fired. Carl expected some kind of *Star Trek* phaser beam blasting out of the aperture, but the beam was completely invisible. In fact, the only way he knew the laser had melted the guidance electronics of its target was when an indicator on the display turned from red to yellow, indicating the missiles were no longer on a threat trajectory. The deck camera showed six of the missiles passing harmlessly over the ship, their melted optics unable to direct the missiles into a terminal attack maneuver.

Then the distant intercept missiles began hitting their targets, and the first wave of inbound missiles was decimated in mere seconds. The laser and missile launchers retreated into their shielded housings, but the long barrel of the rail gun rose out of its housing and tracked the distant targets of the second wave.

On the display, the second wave of missiles was a cluster of more than three hundred red triangles, moving with an ETA of just under six minutes, and four minutes behind the second wave was a formation of thirty-odd solid red plane indicators. Their moving data showed them at a higher altitude. At the far top edge of the screen sat a large red indicator shaped like an aircraft carrier labeled *CSG9*. The carrier strike group was just over three hundred miles due south.

"Mr. Johnson," the commander said, "the president tells me you have a plan to force the admiral to surrender."

"I do," Carl said with a nod.

She pointed at the display. "This would be a good time to deploy it."

"Do we still have the channel open to the chopper?"

The ensign said, "Confirming secure point-to-point transmission status for EMCON Alpha."

Carl said, "Negative. When we talk to the chopper, I want our enemy to hear it too, so they understand the tactical situation."

"Copy," the ensign said.

Carl added, "And open a separate channel to the carrier group, please."

"Channel is now open, but they are not answering. That's standard military procedure in an operation. They're at EMCON Alpha. Complete radio silence."

"Do you have video capability?"

The ensign glanced to Commander Eckels, who said, "Make it happen."

"I want that admiral to see my eyes, so she'll believe what I'm telling her."

"It won't matter," the commander said. "Admiral Janis Montmarkle is old-school. She rose to the top of a pile of male officers who actively worked together to keep her down. She's as tough as they come."

The ensign pointed at Carl and said, "The channel is active, sir…um, ma'am." Then he stammered a bit and looked at his commander like he didn't know who was really in control.

A tiny spoke had extended down from the ceiling with a small ball camera attached to the end. Carl saw his face on the bottom right of the wall screen behind the camera. The rest of the screen was gray.

Carl spoke to the camera. "Admiral, this is Air Force Captain Carl Johnson, retired. The president is aboard this ship. My sole mission is to keep Shirley Mallory alive and protect her from harm. Recall your fighters and self-destruct the missiles coming our way. Make no further attempts to attack this vessel." He looked to his left. "Madam President, if you will step into view of the camera."

She did.

"Admiral, your missiles are putting the commander-in-chief's life in peril."

President Mallory said, "Admiral, I order you to stand down your attack."

Commander Eckels said, "Ensign, transmit encrypted ship ID again to prove who we are."

"Done."

Carl added, "ETA on the next wave of missiles?"

The ensign reported, "Five minutes, ten seconds. The computer will engage the rail gun in thirteen seconds."

Eckels said, "I need mobility, Mr. Johnson. Our battle effectiveness is diminished sitting still in the water."

Carl glanced over at Merc Eight and nodded. Then he glared at the empty part of the screen. The admiral was trying to make him sweat. He had to get her attention.

ETA, four minutes and thirty seconds.

Eckels commanded, "Lieutenant, come to full power on all engines, emergency flank three. CCS, disengage revolution limiters, override engine safeties. Bring the ship to course two-seven-zero and fire rail gun and forward laser. Engage aft laser when clear."

The lieutenant added, "Launch decoys, Commander?"

"Not yet. We're going to need them later."

"Standing by on decoys."

Carl heard *and felt* the rhythmic pulsing of the rail gun as it blasted a Mach 8 projectile toward a distant target on the horizon every four seconds.

"Admiral, I'm gonna kick your ass if you don't talk to me. You've been briefed. You know what I'm capable of."

The channel remained silent as the commander and her officers continued exchanging rapid-fire orders and confirmations.

The lieutenant said, "Commander, we have full-envelope detection. We're being bombarded by multiple terminal homing radar signals."

"Make those targets your top priority. Target the sources with the rail gun and fire."

"Aye, Commander. Three seconds. Done! More targets actively homing."

"Keep firing. Fire missile batteries one through eight!"

"Fire missile batteries one through eight, aye!"

ETA, four minutes.

"Reload one through eight and fire missile batteries nine through sixteen!"

"Engage the rail gun on the targets in the yellow zone. Bring the forward missile intercept laser to bear on targets in the red zone and engage."

"Aye, Commander. Rail gun, yellow zone. Engaging forward laser, red targets."

"Maintain aft laser on yellow targets."

"Aft laser, yellow, aye."

The ship shuddered multiple times as intercept missiles left their launchers. On the tactical display, the intercepts sped into the vast wave of missiles at the five-mile mark. With each impact, an inbound threat disappeared from the display. He felt a rhythmic thumping of hypersonic projectile launches and heard the hum of heavy-duty motors somewhere deep inside the ship as the missile launchers and the rail gun were continuously reloaded. Lights dimmed frequently as the front high-energy laser fired repeatedly.

ETA, three minutes and thirty seconds.

The ensign's voice rose with excitement and panic. "Sixteen missiles in the red zone! Engaging short-range intercept missiles!"

"Steady now," Eckels said. "Ready close-in guns."

"Standing by."

"Release chaff, all sectors, engage guns."

"Aye, Commander. Decoys out. Firing close-in deck guns."

A high-speed rumble swept through the ship as multiple deck guns fired off two-second bursts at the four incoming missiles, engaging just enough to hit specific targets.

It was then that Carl realized one of the enlisted people, a young Black woman who looked barely out of high school, was operating the deck guns with some kind of high-tech joystick. It reminded him of a video game controller. She sat two stations away to Carl's right. She was jerking the joystick and pressing the red firing button repeatedly, but she was panicking, missing her targets. She was talking to herself.

Carl stepped over to her just as she cried out, "There's too many. Too close! I can't—"

He laid a heavy hand on her shoulder. "Yes, you can. Just take a deep breath and hit this one." He pointed a finger at her display. "Now!" Her targeting reticule covered the missile, and she pressed the button. "Now this one." He tapped the screen again, and she destroyed another inbound missile. "Now these four, left to right. Real fast!"

The young woman hit all her targets, the last one a mere twenty yards out. Even deep down in the ship, they all heard the ping of debris off the ship's armored skin. The shooter took another deep breath and shuddered.

Carl said, "Well done, young Sista. Well done." He tapped her left shoulder and added, "You see that woman over there? The president?"

The shooter looked over and nodded.

"She's why you're fighting." Carl raised his voice so everyone in the room could hear him. "This is the most capable ship in the Navy, and you're stationed here because you're the best of the best. We're going to take some hits, but just stay calm and keep doing the best you can...for your president."

Carl stepped back over next to Mallory and saw his image appear again in the lower right corner of the vertical monitor in front of him.

Commander Eckels glanced at Carl. "I'm still waiting for the admiral's surrender."

The ensign said, "Two minutes ten until the rest of the second wave arrive."

"Johnson," Eckels said, "that was only the first wave and the leading edge of the second wave. We won't survive the next wave."

"Yes, we will."

CHAPTER 40

LENORE'S ACRYLIC FACE SHIELD SHATTERED. She'd juked her head at the last moment, knowing the killer had her dead to rights, and stumbled sideways from the impact. The man holding Lisette shot her again—another headshot off the left side of her helmet.

A ringing sound exploded in her ear, and she felt, rather than heard, herself scream in pain.

He shot her again, this time high in the back.

When the impact pitched her forward a step, she dug in her heel and spun, aiming her sidearm at the same time.

Then he shot her in the gut.

The bullet bounced off her armor but knocked her breath away, and her legs wobbled and buckled. She found herself on her knees in the mud again, holding the gun at her side.

The killer expertly stayed hidden behind Lisette, gazing through her hair so Lenore couldn't get a shot. He pointed the gun right between Lenore's eyes, and she waited, even as she heard the sound of boots sloshing through the mud and water.

"Sixteen!" came the merc's identifying call out of the smoke.

"Seventeen!" said another.

The killer started to shift his aim, probably by instinct, but he must also have instantly realized his mistake. In the millisecond before he shifted his attention back to Lenore, she saw a tiny sliver of the man's nose next to her daughter's cheek, and that's what she fired at.

It was a snapshot in desperation with no time to aim. She just raised her gun and fired. The gunman screamed and grabbed his face as he and Lisette fell to the ground. He started to sit up and aim, Lisette still in his grasp, but surprisingly, her daughter elbowed the man right on his bloody nose. He screamed again, and Lisette rolled off him. Seventeen finished him off with a triple tap to the head and another to the chest.

Lisette ran to her mother, and Cummings pulled off her damaged helmet. They hugged while Sixteen approached and stood guard during their tearful reunion.

"Boss, that was the baddest motherfucking fast-draw I have *ever* seen, bar none!"

Lenore nodded and sucked a deep breath as her daughter helped her to her feet. "Check on the civilians and mop up."

Sixteen and Seventeen pressed south in the gully, where only sporadic shots could be heard. They hollered their number designations periodically and were answered by the numbers assigned to the civilians.

Footsteps approached again from the north, and Lenore spun around to keep her armored body between the footsteps and Lisette. She aimed into the smoke.

"Nineteen!"

"Good for you," Rebecca's voice answered. "I forgot my fucking number!" She stumbled out of the smoke.

"You're injured."

"It's nothing. I got nicked in the leg." She limped so badly, one foot dragged, carving a groove in the mud.

"Let Seventeen look at it. He's a field medic."

"Let's get to the truck first. I don't hear any more gunfire, so I assume it's over. But I'd like to get the hell outta here, just in case." Rebecca looked at Cummings's shattered face shield. "So this is how you and Carl spend time, huh?"

"We don't spend—"

Rebecca held up a hand as they moved upstream. "Just kidding. But if a fellow saved me and took a few bullets for my daughter, I'd probably keep him around."

Cummings stopped walking. "He told you?"

Rebecca just shrugged with a side cock of her head. "He called me a while back. Told me a lot about you and the government."

Lisette said, "Carl's not nice. He's scary."

"Yeah?"

Lisette nodded. "He tied us to a table and threatened Mom."

That stopped Rebecca in her tracks. She glanced from Lisette to Cummings. "He did?"

"You remember?" Cummings said.

Lisette nodded and looked at Rebecca. "He blamed Mom because his son died."

"I was responsible," Cummings said. She shook her head sadly. "I killed Mark."

"No, you didn't, Mom." Lisette hugged her mom. "He doesn't blame you anymore."

"He didn't tell me all that, but it's gotta be tough to deal with for both of you." Rebecca looked at the girl. "Do you hate him for what he did to you?"

Lisette shrugged.

"He keeps saving you."

Lisette nodded.

Lenore said, "Let's move."

They met up with the others, and Cummings was relieved to learn they only had two casualties—Merc Six and the Twin Otter pilot. All the mercs had their fair share of scrapes and bruises, and even the civilians were plastered head-to-toe in mud and dirt.

"Let's get safe," Lenore said.

Sixteen replied, "Copy that, Boss. I wonder how Zero is doing?"

Lenore growled. "I hope he blasts these Atlas fuckers off the face of the planet."

CHAPTER 41

CARL LOOKED AT THE COMMANDER, then glanced at the president. To the young ensign, he said, "Is this your first real combat?"

The junior officer nodded.

"First time is always the hardest." Carl looked at the camera again. "Come on, Admiral. You didn't think it was going to be this easy to take me out, did you?"

Silence.

"You've seen my file. You know the FBI sent a full squad of counter-terrorist troops after me, and I defeated them with four mercenaries and a drug-addict computer jock. Then the TER sent their top assassination team after me, and my mercs killed all of them, and I cut the head off that motherfucker while he was still alive! Do you seriously believe I came out into the middle of the fucking ocean without a backup plan?"

The channel remained silent.

Carl shot the commander a look of irritation.

She half-shrugged in return and gave him a look that said, "I told you so."

He leaned forward against the acrylic top of the tactical display desk, looked down as if exasperated, then glanced sideways at Mallory. Then he peered up at the camera under heavy lids because he knew it gave him a sinister look when he wanted to intimidate an opponent. "Look, Admiral, I know you're sitting comfy out yonder on your big-ass boat. You're probably laughing at us, sipping coffee, and thinking you're untouchable, but my patience grows thin. I have three nukes in my arsenal, and I'm going to shove two of them right up your ass."

The console under his fists beeped, and new indicators began to appear on the vertical screen a short distance ahead of the fleet.

Carl glanced at Commander Eckels. "What the hell? What the fuck is that?"

She turned to her left. "Ensign?"

"They're ours, Commander. Contact parameters confirmed. They are modified Harpoon extended-range anti-surface missiles."

Eckels grimaced. "Submarine-launched ship killers. If any *one* of them hits us, it'll blow us clean out of the water."

The beeps stopped, and Carl counted sixteen ship killers. "Well, fuck me sideways," he muttered. He glared at the camera. "Admiral, surely your ship has verified that this is an authentic channel, and the signal is, in fact, coming from the *USS Grace Hopper*." He turned sideways and indicated the president, who still stood beside him with concern in her eyes. "And you can see Shirley Mallory standing beside me."

The channel remained silent.

Carl looked over at Eckels. "Can we engage all those ship killers?"

"You mean if we survive those two-hundred-plus remaining missiles?"

"Yeah, that."

"Ship killers have end-of-trajectory evasive maneuvers programmed into their terminal guidance packages."

Carl nodded. "Yes, I'm familiar with that technology. I intend to use it myself."

Eckels seemed to simply dismiss his statement. "Fully functional, we could hit them with the rail gun and long-range missiles, but our defensive capability will be severely compromised after the next wave...if we have any capability left at all. Our missile batteries will be empty, and our ammo bunkers will be virtually depleted. Our rail guns, if they're not empty, won't be able to track them fast enough through their terminal maneuvers."

Carl pounded the table with his armor-gloved fists hard enough to crack the acrylic. "Fuck you, Admiral! *You cannot kill my president!*" He paused a beat, then shouted at the camera again. "Merc Three, *escalate!*"

CHAPTER 42

G RAINGER KOLL LISTENED TO THE encrypted military comm channel in his private office. He heard the one-sided threats from Carl Johnson to the silent Admiral Montmarkle. He pressed a button on the desktop intercom.

"Thaddeus Leak here, sir."

"Any word from the ranch assault team?"

"Negative, sir. All channels are quiet. Our civilian satellite feed is obscured by a massive smoke cloud over the area from the missile strikes."

"Let me know as soon as you regain contact."

He pushed the intercom button again and leaned back in his chair. Somehow he'd known there would be no further contact from the ranch team. The last thing he'd heard over the channel was screams of pain and explosions, then silence.

Grainger spoke to the empty room. "How the hell did a bunch of civilians with three mercenaries and a washed-out FBI agent overcome a well-armed team of over two dozen professional soldiers for hire armed with cruise missiles and drones?" He took a deep breath and swallowed the bitter pill of defeat. "You trained them well, Mr. Johnson."

On his second monitor, a shout erupting from the speaker grabbed his attention.

"Merc Three, *escalate!*"

Grainger narrowed his eyes. It wasn't like Carl Johnson to lose his cool like that. He watched a missile separate from the tiny helicopter.

Two fighters peeled away from the formation en route to the *USS Grace Hopper* and headed toward the helicopter.

"What the hell is he doing now?" He went into the control room. "Zoom in on that object."

He pointed at the monitor, and in less than a second, the helicopter filled the huge screen, moving slowly over a canvas of blue ocean. Its main rotor looked like a see-through disk with concentric circles, where the outer edges of the spinning blades were painted with Navy markings.

"No, magnify the missile that just left the helicopter."

In another second, the digital optics of the satellite refocused on a fast-moving object. He recognized the old Soviet design.

Not possible, Grainger thought. *Not fucking possible! Hell, even I can't procure nuclear missiles!*

To Thaddeus Leak, Grainger said, "What's the trajectory of that missile?"

The monitor expanded to show the four-hundred-mile-wide swatch of ocean with the fleet at the extreme right side of the view and the *USS Grace Hopper* at the left. The helicopter was about a third of the way to the fleet, and its missile was rapidly closing to intercept the fleet's huge mass of missiles that were well past the halfway point and closing rapidly on the *Grace Hopper*. A dotted vector line extended from the missile to the mass of the second wave of missiles from the carrier group. Speed and time-to-intercept data moved with the helicopter's missile.

He pulled out his cell and sent an encrypted text to Admiral Montmarkle: *I think he has a nuke. Target is the field of inbound missiles.*

Five seconds later, Grainger's phone signaled a reply.

Impossible. He's bluffing.

Grainger fired off his own reply: *Bluffing is not his MO. Take precautions.* Then, turning to his Senior Admin, he said, "Mr. Leak, if that's a nuclear missile, will we lose the satellite when it detonates?"

The young man shook his head. "I'm pretty sure the detonation will be too low in the atmosphere for the EMP to damage the satellite electronics or any mainland systems, but it will very likely overload the optics if we're looking right at it."

"Time to intercept?"

"A little more than a minute."

Grainger nodded. Admiral Montmarkle was on her own, whatever she decided to do. "Turn the satellite away. Refocus on the ship immediately after we have confirmation of a detonation or no detonation."

He turned away from the monitor as the field of view of the satellite began to move away from the ocean battle, so he didn't see the second missile leave the helicopter just seconds before the hapless aircraft was blown to bits by missiles from the two fighters.

CHAPTER 43

"**M**ERC THREE, *ESCALATE!*" THEN CARL said, "Close that goddamn channel!"

Everyone in the CIC looked at Carl, and after looking around the room, meeting everyone's gaze briefly, he focused a sinister smile at the commander, the only person who seemed to understand what he'd done.

He felt President Mallory staring at the left side of his head. "What did you do, Carl?"

He turned to face her. "How do you combat an opponent who possesses overwhelming power, force, and confidence?"

Commander Eckels told her ensign to track the new indicator and leaned on the command console in the center of the CIC. She gazed at Carl from across the acrylic console surface, then nodded down at the tactical display.

"Captain Johnson, what is that?"

"I'm no longer a *captain*, Commander, at least not in a military sense. Military people respond to authority, so I just used that old title to mess with the admiral's head. Maybe she's thinking I was a Senior Air Force Combat Strategist or something. Maybe she's thinking I went to Air War College. Maybe she's thinking I'm some kind of highly trained tactical genius or sump'n." He glanced at the president. "Air War College is where the Air Force sends its officers to learn advanced war-fighting strategy."

Mallory nodded. "I know what it is." She waved at the wall screen. "So, all that shouting and losing your composure—"

"Head fake."

Eckels slammed her palm down on the tactical display. "What. Is. This. Indicator?" she said, pointing at a new blip on the acrylic tabletop display.

"You know exactly what it is, Commander."

A single blue triangular blip had separated from the southbound indicator that was the destroyer's helicopter. Merc Three was a little more than a third of the way toward the carrier group. The new blip was on an intercept course with the field of missiles in the remainder of the second wave.

Carl spoke softly to the ensign across the room. "With the commander's permission, would you please reopen the comm channel with the admiral? Audio only this time."

"Do it," Eckels said. "And quickly!"

Yes, Carl thought. *She knows.*

"Channel open," reported the ensign.

Mallory seemed bewildered. "You plan to save us with *one* missile?"

Carl looked at her and replied, "Madam President, you should know me better than that by now. When you face an opponent who possesses overwhelming power, first you give 'em a bloody nose, like I did with the FBI, the TER, and the Mexican army. Then, while they're reeling from the surprise, you hit 'em again and again." He turned his attention to the camera. "And Admiral Montmarkle is no doubt evaluating her tactical display at this moment, aren't you, Admiral? You know what that new indicator is. I'm fixin' to give you a nuclear bloody nose, so feel free to open a channel and discuss this with me anytime. You still have about one minute before this war becomes irreversible."

The ensign reported in, saying, "I'm receiving a video transmission, Commander."

"On screen."

The admiral's face was shocking in its severity. She was Agent Palmer, Special Agent Cummings, Director McGrath, and all of Carl's mercs rolled into one person. She had a narrow hawklike face with penetrating blue eyes, edged by severe crow's feet. Her gray hair was severely pulled back in what Carl assumed was a bun behind her head.

"This is Admiral—"

Carl waved her silent. "I know who you are. Let's jump to the part where you realize you are not in control here. You'll notice my helicopter has not reversed course yet. That's because its mission is not complete."

"Standard flight range for a chopper billeted for the Zumwalt-class destroyer like the *USS Grace Hopper* is 275 miles. It will fall short."

"It doesn't need to make it all the way. In fact, it's close enough now. When that first missile detonates, it will create a massive curtain of radiation through which you will not see the next two missiles. You should know by now that I'm not real comfortable playing defense. I'm better at offense. So, the first detonation will be your bloody nose, Admiral. The next two will be your ass-whooping. I'm going to destroy your ship and cripple your fleet."

Mallory gasped. "You fired a nuclear weapon at the US Navy?"

"Not yet, Madam President. I fired a nuclear weapon to disable a mass of missiles fired at *this* US Navy vessel. I will fire the next two nukes at an enemy who is trying to murder the president of the United States. The admiral knows you're on this vessel."

The admiral said, "I know that your *transmission* is coming from the ship."

"What you think you know is irrelevant now," Carl said. "I'm prepared to use my two remaining nukes if you do not self-destruct your missiles."

Her eyes darted off camera, and Carl knew someone was updating her. She said, "The *Grace Hopper* does not have a nuclear arsenal."

"Mm-hmm. Well, it's a good thing I brought my own." Carl considered an abstract thought. "I'm guessing your morning national security threat briefing last month didn't include a report on the black-market auction of ten old Soviet nuclear warheads from whatever third-world country that was." He waved off his own comment and directed his attention to the tactical display. "Yeah, I bought them."

The indicator for Carl's nuke was closing fast on the mass of missiles.

"Admiral, you have forty seconds to comply. My guy has orders to launch right before that nuke detonates. The EMP will fry most of the unprotected electronics in your fleet, destroying all but your radiation-hardened systems. What you'll have left won't detect my next two missiles until they're too close. And while my missiles are old, we've installed the latest end-of-trajectory evasive flight package, same as your ship killers."

Mallory touched his arm. "Carl, what are you doing? You can't possibly—"

"Madam President, it's called *mutually assured destruction.*" He turned back to the camera. "Admiral, I know I can't win a shooting war against a carrier group, but I can hurt you. I can hurt you very badly. You will ultimately win this fight, I know that, but if you kill my president, I will kill you, Admiral. I will vaporize your ship along with any vessels within three thousand yards."

Eckels said to Mallory, "The ship killers are fire-and-forget missiles. There is no termination signal for those."

Carl noticed the admiral say something to someone off camera. The tactical display beeped again, and two of the inbound fighter jets peeled off on a trajectory to intercept Merc Three's chopper. "Nice try, Admiral. They'll never get there in time."

Even as he spoke the words, four blips separated from the indicators, closing on Three's position. Carl took in the data stream next to all the indicators on the tactical display.

Twenty-two seconds to detonation of Carl's missile.

One minute and ten seconds until engagement with the nearest of the remaining missiles of the next wave.

Ten minutes and four seconds until the arrival of the fighters, though Carl knew they'd likely launch their missiles long before then.

Fifteen seconds until the missiles from the two fighters intercepted Three's chopper.

Carl said, "Admiral, at least turn your fighters away. All are inside the blast radius of the coming detonation, and there's no need for those men and women to die." He glanced at Commander Eckels. "Make sure no one is topside."

She nodded to one of her enlisted CIC operators. "Prep the ship for nuclear detonation and ready contamination protocols."

"Prep for nuclear, aye, Commander." After a moment, the operator said, "All personnel are below decks."

"Mr. Johnson," the admiral said, "I require your unconditional surrender."

Carl shook his head. "The American Terrorist does not *surrender*, Admiral. I *escalate*." He paused for effect. "However, I will accept *your* surrender. The president must live. That is nonnegotiable."

Five seconds.

Carl and the admiral stared at each other, and he could tell she wasn't going to yield. Suddenly, the wall screen, the tactical display, and every piece of electronic equipment in the CIC blinked off for a few seconds. The red tactical lighting popped on.

Slowly, the destroyer's radiation-hardened computer systems rebooted, and systems came back online.

The ensign swiveled in his seat. "Commander, sensors show a nuclear detonation at the location Mr. Johnson specified."

Eckels gazed at Carl. "I thought you were bluffing."

"I'm sure the admiral thought the same."

The president added, "And Three just launched two more nuclear missiles at the carrier group?"

"Well, that part was a bluff," Carl said. "I only have one more, but they'll be *looking* for two." He glanced around the room and raised his voice for all to hear. "I will do whatever it takes, and I will kill anyone to make sure President Mallory survives."

The young ensign said, "Systems coming back online. We have full acquisition and targeting capabilities." He consulted his computer screen. "The detonation obliterated most of the missile field and…"

The commander glanced over at him. "Let's have it, Ensign."

"The planes, ma'am. I no longer see them on the screen, but we still have seventy-three of the farthest missiles inbound, moving yellow to red."

Carl closed his eyes, though he knew the outcome could be no different. He bounced his fist against the acrylic. *Fuck! Fifty young men and women just died because the admiral…*

No, it wasn't the admiral who killed those people. It was Carl. He heard urgent voices around him.

"Weapons free! Engage lasers and rail gun on yellow targets. Engage missile batteries on red targets. Stand by, close-support guns."

"Standing by guns. Lasers, missile batteries, and rail gun engaged and firing."

The ship came alive again like a living, breathing combat animal. When Carl had told McGrath what he needed, the director had chosen *USS Grace Hopper* as their target without a moment's hesitation. Commissioned barely six months ago, it hadn't seen actual combat, and its weapons systems had only been fired at stationary test targets. Now, the most advanced ship in the US Navy was tasked to defend the life of the leader of the free world against a surface fleet powerful enough to defeat *most countries* on the planet.

Mallory touched his arm. "It's not your fault."

He glanced at her. "I keep asking myself, what would Aaron McGrath do?"

"He would keep fighting until he can't."

"But he's never fought like this. He's always had the best weapons, the best intel, the best people. He's always been the one with the overwhelming force. He's never been the underdog."

"But he always wins. Just like you do."

The ship rocked with an explosion, and Carl saw a red expanding blip appear on the tactical display a mere ten meters from the aft portside of the destroyer. The guns had destroyed the missiles inside the one-hundred-meter defensive perimeter, but now the perimeter was easing closer to the ship, and everyone in the CIC felt the ship shudder under the increasingly closer airbursts.

An alarm echoed throughout the ship, heard over the mélange of gunfire, missile launches, and explosions.

"They're getting too close, Commander. LIDAR can't track them all."

"Stay calm, Ensign. Mr. Johnson was correct. We will survive this." She stepped over to the tactical display with Carl and the president and fingered her jaw like she was considering something radical. Then she tapped a finger on the sixteen ship killers still ten minutes out. Carl could tell she was just about to voice her idea when three impacts shook the ship. The ship shuddered horribly, the vibration worse than the most intense earthquake he'd ever felt.

"Aft impact!" an operator hollered. "Port impact! No response from aft weapon systems."

Commander Eckels bellowed, "Bring the ship to one-eight-zero. Quickly!" To Carl and the president, she added, "We have to make ourselves a smaller target."

The lieutenant added, "Helm is sluggish, Commander."

Merc Eight hollered from across the room. "Computer shows port shaft is down. Zero turns on port shaft. Request permission to redirect damage control teams."

"Granted!"

"Fire in the port magazine!"

"Deploy fire suppression gas."

"No response."

"Flood it!" Eckels commanded. "Seal all compartments, frame seven-two through one-two-four, decks four, five, and six."

"Done," Eight said.

The lieutenant added, "Aft laser destroyed! Rail gun is not responding. Missile launchers seven and eight off-line!"

"Ensign, reconfigure launchers six and fourteen through sixteen for long-range ship-to-air missiles. Prepare to engage blue targets."

"Aye, Commander, but that's going to cripple our yellow zone defense capability."

"I'm aware of that. Fire when ready."

Carl said, "You intend to try to intercept the ship killers at distance?"

Eckels nodded. "Yes, while we still have launchers to fire. Normally, on final approach, they go into automatic threat-evasion maneuvers, so if an intercept missile misses on its first attempt, there isn't enough time to correct course and make another attempt."

"But if you can hit them at distance..."

She nodded. "Or if we can force them to begin evasion while still many miles away, it'll consume all their fuel before impact...maybe." She shrugged. "We're at the extreme edge of their range. It's a shot in the dark."

Carl nodded. "But it will buy us a few more minutes."

"A few more minutes for what?"

Two more impacts violently rocked the ship.

Ensign said, "We just lost the bridge, Commander, and we took a hit on the front hull plate…below the waterline!" He consulted a screen at the station next to his. "Two casualties, one fatal. Three others are trapped inside that compartment."

Carl looked at the tactical display. Seventeen inbound missiles remained, but the guns were making quick work of those. He glanced over at the enlisted gunner. She was calm, working her joystick with ease, destroying targets one after another.

Eckels ordered, "Ensign, how many long-range missiles got off before we lost those launchers?"

"Our remaining complement was eight, and all launched."

The tactical display beeped as the last inbound missile was destroyed.

"Weapons inventory?"

"Rail gun and rear antimissile laser destroyed. Three of four deck guns operational—bow, port, and starboard. Ammunition down to 20 percent. Five of sixteen missile launchers still operational." The ensign swiveled in his chair and gazed at the commander. "We have four intercept missiles left, ma'am, and all are in the launchers."

Eckels nodded. "No use saving them for later, Ensign. Pick your targets and fire."

"Aye, Commander. Ship killers targeted. Last missiles away."

"What's our damage control status?"

"We only have two teams now, ma'am. Both are aft putting out a fire near the ammo locker and fuel bunker. The third team is the one trapped forward. I was on the line with them a few seconds ago, but the line went dead. It sounded dire."

Lieutenant Hawkins stepped up beside the president. "Commander, Captain, damage control is our alternate combat duty aboard ship. Let me take my marines and go forward to see if we can free those trapped sailors." Carl was about to object, but the lieutenant held up a hand. "It was a smart tactical decision to station us with the president in case we were boarded after the missile attack, but with the ship killers on the way, there's no way a Navy SEAL team will attempt a high-altitude insertion."

Carl glanced at Commander Eckels, who nodded.

"Good call, Lieutenant. Deploy your marines." Carl looked at Merc Eight. "Are Fourteen and his team finished with their task?" Eight nodded at him. "Then have all our team members report to Lieutenant Hawkins for damage control." He tried to make sense of the high-tech tactical display and all its indicators and symbols. "Ensign, what's the ETA of the ship killer missiles?"

"Six minutes, ten seconds."

Eckels rapped her knuckles on the acrylic display. "I repeat, a few more minutes for what?"

"Director McGrath told me he'd be here with a ride."

"And if he doesn't show up?"

"Then we go down with the ship."

"So all this"—Eckels waved her hand around the CIC—"is simply a distraction? What was it you said, a head fake?"

"It's how you fight an opponent with overwhelming power. I had to give Atlas a target that would survive an hour of combat while we await rescue. I needed the ship and your crew to put up a good fight, and look sincere and authentic doing it, and you did. I'm sorry your ship won't survive the next attack. Director McGrath and I knew Atlas would just keep coming at us until we were destroyed, so we had to be prepared for this level of engagement."

Eckels nodded and said, "Were you prepared for nuclear war?"

Carl nodded. "That's why I brought nukes." He looked down at the tactical display—*five minutes, forty-five seconds*—then at President Mallory, then at the commander. "When I graduated from Air Force Officer Training School in '91, me and my fellow graduates were still young and immortal. I was only twenty-eight. We promised each other we'd visit. We planned to get together every year at a different member's base. Shortly after graduation, I drove across the country and passed right by the base where one of my classmates was stationed. But it was late at night, and I wanted to get where I was going, so I didn't visit. Next thing I knew, he was shipped off to the first Gulf War, and he was the navigation officer on the only US plane to get shot down over there.

"He was one of those kids that died today. They were him." Carl took a deep breath. "War is a messy business, Commander, and I'm prepared to do whatever is necessary to protect the president. I was prepared to send my second-in-command on a one-way mission we both knew would get him killed. I was prepared to order a drone strike yesterday on my agent who was dying but not dead yet, to kill the enemy combatants around her."

Five minutes and fifteen seconds. "It's time," Carl said. "Ensign, which way is the wind blowing?"

"Westerly, sir."

"Um, is that *from* the west or *to* the west?"

"From the west to the east, sir."

"Copy that. Commander, point the ship due south and stop."

"Do it, Lieutenant."

The lieutenant got on a corded handset. "Engine Room, CIC. All engines stop. Repeat, e-stop all main engines and feather props." He punched some buttons on his console. "We are completing our previous maneuver, steering one-eight-zero."

Carl said, "Eight, blow the charges on the starboard side and make smoke. Flood the lower compartments on the portside. Check the sensors and make sure no one is in those areas. Give me a thirty-degree list to port."

Merc Eight consulted the ensign and then called Hawkins by intercom, then touched a key that activated a preprogrammed set of explosives. The ship rocked violently yet again.

"You're going to scuttle my ship?"

"The *USS Grace Hopper* has one last duty to perform, and that is to cover our escape. Eight, do we still have any topside cameras active?"

The wall monitor flickered, and everyone in the CIC gasped. It wasn't the sight of the enormous expanding fireballs that had just erupted from the starboard side of the ship. It was the condition of the ship. The entire back end of the superstructure was literally scraped from the deck. Blackened and twisted metal was all that remained of the armored radar and comm housings. There was no sight of the aft missile launchers, the rail gun housing, and the aft gun housings. Most of the bridge was gone or in shambles. Without the heavy armor of the stealth ship's construction, the *USS Grace Hopper* would have already been sinking to the ocean floor with its crew.

On the monitor, Carl saw huge plumes of billowing black smoke roll over the deck and obscure the immense destruction. Already, the horizon was beginning to tilt to the right as the deck settled to the left. With his back to the port bulkhead, Carl had the uncomfortable feeling he was being pulled backward, and he and everyone in the CIC leaned against the pitch.

He pointed a finger at the ceiling and said, "Our enemy is watching from a satellite, but I don't want them to see what happens next."

"Mr. Johnson, I most certainly don't approve of your methods and your blatant disregard for military property and lives. You clearly had this all planned out, so you did not need to launch a second nuclear missile at the fleet. As many as ten thousand people will die needlessly."

"Sista, ten thousand is nothing. I released the Contagion in Mexico knowing full well that if the vice president didn't give up his private stash of the antidote, everybody on the planet would die. That's how many people I will kill to protect my president. *Seven billion.* It's ironic, really. In the movies, there's always a lone hero or a small team who saves the president from countless hordes of terrorist attackers. Now, here, in real life, it is a terrorist and his team protecting the president from her own military."

Four minutes and thirty-six seconds.

Carl added. "Commander, we're empty of missiles, right?"

She nodded.

"And the guns fire tracer rounds that can be seen from a satellite?"

She nodded again.

"Then let's keep up the illusion that we're fighting to the last bullet."

Eckels nodded. "Combat, weapons free. Engage computer auto-fire as soon as any target is in range. Empty all ammunition bunkers."

"Weapons free, aye, Commander."

Come on, Aaron. Where are you?

The thought had just tumbled through his brain when a klaxon blared throughout the room.

"Conn, Sonar! Danger close!"

CHAPTER 44

CARL HEARD A TREMENDOUS SCRAPING sound like someone was ripping open the wall behind him. He knew it was McGrath's submarine surfacing right next to the destroyer. Hence the list, so the destroyer's deck would be on the level with the conning tower of the sub.

Commander Eckels shouted over the noise, "Lieutenant, shut off that klaxon!"

In the sudden silence, Carl said, "Commander, get all your people topside and onto that sub!" He glanced at the tactical display for the last time. *Four minutes and two seconds until the ship killers hit the ship.* "Our ride leaves in exactly three minutes, forty-five seconds. Madam President, if you will accompany me topside."

Commander Eckels made the announcement over the ship's intercom to abandon ship. Carl led the president out of the CIC, half-leaning against the bulkhead to stay upright against the severe pitch of the deck. They made slow progress down dangerously tilting ladders, but two and a half minutes later, the commander, Carl, and Lieutenant Hawkins stood at the coaming rail just about level with the top of the conning tower of the sub and watched the president being escorted through the sub's hatch.

"Now I understand why you detonated charges on my ship and wanted it to list." She looked up at the thick cloud of smoke roiling ten feet over their heads, masking their exodus from the eyes of any orbiting satellites. She turned her gaze back onto Carl, and he saw a renewed respect in her eyes like he'd seen in many of his opponents. "Good execution, Captain." She nodded at the sub. "Now get off my ship, Mister."

Carl understood. Commander Eckels had to be the last soul off the ship. After all, the president was safe on the sub, so Carl's mission on the destroyer was complete. He relinquished command of the ship simply by following her order. A sailor in a dark blue uniform stood on the sub's conning tower and reached out a hand, which Carl grabbed to make the two-foot leap.

Hawkins hesitated, looking back toward the bow of the ship. The trapped damage control team had been freed, and all but one marine and one mercenary were on the sub. Corporal Inajosa was still nowhere to be seen. Merc Twelve was missing too.

Eckels bellowed. "You too, Lieutenant!"

"Commander, my corporal—"

"She's well-trained, Lieutenant, and she knows how much time she has. Now move it!"

The lieutenant followed her instructions and made the leap to the conning tower, as did Commander Eckels. They disappeared down the hatch. Over the creaking and grinding of metal on the dying destroyer, Carl heard a squawk from the sub's intercom about being out of time. He knew they had less than thirty seconds before the first ship killer impacted the destroyer. There was an extremely high likelihood that the sub would be damaged by the blast if any part of it remained above the surface.

He gave the *USS Grace Hopper* one final look, surveying its damage. She was a mess from the fantail to amidships. Even the bow had taken some damage. He turned toward the hatch as the sailor made the all-clear-up-top call.

Dive! Dive! Dive!

A tap on Carl's left shoulder made him look up and see the sailor pointing to the front of the destroyer. Two figures in black combat armor moved slowly along the coaming, the corporal nearly carrying the limping mercenary.

The ten feet of conning tower above the water's surface diminished rapidly, and Carl knew the stragglers had zero chance of miraculously covering fifty feet of the mangled deck in time.

Merc Twelve and Corporal Inajosa stopped and stared at him.

Carl did the only thing he could under the circumstances of their certain death, even as surface waves lapped at the top of the conning tower. He stood ramrod straight and saluted them, then he and the sailor dropped through the hatch, and it slammed shut behind them just as the top slid beneath the waves. Five seconds later, a series of tremendous explosions echoed through the sub's hull, but the vessel was already leaving the area at flank speed and an ever-increasing dive angle.

The hatch at the bottom of the conning tower dropped into the back of the conn, or the control room of the sub, where the command staff directed the operation of the vessel.

A short, wiry man of about forty-five or so greeted Carl when his feet hit the deck. "Welcome aboard, Mr. Johnson. I'm Captain Julius Manford. Director McGrath has asked me to extend his gratitude for rescuing the president. I'm told her medical condition requires her to be sequestered in our SCIF, which we've modified to prevent leakage of the radioactive signature of the isotope in her blood."

Carl removed his battle helmet and looked around the room at the dozen or so faces gawking at him. *Must be weird collaborating with the American Terrorist*, he thought, then simply nodded. "You have a bunk for me then?"

"Ensign Reynolds will show you to your room."

A slender woman in a dark blue utility uniform stepped smartly up next to him.

"And, Mr. Johnson," the captain continued, "if you'll relinquish your weapons to the Master Chief."

A burly redhead strode up beside the ensign. "Yes, sir, we cannot have any accidental discharges, especially from armor-piercing ordnance aboard a submarine."

Carl nodded and carefully checked his PDW. "Safety is on," he said.

He popped out the mag and cleared the breech, then handed the assault rifle to the Navy man. With his helmet in one hand, he unbuckled his utility belt, laden with two more handguns, multiple grenades and magazines, and two combat knives, and handed the whole getup over. Then he followed the young female officer out of the conn, through an oval bulkhead door, and down a short corridor. The first room on the right was simply labeled *Captain*. There was no name on the label, but then everyone on the boat would know who the captain was. Reynolds stopped by the second room, named *Two*, no doubt, Carl thought, for the second-in-command, whoever that might happen to be.

Efficient, Carl thought. *If an officer gets reassigned, there's no need to change the nameplate on the room.* "Damn," he whispered as he saw the tiny officer's room. "You folks live cramped up like this for months at a time?"

"Sir, this is an executive room for the command staff. Under water, this is darn good living."

She ended the statement with an upbeat tone, almost a chuckle that Carl found a bit informal coming from a naval officer in the presence of a terrorist. When he looked at her standing in the doorway, though, he saw a mixture of fear, awe, and eagerness.

"You have a question, Ensign?"

She glanced to her left and right as if involved in a conspiracy, then leaned forward and whispered, "The director said you're an officer?"

He nodded as he tore loose various Velcro straps and peeled out of his armor. "US Air Force, way back almost thirty years ago, when I was your age." *Christ, was I ever that young?*

"Why did you…"

"Why did I become a terrorist?"

"Why did you save the president?"

Carl got out of his armor gear and boots and stood in his skintight full-length athletic undergarments and socks. He got a whiff of his own body odor and remembered he'd been running on adrenaline for almost three days straight. He was tired and hungry, and he needed a long, hot shower.

"That story, Ensign, will no doubt be classified way above your pay grade. But I can tell you this. It was the right thing to do. President Shirley Mallory is a good human, and she deserves to live, which is more than I can say about the people trying to kill her."

"Yes, sir." Her posture told him she was ready to get back to her post.

"Can I trouble you for some clean clothes and a towel for a shower and maybe an MRE?"

"The officer's latrine and shower are down the hall. I'll bring you a deck uniform. But we don't have MREs, sir. I'll bring you some food from the galley." She left before Carl could thank her, but she left the door open, obviously intending to return within a minute or two.

He sat on the bunk, reviewing all the new faces that would forever play across the movie screen of his mind, faces that would forever torment him for the decisions he'd made. Corporal Inajosa was there now, as were Mercs Twelve, Three, Thirteen, the helicopter pilots, and now, dozens of young Navy pilots. Nancy Palmer was there along with her support crew, whose names he did not know, heroes who had made the ultimate sacrifice, making sure the president got out of DC alive. Mark was always there.

Carl felt fatigued deep in his bones, then suddenly became aware of a loud banging noise. His eyes flashed open painfully, not because his eyes hurt, but because the effort to reenter consciousness from such a deep and mind-numbing sleep physically hurt. He looked around the tiny room and realized the overhead light was off when it had been on a moment ago. The desk lamp was on, though it had been off before. A pile of neatly folded clothes and a tray of food occupied the top of the desk. He was lying down. The door was closed and being subjected to an insistent pounding.

"Yes, what is it? Come in." Carl found the strength to force himself to a sitting position on the edge of the bed.

The door opened, and the young ensign—*Reynolds,* he recalled— peeked her head in. "Sir, are you okay?"

"Um, yeah, I, uh… What do you mean?"

"I've been knocking for almost a minute. I was about to go get the—"

"I'm fine, Ensign. What's the matter?"

"President Mallory is ready for you."

"Ready for me?" Carl muttered the words because he was having trouble concentrating through the fog that still had its tentacles wrapped around his brain.

"Yes, sir. She wants to see you in the SCIF."

"I must have fallen asleep for a minute."

"Sir, it's been ten hours since I left your clothes and food on the desk." She pointed across the small room.

"Ten hours? Okay, I'll get dressed."

"Yes, sir. Um, and about that shower, sir…" She gave it a California question mark, that uptick of the voice at the end that made it sound like a question when it really wasn't.

"Yeah."

Carl snatched a biscuit from the tray and then grabbed the blue deck uniform—navy blue cargo pants and button-down utility shirt, black boxers and T-shirt, and black socks to go with the nonskid deck shoes. So many years ago, when he'd enlisted, the military underwear had all been white. *How times have changed.*

He slid through the doorway beside Reynolds and headed up the hall, stuffing the biscuit into his mouth on the move. It was cold and dry, but he was so hungry, it tasted magnificent.

"Sir!"

He turned.

The ensign thumbed over her shoulder to the opposite end of the hall. "That way to the latrine and shower. Last door on the left before the next bulkhead door."

The fog around his brain suddenly lifted, and he remembered where he was and what the next step was in the plan. The president still wasn't truly safe until the Kolls had been dealt with and their corporate cabal neutralized.

Carl had one final task to complete, then he could *retire* from his American Terrorist persona.

CHAPTER 45

GRAINGER KOLL WAS WATCHING THE naval battle on his forty-inch HD desktop monitor for the umpteenth time when his brother entered his office. It had been two days since Hollis had arrived at the island. The door was open to the much larger control room that served as the nerve center—the brain—of the underground island bunker. His office measured roughly twenty feet square and was Spartan in appearance. The walls were bare gray concrete, completely unadorned with any kind of art or decoration, and the floor was equally minimalist. The only furniture in the room was the desk with its accompanying plain black leather chair, a corner bookshelf, and the small conference table with four chairs. The room lacked personality, like its current occupant, he figured many might say.

"How's the arm?" Grainger said.

Hollis nudged the sling holding his left arm across his chest. His shirtsleeve was cut off at the shoulder, and his upper arm was wrapped in fresh gauze. "Still hurts like hell, but the meds help." He looked at Grainger's monitor as the final moments of the battle played out.

Multiple submarine-launched cruise missiles, *ship killers*, impacted the *USS Grace Hopper* within a time span of only ten seconds. The first missile ripped the heart out of the listing ship with a tremendous detonation that broke its spine and lifted its bow and fantail completely out of the water. The rest of the missiles merely hit the remaining huge fragments of the dying ship.

From the perspective of the satellite holding in a geostationary orbit a few hundred miles above the ocean, the blast waves of the missile impacts could be seen sweeping outward away from the stricken vessel slowly, it seemed, though they both knew that wave of super-condensed air was moving faster than the speed of sound.

"It's not like Carl Johnson to go down with the ship," Grainger said, rubbing his chin.

"They had time to get off the ship, but he'd know they could never escape the blast wave of those missiles." Hollis nodded at the monitor. "Unfortunately, I won't be able to wring that fucker's neck for shoving his knife in my arm."

"I guess."

"You guess?" Hollis waved his good hand at the monitor. "The only way he could possibly have escaped that blast is—" He stopped in mid-sentence and stared at the monitor for a few seconds longer, then turned his gaze on his brother. "No way! No *fucking* way he has enough money to buy—"

"A submarine hidden under all that smoke." Grainger nodded. "Aaron McGrath wouldn't have to buy one." He paced his office once. "I never figured in a million years those two could ever actually work together, but they are."

"I know." Hollis examined the monitor as the last moments of the ship looped again. "Look at all the damage to the aft part of the ship, but it's not listing aft. And the smoke is coming from the starboard side of the ship, but it's listing to port. Fuck! It's a ruse!"

"He *did* get off." Grainger pressed a button on his keyboard, then said, "Do we have an infrared channel on our Pacific satellite?"

"Yes, but—"

"Well?"

"We're getting something strange in here, Mr. Koll. There's an incoming signal being broadcast to us, but it's a carrier signal only. No audio or video channel." There was a pause, then the voice said, "Um, you'd better get in here, sir."

Grainger looked at his brother, then hurried into the command center. He stopped in mid-stride. He'd half-expected this, but the image still took his breath away, though he tried not to show his shock.

The knock on the door of the command stateroom brought Admiral Mont-markle rather violently out of an unexpectedly deep and disturbing sleep. She lay on her back without a blanket or bed sheet, the way she always preferred. Always fully dressed, she could be awake and alert by the time she pivoted on her butt and her feet hit the deck. This time, though, she was a bit slow in reacting. She sensed the person had been knocking for some time.

She opened the door to see Yeoman Bracker standing there, impec-cably dressed in his military whites. She subconsciously straightened her own blouse, not wanting to be outdressed by anyone serving under her. It was tough with the yeoman, though. His uniform was always flawless, and he was always perfectly groomed.

"Ma'am, you have an 'eyes only' video communiqué holding on Channel One."

"Eyes only" meant she had to get her rotating cipher code from her locker to decrypt the call. Such a call could only come from a higher au-thority, and there were precious few in the US Navy who fit that descrip-tion. That could only mean one thing. She was being reassigned, likely *early-retired* for her bungling of the American Terrorist incident.

"Thank you, Yeoman." She almost asked who was calling, but that would be reckless. The yeoman had a high security clearance—a require-ment to serve as an assistant to a flag officer—but he would not be privy to Eyes Only, above Top Secret information.

She closed the door and stood there for a moment. *Bungling?* She leaned against the door and snorted contempt at herself. That word hardly even began to describe the level of incompetence her superiors would judge of her. She had competed against the most capable male officers her entire career, some at the same time, and had risen above them all.

Now this one man, a former Air Force captain who was one level below the equivalent rank of a lieutenant commander in the Navy, and now a terrorist, had completely outmaneuvered her. And that missile…

She crossed the room and knelt down in front of her safe, input the twelve-digit numeric code, and opened the door, then withdrew a plastic sleeve that held her rotating codes. She sat down in front of her desk and keyed the proper code into her laptop.

The admiral raised an eyebrow at the face gazing back at her. She leaned back in her chair and put two fingers to her chin.

"Huh," she said after a few seconds of wordless surprise.

"How is your ship, Admiral?"

"In one piece, Captain Johnson." She shrugged. "Except for the hole in the superstructure. Your missile tore through the portside wall of the bridge, hit my chair, and got stuck in the opposite bulkhead. Had I been sitting in that chair..."

Carl shrugged. "I'll try to do better next time."

"Why no warhead?"

"I guess my mercs forgot to put the bomb part in that damn thing. I'ma have to get on 'em about that."

"You could have destroyed my ship and crippled my entire fleet," the admiral said. Oddly, she felt uncharacteristically chatty. It was almost as though she'd been bested in a chess match and felt obligated to give her opponent the respect he was due.

The initial nuclear explosion had been a very small yield, barely a kiloton, but radar was disrupted for hours. And that had been Johnson's plan, she now knew. As he promised, his second missile flew undetected out of that nuclear soup and deployed the same end-of-trajectory evasions as state-of-the-art US missiles. None of her escorts' guns or missile batteries could intercept the inbound missile. How and when he had acquired such high-end terminal guidance technology beguiled her.

"Admiral, I simply needed you to be distracted by what you thought was a couple live nukes coming down the pipe. I needed you to be on the defensive for a few minutes."

"While you evacuated the president on what...a sub...under cover of that thick black smoke?" She nodded at the laptop. "Now I understand why the FBI and TER had such difficulty with you."

"They underestimated my willingness to escalate. They underestimated the lengths to which I will go to save my president." He cocked his head to the side. "My only mission, Admiral, was to save the president. Murdering thousands of American service men and women in your fleet and crippling America's Pacific Fleet was not the mission." He paused. "Unlike *your* mission."

Suddenly, the admiral knew why he called. "You know, don't you?"

He nodded. "My people have discovered you have a daughter whose identity you've kept hidden all these years. We discovered she's married." He dipped his head, and the admiral felt those brown eyes slicing into her brain like lasers. "To a man who is a senior member of Hollis and Grainger Koll's staff."

She nodded again, knowing resignation was clear in her eyes. "How did you know to look?"

"You were too driven to kill us, Admiral. You could have easily diverted your attack planes to a safe distance if you even half-believed I had a nuke. You could have saved all those pilots and brought them back around for a second run. Hell, you could have self-destructed those missiles and waited until my chopper ran out of fuel and fell into the ocean. Then you could have launched two or three hundred more missiles at us. I think that's what a prudent flag officer would have done. But no." Carl took a deep breath. "You wanted it too much. Somewhere during the past few years, your officer training and your allegiance to your country was hijacked, co-opted somehow. You owe allegiance only to Atlas." Carl shrugged. "Those pilots didn't have to die, so now *you* have to pay for their lives, either with your daughter's life or your own."

The admiral nodded and then reached into her drawer and withdrew her service handgun. She laid it on the desk in front of her. "Do I have your word as an officer and gentleman that my daughter will be spared?"

"On my honor as an officer and gentleman, your daughter will be spared, Admiral."

She felt oddly at peace. There was no need for any further explanations or discussions. She'd been discovered and would either be arrested and disgraced in a military court-martial or assassinated by the terrorist later. His current offer was far better than either of the other options.

Admiral Montmarkle picked up the gun, put it to her temple, and pulled the trigger.

———— ·◆◆· ————

Three hundred miles to the north, Carl Johnson rose from the communications desk chair in the submarine SCIF adjacent to the sub's CIC. He looked at President Mallory and Aaron McGrath standing to the right of the desk, then at Captain Manford and Merc Three standing to the left. The five of them left little room to maneuver in the cabin.

Three was still sopping wet from being pulled from the ocean. He and the pilot had bailed from the chopper thirty seconds before the fighter missiles destroyed the helicopter. Carl learned Three had added air tanks to his flight kit in case they actually had to deploy the nuke. With air tanks strapped to their backs, they dove as deep as they could to avoid the initial gamma rays of the nuclear detonation. After a minute, they popped their life vests and floated back to the surface. Fortunately, the wind had carried the residual radiation away from them.

"Boss, you actually gave her your word?"

Carl shrugged. "There is no honor available to someone who is trying to kill the president. I will do or say anything to protect her." He swiveled his head toward McGrath.

The TER director nodded. "I would have done exactly the same. Now, our TER analysts have identified sixteen top-level operatives associated with the Kolls, all of whom are assigned to senior government positions or corporate jobs, and your Wizard has located all of them. We also have the location of the admiral's daughter and that woman's husband. I have CIA wet-work teams standing by to execute on all targets simultaneously. Awaiting the commander-in-chief's order…"

"Mr. Johnson." Shirley Mallory stepped forward and put her hand on Carl's arm. "Carl, you've done so much for the country, and for me and my daughter, after what we put you through. Would you like to finish this?"

"I would indeed." He glanced at Merc Three. "Give the word, Three."

Three nodded in return and spoke into the wall phone he held in his hand. "Wizard, all teams execute!"

For two minutes, Three nodded at the phone while wearing a look of intense satisfaction. Finally, he hung up and said, "All targets eliminated. Zero casualties, our teams."

Carl touched a couple keys on the captain's laptop, and Wizard's face appeared on the video stream. He expected the feed to appear patchy like a cell phone video, but the sub had top-grade military comm gear. Wizard's image was crisp in high definition, and the audio made it sound like he was in the room with them.

"All right, Wizard, let's wrap this up, eh?"

"Copy that, Boss. McGrath's people sent me control of a satellite over the island. Tying you in now."

An overhead view of a small three-square-mile island appeared on the laptop. It was almost barren and had only a small airstrip and a few warehouses. Wizard had previously uncovered architectural drawings from a little-known company that had built a massive bunker-type structure buried deep inside the island. The overhead satellite verified the subterranean complex with thermal information.

"And get that reporter on standby so the world can witness this. What was her name?"

"Tying in Miss Logan too."

Ten seconds later, the face of a man resembling Hollis Koll appeared on the monitor. For a split second, he seemed shocked but recovered quickly. Behind him stood Hollis with his arm in a sling. Grainger opened his mouth to speak, but Carl preempted him.

"Hollis! Dude! How's that arm?"

Hollis seemed so visibly angry he couldn't speak, and the man's face was turning more cherry red by the second.

Grainger shook his head and said, "What does it take to kill you?"

"A smarter man than you, Grainger."

"I suppose President Mallory isn't dead, either."

Carl shook his head. "She is not."

"So what now? I suppose the president will try to extradite me from a country none too friendly to the United States."

Carl simply glared into the camera for a few seconds. "Extradite? Pffft! It's just you and me now, so how 'bout I just send a bomb over there and blow your ass up?"

"Good luck with that," Koll said. "First, you have to find me."

"Well," Carl said, "I coated my blade with the same isotope you put in the president's blood."

Grainger's face shaded, and Hollis looked at his wounded arm as if to discover the truth of Carl's statement.

"Mm-hmm. I know exactly where you are, and the bomb is on its way."

A klaxon started to blare on the video as the bunker's defense system detected the inbound missile.

Hollis exclaimed, "One missile? You launched *one* missile at us? We're 150 feet underground, under solid concrete."

Carl shrugged. "I don't think that's going to matter. Or did you already forget I still own nine more nuclear missiles?" After conferencing with the president and McGrath, it was unanimously decided they needed to make sure the Kolls' bunker was completely destroyed. There was no room for chance, so Mallory authorized the use of a nuclear-tipped bunker buster fired from the nearest Navy vessel hundreds of miles away, though Carl saw no benefit in disclosing that fact.

Grainger consulted someone off camera, then banged his fists on the console in front of him. "No, no, *no*! You did *not* launch a nuclear missile at a foreign country!"

"Their fault for harboring a terrorist organization that tried to kill my president…three times."

"The president would never agree—"

"I didn't ask her permission." Carl looked over at Merc Three. "Is Miss Logan getting this transmission and the satellite imagery?"

Three nodded. "We're transmitting live."

Carl shrugged and said, "Like I said, Mr. Koll, it's just you and me now."

Four antimissile missiles blasted away from the north and south ends of the small island and quickly closed the distance to the inbound missile. Right before intercept, though, the inbound went into a spiraling evasion maneuver, and all four of the intercept missiles missed on their first attempt.

Grainger banged his fists on the console. "Carl Johnson, you mother fu—"

The inbound missile hit the island exactly over the center of the underground bunker. It burrowed deep for a fraction of a second. Hundreds of acres of land bowed upward above the subterranean explosion, and then the satellite feed flashed bright white for a few moments, and no one spoke. The satellite optics adjusted, and a huge mushroom cloud could be seen expanding over the island.

Miss Logan's voice could be heard on the silent channel. Her stunned face showed on the left half of the screen, and a high-angle view of the mushroom cloud showed on the right.

"Oh my God! You detonated a nuclear bomb in a foreign country?"

"You think the American Terrorist cares about borders and sovereignty?" Carl said. "Nobody tries to kill my president and lives to talk about it. And I still have eight more nukes for anyone who wants to go after her again."

Carl had insisted on broadcasting the transmission live so that the world's nuclear powers would know the American Terrorist was responsible for the explosion, not President Mallory.

"Is President Mallory alive? Safe?"

"The president is safe in the protective care of the US military." He shrugged at the camera. "I expect she'll want to make an announcement as soon as she hears I exploded a nuclear weapon. But Atlas is decapitated, and its senior leadership incinerated, so my war is concluded."

Carl nodded at Merc Three, and the laptop screen went blank. He faced Mallory and McGrath. For a moment, his gaze lingered on his former nemesis, then he held out a fist.

McGrath fist-bumped him.

"We did good, Aaron."

"We did real good."

"Carl…" Shirley Mallory began.

For a moment, Carl thought she was going to break down in tears.

"I and my daughter, the whole country, we owe you so much."

He smiled mischievously. "Yes, you do, Madam President." Carl turned to the captain of the submarine. "Permission for me and my team to disembark."

Three interrupted, "Me and the rest of the team are getting off at San Diego, then we'll head across the border, lay low, and rebuild a couple of your estates. Regroup and retool, that sort of thing. Nineteen—that's Agent Cummings—and her family are actually in Los Angeles at the Manhattan Beach Pier waiting for you. Wizard took it upon himself to arrange for you to get off there and debrief her, then join us down in Mexico later. If that's okay with you…"

"I could sure use a vacation."

Carl followed the captain out and was assigned a junior lieutenant to escort him topside, where he was told they'd take an inflatable boat to the pier a mile away. On the way, he saw Lieutenant Hawkins and his two marines sitting in the enlisted galley, so he detoured.

"Lieutenant Hawkins," he said as the marines rose and stood at attention. "At ease, Marines. I saw Corporal Inajosa. I was the last one down the hatch, and just before the conning tower went under, I saw her carrying my guy. They were too far away to make it." Carl took a deep breath and looked at each of the marines. "She could have saved herself, but she chose to try to save one of my guys, and she died for it. I suppose that's what being one of 'the few and the proud' is all about. She died a hero, Lieutenant. I *know* that. You're going to have to figure out how to live with that."

Hawkins nodded. "I know, Captain." He nodded, then snapped a precision military salute.

His marines did the same.

Carl saluted them back.

Thirty minutes later, Carl hopped out of the submarine's inflatable boat and walked through the early morning crowd on the beach. Some folks took pictures or videos of the military inflatable. Some were pointing at the conning tower of the submarine parked offshore. He wondered if the beach crowd recognized him.

As he trudged through the sand, he picked out Lenore Cummings's lithe figure easily. She stood with an easy confidence, and her gaze continuously roved around. When her gaze met his, it stuck, and he saw a mix of emotions cascade across her face. He waved, and she gave him a head-nod.

Then he saw Lisette and froze. He knew instantly that the future date of a conversation he'd promised to have with the girl was right then, at that moment. She wouldn't look him in the eye, and as he approached, she took a step back almost behind her mother. The circumstances that had thrust Carl and Lenore's family together were resolved with the destruction of Atlas, and he knew there was absolutely no scenario where he could ever see them again. There was only one more thing to do.

He walked up to Lenore, her daughter, and her mother, and he knelt his right knee in the sand to appear as unthreatening as possible to the girl. "Miss Lisette," he said.

She peeked from behind Lenore's shoulder.

"What I did to you and your mom was unforgivable, and I will never do that to anyone ever again."

Her eyes teared up, and she nodded.

Carl stood. He felt an air of completion, but there was also an emptiness inside him he knew would never fade, a void he would never fill. That day he'd dreaded for the last eight months had arrived.

Today was the first day of the rest of his life without his son.

"Lenore, I tried to blame you for Mark's death. And I tried to blame the others too." He shrugged. "Fact is, he's just gone, and it wasn't your fault." He tried to think of something else to say, but no words came to mind.

Carl turned and walked away, a tremendous burden of guilt lifted from his shoulders. He felt a lightness in his step and imagined that Mark would be proud of him. He found himself smiling as he walked.

"Carl!"

He turned to find Lenore walking toward him. She walked right into him, literally colliding with him, and she wrapped her arms around his neck. They hugged fiercely for a long time.

"I'm sorry, Carl. I'm so sorry."

"I know," he said. "So am I."

They disengaged, and she stepped back. "Is it over, Carl? I mean, really over this time?"

He nodded. "I think so. I hope so."

"What are you going to do now? This whole week—it's a hard act to follow."

"I know, right?" Carl kicked some sand. "I think I'll go back to Taos for a bit and help Rebecca rebuild her little sanctuary. Then maybe I'll head down to Mexico. Alfonso Reyes had some legitimate businesses down there that are now mine."

"Well, check in on us in a while. She's been through a lot, and she's still processing it. I know it'll be hard for you to face her, and it'll be hard for me, but I think it might help her heal if she knows you care about her and that you're there for her if she needs you. I mean, if you want."

"I will."

Lenore walked backward away from him, adding, "You know, after you get done rebuilding Rebecca's house, you still owe me a new one since you blew up my last two."

As she turned away, Carl hollered, "First one wasn't my fault!"

She waved without turning, so he turned away and started walking again.

He didn't know where.

Day one without Mark...

THE END

If you enjoyed this adventure, check out Jeffrey Poston's other action adventure thrillers at JeffreyPostonBooks.com or wherever you buy books. Please let other readers know what you thought of the book by leaving a brief review at your favorite retailer. It only takes a moment and reviews are very valuable to authors.

ABOUT THE AUTHOR

Jeffrey Poston is the acclaimed author of the Jason Peares historical western series, as well as the fast-paced adventure thriller series *American Terrorist* and *Call Sign: Raven*. Blending traditional and revisionist historical research, his historical westerns have been praised as "fast-moving" (Kelton) and "exciting, page-turning" (Zollinger) and "among the best writers of westerns" (Biblio.com). His thriller books are lauded as "so realistic," "powerfully intense," and "action-packed page turners." He is a self-described *Rambling Man* and writes his novels wherever he happens to be in his travels.

Find Jeffrey at http://www.jeffreypostonbooks.com/

Facebook: http://www.facebook.com/JeffreyPostonBooks

Twitter: http://www.twitter.com/BooksByJPoston

ACKNOWLEDGMENTS

As writers, we often go into our creative caves to compose a book, but when we come out, there are often dozens of people who help refine a story and turn it into a really good book. No writer can succeed without this special group of people—critical readers, cover artists, professional editors, marketing and PR specialists, and publishers.

I especially want to thank my critical reader and sounding board, Dr. Stephanie McIver. She's helped me through many of my books, offering insight and analysis that added depth and breadth to my characters and my plot.

Special thanks to Debra L. Hartmann, The Pro Book Editor, and her team for copyediting and proofreading. I also want to give a shout-out to the cover art designers of my books: Deanna Dionne.

I'm also thankful for the active imaginations (and the suspension of disbelief) of all the readers who enjoyed my Western and Thriller adventures. I'm especially grateful to the dozens of beta-readers who previewed the book and sent back invaluable advice. Your help means the world to this author!